LOVE LIKE No Other

jenna hartley

ISBN: 9798386500221

Editing: Lisa A. Hollett
Cover design by Indie Sage

For Angela.

*Thank you for being a consistently positive and encouraging voice
in my life.*

PLAYLIST

"500 Days" by Felix Cartal, Matilda
"Part of Me" by Katy Perry
"I Got You" by Bebe Rexha
"Roar" by Katy Perry
"Butterflies" by William Black, Fairlane, Dia Frampton
"New James Dean" by Kaskade, Tishmal
"About You" by KREAM
"Find Me" by Virginia To Vegas
"Oops (I'm Sorry)" by Lost Kings, GASHI, Ty Dolla $ign
"Yesterday" by Virginia To Vegas
"How You Love Me" by 3LAU, Bright Lights
"As It Was" by Harry Styles
"This Could Be Love" (featuring Dealaney Jane) by Borgeous, Shaun Frank, Delaney Jane
"Don't Wake Me Up" by Jonas Blue
"Into Me You See" by Katy Perry
"Water" (featuring ZOHARA) by KREAM, ZOHARA
"Make It Last" by Virginia To Vegas
"Big Plans" by Why Don't We
"Losing Touch" by Virginia to Vegas

"Cry" by Virginia To Vegas
"Make You Mine" by PUBLIC
"Touch" by 3LAU, Carly Paige
"Unconditionally" by Katy Perry
"I Believe" by Jonas Brothers
"Every Little Thing" by Russell Dickerson

You can find this playlist and more at
https://www.authorjennahartley.com/playlists

Blue River Creek

freedom
tiny homes

pore
over

little bird
studios

alondra valley
animal clinic

Fall River

allen landscaping

Alondra

fall river
estates

bibliolater

wildflour
bakery

lick

alpaca acres

Cortina

woodhouse spa

St. Cecilia

jenna hartley

CHAPTER ONE

Liam

"Routine," I muttered under my breath as I scanned the review. "Predictable," I scoffed at another. *Unbelievable.*

I turned off my phone and placed it facedown on the bar before taking a long gulp of wine. My latest book had been a flop. Readers thought the sex was unoriginal.

I didn't understand. The couple had sex on the gondola up to the ski chalet. They fucked nearly every few chapters. Yeah, so maybe it wasn't the best book I'd written as Meghan Hart, but it was the best I could do at the time.

I had a feeling Tessa would've known how to fix it, but she was part of the reason I was in this mess in the first place. I tried not to take the reader response personally. I knew one book wouldn't make or break my career. That's what I told myself anyway.

But it was harder to convince myself it was true. Especially since my sixth book had been the catalyst for my author career taking off. *Insatiable* had hit the *New York Times, Wall Street Journal,* and *USA Today* best-selling charts and stayed there for weeks. Almost every book I'd written since had hit at least one best-selling list. And last year, I'd finally quit my job and become a full-time author.

It had added more pressure than I'd expected. And while I knew I couldn't please everyone, I'd come to expect mostly glowing reviews. Or at least, I had in the past. Lately, it felt like writing was harder. Editing was harder. Selling books was harder. Everything was harder.

I shook my head and stared down at the contents of my glass, rubbing the pad of my thumb over the Fall River Estates logo. I missed Tessa. I missed talking to someone about my books. I missed having someone to share my secret with.

She'd been my beta reader and my confidante. Tessa's advice and insight had been a big reason for my success. She'd always pushed me to dig deeper, to be a better writer.

And ever since her death, I'd felt lost. Lonely. Straddling two worlds but never fully being myself in either. Never being completely honest about who I really was. At this point, I wasn't even sure I knew myself.

The only two people who had ever known my secret were dead.

"Hey," Asher said, clapping a hand on my shoulder before joining me at the bar. "I would've been here sooner, but I had to finish the pastries for the big wedding tonight."

Right. The wedding. How had I forgotten? Everyone in town had been talking about it for weeks. It was one of the most expensive and elaborate weddings the Alondra Valley had ever seen, and everyone was abuzz with excitement. The last time there'd been this much hype around a wedding had been for Harper and Enzo's—they owned the winery, and he was a retired international soccer star.

Harper's best friend, Juliana Wright, was a famous wedding planner to celebrities in LA. Juliana had planned Harper and Enzo's wedding. But even their celebration seemed understated compared to the upcoming nuptials of the heir to some pharmaceutical fortune—assuming the rumors posted by V in *The Vine* were true.

Though *The Vine* was a local blog focused on local gossip, V had posted about this event—a wedding between two non-locals—multiple times. And while I didn't read it often, I kept an eye on the posts since my alter ego was mentioned from time to time. I had to protect my secret at all costs. I couldn't let anyone know that Meghan Hart—world-famous author known for her tastefully naughty romance—was actually a thirty-three-year-old bachelor.

What would my readers think if they discovered the truth?

Would they feel betrayed? Misled?

Would it undermine their confidence in my work? Their love of my stories?

I thought about it often.

Because if the truth came out, it could wreck my brand and ruin my career.

A career I'd spent years building. I'd invested too much. I'd come too far to reveal my identity now. I relied on the income from my books, and I loved my job. Even if sometimes I hated keeping it a secret.

Sometimes I wanted the credit for my hard work. *Me*, not Meghan.

I'd overhear my younger sister, Wren, gushing about Meghan's latest release. Or my mom—who had the exclusive right to sell signed paperbacks in her bookstore, Bibliolater—would marvel that the signed copies had sold out in an hour. Meghan had even hired Wren's photography studio to take her cover photos. The two most important women in my life were both intimately involved in my business, but I couldn't seem to tell them who was really behind the name.

I was scared.

I knew the air of mystery was part of the allure for my readers. Everyone wanted to know who the elusive Meghan Hart really was. But it was more than that.

I was scared it would change the way my friends and family looked at me. It had certainly changed my grandpa's opinion of me. I shuddered at the memory, knowing that his reaction had kept me from telling anyone else.

I didn't think Wren would judge me, but I was her older brother. Her protector. She'd never been anything but loving and supportive of me.

Then again, I hadn't expected it from my grandpa either.

While I tried to tell myself that Wren would always embrace me for who I was, the longer I kept this secret, the harder it was to tell anyone. I could only imagine the sense of betrayal she'd feel. The only thing worse than a liar was a hypocrite, and I was both.

When I'd learned the truth about my best friend and my little sister's relationship, I'd been livid. Bennett was supposed to be her roommate. And a temporary one at that. He was supposed to look out for her, not sleep with her.

They'd been sneaking around behind my back. Lying to me about their "friendship." I hadn't handled it well.

Granted, the discovery had come on the heels of Tessa's death. But it was weeks before I'd even considered speaking to Wren or Bennett again. I'd taken the protective older brother role too far. Let my own fears almost get in the way of their happiness. I'd since realized how wrong I'd been, and how right for each other they were.

But their betrayal had stung, and they'd only hidden the truth for weeks. How would they feel if they discovered I'd been lying to them for years?

"Fuck. I'm starving," Asher said, glancing around the bar as if searching for someone. "You eaten yet?"

I shook my head as he slid me a menu. "I was waiting for you. Wasn't sure if you'd want to stay here or not."

He shrugged. "We're already here. Might as well stay."

"Sometimes I wonder why you don't just move in," I teased, knowing the long hours he often worked, especially on a day like today.

Though he wasn't the only one. Fall River Estates was busy year-round thanks to its award-winning wines, beautiful scenery, and incredible food. But the fall was especially hectic due to the grape harvest. I was honestly surprised Enzo had ever agreed to hold a wedding during vintage.

"Hey, Lisa," Asher called to the bartender. "Can I get a glass of Sauv?"

"You got it." She was practically stripping him down with her eyes. When I glanced at Asher, he wore a similar look. *Ugh.*

I had a feeling that would bite him in the ass eventually, though maybe not. Women of the AV knew what to expect from Asher, and it wasn't commitment. That was the problem with small-town life; everyone knew everyone else's business.

And it was a big reason why I'd given up on dating long ago. Well, that and the fact that most women seemed to want more than I was able to give. It was much easier to lose myself in the worlds of my characters than to open my heart after what had happened with Diane.

So, I tried to ignore Asher and Lisa's eye-fucking and let my mind wander. Maybe I should write a story about a workplace romance between a bartender and a famous pastry chef. It could be a grumpy sunshine. Or maybe an age gap. Make her ten years younger. Or...

"You want a refill, Liam?" Lisa asked.

"What?" I startled and nearly fell off my stool, my mind spinning with additional story ideas. About a best friend's ex… I was always analyzing. Brainstorming. "Yeah. That would be great. Thanks."

Was that what readers wanted? Something more angsty or "on trend"? Was that responsible for my decline in sales?

And since when did I write for anyone but myself? I groaned then emptied my glass.

"What's up with you tonight?" Asher asked.

I lifted a shoulder. "Nothing. Just a long week at work."

He nodded and swirled his glass, appreciating the wine before savoring it. My friends and family thought I was still an electrical engineer who worked on a contract basis for the government organization that regulated nuclear power plants. Tessa and my grandpa were the only ones who had known my secret, and as far as I knew, they'd taken it to their graves. If she'd told Tristan, he'd never mentioned it.

I hadn't even planned to tell Tessa. But I'd admitted the truth in a moment of painkiller-induced bravery after surgery to repair my ACL. She'd come over to bring me dinner and check on me, and I wasn't as careful as usual. She'd happened to see Meghan Hart's manuscript open on my computer, and when she asked, I couldn't lie. Not to Tessa.

She'd always been the conscience of the group. If I had to describe my best friends as characters, Tessa was the All-American Girl Next Door. Her husband, Tristan, was her perfect counterpart. They were childhood sweethearts, dubbed the town's Golden Couple. Or, well, they had been. Now, he was a widower and single dad.

Asher was this rock star of the pastry world. Brooding. Conflicted. Fucking talented.

Before moving back to the AV from LA, he'd been engaged. But then everything had happened suddenly. He'd left his job at a three-star Michelin-star restaurant, broken things off with Bianca, and returned home grumpier than ever. I still didn't know why. None of us did.

"Is Bennett coming?" Asher asked.

Bennett—total cinnamon roll hero. Loyal. Nurturing. A family man.

"He and Wren are binge-watching the latest season of GBBO."

"Of course," he muttered, but there was a slight uptick to his mouth. If he had a comment about Netflix and chill or whatever, I was grateful he kept it to himself. "And Tristan?" There was a subtle shift in his tone. A hint of sadness. Not many would pick it up, but I'd known Asher my whole life.

I shook my head. We both knew Tristan was still recovering from the shock of losing his wife. We all were, but he had his hands full with two kids, a growing company, and his grief. We all missed Tessa; and Bennett, Asher, and I tried to be there for Tristan in any way we could. Even when he pushed us away. Even when he tried to shut us out.

Conversation shifted to lighter matters, and the meal was delicious as always. Locally sourced produce. Homegrown wine. It was definitely one of my favorite parts about living in the Alondra Valley.

While we waited for the check to arrive, I headed to the bathroom. Noise from the kitchen spilled into the hallway— the clatter of pans, the hiss of something cooking on the stove. A woman rushed by me, white fabric billowing around her, the scent of peppermint and eucalyptus hanging in the air as her hair bounced and swayed.

I was so captivated that, for a moment, she was the only thing that existed. Everything else faded away.

I was flooded with a rush of excitement or…something. I wasn't sure quite how to explain it other than to compare it to the feeling I had when struck with a new idea I couldn't wait to write. Like a firework with a fuse that had been lit and was ready to fucking explode.

At least until the kitchen door slammed into me, jolting me back to reality.

Everything seemed to happen in slow motion, yet I didn't move quick enough to get out of the way. One of the waitresses backed into me with her tray. She somehow managed to keep the plates from falling, but a ramekin of ketchup spilled on my shirt. I cringed.

"Oh my god. I'm so sorry."

The woman in white—a bride, I now realized—stopped. Her eyes were frantic, and she glanced around as if searching for an escape.

"It's fine." I waved away the waitress's concern and stepped closer to the bride, ignoring the ketchup on my shirt. "Are you okay?"

"I need…" She gulped, wide-eyed. "Hide. Can you help me hide? I can't—"

I didn't know her, but I felt compelled to help. She looked so lost. So scared. It spoke to something deep inside me.

"Of course. This way." I headed down the mostly deserted hall. I opened the door to the tasting room. It was dark. Empty. I flipped on the lights and gestured for her to follow.

A runaway bride. I'd never written a story with that trope, but I was definitely feeling inspired by this encounter.

She took a few tentative steps inside. "Are you sure we aren't going to get into trouble for this?"

I chuckled as I closed the doors behind us. It was cute— her concern about getting in trouble. All my life, I'd been getting myself into trouble.

"It's okay." I smirked. "I know the owner. I'll text him."

The ketchup was seeping through to my undershirt. And I started unbuttoning my shirt, needing to get it off.

"Wh-what are you doing?" she asked.

I pointed at the ketchup. "Taking this off."

"Oh. Right." She shook her head.

"What are *you* doing?" I asked, grabbing an empty steel pail and pouring in some water from a pitcher before adding my shirt.

"Trying to disappear." She yanked off her veil, some of her hair tumbling down around her face. I couldn't imagine someone as striking as this woman ever being able to vanish. To blend in.

Now that we were alone, I had a chance to get a good look at her. Long, wavy hair the color of sable. Expressive brown eyes framed by long, dark lashes. Lush lips, fuller on the bottom.

She was tall, almost as tall as me. With delicate shoulders, breasts that all but spilled out of her dress, and full hips.

Fuck me. I swallowed hard and then glanced away.

"Am I going to be arrested for aiding and abetting a criminal?" I teased. Considering her concern over breaking the rules by being in here, I considered it highly unlikely.

"No," she sighed. "But I would murder for a glass of wine."

Her tone held an edge that told me she wasn't as okay as she wanted me to believe. Which prompted me to ask, "Are you sure there isn't somewhere I can take you? Someone I can call?"

"All I want is to drown myself in wine and forget this evening ever happened." She went over to the wall of bottles, her gaze challenging as she met my eyes over her shoulder. "I assume you can also text the owner about any wine I'd like to purchase?"

I joined her. "What are you in the mood for? Chardonnay? Cabernet—"

"Whatever will get me drunk the fastest." She grabbed two glasses and set them on the table before taking a seat. "You pick."

I pulled my phone from my pocket and selected Enzo's name from my contacts.

> Hey. I'm renting out the tasting room tonight. I'll pay for all bottles consumed and use of the space.

Enzo: Should I ask?

> Probably not.

Enzo: Do you want me to send someone to explain the wines?

> Some food would be awesome. Maybe a charcuterie plate.

> And some of Asher's pastries.

Enzo: I'll have it sent over.

> Thank you. And a "Closed for Repairs" sign would be a nice touch.

I could hear his sigh through the phone. Three dots danced on the screen then disappeared then reappeared.

Enzo: This is not what we mean when we say we offer "private tastings."

I chuckled but didn't respond since a new text came in from Asher.

Asher: Did you fall in the toilet?

> I'm going to be here a while.

Asher: First of all, TMI. And second, I can't believe you're trying to stick me with the bill.

I didn't correct his assumption. I didn't feel like explaining where I really was. Or who I was with.

I'll pay next time.

Asher: Don't worry about it. Feel better.

Thanks.

"Okay," I said, sliding my phone into my pocket. "It's all taken care of."

I grabbed a bottle and removed the cork, pouring us each a glass. She gulped it down, and I watched her throat work with every swallow. She filled her glass and started drinking again. If she kept going at that rate, she was going to pass out on the floor before long.

"You want to talk about it?" I asked.

She was slouched against the table, head propped up in one hand, the other teasing the stem of the wineglass as she stared straight ahead. "No."

"How about a game, then?" I suggested, curious about her. If she didn't slow down, I was going to be babysitting a drunk bride on what I assumed was her failed wedding day.

"Not in the mood."

"Humor me," I said, snagging the bottle before she could pour herself yet another glass. "Truth or drink."

CHAPTER TWO

Penny

His brows were furrowed with concern, corded forearms resting on the table. Everything about him radiated confidence and control. If he'd told me he owned the vineyard, I wouldn't have been surprised.

I shook my head and drank, then asked, "Why are you being so nice to me?"

He lifted a shoulder. "Because you looked like you needed help."

He said it like it was *that* simple. Like everyone was so kind and caring. After spending the last six years in New York, I found that difficult to believe. Or maybe it was that I'd lost all faith in men after my fiancé had left me at the altar.

But even I knew my trust issues went deeper than that. When my dad had died of suicide, my mom and I had been both shocked and devastated. I'd been a senior in high school, and our whole world had been turned upside down in an instant. I still didn't understand why.

Erik's seemingly sudden decision to end our engagement and cancel our wedding made me feel like I was that scared girl again. The one who was simultaneously filled with rage and heartbreak but didn't have much time to dwell on it because my mom and I found ourselves both broke and homeless.

Fortunately, I was neither this time, but I still felt like that same naive, hopeless, and confused girl.

Ugh. I hated that I was in this position. That I'd allowed myself to believe in happily ever afters or the fact that a man might actually want me.

I was done being polite and quiet. I was done trying to be small or swallowing my needs for a man.

"Would you ever leave a woman at the altar?" I asked.

"As a matter of fact, it's my turn," he said, then leaned closer. "He's a fucking idiot, by the way."

I ignored his comment about Erik, though it did make my chest puff up with pride. Erik *was* an idiot. But I was the fool who thought they'd fallen in love with him.

"No." I held up my glass, grateful there was a bathroom just down the hall. Though, hopefully, I wouldn't need it. "You want me to play a stupid game, you have to answer a question first." I was done letting a man's decisions define me or my life.

"No."

"No, you won't answer? Or no, you wouldn't leave a woman at the altar?"

"I don't intend to get married, so it's a moot point."

"Ever?" My eyes bulged, though I wasn't sure why. After tonight, I wasn't sure I'd ever walk down the aisle again either. Despite everything that had happened, I wanted to believe in love. Marriage.

He shrugged. "It seems like a big waste of money. You spend money getting married, only to spend even more getting divorced."

I scoffed. "Wow. That's...jaded."

His phone buzzed, and he glanced at the screen before standing and heading for the door. "Am I wrong?" he called over his shoulder. I tried not to check out his ass as he crossed the room.

I considered it briefly then admitted, "I guess not, though I prefer to believe in love." Or at least, I had. Now, I wasn't sure what to think.

I shifted in my dress, unable to get comfortable. There was too much fabric and not enough room to breathe. It was digging into my ribs, reminding me of all my shortcomings.

Was that why Erik had left me?

I wasn't thin enough? Wasn't the right type of woman to marry the heir to Cartwright Pharmaceuticals? Or was he annoyed by my career? It had definitely caused friction in our relationship in the past. And I was still pissed about my phone. Perhaps that incident the night before our wedding should've alerted me that something was wrong.

"It's not that I don't believe in love," he said, returning with a tray of food. The game was temporarily forgotten as we sampled the cheeses, meats, and other items from the platter. "I just don't think you need a ring or a marriage certificate to prove it."

"Are your parents divorced?" I asked, our hands brushing as we both reached for the bottle to refill our glasses.

I yanked my hand back as if I'd been scalded, and he shook his head, a strange look crossing over his features.

"Happily married," he finally said. "But my best friend is dating my sister, and—"

"Ooh. Scandalous."

He chuckled. "Yeah. I was pretty pissed at first."

"Sounds like a good story," I said, thinking of how much I loved that trope in romance novels. I'd been toying with writing one myself.

"My point is, my sister has a kid—River. My best friend,

Bennett, isn't my nephew's biological dad, but he's always loved River as his own. Why should the relationship between couples be any different?"

"Have you ever been in love?" I asked, popping a cheese cube into my mouth.

He drank, and I suspected the answer was no. Or maybe it was yes, but he'd been hurt. I was still thinking about that when he asked, "How long were you together?"

I sighed. "Three years, but I really don't want to talk about him."

If I'd wanted to talk, I would've called Brinkley. I briefly considered asking to borrow the guy's phone to let my best friend know I was okay, but I wasn't ready for more questions. I didn't want to face reality, even if that meant ignoring the fact that my body would hate me for this in the morning.

We settled into a comfortable silence, enjoying the charcuterie board and the wine. I could feel his eyes on me, watching me. Though I didn't understand why.

"What?" I snapped, immediately regretting it.

"I just—" He rubbed the back of his neck. "This is going to sound crazy, but I feel like I know you. Like we must have met before."

I lifted a shoulder but said nothing, quickly changing the topic to something else. I wasn't ready to face the world. I wasn't ready for judgment or snide remarks. I dealt with enough trolls online, and I seriously doubted this guy read romance. Not that men couldn't read romance. I just didn't think *he* did.

He was hot. Like cover-model hot. The type of guy romance novels were written about.

And interesting. Intelligent.

We spent the next several hours discussing wines and local attractions, places we wanted to travel and favorite foods. If it weren't for the fact that I was wearing a wedding dress and had just been dumped by my fiancé, I could've almost believed it was a date.

Even so, we had an easy familiarity between us. And maybe because we both knew nothing would come of our time together, there was no pressure. No expectations.

Which got me thinking. They always said the best way to get over a man was to get under a new one. Maybe...*maybe* it was the wine talking, but it didn't sound like such a terrible idea.

I let that idea percolate while we continued playing truth or drink. I wasn't sure whether it was the wine or just the fact that this guy was *that* cute and considerate, but I found myself flirting with him from time to time. And he flirted back. I got the feeling he was attracted to me—and I was certainly attracted to him. But he was holding himself back, always letting me take the lead. He'd answered my last question, and now it was my turn.

I summoned up all my courage, channeling my inner romance novel heroine. "Have you ever had a one-night stand?"

That made him pause in his movements and raise an eyebrow. But then when he answered, he didn't flinch. Didn't blink. "You haven't?"

"That's a question."

"So?"

I shook my head. "You can't answer a question with a question."

"Yes, but in it lies my answer. Besides, we never stated that was part of the rules." He smirked.

I drank again, mostly to cover my embarrassment. I mean —could I be more pathetic? His cryptic riddle of an answer certainly made me feel foolish for asking.

"Let me guess." He tapped a finger to his lips, his eyes

scanning my body in a way that made my skin heat. "The answer to that one is no. But you want to."

"Uh-uh." I wagged my finger. "That was more than one question."

"It was an observation."

"Semantics."

He smirked and stood to grab another bottle, refilling each of our glasses. "How drunk are you?"

"Buzzed but still cogent enough to make decisions, if that's what you're asking."

"Cogent, huh?"

"What?" The wine sloshed against the sides of the glass as I lifted it to my lips for a sip. *Shit. Maybe I need to slow down.* I glanced at the bottles littering the table, knowing my stomach would likely hate me for it in the morning. *Maybe I'm about to make a big mistake.* "My best friend is an attorney."

And I'm a writer, dammit. Though, many people looked down on romance novels, as if reading about people's innermost thoughts and intimate relationships was somehow inferior. *Psh.*

"Well, then I think your friend would advise you to use the word 'coherent,' not 'cogent.'"

"That's the one." *I knew that! Ugh.* I tried to hide my chagrin with a smile but then grimaced when the dress dug into my side again.

"That looks really uncomfortable. Beautiful..." His eyes lingered on my collarbones, sweeping over my cleavage. "But uncomfortable."

I bit back a smile. "Oh, it is. I feel like my ribs are being crushed." I squirmed in the seat. "There must be some rule that the more expensive an article of clothing, the more uncomfortable it is."

He glanced around. "As I see it, you have two options." He walked over to a stack of blankets and picked up one. "Well, three, actually. We can get you a ride back to where you're staying."

My shoulders slumped. "I don't want to go back to the hotel." The idea of going to the honeymoon suite alone was beyond depressing.

Nor did I want to chance running into…well, anyone I knew. Not Erik. Not the guests. And certainly not my mom. She was going to be *so* disappointed. She and Erik's mom had been envisioning our wedding nearly as long as they'd been friends.

"You can stay in your dress."

I grimaced. "What's option three?"

"Change into this." He held up the blanket. "We use them on cooler nights around the fire pit, but I'm not sure the last time it was washed."

His expression said he assumed there was no way I'd go for it. I couldn't wait to prove him wrong. To wipe that smug grin off his face that said he believed I was too uptight. Too "proper" to consider ditching my designer gown for a flannel blanket.

"Winner winner chicken dinner." I stood and wobbled. He rushed over and steadied me, and when I smiled up at him, we both stilled. Dust motes danced in the air like we'd been dancing around each other all evening. Falling softly before floating to the floor. It was inevitable—gravity. And in that moment, the pull I felt toward this man was just as undeniable. Just as powerful, like a force of nature.

"No problem." He didn't release me, and I didn't move away. I couldn't.

He was kind and genuine and sexy. God, he was sexy.

"Thank you," I finally said when I felt more stable. I took a step back and kicked off my heels. "That's better," I sighed, having shrunk by a few inches. The top of my head was now level with his chin. "I wish I'd done that hours ago." I rolled my neck and picked up another cheese cube and held it in front of my face. "Oh, how I've missed you." And then I devoured it.

He chuckled. "I can't believe you haven't touched the éclairs. People travel across the country for them."

"Meh." I lifted a shoulder. "I have more of a salt tooth." I started laughing. "That sounded ridiculous. Whatever the salty version of a sweet tooth is. That's me. If it's salty, I'll eat it."

"Mm," he hummed. The way he was looking at me caused visions of dirty fantasies to play through my head. I wondered if he tasted salty when he came.

"Bad idea," I murmured.

"What's a bad idea?" he rasped, his eyes on my lips.

"This," I said, and then I leaned in and kissed him. Softly. Tentatively at first.

Judging from his expression when he pulled back, he hadn't been expecting it. I worried that I'd made a mistake, but then he stepped closer and cupped my cheeks. His hands were warm yet callused, his gaze intense.

I stilled, my breath whispering across his lips. My chest rising and falling rapidly. And then, in a rush, our tongues were clashing, teeth nipping, hands exploring. He tasted of wine—notes of plum and the promise of adventure, and I wanted to get drunk on him.

Him. A stranger. Not your fiancé.

I pressed my palms to his chest, ending the kiss. We stared at each other, the air between us heavy with tension. My thoughts were clouded with lust, the needs of my body overriding my better judgment.

My lips were still throbbing from that kiss.

My core was aching for release.

Erik had left me, but this man wanted me. He seemed just as desperate for me, if his ragged breaths were any indication. Not to mention his raging hard-on that tented his pants and appeared to strain my direction.

"I should take you back to your hotel," he rasped. His voice was raw with desire, his blue eyes pools of liquid heat.

He'd been nothing but a gentleman all evening, despite my vulnerable state. And it only made him that much more attractive to me.

"Probably," I said, tugging at the hem of his shirt. I'd gone too far down this path to back out now. "But that's not what I want."

"What do you want?" he asked, hands clenched at his sides as if he were trying to resist touching me.

"Just for tonight," I panted. "I want to know what it feels like to be bad."

That seemed to be the answer he was waiting for. He teased the tops of my breasts with his finger. Running it back and forth over my cleavage in a tantalizingly slow motion.

"Are you sure?" he asked.

I nodded. "Yes."

He reached behind his neck and pulled his shirt over his head. My mouth went dry at the sight of his bare chest. I didn't even try to hold back, allowing myself to roam all the glorious skin, discovering his body as he devoured me.

He fumbled with the buttons at the back of my dress, both of us impatient to remove the layers of fabric between us. Finally, he spun me around and tugged at the material, sending several buttons flying. I gasped, both surprised and incredibly aroused.

I needed more. I wanted him inside me. I pressed my ass back into his hard-on, reveling in the feel of it.

"Mm. That was satisfying." I could hear the smile in his voice, and I liked the idea of another man destroying some-thing of Erik's. Destroying me.

I smiled at him over my shoulder, and he kissed down my

neck, my spine, as the dress slid closer and closer to the floor. The air was cool on my skin, but I felt hot beneath his gaze.

When he reached the clasp of my bra, he ran his palm over it and down my back. It was both sensual and soothing. And I could feel him taking in every inch of my body as if he were memorizing it. I couldn't think of a time that a man had looked at me with such reverence and raw desire. I couldn't think of a time I'd ever felt so wanted.

I bent forward to push the dress all the way to the floor.

"Fuuuuck," he groaned.

And when I stood and spun to face him, he captured my lips with his. Shoving down my bra so he could tease my breasts, pinch my nipples. And then he replaced his hands with his mouth, savoring me like the finest wine.

I shuddered, needing his touch there. *Everywhere.* Feeling even more brazen, I grabbed his wrist and slid one of his hands down my stomach to my underwear. He swallowed hard and started rubbing my clit through the silky material until I was riding his hand.

"Oh god. Oh god. Oh god," I chanted, undulating. I'd never felt so sexy. "That feels so good. So, so good."

In the past, I would've felt the need to touch him back. To reciprocate. But tonight was about what I needed. And I was going to take what I wanted.

"Mm. I think someone likes being bad." He bit my nipple, and it sent a jolt of pleasure through me.

I was so close. Apparently, I *did* like being bad. Or at least, my body did.

I wasn't sure I'd ever felt more alive. More liberated than I did in that moment.

This buildup was like the anticipation before a big release. Then my book would go live and positive reviews would start flowing in. It was overwhelming and exciting and all-consuming.

Between the way he was touching me and the sense of empowerment I felt, I soon went careening over the edge. I jerked in his arms, sensations flooding my body as he rubbed me harder. Faster. When he pinched my clit between his fingers, my eyes closed and my lips parted on a sigh.

"Fucking gorgeous." He kissed me again, cupping my cheeks, tangling his fingers in my hair.

I loved the feel of his touch, and he seemed to be enjoying himself just as much. My pleasure was his pleasure. My needs were…well, neither a burden nor an afterthought.

I wanted more. *Needed* more.

"I need—" I poked my tongue out from between my teeth as I focused on undressing him. But my hands were shaking from adrenaline and nerves. He was right; I'd never done this before. Never had a one-night stand. "This off." I finally unbuckled his belt and yanked it from his pants.

"That was hot." He smoothed my hair away from my face as I concentrated on his pants. Undoing the button, lowering the zipper. Pushing them and his boxers over his hips.

"Wow," I breathed as he kicked his pants aside, but not before grabbing a condom from his wallet.

I hadn't meant to say the word aloud, but his cock was, well…dang. Hard and proud, jutting toward me with a dot of precome beading on the tip.

"I'm going to fucking explode if you keep looking at me like that." He looked like it too. Vein bulging in his forehead. Jaw clenched as he slid on the condom with ease. It was sexy AF.

He pulled me to him, scrambling to unhook my bra and push my panties aside. "One more question."

"No," I groaned. "No more games."

"What's your name?" he asked, picking me up as if I weighed nothing.

I wrapped my legs around his waist, my arms around his

neck. Our chests pressed together. He set me down on one of the chairs then slowly dragged my custom garter down my thigh.

I hadn't realized it was digging into my skin until it was gone. "Thank you."

He lined himself up at my entrance, and I swallowed hard, my eyes glued to where our bodies nearly connected.

"Penny. Yours?"

"Liam," he said. "You sure this is what you want?"

I didn't hesitate. "Yes."

"Good," he responded and pushed into me in a single thrust that stole the breath from my lungs.

Oh yeah. This was definitely what I wanted. Then I threw my head back and let go. "It's a pleasure to meet you, Liam."

# CHAPTER THREE

Penny

"What the…?" I whispered as I blinked a few times, my vision still blurry.

My contacts were so dry it was difficult to pry open my eyes. I held a hand to my head, which was pounding. And tried to figure out where the hell I was.

The ceiling looked like a maze of tubes and pipes. Industrial. The floor was hard. And cold. I sat up slowly, clutching the blanket to my chest as I glanced around.

Have I been kidnapped?

As the space came into view, I realized I was in the tasting room. At the vineyard where I was getting married. *Supposed* to be getting married. And I was naked. And alone.

It came to me in bits and pieces. Erik's back as he left the bridal suite. The handsome stranger who'd rescued me. The… I gulped. Oh god. Liam's hands. His mouth. His…

Where was he? I glanced around, but there was no sign of him. Not even a freaking note.

And here I'd thought we'd had a connection. It wasn't as if I was looking for a relationship—far from it. But Liam seemed too thoughtful to cast me aside so carelessly.

Right. Because men are always so considerate.

I should've known better. I should've seen it coming. Wasn't this the story of my life after all? Trusting a man, only to have him let me down.

That said, this was definitely a new low.

Abandoned not only by my fiancé on my wedding day, but also my one-night stand the morning after. Was I wearing man repellent? Did I have a neon sign on my forehead that told men to run the other way? I was beginning to wonder.

Perhaps it should be flashing "idiot" in bright lights. Because I certainly felt like one.

Actually, I felt like a character in one of my romance novels, except this was real life. And I needed to find a way out before I had to do the walk of shame in my wedding gown.

My stomach rumbled, protesting my bad decisions from the night before. I drew my knees to my chest and buried my head in my hands. It was so much worse than that, though.

All my followers. All 61,000 of them knew I was supposed to be getting married this weekend. They'd been there for the proposal, cheering us on and wishing us well. They'd seen the preparations. The shoes. The… I slumped.

I wasn't just a jilted bride. I was a romance author who'd been left at the altar on her wedding day. As if having to face my family and friends weren't mortifying enough, I'd be the laughingstock of the internet.

I tried to think back. To figure out what the hell had happened and where it had all gone so wrong. In the span of twenty-four hours, my life had completely and utterly changed. I'd gone from being engaged to the crème de la crème of New York society to being cast aside like an empty bottle of wine.

I frowned at the empty bottles on the table, one of which

had my garter thrown around the neck. I'd selected the design because it was named "Floral Fairy Tale," and the company donated a portion of the proceeds to an organization that helped domestic sex trafficking victims.

Erik wanted to splash cash on the wedding. If we were going to spend an obscene amount of money on the celebration, I was determined to spend with purpose. Every item I'd had a hand in selecting had been to benefit female-owned businesses or ones that served their communities.

I glanced back at the empty bottles. None of that mattered now. And my head hurt just thinking about it.

Or maybe that was from the wine. I was positive Liam and I had consumed three bottles. Maybe it was just the two on the table. I'd lost count.

Just like you lost count of the number of orgasms Liam gave you last night.

Shut up!

I lifted my wedding dress from the floor. The white organza was now stained with dirt and speckled with wine. Several of the buttons had gone missing, and I remembered Liam ripping it open in his haste to undress me.

A rush of heat flooded my core.

I could never imagine Erik doing something like that.

Up until yesterday, I never would've imagined him leaving me at the altar either. Or "dropping" my phone when he was frustrated with me.

"WE'RE GOING TO BE LATE FOR OUR REHEARSAL DINNER." HE leaned against the wall, arms crossed.

I adjusted my dress and smoothed my hair. "I just need a few pictures for content, and then I'll be done. Can you please take another one?" I posed.

He grumbled. "This isn't how I envisioned spending the night before our wedding. I'm not taking any more photos."

"It'll just take a second."

"No." He tossed me the phone, but he hadn't given me any warning. It crashed to the tile with a sickening "crunch."

When I picked up the phone and saw the screen was cracked, I tried not to panic. But when it wouldn't turn on, my stomach twisted with anger and dread. "What am I going to do now? My work, my calendar, my whole life is on there."

"It was an accident, babe. I'm sorry." But he didn't seem remorseful.

I still wasn't convinced it had been an accident. Erik typically had much better aim. But I hadn't wanted to risk an even bigger fight the night before our wedding by asserting it was intentional. And while he'd promised to replace the device, the new one wouldn't arrive for a few more days. Conveniently leaving me without a phone.

What a disaster. I dropped the dress and rubbed a hand over my face. The whole thing was a huge mess, but more importantly, what was I going to do now?

I had nothing to wear. No phone. No money. I was fucked.

But as my best friend Brinkley often reminded me, I was resourceful. And creative. I would find a way out of this.

Now...if I were a character in one of my novels, what would I do?

I would start by finding something to wear.

I wrapped the blanket around me, trying to fashion it like a dress. I found some cord in a spare drawer and tied it around my waist. It felt very Ariel from *The Little Mermaid*, but it was better than being naked. I stepped into my Manolo Blahniks with "Mrs. Cartwright" and the date of our wedding etched into the bottom. I stomped and scuffed my feet against the floor in a burst of anger as I tried to erase it from my shoes. Like I wanted to erase the past twenty-four hours—and Erik freaking Cartwright—from my life.

Well, maybe not all of it. *Not* all *of the past twenty-four hours anyway.* The part with Liam hadn't been terrible.

Reckless, perhaps. But *definitely* not terrible. Quite the opposite, in fact.

He'd been so passionate. Like the men I wrote about in my books. He was intense. Sexy. That blond hair and those endless blue eyes.

Last night had been incredible. But then he'd left. They always did.

I stared at my dress crumpled on the floor. I'd spent months working with a designer. Attended countless fittings. Worked out and monitored my food intake closely to make sure it would look perfect. All for what?

I scoffed and hefted it into my arms, dumping my wedding gown into the trash by the door. What a waste. A $24,000 waste.

A few years ago, that was more than I made in a year. But to Erik, it was nothing.

I was tempted to try to salvage the dress and sell it at a secondhand shop, but I wanted nothing to do with it. Nothing to do with Erik or his money. I glanced down at my hand where his grandmother's vintage five-carat solitaire Tiffany ring sparkled. What a joke.

I wondered if that's all I was to him. A joke. Someone he could push around. Who would be an obedient and dutiful wife.

I took a deep breath and straightened. Now was not the time to dwell on it. Not when my stomach was gurgling and cramping, and I knew what was coming. *Thanks, IBS.* I needed to find a bathroom—soon.

I opened the door and peeked my head outside. The coast was clear, so I scurried down the hall to the restroom. When I finally felt like my stomach might cooperate for a few minutes, I washed my hands and tiptoed the rest of the way down the hall, until I came to the host stand. I ducked behind it and quickly dialed Brinkley's number. I'd had it memorized since college. And it was the only phone number I knew by heart since my mom had changed hers when Erik had given her a new iPhone for Hanukkah last year.

I tapped my fingers against the stand while I listened to the phone ring and ring and ring. My stomach was still roiling, and I hoped I'd make it back to the resort without having to stop again. When Brinkley didn't answer, I hung up and dialed her number again. This time, she answered on the third ring.

"Hello?" Her tone was terse. Expectant.

"Ink," I whispered. "It's Pen."

"Penny?" she gasped. "Where are you? Are you okay?" She rattled off a string of questions.

"Listen," I said, trying to get her attention. "I need you to pick me up at the winery and bring me some clothes."

"Clothes? What's—"

"Don't ask." I cringed, the bright sunlight and her loud tone hurting my head. "Just come. *Please.* I promise I'll explain later. But hurry!"

"Okay. Okay." I could hear shuffling in the background, and I hoped she'd get here soon. "Where will I find you?"

"Um—" I glanced around. "I'll be outside. Out of sight. Just park near the side entrance."

"Okay. See you soon."

I glanced back at the bathroom once more before I rushed outside and hid behind a pergola. While I waited for Brinkley to arrive, I prayed no one would see me. The gardens were dappled with dew, my blanket not warm enough for the cool autumn morning. I shivered and clutched it to me, praying she would come soon. Praying my stomach would settle, while I tried to focus on my breathing exercises.

Someone pulled into the parking lot, but when I peeked my head out, I almost immediately ducked back out of sight. The driver of the car was facing away from me, his dark brown hair wild. Definitely not Brinkley.

I held my breath, listening as he closed the car door. Straining to determine the direction of his movements as his footsteps crunched against the gravel path. Finally, a door opened then shut, and I let out a sigh of relief.

Another car arrived, and I hesitated before taking a look. *Oh thank god.* It was Brinkley. When she spotted me, her eyes went wide, her mouth agape. I couldn't be sure, but it looked like she mouthed, "Holy shit."

I walked to the car, though I wanted to run, but the gravel made it difficult in my heels. I opened the door and hopped inside, grateful she'd rescued me.

I pulled my blanket dress tighter around me and cranked the seat heater all the way up. "Thank you."

"Thank you." She jerked her head back. "*Thank you?*"

"Um. Yeah." I sank down even farther into the seat, trying to hide. I didn't care about changing; I just wanted to leave. Preferably before I had to run to the bathroom or face Liam. "Can we please just go?"

"What the hell happened, Penny? Are you okay? Do we need to call the cops?" She was in lawyer mode now.

"What? No. Why would we need to call the cops?"

"Um, maybe because I've been worried sick about you? You go missing, and no one can find you. And you've been here the whole time? What the hell?" She pulled out of the parking lot.

My head really could not handle her volume level. I groaned.

"And then you ask me to pick you up and bring clothes. What happened to your dress?" She waved her hand around.

"Please pay attention to the—" She swerved, and I gripped the door handle tighter. "Road," I said more softly.

"I mean, where the fuck is your custom dress that you spent a year of your life designing?" She glanced over at me then softened, probably because she'd seen me wince. "I'm sorry. Did you have an accident?"

"No." Thank goodness. "And *I'm* sorry," I sighed, knowing that she was upset because she cared about me. "I should've found a way to call you, but I was freaking out. So, when I saw an opportunity to escape, I took it."

"I want to hear more about that later, but—" She placed her hand over mine, her expression full of concern. "First tell me, are you okay?"

"I will be—" I pumped an imaginary brake as she veered toward the wrong side of the road. "As long as you don't kill us on the way back to the hotel."

God. Her crazy-ass driving was *so* not helping my stomach.

She rolled her eyes. "Fine. Deflect. I'll allow it. For now."

"I just…" I sighed and stared out the window at the rows of grapes. Rows upon rows of them, as far as the eye could see. I'd lived in New York so long, it was almost as if I'd forgotten how much I loved nature. Erik, on the other hand, did not. We'd taken so many vacations where I would've loved to have spent more time outside. But unless we were on a golf course, he wasn't interested. "I want a hot shower and some peppermint tea, and then I promise I'll tell you everything. I'm really sorry, Ink."

She nodded and pulled into the front entrance of the resort behind a Bentley. A valet from *Ensueño* came to open my door, and I cringed as I remembered my current fashion statement. But, hey, it wasn't the first time I'd had to improvise with my clothing. Thanks to my IBS and the lack of public restrooms in New York, I'd had to get creative or buy something new to wear more than once. It was probably my least favorite thing about living there.

"Good morning, ma'am."

"Good morning."

Brinkley grabbed my arm and led me inside. I disappeared into the bathroom while she talked to an employee at the front desk. When I returned, she was having a discussion with the manager before she was finally given a key to the room. An employee led us to the Treetop Suite, where I hoped all my luggage would be waiting as promised.

The plan all along had been for Erik and me to stay in separate rooms the night before the wedding at the same hotel as the guests. During the wedding, his staff would move our things over to *Ensueño* for our honeymoon. Well, just my stuff now since he wouldn't be joining me.

Because there would be no honeymoon.

I tried to distract myself by focusing on the hotel. It exuded the type of quiet luxury that I'd come to expect from traveling with Erik. I had a feeling it was even more expensive than I'd suspect, but at the moment, I didn't care.

All I wanted was to shower, drink some soothing peppermint tea, and forget yesterday ever happened.

"What if Erik's here?" Brinkley whispered as we walked down the hall.

"He's not," I said with certainty. Though, really, I wasn't sure I could trust my intuition anymore.

CHAPTER FOUR

Penny

Brinkley's gaze was questioning, but she remained silent until we got to the room. Once the door was closed, she rounded on me.

"Nope." I held up my hand. "Shower and tea first."

Fortunately, I could enjoy this place without it being tainted by memories of my ex. Or without fear of running into anyone who had come expecting to celebrate our wedding. All the guests would've already left or were staying at a different hotel in Fall River that was closer to the wedding venue.

She headed for a small desk with a phone on it. "Fine. I'll order breakfast."

"Great. Thank you."

I escaped to the bathroom, closing the door behind me and sinking against it while the water heated in the shower. I caught sight of myself in the mirror and almost didn't recognize the woman staring back at me. She looked unkempt and wild. But also…vibrant and full of life.

My hair was everywhere. My eyeliner smudged. And I couldn't help but laugh.

This was just too crazy.

Too unbelievable.

Definitely a story worth telling. Maybe someday when it didn't feel so raw. When it wasn't so personal. For now, it was easier to imagine myself as a main character in one of my novels than face reality.

I removed the blanket and folded it up. I hovered over the trash can, ultimately dropping it on the floor instead. As if it were another piece of laundry needing to be washed. I didn't know why, but I wanted to keep it.

I'd tossed my high-end wedding dress in the garbage, but I couldn't seem to part with a flannel blanket.

So what if I wanted a memento from my sexy one-night stand? I told myself it was because Liam had made me feel wanted in a way I hadn't in a while, but it was more than that. Liam had made me feel more alive than I had in a long time.

Again, I wasn't going to dissect that one too thoroughly.

I took my time showering and dressing in my favorite cashmere joggers with a matching oversized sweater. I was tempted to hide out in the bathroom all day, but Brinkley would never allow it.

I grabbed a blanket from the back of the sofa and wrapped it around myself before heading out to the terrace where Brinkley was waiting with breakfast. I sank down in the empty chair across from her, scooping some of my tea into an empty cup before adding hot water. The familiar scent of peppermint immediately put me at ease. I started picking at the bowl of plain oatmeal, wondering how much my stomach would tolerate. When I glanced up, Brinkley was staring at me, mouth agape.

"You keep doing that," I said between bites.

"What?"

I pointed at her face and made a circle. "*That*. That face."

She closed her mouth and let out a deep sigh. It was then I noticed the dark circles beneath her eyes. The hair hastily thrown in a ponytail. "I'm exhausted. Your mom and I were up all night, trying to reach you or figure out where you were. We were really worried about you."

"Oh my god. My mom." I groaned, burying my head in my hands.

I'd avoided her yesterday because I knew how disappointed she'd be. I didn't want to upset or worry her, but I also knew that I couldn't put on the brave face she'd hope to see. I couldn't force myself to smile and act like everything was going to be okay.

"It's okay," Brinkley said. "I covered for you."

I felt my shoulders relax. "Thank you. I'll call her in a little bit." I sat back down. "And I'm sorry you were worried. Last night was crazy."

"I'll say." She leaned forward, resting her arms on the table. "Tell me everything that happened after I left you in the bridal suite with that douche canoe."

"Well," I sighed, not sure I was ready to talk about it but knowing she deserved an answer. "Erik seemed really nervous." He'd seemed on edge for weeks leading up to the wedding, in fact.

"I noticed that too. Which is odd because he's typically so calm."

I nodded. "He started pacing, asking me questions like, 'Do you really see yourself spending the rest of your life with me? Raising a family with me?'"

At the time, I'd been shocked. And despite a pinprick of doubt, I'd been more outraged than anything. Of all days to end things, why had he waited until our wedding day?

"What'd you say?" Brinkley asked.

Rage churned through me, along with embarrassment. "I

told him I wouldn't have said yes if I didn't see a future together."

"Right? Ugh." She rolled her eyes.

"And then he said, 'I'm sorry. I can't marry you.'"

I grasped my joggers and squeezed the fabric, remembering how I'd gathered the silk layers of my wedding dress in my hands before marching over to him. Five hundred guests were waiting outside to watch our wedding, and he wanted to do this now?

"You've had months, years, to decide. And you want to change your mind now? Minutes before we're supposed to walk down the aisle?"

I would never forget the look he gave me as he backed toward the door. His eyes were full of regret and remorse, but also...relief. "I can't." He nearly tripped. "I have to go."

I took a step toward him, surprised by the strength of my voice. "Go where? What about our guests?"

"I'll tell the wedding planner. She'll handle it. And feel free to stay in the honeymoon suite for the week. Charge food or whatever to the room."

"That's right, because all you have to do is throw money at a problem to make it go away."

I thought about my broken phone. About the times he'd bought me extravagant gifts when he was late or forgot our anniversary. And now this...

"Did he say why?" Brinkley asked, bringing me back to the present. I shook my head. "That's it? What a bastard." She blew out a breath. "Fuck. I'm sorry, Pen."

I nodded and stared at the table. I kept thinking I'd cry, but I hadn't yet. Maybe I was still in shock, or maybe I just didn't care enough. Crying over Erik—spending any more time thinking about him apart from killing off a character bearing his name in one of my novels—felt like a waste of time.

"What happened after that?" Brinkley asked.

I laughed a little and tried to ignore the arch of her eyebrow.

"After that, I ran. I ended up hiding in the tasting room."

"Alone?"

"Um—" My cheeks heated. "One of the locals may have pointed me in the right direction."

"And did *said local* also help with the removal of your dress?" Her self-satisfied expression was annoying, so I didn't answer. Instead, I went into my room to grab my laptop. I'd put this off long enough.

I was powering it on when she shut it. "Trust me, you don't want to do that."

My stomach clenched, and I took another sip of tea. It must be even worse than I'd feared. "That bad?"

"I just think you should give yourself some time to digest what happened before going online."

I sank down on the couch. We both knew it was more than that. All my readers were probably wondering why I hadn't posted anything. I never went a day without posting *something*. And my wedding, of all things…

"You're right. I really don't have the energy to deal with it right now." With the way my stomach was acting, I just wanted to curl up on the bed with one of Meghan Hart's books.

"You know what will make you feel better? A massage. The clerk at the front desk informed me that you have a couple's massage scheduled for noon."

I assumed that was *after* their discussion. *After* the manager had been summoned.

I didn't know what she'd told them, but they kept calling me Mrs. Cartwright. Ugh.

"I don't know, Ink. My stomach's a mess this morning."

"The massage might help you relax."

True. Stress was not good for my IBS. And the past twenty-four hours—the past few months—had been incredibly stressful. Planning a wedding on the opposite side of the country. Making preparations to move in with Erik full time and become his wife. All while still trying to finish writing a book.

A trip to the spa did sound nice. And as long as I wasn't having a terrible flare-up, a massage was okay.

But still… "I'm not going alone. No way." How mortifying.

"You don't have to." She stood and turned the key card in her hands. "Because I'm going with you."

The idea had merit. Though…did I really want to accept any more of Erik's money?

Erik had always insisted on paying for everything. Many times, he'd been aggravated with my job and had tried to convince me to quit. I loved writing too much to ever consider that. But now more than ever, I was thankful I hadn't listened. I was also thankful I still had a few months left on my lease.

If it had been up to Erik, I would've terminated the lease long ago. And despite having mostly moved in with him after we'd gotten engaged, I'd struggled with giving up my apartment, even if it was only used as a place for me to write in peace. So, we'd struck a compromise. I'd keep the apartment as my "office" until the wedding.

Now that the wedding was off, I needed to be mindful of my spending. Not blowing money on an expensive massage at a luxury resort.

"It's already paid for," Brinkley said as if reading my

thoughts. "Come on." She grabbed my arm and dragged me toward the door. "We're going to make the bastard pay, and you're going to enjoy the hell out of this honeymoon."

He *had* told me to charge it to the room, but still… I wasn't sure why I even cared. "It's not like he'll even notice," I muttered, following Brinkley as she navigated us to the spa. "He has more money than god."

"Then you shouldn't feel guilty about spending some of it." Brinkley smiled at me over her shoulder.

I rolled my eyes but followed her anyway. I wasn't sure I'd ever look at money and not feel guilty. Grateful, yes. But guilt was a different matter. It was impossible to forget all that I'd overcome. How hard I'd worked to put myself through college, to start my writing career to, well…all the steps I'd taken to get to this point. Which was why I found it difficult to be blasé about money.

We changed and settled onto our tables. As the massage therapist kneaded my muscles, I let my body relax and my mind wander. I didn't want to go home, not yet. But did I really want to stay here? Alone. On what was supposed to be my honeymoon?

The longer I thought about it, the more I realized the answer was yes.

I'd always wanted to explore the Alondra Valley. I dreamed of shopping in the stores Meghan Hart did. Of writing at the coffee shops where she might write. Of running into her. Perhaps it was foolish—especially since no one knew what she looked like. But I'd come here wanting to feel closer to her. To her stories. They always made me feel so hopeful.

Her books had been my escape after my dad had died. When my mom and I had to completely start over and struggled to make ends meet. And any time my stomach acted up, which was more often than not, thanks to my irritable bowel syndrome, Meghan's books got me through.

"So," Brinkley asked once we'd returned to the suite, boneless and relaxed, "what now?"

"I'm going to hang out here. Take the vacation as you suggested."

"Do you want me to stay? We could make it a girls' trip."

I appreciated the offer, but I knew she had to get back to work. It had been hard enough for her to take off for the wedding. Her firm didn't offer much vacation time for associates. And what little time off she had was often over-shadowed by emails and phone calls. Yet she'd come to my bridal shower, bachelorette party, and the wedding.

"Thanks, but I'll be okay on my own. It might be good for me." And it would be nice to do whatever I wanted. Not what Erik had planned for us.

"Is this about the local?" she teased.

I tried to steady my voice and ignore the way my heart raced at the reminder of Liam. "Who?"

"Oh, come on," she said. "You really think I bought that story that you were in the tasting room alone? You totally had that fresh-fucked face. And your hair…" She raised one eyebrow with a knowing smirk.

I laughed but shied away from answering. "Does that sound like something I would do?"

"Ordinarily, I'd say no. But after what happened yesterday, I wouldn't blame you. Besides, I'd much rather imagine my best friend having a sexy-revenge one-night stand than drowning her sorrows alone."

I cringed. "You imagine me having sex?"

"Again with the deflection." She rolled her eyes. She'd known me long enough that she could spot my bullshit and call me on it. "Clearly, you don't want to talk about it."

"Clearly," I deadpanned.

After my dad's death, I'd tried to shut off my feelings. I didn't like to think about them, let alone talk about them. But in the past year, I'd started seeing a therapist to process some of my grief. And while I knew it was healthier to talk, I just… I wasn't ready yet.

It was a big part of the reason I loved writing romance. It allowed me to explore my feelings on a diverse array of subjects and to try to understand a variety of viewpoints. Writing was both cathartic and healing. But even that didn't sound appealing.

"But I'm here if you do. Okay?"

I wrapped my arms around her. "I know. I'm your Pen, and you're my Ink."

"And no matter what happens…" She held me tight, clinging to me as I did her.

"We'll always have each other," we said in unison.

CHAPTER FIVE

Liam

"I'm going to the back for a few minutes," Mom said to Lizzie. "Can you keep an eye on the register?"

I kept my attention on the bookshelves, debating what type of character I wanted to write next, though my mind was still stuck on last night. On Penny. The jilted bride who'd disappeared the morning after our one-night stand.

I didn't know why I was still thinking about her. Or why I cared that she'd left. All I knew was that I'd gone to get her some clothes and coffee. Some breakfast. I didn't think I'd been gone that long, but by the time I returned, she'd vanished.

I slid my hand into my pocket and rubbed her garter with my thumb and forefinger. I'd found it on the neck of a wine bottle, and for some strange reason, I'd kept it. I had no use for a bridal garter covered in rhinestones and flowers, but having that piece of Penny made her feel all the more real to me.

I stared at the shelves, willing myself to focus. Thinking about last night wouldn't help me write my next book or gain new readers. I was here to find inspiration. To find something that sparked an idea I might want to write about, like parkour.

Researching parkour had been fun, even if Wren had wanted to kill me for it. River had been a little too enthusiastic about the sport for her taste, though I knew he'd move on to something else eventually. He was like me in that way.

Maybe an Olympic athlete? I grabbed a copy of Lindsey Vonn's latest book. I could give the story a twist: an athlete struggling to find her purpose after a career-ending crash.

"Did you read Meghan Hart's latest?" I overheard a woman ask from nearby. She was standing at a table featuring books by local authors, my latest release in hand.

My ears perked up, and I strained to hear her friend's response.

"Not yet, but I can't wait."

I smiled to myself, though I half wished I could go over and remove the book from their hands. I hated the idea of disappointing my readers. I hated the comments that had circled my brain on repeat since the release.

Boring.

Unoriginal.

Not all of my readers felt that way, but enough of them that it made me worry.

I shook my head and pushed away the negative thoughts. I needed something that inspired me. Something like—

The bell over the door chimed, and that was when I saw her. *Penny.*

She looked different today. Her waves stuffed under a New York Yankees baseball cap. Her skin devoid of makeup. She looked nothing like the frightened bride I'd encountered last night. Though I—of all people—knew appearances could be deceiving.

I mean, who would've suspected that I was a famous romance author?

Me. Liam Beaudin. An engineer who inspected nuclear power plants. Or at least, that's what I'd been until about a year ago when I'd quit to write full-time.

Penny ducked her head and made a beeline for the romance section. *Hm. Interesting.*

I couldn't help myself; I decided to follow. She pulled out a book, and I watched as she read the back cover then replaced it. She did this a few times, her shoulders relaxing a little more the longer she lingered.

I strode up next to her and grabbed a book from the shelf. She glanced up and smiled but then jumped back when her eyes met mine. "Jesus. Are you stalking me?"

"My name's Liam," I teased. "Though you certainly called me 'God' a lot last night."

Her cheeks turned a beautiful shade of red, much like the wine we'd shared the night before. But then she narrowed her eyes at me. "Leave me alone."

I frowned. Why was she so upset? *She'd* ditched me.

Was she embarrassed? And then a worse thought occurred to me. Had she reunited with her ex?

I should drop it. Leave her alone. But I couldn't. Something kept pulling me back to her. If nothing else, I needed to know she was all right.

"Are you okay?" I asked in a gentle tone.

"What do you think?" she snapped. She huffed and placed a book back on the shelf before grabbing another. I smiled when I saw the author's name—Meghan Hart. "And why are you smiling?"

I schooled my features into a neutral expression. "Sorry. Um—" I cleared my throat. "Just thinking about all the fun we had last night."

"You know what wasn't fun?" She stepped closer, careful to keep her voice low. "Waking up on a concrete floor, naked and alone."

Shit.

"I—" I started to explain, but she was on a roll.

She crossed her arms over her chest. "Save your excuses. You're like all men. When things get too real or too difficult, you bail."

Ouch. Was this about me or the groom? Or someone else? I started plumbing ideas about her backstory as if she were a character.

Stop. Just stop.

"I could've been arrested for trespassing," she hissed.

"The owner gave us permission to be there. And I was coming back," I said, and when she glared at me, I added, "I swear. Didn't you see my note?"

"Right," she scoffed. "A note."

"I left you a note. I went to get breakfast and coffee. Clothes," I said. "But when I came back—" she pretended to ignore me, but I was determined to convince her "—you were gone."

She crossed her arms over her chest. "Excuse me for not wanting to wait around *in case* you *decided* to show up again."

I had, though. I'd borrowed some clothes from the gift shop, snagged some coffee and breakfast from the kitchen. And then when I'd returned to the tasting room, Penny had vanished. Almost as if she'd never been there. As if it had all been a dream.

"Look," I continued. "I came back. I did. And I know you don't believe me, but let me make it up to you."

"I don't want anything from you." She turned and walked away.

I followed her past the stage used for children's story time and author readings and down another row of books, my attention landing on the one in her hand. I puffed up my chest. "I'll get you a signed copy of Meghan Hart's latest novel."

She frowned at the shelf in front of her. *"That's* how you're going to make it up to me?" she hissed. "By buying me a fifteen-dollar book?"

"A signed book," I said. "And no. That's just the start. Clearly, you're a fan, right?"

"I'm not *just* a fan." She clutched my book to her chest, her anger melting into an expression of pure adoration. "She's my idol. She inspired me to write romance."

I wanted to bask in her compliment, but I stilled, everything crystallizing in that moment. We'd only met last night, but all along, Penny had seemed so familiar. As if I knew her. When she'd told me her name, I hadn't made the connection, but I did now.

Penelope Glass.

Her attention jerked to me, making me realize I'd said the name aloud. "What did you say?"

I rushed to grab one of her books from the shelf and flashed her the back cover. "This is you, isn't it?" She looked a lot more formal—posed—in the picture. But it was still clearly her. "You're the romance author Penelope Glass."

She grabbed my elbow and dragged me deeper into the store, away from anyone who might overhear. "How did you know that?" she hissed.

I scrambled for an explanation. One that didn't involve divulging my pen name. I was already playing a dangerous game. I knew way too much about her. Things I shouldn't know.

Her birthday was in May. She was twenty-five. She had an obsession with alpacas. She looked amazing in the color red. She loved popcorn. And she was a talented writer whose stories resonated with readers. Fuck. They'd resonated with me. Not to mention given me one hell of a book boner.

"So...?" Her arms were crossed over her chest.

"My mom owns this store. She and my sister, Wren, love

your books. They also may have mentioned you were getting married soon. They talk about your wedding almost as often as they do the new season of *Outlander*."

They'd talked about *Outlander* so often that Dad had finally caved and watched it. I wondered when he'd finally relent and read a Meghan Hart novel.

Penny laughed, tucking a strand of hair that had come loose behind her ear. But then her expression darkened.

"What is it?" I asked.

"I have to go." She dropped the book on an empty shelf and brushed past me.

"What?"

She hurried out of the shop, and I stood there for a minute, watching her. I grabbed the last book she'd been looking at and followed.

"I'm taking this." I held it up as I passed Lizzie and the register. "And this one," I said, realizing I still had Penny's book in my other hand. "Add them to my account."

"Interesting choices."

I ignored the teasing in her tone and backed open the door. "They're a gift. For a friend."

"Mm-hmm. Sure they are."

I rolled my eyes and glanced both ways, searching for any sign of Penny. I finally spotted her standing outside of Lick ice cream about a block down.

I jogged over to her. "What happened back there? Are you okay?"

"I—" She pulled her lower lip between her teeth. "I freaked out, okay? I'm not ready to face my readers after the wedding, so the fact that you knew my pen name…"

I nodded, understanding better than she could imagine. "Your secret is safe with me."

Her shoulders relaxed. "Thanks."

"Here." I held out the book. "You forgot this."

"Did you—" She glanced back at Bibliolater with wide eyes. "Did you steal that?"

I lifted a shoulder. "I asked them to put it on my tab."

"Like at a bar?" She shook her head when I nodded but didn't take the book from me. "Wow. It must be nice to live in a small town."

"It is. It's nice to be surrounded by people I've known almost my whole life." I indicated to a few shops and told her a little about each of the owners.

"Next you'll tell me you know Meghan Hart." She scoffed, as if the idea were preposterous.

"I do," I blurted, wanting to impress her. To keep her from leaving again.

Shit. Why did I say that? I immediately wanted to take it back.

She arched an eyebrow. "*You* know Meghan Hart?"

I nodded. "Yep."

Fuck. What are you doing? Stop!

"*No* one knows Meghan Hart. So why should I believe you?"

"Maybe because you said I was the best sex of your life. That's gotta count for something."

"Hmm." She tapped a finger to her lips. "Was that me or the alcohol speaking?"

I grinned. "There's only one way to find out."

Her lips parted, and I licked my lips, remembering the taste of hers. But then the lust cleared, and she scoffed. "As if I'd sleep with you again after…well, what you did."

I leaned in and whispered, "Which thing are you referring to? The one with my tongue? Or with my—"

She moaned, her body drifting toward mine. "Don't tempt me, Liam."

"Why shouldn't I?" I settled my hand on her hip. "Unless you got back with your ex."

She jolted, and I hoped that meant she was repulsed by the idea. Then she said, "No, but I'm only here for the week."

"So?" I wasn't sure I saw the problem. She'd just ended a relationship and wasn't looking for anything long-term, and neither was I.

She frowned. "You're forgetting the fact that you left me naked and alone."

I threw up my hands. "I came back." But then I was struck with an idea. "And I can prove it."

She popped out her hip, skepticism written across her features. "*Really?*"

"Yes, really." I reached into my pocket and pulled out her garter, twirling it around my finger. "Look familiar?"

Her eyes widened briefly, and she tried to yank it from my hand. "Give that back."

I quickly stowed it away, and she glared at me. But we both knew she was teasing. At least maybe now she believed me.

"Finders keepers," I teased, shoving it even deeper into my front pocket. I rocked on my heels. "So…"

"So if I agree to what you're proposing, I'd be using you as a rebound."

"And that's a problem how?" I joked.

She didn't answer, instead asking, "Don't you have work?"

"I'm between projects."

"So you're unemployed."

"No," I huffed, trying to ignore the couple that skirted around us on the sidewalk. I was relieved it was no one I recognized. "I'm between projects."

I considered giving her my usual explanation, but I didn't feel like lying. Not to Penny. And it was true. I *was* between books, stuck on a tricky plot point when my release had flopped and my inspiration had dried up.

The only reason I'd even published my last book was

because I'd already put it up for preorder before Tessa died. I hadn't wanted to disappoint my readers by canceling it or even postponing. And I hadn't wanted to risk losing my preorder privileges on the vendors because I'd failed to meet the deadline. Considering how much of a disaster it had turned out to be, I was beginning to wonder if that would've been the wiser decision.

"Do you have an answer for everything?" she asked.

I flashed her my most charming smile. "I can be pretty persuasive when I want something."

"Oh yeah, and what do you want from me?"

"I think you know."

"Let's pretend I don't. Spell it out for me." She crossed her arms over her chest.

I laughed. The more I got to know Penny, the more I liked her. Not just her online persona—Penelope Glass—but the *real* her.

"A rematch of truth or drink."

"No." She groaned, covering her face with her hands. "No more wine."

I laughed. "Fine. One week. That's all I want."

She shook her head. "It's a bad idea."

"And here I thought you wanted to be bad."

The corner of her mouth tilted, and she tried to fight a smile. Instead, she stared at the sky as if searching for answers then finally returned her attention to me. She blew out a deep breath. "I can't believe I'm actually considering this."

I lifted a shoulder. "It's not like we haven't slept together before."

She rolled her eyes. "One night can be passed off as a mistake. One week…" She shook her head. "That's different."

I hated the idea of being a "mistake." A regret. It was almost as bad as when a reader DNF'd my book. Not finishing was far worse than a one-star review. At least the one-star reviewers had finished the book. And usually, they hated it, which meant I'd made them feel *something*.

Farther down the street, I spotted River hugging my dad with my sister and Bennett watching on. *Oh shit.* I couldn't let them see me. See Penny and me. I pulled her into an alcove between the stores.

"What are—"

"Shh." I placed a finger to her lips, ignoring the sparks dancing along my skin.

Instead, I glanced around for Wren or anyone else I knew, as I wondered if this was going to end up in *The Vine. God, I hope not.* For both my sake and Penny's. I had a feeling being featured in *The Vine* was the last thing she would want.

"Is something wrong?" Penny whispered, brow furrowed.

I chuckled and shoved my hands into my pockets, embarrassed by my behavior. Wanting to downplay it. "It's nothing. It's stupid, really." When she continued to stare at me expectantly, I said, "There's a popular local gossip blog, *The Vine.* I don't want us to end up in it."

Her eyes went wide. "Oh my god. Are you serious?"

"They generally go pretty easy on non-locals. I'm guessing they don't want to scare them off. But since I'm a local..." I lifted both hands in the air.

"Is it like Lady Whistledown?"

"No. V isn't nearly as mean."

Her jaw dropped. "You watch *Bridgerton?* Or maybe you've read it?" she mused, sounding even more stunned.

"That's what you're most surprised about?" I shook my head. "I have a younger sister, remember?"

"My ex refused to watch it with me. Said it was a waste of time."

"Waste of time?" I shook my head. "He clearly wasn't paying attention." And not just to *Bridgerton.*

"Right?" Her smile could've lit up downtown Alondra. "That show demands your full attention."

I stepped closer, my gaze intent on her. "*You* demand my full attention."

She smiled but then rolled her eyes. "Are you always this cheesy?"

"I thought you loved cheese." I mimed picking up a cheese cube from a charcuterie platter and held it up in front of my face before saying, "Oh, cheese. How I love thee." I puckered my lips, and she slapped my shoulder.

"Oh my god. Stop it! I did not do that!"

"You didn't, huh?" I chuckled. "I distinctly remember your ode to cheese."

"Wow. Excellent. Good to know that's the memory that stuck with you from last night." She pulled her baseball cap lower on her face, as if to hide her embarrassment.

"Oh, it's one of many." I tapped my temple. "I think my favorite was when you—"

"Okay." She hooked her arm in mine, dragging me out of the alcove and back onto the sidewalk. "Time to go. I think that's enough."

"Are you sure?" I teased. "You don't want a Lick?"

"Liam!" She pinched my bicep, but it only made me laugh harder.

"What?" I pulled an innocent expression. "I meant the ice cream." I gestured to the sign.

She rolled her eyes and tugged on my arm. "Let's go before I change my mind."

"Where are you taking me?" I asked, following her to a parking lot.

The lights on an emerald-green Aston Martin flashed. I let out a low whistle and circled the car, admiring the sleek lines and the body styling. *Ho-ly shit.*

"Should I give you two a moment alone?" Penny teased, leaning against it with her arms crossed.

"Aw." I set the books on the ground and caged her in with my arms. "Is someone jealous?"

"No." She glared at me.

"Don't worry." I chucked her chin. "I'll have you purring before too long."

She rolled her eyes and turned to open the door. "So full of yourself."

I placed my hand over hers. "Allow me."

She stepped back and waited for me to open the door. Then she slid inside, and the sight of her behind the wheel made my cock strain against my zipper.

"What?" she asked.

I rubbed the back of my neck. "I'm not sure I've ever seen anything sexier." I took out my phone and snapped a picture.

"Liam!" she chided.

I didn't respond, merely pocketed my phone and grabbed the books before heading around to the passenger side. I slid into the seat, grateful the window tint was dark. This car was definitely going to turn heads. Not that there weren't luxury cars on the streets of the AV, but an Aston Martin? I sighed, running my hands over the buttery leather seat.

"You're doing it again," she said.

"What?"

"Fondling the car."

I placed my hand on her leg, slowly sliding it up her thigh. "Is that better?"

She smirked but kept her attention on the road. I glanced around at our surroundings and then at the speedometer. We'd left the center of town and were out on the open road, and yet she was still driving thirty-five miles per hour.

"Why are you driving so slowly?" I asked.

"I just...don't want to get a ticket."

"Are you kidding?" I gave her leg a squeeze. "Who cares about a ticket? Let 'er rip."

She shook her head, as did I.

I pinched the bridge of my nose. "You're killing me."

All this power. Right at her fingertips. An engineering marvel. And she was going to let it go to waste.

"You're a bad influence."

"Ooh, speeding. *So* bad." I bit my lower lip.

"Not just speeding. Last night…" She scanned me from head to toe, her eyes full of desire. Definitely no regrets there.

I slid my hand closer to the apex of her thighs. "It's not too late to reform yourself. To turn around and take me home."

She swallowed hard, twisting her hands on the wheel as I began to rub her through her jeans. And then she punched the gas, and we went flying down the road. My body was pressed back against the seat, and she squealed.

When I looked over at Penny, she was smiling. The vine-yards and mountains flew past, the engine purring, my heart pounding—a rush of lust and adrenaline making me impatient to reach our destination.

I'd only just met Penny, and yet I could already tell I was in over my head.

CHAPTER SIX

Liam

Penny slowed as we reached the stone archway that led to *Ensueño*. I should've known this was where she was staying. It was the most expensive resort in the AV after all.

She pulled up to the valet stand, and he took the keys from her. "Thank you, Mrs. and Mr. Cartwright."

Her expression hardened, at least until I wrapped my arm around her waist. "Come on, wife." I leaned in and whispered, "I have some very naughty plans for you." I squeezed her ass, unable to resist touching her.

She batted my hands away but laughed as she led me to her room. All the while, I was cataloging details, taking note of things for future inspiration.

"I've always wondered how swanky this place was," I said once we were alone in her room. It smelled of peppermint, like Penny. Peppermint and…eucalyptus or something.

She laughed, removing her baseball cap and tossing it aside before shaking out her curls. She was stunning, and she seemed right at home. "You've never been?"

"No reason to. I live here, remember?"

"Mm. I remember." She tossed me a menu. "Want to order room service? I'm starving."

"I'm starving, all right." I ignored the menu and pulled her closer to me. She gasped, and my body flooded with sensations.

"I'm not a twenty-four-hour all-you-can-eat buffet." She pressed her hand to my chest as if pushing me away, her tone full of sass.

"Maybe not, but you are my new favorite meal," I said, kissing down her neck, craving another taste of her.

She sighed, but then her stomach growled. So I said, "After lunch," and gave her ass a playful swat.

I explored the space while she called down to order. It was both luxurious and cozy, and I was definitely going to use it as inspiration in a future novel. Hell, I might have to come back and write here. It wasn't unusual for me to stay at my cabin a few hours north when I was on a deadline.

My cabin was sparse. Spartan, in comparison.

And this was filled with light. The sun bouncing off the white wood of the ceiling. The shadows of the leaves on the oak tree outside rippling across the desk. The TV was hidden behind a panel—that was a plus. No distractions. I could turn off Wi-Fi. Go to the spa.

This was...*mmm*. I could already feel the creative juices flowing, and I was excited. Or maybe it was my lust talking, my excitement over the prospect of spending time in such a beautiful place with an even more beautiful woman.

"Why did you want to get married in the AV?" I asked, pushing open the doors to the balcony. A private seating area overlooked acres upon acres of vineyards and gardens. "I mean, it's gorgeous, don't get me wrong. But I figured you'd want something closer to...home." I caught myself at the last minute, remembering that I wasn't supposed to know where she was from. Then she really would think I was a stalker.

She sighed and sank down onto the couch. "The only thing I had a say in was the location. And I think my ex only agreed because he does a lot of business on the West Coast."

I blew out a breath and took a seat in the chair opposite. "Ass." Though I already knew that. I mean, who left a woman like Penny at the altar?

She said nothing, and I didn't push. I could remember when Kade left my sister. She'd been young. Pregnant. And devastated.

I found myself wondering if Penny had support. An older brother or someone to look out for her. I tried to remember anything from her social media, but nothing came to mind apart from her fiancé and maybe her mom. But as I knew, social media could all be very carefully curated. Edited.

Room service arrived, and I ducked into the bathroom, trying to stay out of view. No one knew who V from *The Vine* really was, and the last thing I wanted was for her to post about my tryst with Penny. More for Penny's sake than my own.

"So...the AV," I said, taking my seat across from her at the table. The meal had been laid out, and the presentation was phenomenal. I met her eyes, admiring the rich brown color. If she were a character in one of my novels, I would've likened them to the most decadent chocolate ganache. "Was it all about the scenery, or did you have some other tie to the region?"

She covered her face with her hands. "This is embarrassing to admit, but...Meghan Hart."

"Wow." I leaned back, crossing my ankle over my knee. Trying to hide the giant fucking grin that wanted to overtake my face. "You really are a big fan."

"I've read all her books. Some multiple times." She ducked her head, the glow from the fireplace lighting up her cheeks.

The heat crackled as the flames consumed the logs. Just as

I wanted to consume her. I wanted to be consumed by her. My body felt as if it had been ignited in her presence.

It made no sense. I hardly knew her, but I blamed it on the setting. It was intimate and romantic. I couldn't have picked a better setting for a scene in a romance novel myself.

But the more she talked about Meghan, the more I was torn between keeping my secret and wanting to blurt out the truth. I wasn't going to, but it did make me wonder. How would someone like Penny—a superfan—feel if they knew that I was the writer behind the name?

It felt as if the universe was handing me an opportunity. A chance to gain insight from a reader who had been there since the beginning. I knew this was a bad idea, but I couldn't seem to help myself.

"Even the latest one?" I asked, cutting into my meal. "It got slammed. Or at least, that's what I heard." I took a bite so I'd shut the hell up.

"It's unfortunate, but it happens."

"Why do you think readers hated it so much?"

She paused, glass midway to her mouth, a funny expression crossing her face. "Hate is a strong word. But you really want to know?"

I nodded, scared to speak and risk betraying my true feelings.

"It's hard to put my finger on, but if I had to guess, I think it's lacking intimacy."

"Really?" I furrowed my brow, resisting the urge to point out all the places and all the positions in which the characters had sex.

"There's a difference between sex and intimacy. Usually, Meghan nails it, but this one felt off somehow from her usual work. Not bad," she hastened to add. "Just different."

I considered her words, tempted to defend myself but knowing it would only cause more trouble. Besides, it wasn't going to change anything. The book was already out there; I wasn't going to re-edit it now. The only solution was to publish another book, a better book.

The more I thought about it, the more Penny's comments reminded me of something Tessa would've said.

"Are you sure you haven't read any of her books?" she asked, coming over to sit on my lap. I rubbed my hands up and down her hips, loving this more assertive side to her. Loving that she felt comfortable with me.

"Why do you ask?" I purposefully evaded answering her question.

"Well—" She dragged her teeth along the shell of my ear. "There's this one scene that I've always wanted to act out."

"Mm." I closed my eyes as I wondered which scene she'd selected. Her hand dipped below the waistline of my pants, and I groaned. "Tell me more."

"I HAVE A SURPRISE FOR YOU," I SAID A FEW MORNINGS LATER, trailing my finger down the bare skin of Penny's back.

"I'll bet you do," she said in a suggestive tone as she wiggled her hip against my hard-on.

I growled, smoothing my hand down farther, over her full hips and luscious ass. "Damn, I love this ass." I leaned forward and kissed her globes, squeezing them in my hands.

"Tell me more about this surprise," she said, as if trying to keep me focused.

It wasn't working. Not with her naked body on full display. At this rate, there would be no surprise because we'd spend the day in bed. *Again.* Not that I was complaining.

"You have a choice to make," I said, caressing her skin and

wondering why I'd thought it was a good idea to leave the resort. But then I remembered how excited she'd been when she'd talked about the AV. So I added, "If you're willing to venture into town."

"I don't know." Her words were muffled by the mattress, her body laid out for me like a feast. "I'm pretty happy here."

I laughed, leaning over to press kisses down the length of her spine. She wriggled and sighed, and I was tempted to keep her here all day.

"We can go back to the bookstore and pick up some reading material," I said. "Or we can spend the day with alpacas."

She shot straight up, arms extended as if she were doing a push-up. "Did you say alpacas?"

I laughed, though I was captivated by the sight of her naked form. "I did."

She spun around and sat on the bed. "Really?"

"Yes, really." I grinned, loving her excitement. *This* was why I'd considered leaving the resort. Because I knew it was something Penny would love. "I was thinking we could spend the day at Alpaca Acres and have lunch."

"That sounds amazing." She wrapped her arms around my neck, her breasts crushed to my chest. My cock was aching for her. "And then maybe swing by Bibliolater on the way home?"

I smirked, pressing my lips to her temple as I tried to ignore my hard-on. "I think we can make that happen."

"What about *The Vine*?" She wrapped her hand around my erection and started stroking. *So much for waiting until later.*

"Liam?" she asked, making me realize I'd forgotten to answer her question. I'd been more focused on the feel of her hand wrapped around my cock.

And then she bent forward and took me in her mouth, and dear lord... I inhaled, but it was shaky. I wasn't going to last long. Not with the way she was licking and sucking the tip, teasing my shaft with her hand. I lost myself in the feel of her.

I reached out for her breasts, her clit. Wanting—no, needing—to touch her. She wiggled her hips as I drew circles around the bundle of nerves.

"Come here," I rasped, wanting to touch her even more than I wanted her mouth on me.

"What about *The Vine?*" she asked on a gasp as I slid a finger inside her.

We'd scrolled through some of the posts on *The Vine* together on my phone last night, but there hadn't been anything about her wedding or Penny.

I'd read some gossip about Asher's grandma and her—alleged—harem of adoring men. I wondered how he felt about it and couldn't wait to ask, just to see his reaction. A new ax-throwing place that was coming to town. And a mystery involving the little lending libraries in town and the reading contests that had suddenly started appearing inside. With prizes like a new tablet or a gift card to some of the local businesses. No one seemed to know who was responsible, but everyone was talking about it.

Penny hovered over my lap, riding my hand. I swallowed hard, sucking her nipple into my mouth as I smoothed my free hand down her hair, her back.

"Up to you," I said, barely able to think straight. "I certainly don't mind having you all to myself."

"Mm. I know what you mean." She hummed as we got into a good rhythm, continuing to stroke my cock while I made her moan.

"What do you want to do?" I asked.

"Fuck," she panted, tits bouncing in my face. "*The Vine.*"

"No." I smoothed my hands over the soft skin of her stomach, our eyes meeting. "Fuck me."

"Yes," she hissed, starting to unravel. "Right there, Liam. That's it."

She moaned when I took her other nipple in my mouth. Biting and sucking in the ways that made her arch her back and dig her fingernails into my skin. I was bathed in her peppermint scent, and it was intoxicating.

And then her movements became jerky, her eyes closed and lips parted as she came. I nearly came watching her. She was so fucking sexy. So…free.

"Condom," she gasped, still coming down from the high. She leaned over and grabbed one from the nightstand before rolling it on me.

She climbed on top of me and sank down inch by inch, both of us groaning until I was fully seated. I cupped the back of her neck, her forehead pressed to mine. Our eyes locked. It was intense. All-consuming.

She cried out, her walls clenching around me. Hot. Tight. Wet.

There was sex, and then there was…this. And this was the type of sex I wanted to write about. A connection that seemed to eclipse everything else. The type of release that seemed to both deplete and restore. Until all I saw, all I felt, all I could think of, was her.

It was incredible. Like nothing I'd ever experienced. And after my body finished convulsing, I pulled her onto my chest. We were both panting and sweaty.

"Wow," she said, her tone echoing the awe that I felt.

I chuckled, brushing her hair away from her face. "Yeah."

She rested her chin on her hand and smiled at me. "You've definitely given me some new material for my books."

"Oh yeah?" I teased, wishing so badly I could admit the same to her.

And then I shut that shit down real quick. I'd kept this

huge secret for six years. I wasn't about to divulge it now. To a woman I'd known less than a week. To a fling. Though it certainly felt like more than a fling.

Aw. Fuck. What am I doing?

I stood and grabbed my clothes, needing to put some distance between us. "Let's get ready to go see some alpacas."

She jumped out of bed, tits swaying. Ass jiggling slightly with every step toward the bathroom. "I can't wait."

When we arrived at Alpaca Acres, Susan waved from the gate. "That's Susan. She owns Alpaca Acres. Super cool, but nosy."

Penny groaned. "Don't tell me. She's your aunt."

I laughed and climbed out of the car. "No. Family friend. I told you I knew almost everyone. Not that we were related."

"Hey." She lifted a shoulder, lowering her sunglasses to shield her eyes. "It's a small town. You never know."

I rolled my eyes and headed for Susan. "Hey!"

"Liam. It's good to see you." She pulled me in for a hug.

"Hi, Susan." I gave her a squeeze, and she released me. "This is my friend Penny."

Penny stepped forward and held out her hand to shake, but Susan just pulled her into a hug. Penny's eyes went wide, and I laughed at her surprised expression. But to her credit, she rolled with it.

"Come. Come. Let me introduce you to my babies." We followed her down the gravel path to the paddock. This time of year, the wild flowers were still in bloom, the summer varieties giving way to fall. Her gardens were well tended, and the old Victorian house was inviting.

On the outside, my house looked as charming as hers. But inside, it was a disaster, a work in progress.

Susan stopped next to the fence, and one of the alpacas trotted over. "This one's Daisy."

Penny squealed as she approached. "Oh my gosh. They're

so cute." Her expression darkened. "I wish I had my phone so I could take pictures."

She hadn't told me the story behind her broken phone, but I had a feeling the ex had something to do with it. I refused to let him ruin anything more for her.

"I'll take pictures and send them to you," I said.

"Thanks." Penny stepped forward to greet the fuzzy creatures. "Hi, Daisy," Penny cooed.

"Over there is Larry." Susan pointed to an alpaca chewing some hay. "And that one is Willa."

"Oh, they're all so cute." Penny looked like she was going to burst out of her skin with excitement.

"Would you like to take them for a walk?" Susan asked.

Penny lit up. "Really?"

"Absolutely. I think you and Willa would make a good pairing." She handed Penny a treat bag and called for Willa. "Liam, you can have Larry." She handed me another treat bag. "Have fun, you two!"

"Oh, we will," Penny said, then laughed when Willa pulled on the leash, dragging her along.

I shook my head and then followed them down the trail that led to the vineyards. It was a crisp fall day, but we were walking at a brisk pace and Penny didn't seem to mind. Her ass looked amazing in the jeans that clung to her curves. Sable riding boots encased the lower part of her legs. She looked like a sexy equestrian, and I wanted her to ride me.

"Liam."

"Huh?" I snapped my eyes up to her face, where amusement played across her features. "What was that?"

"I asked if you were having fun."

"Yeah. I am, actually."

"You sound surprised."

I chuckled as Larry nudged the treat bag. I pulled one out for him, and he ate it from my hand. "I am. I guess I figured it would be super touristy or something, but these guys are surprisingly personable."

"I know!" She smoothed her hand over Willa's side. "You're a cutie. Aren't you?" she asked in a baby voice. Then she turned to me. "It's so peaceful out here. The opposite of New York."

"Do you like living there?"

She turned and continued down the path. "Sometimes."

"Is that where you're from?"

"Oh no." She shook her head. "I'm from Wisconsin."

"You don't sound like it."

"I trained myself not to have an accent."

I tilted my head to the side. "Really? Why?"

"Because people judge you for it."

I wondered if she was referring to her ex.

"Do you miss Wisconsin?" I asked.

"It hasn't been home for a long time. I miss wide-open spaces and watching the sunset over the fields. But that's about all."

"What about your friends? Your family?"

Apart from the few years I'd spent away for college, I'd lived in this town my whole life, and I couldn't imagine living anywhere else. I loved my friends, my family, my community. And I liked feeling as if I was part of something bigger than myself.

"Mom lives in New Jersey now. And my best friend, Brinkley, moved to New York when I did. There's nothing left for me in Wisconsin."

I nodded. I wondered if she'd ever feel the same way about New York. I wondered how she felt about going back after what had happened with her ex, but I didn't ask. Those weren't the types of questions you asked a fling, no matter how much I wanted to.

We were quiet the rest of the walk, both absorbed with

our thoughts. When we returned to the paddock, Susan was waiting.

"Have fun?"

"Oh yes," Penny said, her cheeks flushed. "Willa was wonderful."

"Good." Susan led the alpacas back into the fenced area and then turned to us. "Ready for some lunch?"

"For sure," I said, dropping into step behind the two of them.

When we reached the main house, Susan led us to a table by the window, but not before saying, "I have a favor to ask."

Oh no. Here it comes.

"Penny, would you be willing to sign some books for me?"

I'd expected Penny to recoil, but she lit up, nearly bouncing on her toes. "I'd be happy to. It's not every day I get to meet a reader in person."

As I watched Penny sign books, it struck me. As happy as I was for Penny, I was jealous. She was able to interact so freely with her readers. To talk with them and sign books for them. To hear their praise. Unlike me, she was free to be herself—fully.

CHAPTER SEVEN

Penny

"Here," Liam said, handing me a steaming cup of peppermint tea.

I'd just emerged from the bathroom for the second time in less than an hour, and my stomach was still grumbling. I'd tried to follow my usual eating habits as much as possible, but my body did not like eating out this often. I felt bloated and crampy and nauseous and completely unsexy.

But the way Liam was looking at me told me that he thought I was beautiful. That he cared about me, and he was worried.

"Did you get your period?" he asked, joining me on the couch and curling a blanket around me. We were still in our hotel bathrobes.

I blinked a few times, wondering if I'd misheard him. "What?"

"Oh, I, uh, just assumed—" He rubbed the back of his neck. "Sorry."

"No. Not at all. It's not my period, though I appreciate you being so chill about the subject."

He chuckled. "I do have a little sister, remember?"

"Yeah, but most guys are weird about it. Grossed out." Erik certainly was. Though he always insisted on showering immediately after sex too. Forget cuddling.

Liam lifted a shoulder. "My parents always normalized it, so I guess I just saw it as a bodily function. Nothing to be embarrassed about. Nothing to hide."

His response nearly brought tears to my eyes, and it made me feel safe enough to say, "I have IBS. Sorry, um, irritable bowel syndrome."

"Can I do anything to help?"

I shook my head. "You already have."

More than he probably realized. The tea. The blanket. The...acceptance. It was so incredibly comforting.

He took my hand in his and rubbed his thumb back and forth over my skin. "Is this okay?"

I nodded. "Thank you. That feels really good."

"If you ever need a bathroom or something, just tell me. A few years ago, my sister had a health issue that created a lot of bathroom anxiety. So I definitely got used to knowing where the bathrooms were and how to get her there quickly."

"Oh no." I frowned. "I'm sorry to hear that."

"Thanks. She's better now, but I guess I'm just trying to say that I'm used to my family talking about bowel movements."

I smiled and leaned my head on his shoulder. "I'm glad she's okay."

"Me too," he said. "She's been through a lot, but she's resilient. She deserves to be happy."

"Even with your best friend?" I asked.

"Especially with my best friend," he said. "Maybe I wasn't happy about it at first, but I'm really glad they're together. Actually—" He glanced at his phone. "I'm supposed to hang out with Bennett and River this afternoon."

"I'm sure you'll have fun," I said, trying not to let my disappointment show. I knew it was unreasonable to feel so possessive of Liam, but our time together was limited.

I leaned over and grabbed my new phone from the side table to check the time. It had arrived last night. There was no note. Nothing other than the newest phone with a new case and PopSocket, everything set up and completely charged.

Typical Erik. His solution had been efficient and expensive but completely devoid of emotion. In his world, money was always the answer.

"Do you want to get back in bed and watch something?" Liam asked.

I turned to him, eyebrow raised. "Are you asking me to Netflix and chill?" I teased.

"Netflix." He smiled, tucking my hair behind my ear before kissing my cheek. "And cuddle."

I grinned. "Sounds perfect to me."

He led me over to the bed, grabbing the remote and my tea before joining me. He was so attentive. So thoughtful. I could never imagine Erik doing something like this with me. He was always too busy working or something else. And like my pleasure, my IBS often felt like an inconvenience.

Liam and I watched two episodes of *Sex Education*, dissecting the plot and character motivations. I was surprised by how knowledgeable and passionate he was about the craft of storytelling, but I chalked it up to the fact that his mom owned a bookstore. It might seem silly, but if someone had asked me for my idea of a perfect date, this was it.

My stomach was finally feeling better, and I pushed out of bed and stretched. The robe fell from my shoulders, and I relished the way Liam's eyes drank me in.

"I have some places I want to visit in town." I had a whole

vision board of places, in fact. And now that Erik wasn't here, I could do whatever I wanted. After I called my mom, anyway. I knew she was worried.

Liam groaned, and my nipples hardened to tight peaks. "I should shower. But if you keep tempting me like this, you're going to make me late."

"Am I?" I teased, enjoying the feel of his body against my back as he came to stand behind me. The way his golden skin contrasted against my own in the mirror.

He gnashed his teeth, his erection digging into my butt. "I don't want to leave, but I promised my nephew I'd be there."

He brushed my hair aside, kissing my neck as he cupped my breasts. I reached back and rubbed his erection through his robe, loving the way his hands looked on my skin. Drinking in his scent. It was intoxicating. He smelled of clean laundry, sunshine, and something that was unique to him.

"You should get ready," I said, not wanting to be the cause for him disappointing his nephew.

"Come with me," he rasped, sliding his hand between my legs.

"What?" My breath caught in my throat as he began to massage my clit.

"Come with me. Please?"

I met his eyes in the mirror. "You're serious?"

"Yeah. We're going to help Bennett at the animal shelter. You'd get to cuddle with puppies."

A hot man and adorable puppies? It sounded too good to be true. The only thing that might rival it was the alpaca walk we'd taken the other day. Both activities were something I could never imagine my ex being interested in. With Erik, it had always been elaborate and expensive dates. Dinner at an exclusive restaurant. A surprise weekend trip to Paris.

I'd thought that was what I wanted. I'd thought that was romance. But I was coming to realize that maybe that wasn't the case anymore. Maybe it never had been.

This quiet contentment I felt with Liam was new. It was like curling up with a Meghan Hart novel—cozy yet exciting. Comforting yet full of unexpected surprises.

"Count me in. That is, if you don't think your nephew will mind me crashing."

"River?" He shook his head. "I'm sure he'll be delighted."

I gasped, arching my back as he slid a finger inside me. I squeezed my eyes shut as the pleasure mounted. I wanted to clamp my legs together. I wanted him to rub me harder. I wanted—

"Inside me. Now." I panted, reveling in the newfound power in my voice. The freedom in asserting my wishes.

"Later," he said, our eyes meeting in the mirror. "This is about you."

It didn't take long before I was crying out, bracing myself on the mirror as my release barreled through me.

We ran out of time to shower, but Liam didn't seem to care. We dressed quickly, and I braided my hair in the car as Liam flew down the road.

When we arrived at the Alondra Valley Animal Clinic, a man in scrubs came to greet us, the turquoise material matching his eyes. He had a stethoscope draped around his neck, his blond hair glinting beneath the fluorescent lights.

"Hey, Bennett." Liam shook the man's hand then gave him a hug. "Where's Riv?"

"He'll be out in a minute. Thanks for coming." Bennett smiled at me, his eyes filled with curiosity.

"Of course." Liam glanced back at me then made the introductions.

"Nice to meet you," Bennett said and shook my hand. "Are you new in town?"

"Just visiting," I said.

He tilted his head back. "What do you think of the AV?"

"I love it here." The more time I spent here, the less I wanted to go home. The AV was idyllic, and I could see why Meghan Hart loved it so much.

"Uncle Liam!" A kid ran down the hall in a blur of rainbow and glitter.

"River!" Liam said with just as much enthusiasm, opening his arms in time for the kid to fly into them. They hugged, and then River stepped back.

Liam had told me that River was unique, and while that was certainly a fitting description, so was the word fabulous. River would be right at home in New York with his fun sense of style that didn't conform to traditional gender rules. I loved his rainbow overalls with a ruffled blue shirt and glitter high-tops.

"Wait till you see the puppies!" River said.

"I'm so excited." Liam ruffled River's hair. "I hope it's okay. I brought a friend to help."

Friend, huh? We were a bit more than friends, but River didn't need to know that. Besides, it was only for a few more days. Then I'd go home. Back to reality.

I didn't want to think about it.

"River, this is Penny. Penny, River."

"River," I said, feeling out the name. I liked it. I liked this kid. He had pizzazz. "Nice to meet you."

"I like your hair," River said. "Very Anna from *Frozen*."

"Thanks." I pointed at his outfit. "Love those overalls."

"My nana got them for me. Come on." He grabbed one of Liam's hands and one of mine and dragged us down the hall behind him. "You've gotta see the puppies. So cute!" he squealed.

Liam just smiled at me, and I wondered if this was a

regular day for him. Hanging with cute dogs and even cuter kids. The more I got to know Liam, the more I liked him. The more I could see a life for myself here. With him and all this small-town goodness.

And that way of thinking was dangerous.

This was a fling.

My life was back in New York.

I'd traded one fantasy for another. New York billionaire for small-town sweetheart. I mean, what did I even know about Liam? I had no idea where he lived. Where he worked. Because it didn't matter.

Or at least, it shouldn't. Not if this really was just for one week.

"One of our patients had a litter, and we could use some help in the nursery," Bennett said. "Come meet Nana and her puppies."

"Nana?" I laughed. "Like the dog in *Peter Pan?*"

"One and the same."

I heard some sniffing and shuffling, little mewls, and then I saw them. All six fur balls rolling around in their little towel nest.

"Here you go," Bennett said, handing me one as Liam helped River get a puppy. "This is Peter."

"Do you have any pets?" River asked me.

I shook my head, cuddling the little fluff ball, Peter, to my chest. "No. I've always wanted a dog, but my—" I grimaced when I nearly said fiancé "—my ex was allergic."

"What a bummer!"

"Right?" I laughed.

"Is this Wendy?" Liam took one himself, his large fingers stroking the dog's fur protectively. With care and affection. *This man...this town. They were going to kill me with adorableness.*

Bennett chuckled. "That's Smee."

"Hey, Butter Butter," River said to Bennett, and I kissed the puppy to hide my smile at the nickname. I wondered where that had started, because it was adorable.

"Yes, Butter Bean?" Bennett replied automatically.

I smiled, unable to hide it anymore. I felt like I was eavesdropping on a private conversation, but they didn't seem to mind.

"Can we keep one?" River—or rather, Butter Bean—asked.

"What about Toodles?"

"Who's Toodles?" I mouthed to Liam as my puppy started gnawing on my skin. I gently stopped him then returned him to the box with the others.

"Their French bulldog," Liam said to me.

"*Maybe* he needs a friend," River said, batting his eyes. *This kid.* He was too freaking cute. If it were up to me, River would already have the whole damn litter.

"And *maybe* your mom might kill me," Bennett teased.

"Nah. She *loves* you," River said in a singsong voice. "Can I go with you to get the ring when it's ready?"

Liam's head snapped up, his attention on the two of them. I assumed it was an engagement ring, and I only hoped their story would have a happier ending than mine. I had a flashback to my wedding day but quickly pushed it away. It had happened less than a week ago, but it felt like a lifetime.

Bennett placed his finger to his lips, though he was smiling the entire time. "You know that's supposed to be a surprise."

"I know," River whispered. "But I'm excited. I want you to ask her. I want us to be a family."

"We *are* a family." Bennett pulled River to him just as Liam asked, "You're going to propose?"

Bennett nodded, his expression solemn.

Liam held Bennett's gaze. Tension filled the room before Liam's face split into a huge smile. "It's about fu—"

Bennett coughed into his fist.

Liam took a breath, and I could tell both of them were trying not to laugh. "About freaking time."

"Whew." River wiped his forehead dramatically. "I thought you were going to punch him again for a second."

My eyes went wide. "Again?"

Liam hooked his arm around Bennett's shoulder. "Yeah. I was an idiot."

"We both were," Bennett said, and I could see the strength of their bond. The love between them. These two men weren't just friends; they were brothers.

Liam's relationship with Bennett reminded me of mine with Brinkley. She'd always been more than a friend to me, more like a sister. So, when Liam stayed in town to have lunch with River, I headed back to the resort. I figured they'd appreciate some alone time. But it was more than that. After spending time with Liam's family, I needed a minute to catch my breath and check in with Brinkley. I hadn't talked to her since she'd left.

The first few days without my phone had made me realize just how absorbed I'd been with my device and work. How much I'd been using it to distract and numb myself. Back in New York, my phone was like...another limb. But I didn't feel the desire to do that here. So, I'd been leaving it in the safe.

I opened the safe and ignored the engagement ring, bypassing it for my phone. I ignored all the missed calls, instead focusing on the messages from Brinkley and my mom. I called my mom and spent the first ten minutes trying to reassure her that I was okay, despite the fact that we'd spoken just the other day. Then she spent the next five nagging me to take care of myself. After promising to check in again soon, I called Brinkley.

"Hey," I said when Brinkley answered.

"Run into Meghan Hart yet?" she teased. I smiled to myself. It was good to hear her voice.

"Not yet. Though—" I cleared my throat. "My local contact claims to know her."

"The local, huh?"

"Yeah." I bit the inside of my cheek.

"Nuh-uh. I let you off easy before. I need details. What's his name? How old is he? What's his social security number? What's he like?"

I started laughing at her ridiculous, rapid-fire questions. "Even if I knew his social, I would not give you that."

"What? *Girl*, I thought I'd slipped that right in there."

"Mm-hmm." I laughed. "Not so subtle."

"Can you blame me? I feel like we need to run background checks on any future men in your life."

"Ha-ha."

"At least tell me his name. You know you want to."

I laughed. "Liam."

"Hot."

"Right? It means 'strong-willed warrior' or 'protector.'"

She laughed, all too familiar with my obsession with the meanings behind names. What could I say? It was an occupational hazard.

"Does it fit him?" she asked.

"I think so, but who knows. Erik obviously didn't live up to his name's potential."

She snorted a laugh. "True. What was it? 'Ever'?"

"Yep. Ever or always. Or ruler." I pulled a face. I didn't want to admit how much that rang true.

"Still more exciting than 'woodland clearing,'" Brinkley said, referring to the meaning of her name.

"Right? Or 'weaver.'" Not that I had anything against my name. Penelope Glasner was a perfectly suitable name. I'd changed it slightly for my pen name, though I'd only ever gone by Penny to friends or family. When I was at signings or online, I was Penelope.

"So, back to Liam," she said. I knew she wouldn't be deterred for long. Brinkley had an incredible memory, and she was tenacious. It made her a formidable opponent in the courtroom. "Do you really think he knows Meghan Hart? You sure he didn't tell you that just to get in your pants?"

"He told me *after* we'd slept together, thank you very much."

Though now that I thought about it, he'd told me when I was pissed at him for leaving me naked and alone. He hadn't. I knew that now and not just because he'd kept my garter as a souvenir. Liam was too considerate to do something like that.

"Is he going to introduce you?"

I shook my head before remembering she couldn't see me. "I asked, but Meghan's out of town this week."

"Oh, bummer."

"I know, right? So close."

She laughed. "*So* close. Though, really, you know what they say about being careful about meeting your heroes…"

"Yeah. Yeah." I rolled my eyes. "Don't ruin this for me."

"I wouldn't dream of it." I could hear the smile in her voice.

"Good."

"So apart from all that, are you doing okay? You sound… relaxed. And I get the impression you're having fun."

"I am." The answer rolled off my tongue. Life was so simple—at least on vacation. This conversation was the first time I'd even remotely dealt with reality, apart from talking with my mom earlier. "I've been busy."

"Having all the sex!" she said in a singsong voice.

My cheeks were on fire, but when I opened my mouth, it sounded more like a frog croaking.

"Ooh, girl. Don't even try to deny it."

I laughed. "Fine. I am, but it's not just sex. We've done so much more."

"Sounds kinky."

I rolled my eyes. Of course she went there. Brinkley was often telling me to up the heat in my books. Demanding another sex scene. Though, she was usually right. Many times I'd tried to get away with a fade-to-black scene, and she always busted me for it.

"We took a brewery tour that was super fun. I think you'd really enjoy it. And we went for a walk with alpacas."

"No fucking way. Did you tell him that was on your bucket list?"

"No. I never mentioned it. But it's crazy. It's like he knows me." I'd never been with a man who seemed to genuinely care about me and my interests—until Liam.

"Elaborate, please," she said, and I could hear the wariness in her tone.

"I don't know. I just—it's like he gets me." We had so many common interests, but it was more than that. It was like he *knew* me. Like we'd met before or were old friends.

"Whoa. Whoa. Whoa. Back the bus up."

"What?"

"Do you think he's a fan? Does he follow you online?"

"I mean…he did recognize me. He realized that I was Penelope Glass the romance author."

It was like a record scratch.

"I know you've read some stalker romances, but that is *not* okay in real life."

I burst out laughing. "No. No way." I shook my head.

"Liam's not a stalker. His mom follows me online, but I don't think he does."

"You met his mom?" she yelled. "Holy shit," she said more quietly, more to herself. I could hear shuffling in the background. "I need to get out there ASAP."

"No. No," I said, appreciating Brinkley's concern but wanting her to calm down. "He's mentioned her—Debbie. She owns this adorable bookshop in town. Apparently, she's a fan."

"Oh. Okay. I was really starting to wonder what the hell was going on out there."

I frowned. "What's that supposed to mean?"

"You *just* got out of a three-year relationship. Because the asshole you were engaged to left you at the altar."

"Thanks," I deadpanned, my mood souring. "Didn't need the reminder." I still didn't understand what had happened with Erik, and I hated feeling like a failure. Especially when I'd always done everything to please him, even at the expense of my own happiness. No more.

"I know. Sorry. I just—" She huffed. "I don't want you to get hurt again. And it seems like you're getting really invested in a guy you barely know."

"I'm not invested. I'm having fun. Isn't that what you always tell me to do? Let go. Loosen up. Live a little."

"Yes to all of the above, but I know you, Pen. I know how much you want the fairy tale and the happily ever after. And anyone can seem perfect for a week."

"I know what this is and what it isn't. It's fun. It's temporary. And after it's over, I'm coming home and swearing off men."

Even if I weren't, Liam was making it hard to believe that anything could top this week. That another man could ever compare to him and what we'd shared.

"Even the fictional ones?" she teased.

Some of the tension between my shoulders eased. "Oh, hell no. I love my book boyfriends too much to ever consider abandoning them."

They were the only men I could truly count on.

Liam

"Gah. This whole town is so freaking cute!" Penny squealed. "I never want to leave!"

I smiled at her as we walked down the sidewalk. We'd just finished a visit to the AV Farmers Market, where we'd sampled goat cheese and enjoyed drinks from the Pore Over stall—coffee for me and peppermint tea for her. I'd bought her a mug made by a local artisan, and we'd stopped by Bennett's stall briefly, saying hello to the animals he was trying to find homes for.

As we walked through downtown, Penny kept peering in every window we passed. Sighing over some dress or smiling at a display of flowers. I'd lived in the AV my whole life, but she was giving me a whole new perspective.

"Where to next?" I asked.

"I was really hoping to go to Bibliolater. I'd like a new book for the flight home."

I didn't want to think about the fact that Penny was leaving in two days, so I hugged her close to me and said, "I'm always happy to get you more books if it inspires you like it did last night."

She dipped her head, and I pressed a kiss to her temple. Last night, we'd been reading in bed when she put her book down suddenly and straddled me. It had led to one of the hottest nights of my life. Though, every night with Penny was incredible. And not just the sex.

She was thoughtful and wise. Sweet and sexy. It amused me that she could write such filthy scenes yet be so shy at times. She was a dichotomy. A puzzle. And I wanted more time to study her. To get to know the pieces of Penny.

"What are you going to read this time?" I asked.

"I don't know. I want something different. Maybe something a little more slow burn."

"Are you trying to tell me something?" I teased.

"No." She grinned. "I just enjoy a change of pace every now and then."

"Do you ever read nonfiction?"

"Absolutely. I read a ton of nonfiction for my novel about the zookeeper."

"I could tell," I said and then kicked myself. Desperate to cover my mistake, I quickly added, "I mean, I assumed that was the case when you mentioned it the other day. Seems like the type of subject that would require a lot of research."

She nodded and continued on, seeming to accept my explanation. "I also love reading autobiographies as research for my stories."

"Me too," I blurted, but then realized I needed to backpedal quickly. It was almost as if I was *trying* to tell her about Meghan. "I mean, I enjoy reading autobiographies. I watch a lot of YouTube videos too."

"Totally addictive, right? Dangerous, though, because they can be such a rabbit hole. I've lost hours on YouTube."

"Yes. For sure. River and I are obsessed with a parkour athlete, Nick Pro."

"Oh yeah. I think I saw some of his stuff after Meghan

Hart's book *Flow* released. She did such an amazing job describing the sport that I had to see what it looked like in action. Pretty incredible, really."

My chest expanded, air filling my lungs completely. It was a rush to hear such high praise not only from a reader, but a fellow author. And an author whose work I respected.

"It is," I said, afraid to say more and risk exposing my secret.

"I wish she'd publish another book in the series. I loved *Flow* and *Leap*."

"You love all her books," I teased.

"You're right," she sighed. "They're my happy place."

Her compliments made me feel bigger, taller, stronger. Like I could do anything. Write any story. But beneath that excitement was a whisper of doubt and regret: she had no idea who I really was.

She stopped walking, and so did I. "Hey," she said in a gentle voice. "Where did you go?"

"Just got in my head a bit. Do you ever do that?"

"All the time." She laced her arm through mine. "My ex used to make fun of me for... Well, never mind."

"Don't tell me he made fun of you for reading and writing romance. Because I will—"

"No." She gave my arm a squeeze. "I, um, have this tendency to pretend I'm a character in one of my novels. Not all the time," she added quickly. "Mostly when I'm struggling with a situation."

"And he made fun of you for it?" I shook my head. The more I heard about this ex, the less I liked him. "How did he feel about your job?"

"I mean, I never really felt like he was supportive. He was always encouraging me to quit my job. To let him take care of me."

I clenched my jaw to avoid commenting. I was more interested in hearing what Penny had to say.

"But that's not who I am. That's not what I want. I've worked too long and too hard to get to where I am. And I'm not giving that up for anyone, especially not a man."

"I'm glad to hear it. You should never be asked to sacrifice the thing you love. The thing that lights you up inside."

She nodded. "Exactly! That's why I loved *Belonging* by Meghan Hart. It really spoke to me. It really encouraged me to embrace my creativity. To put myself on the page. To be vulnerable."

Belonging was one of my less popular books. I'd written it earlier in my career, and it had never hit any lists. Had never made much money. But it was significant to me.

And the fact that Penny loved it, the fact that she got it, that it had resonated with her in such a powerful way… Well, that was the greatest gift any author could hope to receive. We'd connected through my words, even if she didn't know I'd written them.

"I'm sorry," she said. "I'm fangirling again."

"Don't apologize," I said, bringing the back of her hand to my lips. I inhaled her peppermint and eucalyptus scent and kissed her skin. "I love how passionate you are about it."

"I'm going to blame it on being in the AV. God, can you even imagine what I'd do if I actually met her?" She shook her head, her eyes focused on something in the distance. "I would be such a mess."

She turned the guilt screw a little tighter. Anytime Penny talked about Meghan Hart, I was torn between pride and self-disgust. I was torn between telling her the truth then worrying that wasn't what she'd really want.

"I doubt that. You're a talented writer, Penny. It would be a meeting of equals."

"How would you know? It's not like you've read either of our books."

I'd never said that. She was making an assumption. One I could easily correct without sacrificing my secret. Yet…how would I explain it?

"I was *trying* to read one the other night," I teased. "But *someone* kept distracting me."

"Yeah. Because you were trying to read my book while I was sitting there. I just—" She shuddered. "No. You can read it when I'm gone."

I frowned. I didn't like thinking about when Penny would leave. The clock was ticking, and I intended to make the most of our time together.

"It won't be the same." It was the closest I'd come to telling Penny I'd miss her.

We hadn't discussed what would happen after she left. Probably because we both knew it would be pointless. She lived on the East Coast. She'd just gotten out of a three-year relationship. She didn't know the truth about who I was. And besides, I was just the rebound, right?

As we approached Bibliolater, the door opened and Linda Allen exited the shop, bag in hand. She paused on the sidewalk, smiling as she glanced between Penny and me. "Good morning, Liam."

"Morning, Linda. Find some new reading material?" I asked.

"For Aiden." She tilted her head to the side, turning her attention to Penny. "You look really familiar. Have we met before?"

"You get that a lot. Don't you?" I asked Penny, and she nodded, hiding her smile behind her hand. I moved to hold open the door. "Good to see you, Linda."

"You too."

My mom glanced up from the front counter when we walked in. "Liam!" She came around, greeting me with a hug.

My eyes widened, and I tried to stay calm. "*Hey...*Mom."

She stepped back, her eyes darting to Penny. Her mouth opening and closing like a fish. "Penelope Glass?" she whispered. "In my store?"

Shit. I should've known she'd recognize Penny. But I didn't think Mom was supposed to be working today.

"I thought you and Dad were hanging out with River today."

She waved a hand through the air, her eyes still on Penny. "Aiden invited him and Savannah over. Seriously—" Mom stepped forward and held out her hand to Penny. "I'm honored."

"Thank you," Penny said, blushing. "And same. You have a fantastic store."

She was as gracious as ever, and I tried to imagine what I'd do if I were in her shoes. I tried to imagine what it would be like to meet a reader as myself. Not hiding behind a screen or wearing a mask. But seeing them face-to-face.

"We've met before," Mom said. "Though I'm sure you don't remember me. It was at the Books by the Bridge signing in San Francisco last year."

Penny nodded, her smile knowing. "Such a great event."

"So fun," Mom said, leading Penny farther into the store. "Watch the door for me, Liam. Would you?"

"Penny?"

Penny glanced at me over her shoulder, but she seemed delighted by the entire interaction.

"Oh, she's fine." Mom sliced a hand through the air, and Penny nodded.

"Sure," I said, knowing they were both too absorbed in their conversation to pay me any attention. "I'll just be here. Minding the register."

"Don't pout, dear," Mom said. "It's not attractive."

Penny's shoulders shook with laughter, and I briefly regretted bringing her to Bibliolater. It was her vacation; she didn't want to be harassed by a fan. By my mother, of all people.

But Penny seemed to be enjoying herself. So, I rolled my eyes and grabbed one of the chocolate candies from the basket next to the register. I opened it and popped it into my mouth, watching them as they headed for the romance section. I waited until Lizzie came back from her break to join them.

"Oh. You're going to work on inventory now? Cool," Lizzie said.

I flipped her off over my shoulder. I'd helped with inventory before, and it sucked. No thank you.

Mom and Penny were standing in the romance section, comparing notes on different books. A stack of Penny's books rested on a table nearby. I sighed. Mom hadn't wasted any time.

"Can you grab a Sharpie from the front?" Mom asked me.

"Mom," I groaned. "Please don't make Penny sign books. She's on vacation."

I turned to Penny. "You don't have to do this."

"I offered to." She smiled. "I'd be happy to."

I let out a sigh and trudged back to the front to grab a Sharpie. When I returned, Mom was stacking even more books on a nearby table for Penny to sign. I groaned and handed Penny the marker. We were going to be here all day.

"You know my Liam once had aspirations of being an author," Mom said, handing Penny another book to sign.

Penny glanced up at me, a soft smile gracing her lips. "Did you? What were you hoping to write?"

"Thrillers. He had one published." Mom went over to the local authors table and grabbed my debut novel, a thriller that had totally tanked. The one and only book I'd written under my real name.

Mom always told everyone about it—heaping on the praise for my accomplishment. But every time she mentioned it, it only made me feel worse. About the fact that I'd written nearly twenty books that she knew nothing of. About the lies I'd told for the past six years.

"That's so cool," Penny said, skimming the back cover. "Can you add one to my tab?"

"Sure." Mom winked at me.

Penny resumed signing, then asked, "Is that how you know Meghan Hart?"

Mom turned to me, her eyebrows nearly disappearing into her hairline. "I didn't realize you knew Meghan Hart."

I am Meghan Hart!

This was it. The perfect opportunity to confess to Mom and Penny. The words stuck in my throat as I imagined their shock. Their laughter. Their anger and disappointment. My heart was racing.

I couldn't do it. I...I'd never forget the way my grandpa had looked at me when I told him.

A man I'd respected and admired my entire life. A man beloved not only by his family but the entire town. He was someone I'd always confided in, and his rejection had hurt me deeply.

Mom furrowed her brow. "Liam?"

I shook my head. "Huh?"

Mom placed her hand on my shoulder. "Are you okay, sweetheart?"

"I'm great. Yeah. I'm good." I brushed away her concern. My mom was too perceptive. She knew me too well. And if I wasn't careful, she'd realize I was lying.

The way she wrinkled her nose told me she smelled

something rotten. She knew I was hiding something. And it made my feet itch to move.

"Wait," Penny said. "So, you don't know Meghan, but Liam does?" Penny held the cap of the marker to her lips.

Why couldn't she let this go?

Why had I ever opened my big mouth?

"Nope. I have the exclusive right to sell her paperbacks, but I've only ever communicated with her assistant through email."

I tugged on my collar, wishing I hadn't worn a gray shirt that was going to start showing my sweat any second. *Fuck. Fuck. Fuck.*

"She doesn't deliver the paperbacks?" Penny asked, sounding disappointed.

Was that why Penny had wanted to come back to Bibliolater? She was hoping for a chance to run into Meghan Hart?

Mom shook her head. "Nope."

Both of them turned to me. My blood thumped in my ears, the sound of my heart racing. I opened my mouth to respond, not entirely sure what I was going to say, but knowing they expected an answer.

"Well?" Mom finally asked.

I swallowed hard, sweat beading down my back. "I can't talk about it."

"Can't or won't?"

"Both," I said, then she and Penny shared a look.

"I figured she was an aunt or something."

Mom shook her head. "No relation that I know of." But then she narrowed her eyes at me as if an idea had just occurred to her. "Liam, can you help me grab more books from the back for Penny to sign?"

"I really don't—" I was cut off when Mom pinched my ear, and my words morphed into a yelp. "Yep. Sure. No problem."

Penny bit back a grin, and I followed Mom to the back, head bowed. As soon as the door had shut and we were alone, she rounded on me. "William Edward Beaudin, you better tell me what the heck is going on."

"Nothing, Mom. Nothing is going on." I couldn't keep my eyes from darting toward the door.

She crossed her arms over her chest, her brows knitted. "I don't buy that for one second. You show up here with Penelope Glass, who vanished from social media the past week after her wedding. Then she tells me that you know Meghan Hart. *I* don't even know Meghan Hart, and I sell her books."

"Is that what this is about?" I teased, though, really, I was desperate to escape.

"Tell me the truth. Did you have a fling with Meghan Hart?"

"What?" I jerked my head back. And then I started laughing, deep belly laughs that shook my shoulders and boomed through the space. "No."

A fling. With Meghan Hart.

"How do you know her?"

My stomach churned, and my earlier amusement vanished. I was going to throw up. "I—"

I was on the verge of telling her the truth when the door swung open, and Lizzie walked in. "Oops." She stopped short. "My bad, Mrs. B. Sorry to interrupt, but I need your help with a shipment."

"Sure thing." Mom smiled at Lizzie. "Be right there."

As soon as Lizzie was gone, Mom turned back to me. "Have I met her?"

I lifted my shoulders, unwilling to give anything away. I held the door open for her but said nothing.

"Mm." She tapped a finger to her lips, interpreting my silence as a yes. "Is it Marcia?"

I rolled my eyes, mostly to disguise my discomfort. "What? Mom, stop."

"Trish?"

"Mom," I chided. "Drop it. Please." I darted ahead of her. "Come on, Penny. Time to go."

"William Edward—" Mom hissed. "This conversation isn't over."

I ignored her and sped over to where Penny was waiting. "You ready?"

"What?" Penny glanced around at the stacks of books. "I thought your mom had a few more for me to sign."

"I guess she already sold them. Anyway…" I glanced toward the back of the store where Mom had been waylaid by a customer, then to the front door. I calculated our chances of escape. "Grab the books you want, and we'll put them on my tab."

"Liam," she asked. "Is everything okay?"

"Yep. It's great. But I have something planned for us, and I wasn't expecting to spend so much time here."

"Oh." She perked up. "I'm intrigued."

"Here," I said, taking the books from the table. "Any others?" She set one more on top then smiled. "What?"

She pulled her lower lip between her teeth. "It's sexy. *You're* sexy, holding all my romance novels like that."

"Yeah?" I smirked. "Wait till you see me reading one shirtless."

She fanned her face. "I can't imagine anything hotter."

Mom's voice was getting louder. We needed to get a move on.

"Time to go," I growled and grabbed her elbow, directing her to the front. "Add these to my tab," I said to Lizzie on the way out. She just rolled her eyes then waved.

"I feel bad that I didn't get to say goodbye to your mom,"

Penny said once we'd exited the store and were halfway down the block.

"I'm sure she'll understand. Besides, she was just thrilled to meet you and have you sign some books."

"How awesome that she owns a bookshop." She nudged me. "And that her son's an author."

"I'm not—" I stopped myself. "That was embarrassing."

"I thought it was cute." Penny leaned into me and kissed my cheek. "Your mom's proud of you."

She might be proud of me, but at the moment, I was pretty sure she wanted to kill me. Or at the very least, interrogate me. After Penny left, I might have to escape to the cabin and lie low until Mom forgot about it.

Who was I kidding?

My mom had a mind like a steel trap. And there was no way she was going to drop this. Even so, I needed to reveal my secret in my own way. In my own time.

It's been six years. How much more time do you need?

"What was that?" Penny asked.

"Nothing. Just talking to myself." I opened her door before placing the books in the trunk and joining her.

"Where to?" she asked.

I plugged the address into my phone and then hooked it up to the car. "There you go."

"Yes, but where is it?"

"Do you trust me?" I asked.

She arched her eyebrow and then peeled out of the parking lot. We drove away from town, closer to Fall River, finally slowing as we reached the sign for Around the World Balloons.

"A hot-air balloon ride?" she asked.

I nodded. "There's a bathroom here, and we'll be in the air about an hour. Is that okay?"

"You—" she turned to me with such affection in her eyes "—are incredible, Liam."

She shook her head and pulled off the main road and down a gravel one. The tires kicked up dust. The horses swished their tails in the distance. And up ahead, I could see someone setting up the balloon. I glanced in the side mirror, wondering if my other surprise would make it in time. I'd really pulled out all the stops, wanting to end our time together in a way that was special and memorable.

While we waited for Cassandra to set up the balloon, a courier arrived. He climbed out of the truck and glanced around. "Penelope Glass?"

Penny frowned. "That's me."

"This is for you." He handed her a thick envelope.

All along, I'd planned to give her something special from Meghan Hart. Something I knew she would appreciate more than anyone else. And after hearing her talk about her love for *Belonging* and how it had really resonated with her, I'd put a plan into place.

I'd considered sending the manuscript to her place in ·New York, though I would've had to ship it to her PO Box since I didn't have her home address. But selfishly, I wanted to be there when she opened it. I wanted to see her expression and hear her excitement. I was taking a risk, but I wanted to give her a piece of me. Something true and real.

Maybe if we had longer. Maybe if we had a future…

I shook my head, surprised I was even considering a future. Let alone after being together for such a short time.

Penny tore open the envelope and then pulled out the thick manuscript. An original copy of *Belonging*, signed by Meghan Hart.

"Oh. My. God." Her hands shook as she held the book. "No fucking way." She glanced up at me. "Did you know about this?"

I nodded, captivated by the way the sunlight hit her face. The breeze gently blowing her hair. Her lips curved into a smile. Enticing me.

"Seriously? This is for me?" She kept glancing down at the manuscript then back to me.

I chuckled. "For you."

Her eyes widened. "I can't even…" She placed a hand over her heart. "I can't…" She was panting, and were those tears? "How did you—" She glanced down at the book then back at me. "How did she—" She held it to her chest. "Thank you."

"Are you okay?"

"I'm so incredibly honored. I'm…" She sighed. "Wow. Just wow. This is a dream come true."

"Ready?" Cassandra called.

"Yes." Penny swiped away tears.

"I guess you didn't lie about knowing her after all," she said.

I hadn't lied, but I hadn't told the entire truth either. Still, I wasn't ready to tell Penny. I wanted to, but… What would be the point? She was leaving in two days.

"You doubted me?" I feigned injury.

She shook her head and slipped the manuscript back into the envelope then carefully placed it in the trunk. Cassandra helped Penny into the basket, and then I joined them.

As we rose into the sky, I tucked Penny into my side. The familiar landscape of the AV faded below us, the individual rows of grapes blurring into a tapestry of red, yellow, and orange. And I couldn't imagine a more perfect ending to one of the best weeks of my life.

CHAPTER NINE

Penny

I was curled up on the couch beneath a blanket, my feet resting in Liam's lap. He'd run his hand over them from time to time, the move comforting. Familiar, almost. I'd barely known him a week, and already I felt like I knew him better than I ever had my ex.

My ex. I rolled my eyes.

Erik was probably back in New York. Back at work. I neither knew nor cared.

I'd have to deal with him—and my feelings about our broken engagement—at some point. But for now, I was cozy and warm and cared for. And Erik was as far away from the Alondra Valley as he was from my thoughts.

Brinkley and my mom were still calling or texting every day to check in, and I knew they were worried. Ever since Dad's death, Mom had become a worrier. But lately, it was bordering on hypervigilance. She was convinced that this was all a big mistake, and Erik and I would get back together. I was beginning to wonder if she was more invested in the relationship than I was.

Liam rubbed my shoulder, and I realized I'd been staring

at the same page for the past few minutes. The fire crackled in the old stone fireplace. Outside, it was quiet but for the hoot of an owl. No traffic. No horns. Nothing but the two of us.

It was nice.

I couldn't remember the last time I'd stopped. The last time I'd enjoyed simple moments and quiet evenings. Not since I'd left Wisconsin and moved to New York. And certainly not since I'd started writing.

The silence was punctuated by the sound of Liam turning the page in his novel. A minute later, I turned the page in the book I was reading. Or rather, rereading—my favorite Meghan Hart book of all time.

I glanced over at Liam, smiling at the sight of his brow furrowed in concentration, glasses perched on his nose. The flames made his skin seem almost golden. Like something from another world or perhaps a dream.

This time with him had been a dream. More than anything, they'd been exactly what I'd needed. No social media. No computer. Just fun. With Liam, of all people. My one-night stand turned…well, vacation fling. Though this certainly felt like more than a fling.

From the way he'd handled my IBS to the surprise today…a signed manuscript of my favorite Meghan Hart book? I'd never received something so thoughtful. So meaningful to me.

I wasn't sure I'd ever be able to express my gratitude, but I wanted to try. Not just to Liam, but to Meghan. As a fan, as a fellow creative.

"Thank you again for arranging that surprise with Meghan," I said.

"My pleasure."

"I'd like to thank her as well. I don't know if it would be possible, but can I have Meghan's email address?" I asked.

I was curious how he knew Meghan Hart, but I was trying to respect his boundaries. Liam hadn't brought her up, and I could tell he was uncomfortable with the subject. So I let it go. It didn't matter *how* he knew her; the fact was, he did.

He stilled but then grabbed a piece of paper and scribbled something on it. He held it out to me, but when I reached out my hand, he pulled it back. "You promise not to share it with anyone?"

"Of course not." It was clear that Meghan valued her privacy. I respected that. And I respected her.

He seemed reluctant but handed it to me anyway. On it was the email address <u>romancequeen@meghanhart.com</u>. I smiled to myself and resumed reading, or rather, pretending to. Between Meghan Hart's email resting on the table and the man sitting beside me, I absolutely could not concentrate.

I wiggled my feet in Liam's lap, and he held them still, pushing against them so I could feel his erection. The man should've come with a warning label like Meghan Hart's book. *Insatiable*. But I was just as bad. Every chance I got, I was touching or kissing him.

I had two days left of vacation, and I was already dreading returning to New York. It wasn't even about dealing with the wedding gifts or the idea that I might have to see Erik. It was the fact that I was going to miss this. Miss Liam.

"Why so serious?" he asked.

"Hmm?" I glanced away from the fire.

He leaned over and caressed my cheek. "You're beautiful. You know that?"

I dipped my head, and he tilted my chin back up. He held my gaze then dragged his thumb across my bottom lip, rubbing back and forth like he'd done with his cock earlier. The memory of it had my lips opening, mouth salivating for more.

More. Again. Over and over.

It had never been like this. Not with Erik nor with anyone else. And it wasn't just about the sex. Liam and I connected on a deeper level, his love of books rivaling my own.

Liam brought out something in me—a different side of me from who I usually was in New York. Someone who took what she wanted without hesitation or regrets or what-ifs. I wasn't thinking about tomorrow or the past or other people's opinions. I was living in the now.

I moved so I was straddling his lap. "Want to take a bath?"

"Hell yes." He stood, carrying me over to the bathroom. He set me on the edge of the tub and switched on the water.

I started to remove my clothes when he said, "Stop."

He tugged on my hand, pulling me so I was facing him. With his eyes on mine the entire time, he stripped me slowly. First, he removed my shirt, gently pulling it over my head. My nipples pebbled, and it wasn't from the cool air. Off came my joggers, the material sliding down my legs, followed by his hands. He pressed his nose to my mound, inhaling as he wrapped his large hands around my waist, spanning my hips. He wasn't in a rush. He was unwrapping me like a gift, taking his time until I stood before him completely naked.

"My turn." I licked my lips, then stripped him of his shirt, reveling in the hard planes of his chest. The broad shoulders. The golden hair dusting his muscular pecs.

He sighed with every brush of my hands. Swallowed hard when I pushed his pants over his hips. Moaned when I kissed the tip of his erection.

Then he turned off the water and sat in the tub before offering me his hand. I settled between his legs with my back to his chest and his cock digging into me.

"Hi." His voice coated me with warmth like the water, his lips murmuring against my ear.

"Hi." I smiled, glancing back over my shoulder for his mouth.

He smiled and kissed me. He massaged my shoulders with his hands, sliding over my breasts, taking his time to caress and worship my body just as he had every other time we'd been together.

There was never any rush. It was a big reason why being with Liam felt indulgent. Relaxing. Right.

He paid special attention to my stomach, keeping his pressure gentle as he smoothed his hands over my skin. His touch made me feel like the sexiest woman in the world as he slid his hands up and over my breasts, teasing my nipples briefly before making his way to my jaw. Then he'd glide his hands back down my neck, applying gentle pressure as he continued his exploration.

And when he finally ventured farther south, I parted my legs, granting him access. It was as if his hands were everywhere. Prying my pussy open and applying pressure to the outer lips. Massaging my most sensitive area with passion and care.

"Liam," I sighed as he increased his pace and pressure.

"You like that, baby?"

"Yes." I arched my back, angling my hips closer to his hand. "Just like that."

My shaky breaths echoed in the bathroom. The water sloshed around the tub, nearly going over the side. But all I could focus on was the rising wave of my pleasure, carrying me away with it. Pulling me higher and higher like a bubble floating on the air. Until my body tensed, drawing everything up tight. And then finally, releasing, everything relaxing.

I spun so I was facing him, straddling him. He'd spent so long pleasuring me, ensuring that my needs were taken care of, that the water was growing cold and my fingers wrinkled.

"Bed. Now," he said, gripping my hips, his fingernails digging into my skin.

I climbed out of the tub, and he followed, wrapping me up in a towel before carrying me over to the bed. He deposited me on top, and I propped myself up on my elbows so I could watch him. His muscles flexed as he crawled onto the mattress, prowling toward me. He pushed the towel aside, and my toes curled in anticipation of the delicious pleasure I knew I was about to receive.

I wrapped my arms around his neck and pulled him to me for a kiss. Our bodies were still damp from the bath, our skin slick with moisture as his hard-on slid between my folds.

"Need a condom," he rasped but didn't stop. Instead, he pressed his forehead to mine, our eyes locked. I felt vulnerable but also…seen.

I didn't want to stop. I didn't want to stop what we were doing. And I didn't want to stop feeling like this.

"Just hot dog it."

He stilled. "What?"

"You know—" I hooked my legs around his back and rolled us so I was on top. I closed my legs and started sliding up and down his cock. "Use me like a hot dog bun."

"But what if I want to fill you up with my cream?"

I laughed, even as he made me moan. "I think we're mixing metaphors."

"I don't really care what we call it. It feels fucking amazing."

I kept sliding against him, loving the feel of his cock against my clit. My nipples brushed against his chest, and I rode him until we were both sweating. I'd never felt more like myself than when I was with Liam.

He cupped the back of my neck, our skin feverish with

passion. Our bodies aching for release. It was sexy as hell—the way our bodies worked together.

"I'm never going to look at hot dogs the same way again," he said through gritted teeth.

And then he flipped me onto my back and took himself in hand. With a few tugs, he was spilling on my skin. Like lava erupting out of him and onto me.

He groaned, his cock twitching. "Fuck. That's hot."

And then he spread my legs and licked and sucked and fucked me with his hand and his mouth until I completely unraveled once more. I'd never been with a man who was so intent on my pleasure. Who was so determined to make sure I orgasmed both first and often. Not that I'd been with *that* many men, but still. Liam was in a league of his own.

Later, after we'd showered and were eating room service, I glanced over at him. His blond hair was still wet, his chest bare, and I couldn't help but smile. For the first time in a long time, I felt inspired. Invigorated. I wasn't going home with a broken heart as I'd feared, but with new memories and new material for my stories.

Heck, maybe being a jilted bride wasn't such a terrible thing after all. In fact, I was beginning to think it was the best thing that had ever happened to me.

I STARED OUT THE WINDOW OF THE COFFEE SHOP, WATCHING the copper and golden leaves blow down the street as taxis zipped by. I was supposed to be writing, but I kept wishing I were back in the sunny Alondra Valley rather than chilly New York. Back with Liam.

I sighed and glanced down at my phone. I needed to stop

living in a fantasy. I'd returned to New York a week ago, and I'd thought about Liam every day. But when he'd dropped me at the airport, he hadn't mentioned staying in touch. And I hadn't asked.

Besides, I'd just gotten out of a three-year relationship. A broken engagement. I wasn't ready for another relationship. And even if I were, that wasn't what Liam wanted.

So why was I still thinking about him?

And not just now. I couldn't stop thinking about him. About the amazing time we'd shared. But it was a fling. *One week.* That's all it was.

I shook my head and focused on my phone. I'd put this off long enough. My assistant, Raven, and I had talked about it at length, and I'd finally decided what to say. But that didn't make it any easier.

I opened Instagram, ignoring all the notifications that came flooding in. I hadn't been online in weeks, and I'd missed a lot. Honestly, though, I felt like I'd missed nothing at all. I'd been so busy having fun with Liam that my life in New York had seemed so far away.

Now it was back to reality, and I knew my readers deserved an explanation. I would need to start promoting my next release soon, hyping everyone up, and I couldn't do that if I had this shadow hanging over me.

Despite the chill in the air outside, I started sweating and decided to focus on my newsletter first. It felt more intimate somehow. Like I was merely emailing a few friends, not putting my life out there for the entire internet to see.

I scrolled down to the picture of me at Bibliolater. I was smiling and happy, and I definitely didn't look like a heartbroken, jilted bride. Probably because I wasn't.

Was I angry? Yes.

Embarrassed? Absolutely.

But I would survive this.

No. I clenched my fists, remembering everything I'd already overcome. I would fucking thrive.

I read over the email one more time before hitting send. And then immediately regretted it. I wanted to take it back, despite the brief feeling of relief that had accompanied it. Oh well. Too late now.

It was much like the rush I got when releasing a new book. There was this nervous excitement and also a constant feeling of wanting to throw up for being so vulnerable. I knew it wouldn't go away, at least not immediately.

I went back to Instagram. Same picture. Similar content, just more condensed. Okay. *Okay.* I psyched myself up. *I can do this. Just freaking do it,* I told myself as my finger hovered over the "Post" button.

And then I posted. I immediately logged off. I couldn't— my chest was tight. I'd done it, and now I needed to take a breath. Take a step back.

My phone vibrated with a new text message.

Raven: Way to go.

I smiled. She'd seen the post.

Thanks.

Raven: Now get off the internet and get back to work.

Okay. Okay.

I laughed and set my phone facedown on the table. I'd been working on a story before my honeymoon, but it wasn't clicking. In the time I'd spent away from it, I'd lost interest. Usually, I would've forced myself to keep writing, to push through. But the idea filled me with so much dread that I just couldn't.

The only thing that sounded worse was a run-in with my ex. I hadn't seen Erik since our canceled wedding, nor did I intend to. When I'd returned to New York, I'd texted his assistant, and she'd had my things delivered to my apartment. She'd come with the movers, hugging me when I'd opened the door. I was beginning to think I'd miss her more than Erik.

I'd also asked her to return the engagement ring. We were over. We had been for a long time. In fact, he'd done me a favor by breaking things off, even if his timing was far from ideal.

Raven: Okay. I take it back. Are you seeing this?
Me: Seeing what?
Raven: Get online.

My stomach rumbled with unease, even though I knew Raven had my best interests in mind. And it was so rare that she told me to get on social media that my curiosity was piqued.

I logged back in and found so many comments and likes that my head spun. Authors and readers expressing their sympathy. Sending positive thoughts or sharing their own stories of heartbreak. I'd done my best not to cast Erik as the villain—though, he would've deserved it. Instead, I'd focused on the lessons I'd learned and the message of hope I wanted to promote.

As I scrolled through comment after comment, I was overwhelmed by all the heartfelt messages. By the kindness of the book world. I didn't know why I'd expected anything else. It was one of my favorite things about my readers and the online romance community. Everyone was so uplifting and supportive.

Even so, it was such an immense relief. I texted Raven and then Brinkley.

Wow. Check this out.

Brinkley: I hate to say it, but Erik's stupidity might be the best thing that ever happened to your career.

I laughed, though she wasn't wrong. At least not completely. I knew that my success was due to my hard work. My talent. It was my sacrifices that had gotten me here, and regardless of my relationship with Erik—or any other man—I was the one who would determine my future. *Me.* Not anyone else.

I responded to some of the comments, interacting with my readers. And then I finally returned to my document and tried to make sense of the story. I hadn't put it up for preorder yet, but I had set a deadline with my editor.

I lost track of time, my brain twisting like a pretzel from all the mental gymnastics I was trying to perform to make this story work.

Why are you being so difficult?

Ugh. I went to get a refill, taking my time to chat with the barista. Finally, I dragged myself back over to the table where my computer waited.

Looking for any excuse to stall, I checked my inbox and stilled.

Oh my god.

Oh my god.

Oh my god.

I ignored the curious stares from nearby patrons and tried to calm my breathing. But seriously? If they had any idea!

Meghan Hart. *The* Meghan Hart—my idol—was emailing *me?*

I'd sent her a thank-you email when I'd landed in New York, but I'd never expected to hear back from her. If Liam didn't live across the country, and I hadn't sworn off men, I'd definitely be calling him right about now. Though…a little thank-you text wouldn't hurt, would it?

But we'd agreed it was only for one week.

So I shook my head and turned my attention to the screen.

DEAR PENELOPE,

IT WAS SO NICE TO HEAR FROM YOU AND TO HAVE THE CHANCE to connect with a fellow author. I'm so glad you enjoyed my gift and your visit to my hometown. The Alondra Valley is magical, isn't it?

SPEAKING OF MAGICAL…I HEAR YOU'RE A FELLOW FAN OF *Bridgerton.* Have you seen the latest season? If not, I highly recommend watching it. It is a master class in plotting, and the tension and drama and ugh… It's so good.

XO,
    MH

MY SMILE STRETCHED ACROSS MY FACE, AND I KNEW WHAT needed to be done. I moved the story to my discard pile and opened a new blank document.

I wanted to write something personal. Something vulnerable.

I wanted to write about my week with Liam so I could preserve it and relive it whenever I wanted. I'd change the names, of course.

Despite my broken engagement, I felt excited to write about romance. I wasn't heartbroken as I'd expected. If I was being completely honest, part of me was relieved.

My fingers went flying across the keyboard as I typed the beginning of a new story.

"Once Upon a Wedding…"

CHAPTER TEN

Liam

I picked up my mug and drank, nearly spitting out the cold coffee on my laptop. The cup was still almost full, but I'd been so absorbed in my task that I'd forgotten all about it. I sighed and stood from the desk, stretching as I walked around the cabin.

I'd bought the A-frame a few years ago, and I'd always loved my escape. It was a bit rustic, but it was cozy and warm. A wood-burning stove for the winter. Floor-to-ceiling windows that led out to a large deck overlooking the valley. It was secluded and quiet. Distraction-free. Apart from my thoughts anyway.

My stomach growled, and I padded over to the fridge. The clock in the kitchen told me it was nearly four. But all I could think was that it was almost seven in New York. As I peeked into the fridge, I wondered what Penny was doing.

I'd kept tabs on her through social media. I'd seen her first post since the honeymoon. Her announcement about the wedding being canceled. Since then, she'd returned to her regular content, and I was glad for it. I hoped it meant she'd moved on from her ex too.

Because I couldn't stop thinking about Penny. But I didn't know how she felt about me. Did she still consider me a fling? A rebound? Something more?

I pushed aside a head of wilted lettuce. I hadn't contacted her since she'd left the AV, despite wanting to. Well, at least if you didn't count *Meghan's* email back to Penny. Something I was still kicking myself for.

I'd half hoped she'd lose Meghan's email address or her nerve to send something. And when she'd emailed to thank Meghan for the gift, I'd considered not replying. But I couldn't bear the idea of disappointing her. Or worse still, of Meghan disappointing her.

I mean, what was I supposed to do—not respond? Penny was a superfan. A fellow author in the romance community. And I knew that hearing from Meghan would mean the world to Penny. No response, well, that would cast Meghan in a negative light. So, I'd tried to keep it personable and professional, neither encouraging nor discouraging correspondence.

I sighed and closed the fridge. Ugh. Why had I done this to myself?

I dressed and grabbed my keys before locking up. I inhaled deeply as I rounded the bed of the truck. I drove down the winding dirt road to town, granite peaks rising in the distance, the mountains as majestic as the lake that shimmered in the sun.

My phone started humming to life with missed calls, messages, and emails the closer I got to civilization. I wondered if any were from Penny as I parked in front of Deja Brew. The coffee shop had the best coffee—and internet connection—in the area.

After I'd ordered a coffee and a muffin, I took a seat at a table where my back was to a wall so I could read my messages in private.

Wren: You'll be home for Bennett's birthday party, right?

Wren: It's on the sixth. Seven o'clock.

Asher: You still alive?

Dad: I checked on the house. Everything looks good.

Bennett: You'll be back before the sixth, right? It's game time.

I smiled, imagining Wren's reaction. Bennett was going to propose to my sister, and I was thrilled. I responded to him first.

Glad you're finally going to make an honest woman of her.

Bennett: I never pegged you as an outdated misogynist who supported the patriarchy.

Jeez, B. I was joking.

But I'm glad you passed the test.

I chuckled when Bennett's next text came through—a middle finger emoji.

Love you too, brother.

Bennett: You'll always be my #1, boo.

I rolled my eyes and turned my attention to my email. The other texts could wait. I skimmed my Meghan Hart inbox. A few messages from my assistant. A mock-up for my next cover. And…a new message from Penny!

Aw. Fuck. I shouldn't be this excited.

My fingers hovered over the keyboard. Communicating

with Penny as Meghan felt wrong. She wasn't just a fan or a fellow author who I was deceiving. She was someone I'd had a relationship with, albeit briefly. Someone I cared about and respected.

I'd told myself I couldn't continue a relationship with Penny as Liam while I was hiding the truth about Meghan. I told myself I was trying to give her space, but it was so much more complicated than that.

Hey Meghan!

I loved the newest season of Bridgerton. Have you ever considered writing a historical romance? I couldn't handle all the research that goes into it. But I do love reading and watching them.

How's your latest project going? I was stuck until recently, but I'm now humming along and loving these characters. Guess I just needed a change of scenery and some new inspiration.

XX,

Penny

Ooh. Did that mean I was responsible for her inspiration?

I groaned, remembering that Liam wasn't supposed to know that. Because Penny thought she was communicating with Meghan.

Why couldn't I have just said no when she'd asked for Meghan's email address?

But now I was stuck; I had to reply.

As I was responding to Penny's email to Meghan, a new text message came in from her on my cell phone. God, this was getting confusing. I was pretending to be Meghan Hart —Penny's idol and author friend—in our emails. And now I was going to have to keep that separate from me—Liam—in our text messages.

> Penny: Totally freaking out. Meghan emailed me back. Thank you. #DreamComeTrue

I laughed, my guilt fading to the background momentarily. I was so fucking happy to hear from her that I kept staring at my phone, rereading her message. Hoping that maybe, just maybe, she missed me too.

"HEY, TESS." I LAID THE BOUQUET ON THE HEADSTONE, dragging my fingers over her name.

My grandpa was farther back in the cemetery. He'd died nearly a year ago, and Tessa six months after that. He'd been seventy-two. Tessa's life had been cut far too short at just thirty-three years old.

"How have you been?" I listened to the silence, though I wasn't sure what I'd expected to hear.

I knew what I wanted. Tessa's advice. On my books. On love. On Penny.

"I just came back from the cabin. The words were flowing. God, I wish you were here to read this story. It's about a jilted bride on her wedding day." I chuckled, thinking of Penny. "I'm sure you'd tell me parts of it are unbelievable, but I think you'd love it." I sank down on the grass. "I'm really proud of it."

It was the first time I'd felt that way about a story since my grandpa's death. It was as if his disapproval had taken something from me. A confidence and joy, a freedom I'd always felt from my writing. Then Tessa's death had followed, and my support system had died with her.

I let out a deep sigh, glancing around to confirm that I was alone. Which, of course, I was. Most people didn't spend their Friday nights at the cemetery. It wasn't the liveliest place in town.

"I'm sort of—well," I huffed. "I got myself into a situation."

I closed my eyes, and I could imagine Tessa's blue eyes sparkling with interest and curiosity. She'd lean forward and ask, "Liam, what have you done now?" in a knowing tone.

I smiled, though it was tinged with sadness. I missed my friend.

And even though she wasn't here, I already knew what she'd say: tell her the truth.

For years, Tess had encouraged me to tell my family the truth about my job. Of course, when I had told my grandpa, it had gone terribly. And while I'd felt conflicted about the lies I continued to tell my parents, Wren, my best friends, it wasn't until Penny—until now—that I'd been motivated to do anything about it.

Penny was…well, being with Penny was like the high I'd get from releasing a new book. Excitement and nerves mingled with euphoria.

The past few weeks without Penny had shown me that one week wasn't enough. But I also couldn't continue down the path I was on. I'd thought I could separate the two—Meghan and Liam—but I saw now that it was impossible. So, I knew I could either tell Penny the truth or let her go. Maybe it was selfish of me, but I wanted her. Or at least the chance to be who I really was with her.

"Liam?" Tristan's deep voice startled me out of my

thoughts, and I wondered how long he'd been standing there. How much he'd heard.

I stood and turned to face him. "Hey." There was an awkward beat of silence where we both stared at the ground. And then I said, "Well, I'll leave you to it."

"It's okay. Stay. It's nice to have some company." He stepped closer and laid a fresh bouquet of flowers on the ground next to the headstone. "It's nice to know that someone else visits her."

"Of course."

We stared at the headstone in silence, the crickets chirping in the grass. I wondered where the kids were but didn't ask.

"You and Tessa were always close," he said, kicking at the ground. "I guess it shouldn't surprise me that you're here."

"Yet it does."

He shoved his hands into his pockets. "Sometimes it feels like everyone's moved on."

I placed my hand on his shoulder. "Tessa will never be forgotten. She lives on in you. In Savannah and Maddox. In the hearts of the community." And hopefully in the new branch of the library I was trying to make a reality.

He nodded slowly. "I know. You're right. But I miss her so fucking much." His voice cracked with emotion.

I pulled him into a hug, holding him tight, overcome myself. It was the first time I'd seen him break down. And I wondered how much I'd missed. How badly he'd been struggling and hiding it.

Despite the fact that I wrote for a living, I had no idea what to say to him. How to comfort him. I wanted to, but I was at a loss for words.

"Sorry," he said, pulling back and wiping his eyes.

"Don't apologize," I said. "You can't keep this all bottled

up. It's not healthy for you or the kids. It's not what Tessa would've wanted."

"Yeah? Well, what do you suggest? Huh?" He stepped forward, fists clenched. "She's gone, and I'm fucking lost without her."

I rubbed at a spot on my chest. I was hurting, but Tristan's pain was a million times worse. I only wished I could help him somehow.

"We're *all* a bit lost without her," I admitted, knowing it would be of little comfort. Even so, I wanted to reassure him that he wasn't as alone as he felt. That we all cared about him.

"She was *my* wife." He jabbed at his chest. "My soul mate."

"I'm not trying to compare my loss to yours." It *wasn't* the same, and it wouldn't help. "But I knew her my whole life."

I wanted nothing more than to calm my friend. And maybe it was the reminder of the fragility of life or the fact that Tristan was being so vulnerable, but I found myself saying, "And we spent a lot of time together working on my books."

His shoulders relaxed, and he stared at the headstone with a profound look of sadness. "She never told me your pen name, you know?"

I shook my head slowly. "I told her she could." I'd never wanted Tristan to question my relationship with his wife. We'd never been anything more than friends. "I dedicated my last book to her."

The corner of his mouth tilted upward, and it was good to see him attempt to smile. "She would've loved that."

"And I personally acknowledged her in every book she helped me with. Her advice was invaluable. I miss being able to talk to her about my stories."

"How many have you written?"

The longer we talked, the easier it was to unload this secret. "Twenty."

His eyes went wide. "Twenty?"

"Yeah. Sometimes I can't believe it myself. I can't believe that I support myself doing something I love."

"I thought you still worked as a contractor for the government."

I shook my head. "As of last year, I write full time."

"No shit." He rubbed a hand over his chin. "Congrats, man."

"Thanks." It was both strange and wonderful to talk about this with someone.

"Why don't you tell anyone? I mean, I totally get wanting to keep a low profile."

I rubbed the back of my neck. "I have...a number of reasons." I shifted from one foot to the other. "Tessa never told you anything? Not even the genre?"

He shook his head. "Nope. Just that you were an author. She was helping you. And if I ever breathed a word of it to anyone, I'd never get laid again."

I chuckled. That sounded like Tessa. Loyal. Fiercely protective. Sweet but steely. "Weren't you curious?"

"I guess. But I figured you'd tell me if you wanted to."

I inhaled a shaky breath and let it out slowly. Of all people, Tristan had proven himself able to keep a secret. Maybe telling him the truth would be good practice. Maybe...

"You *cannot* tell a soul," I said.

Tristan shook his head. "You don't owe me an explanation, Liam."

"I'm Meghan Hart," I blurted before I could reconsider.

He furrowed his brow. "What?"

I leaned in and lowered my voice. I'd already said it once. I could do it again. "I'm Meghan Hart. The romance author."

He stared at me a beat and then burst out laughing. "I'm sorry." He was laughing so hard, he had to bend over to clutch at his stomach. "You?"

Fuck. I shifted back and forth on my feet, fighting the urge to run. This was exactly what I'd been afraid of. And it was a big reason why I never told anyone. "Yes."

"No." He shook his head, still laughing. "If you're Meghan Hart, then I'm the Dalai Lama."

I rolled my eyes. I should've anticipated this reaction. I mean, why would he believe me? And if Tristan—someone who knew I'd secretly been publishing books under a pen name all these years—didn't believe me, why would anyone else? Why would Penny?

"I'm telling the truth," I said. I let out a deep sigh and glared at Tessa's headstone. "If you were here, you could tell him it's true."

Tristan's eyes went wide. "Oh shit. You're serious?"

"Yes," I huffed, wondering why that was so unbelievable.

He immediately sobered, glancing between me and his wife's gravestone. "You talk to Tess?"

"Yeah. You don't?" Hell, I talked to myself all the time. It really wasn't much different.

"I—" He glanced toward the sky. "I can't. It's too painful. Too raw."

"Maybe you should try writing. It can be cathartic."

"Is that why you write romance? For the 'catharsis'?" He used air quotes, clearly trying to avoid the real topic.

I rolled my eyes. "Romance novels are about so much more than just sex."

"Oh, *I* know that," Tristan said. "But I'm surprised to hear you say it. You always act like such a player."

I scoffed, but then I realized he was serious. "Tristan, when was the last time you saw me take a woman home? Or go home with someone? Apart from Penny."

Thanks to *The Vine*, everyone knew about Penny and me. Though luckily, V hadn't gone into too much detail in her post a few weeks ago. She'd just mentioned briefly that we'd been seen around town together.

He seemed to consider it. "I—" He frowned. "Now that you mention it, I'm not sure. Though I've been too busy to pay much attention."

"Even if you were paying attention, you'd realize that I haven't dated. Haven't hooked up with anyone in a long time."

"Why?"

"I want a relationship, but that seems impossible while I'm keeping this huge secret."

"Is that why you're telling me now?" He arched his brow. "You want to take this relationship to the next level?" he teased.

I rolled my eyes. "Of course. *Of course* the male romance author is gay."

"I'm just teasing you. Lighten up, man. You're the one who's so concerned about what people will think about your secret career. I mean, shit. You're a brilliant writer, and no one knows. That's gotta suck."

"You're right. It does suck." I paused. "Wait. You think I'm a brilliant writer? Does that mean—"

"Yeah." He rubbed the back of his neck. "I've read some of your books."

I jerked my head back. Now I was the one who was surprised. "You have?"

"Tessa was always so obsessed with them. Everyone around here is. And I was curious. Plus, at one point, things had gotten a little…stale. Between kids and work and everything else, we'd kind of lost the spark."

I'd never known that. Never would've suspected it. Tristan and Tessa always seemed so content and in love.

"Really?"

"Yeah, really. Relationships—marriage—are work. Where your books end is really only just the beginning."

Huh. I'd never thought of it that way.

His phone buzzed. "I have to go pick up the kids."

I fell into step beside him as we headed for the parking lot. "See you tomorrow night for Bennett's birthday?"

"Maybe."

I frowned. But then my phone buzzed in my pocket, and I glanced at the screen. It was a picture of Penny eating a hot dog. I groaned, both at the image and the memory it sparked.

"Thanks again for visiting Tessa," he said when we reached our cars. "It means a lot."

"Of course." I paused with one hand on my car door. "The real relationship stuff. The stuff that happens after my books end. Is it worth it?"

His smile was wistful. "Abso-fucking-lutely."

CHAPTER ELEVEN

Penny

The saleswoman at Saks Fifth Avenue smiled at me from over the register as she typed something on the keyboard. "Thanks for coming in. Sorry for any inconvenience."

"No problem." I crossed my arms over my chest. I just wanted to get this over with. And I couldn't understand why the store had insisted on having me come in to clear up whatever issue existed with the registry. Why couldn't Erik just pay one of his minions to handle it like he always did?

"Mr. Cartwright."

My head snapped up at the mention of Erik's name, his leather shoes clicking against the tile. *What the fuck?*

He tilted his head to the saleswoman in acknowledgment before turning his attention to me. "Penny." His tone was smooth. His hair impeccable. The bouquet of red roses over the top. "I've been trying to get in touch with you."

I was aware. He'd called several times the past few weeks. Texted. But I'd ignored them. I didn't owe him anything, least of all my time.

His whole life, Erik had gotten everything he'd ever

wanted. Often without much effort on his part. He wasn't used to being told no. He wasn't used to losing.

"I've been busy." I kept my attention on the dishes, on anything but Erik.

Less than a year ago, we'd been standing here. Selecting our wedding china. Happily engaged—at least, so I'd thought. Now, he seemed more like a stranger than the man I'd planned to spend the rest of my life with.

His suit was immaculate as always, but he seemed agitated. Dark circles beneath his eyes showing evidence of long, sleepless nights.

"Yes," he gritted out, gripping the bouquet so tightly I thought he might snap the stems in two. "I'm *aware*."

Wait. Did he...? Was he referring to Liam?

Even if he was, so what? Erik had left me at the altar. He didn't get a say in my life anymore. And he certainly didn't get to judge my decisions.

"We need to talk," he said, glancing around with a smile for everyone else.

"About what? We don't have a relationship anymore. Remember?"

He grasped my elbow and dragged me toward a more private spot. "Look, I can understand that you might be upset—"

"Upset?" I scoffed. "Right."

I hadn't realized how upset I was until I was forced to come face-to-face with him. I'd planned to marry this man. He was going to be my husband. And he'd betrayed me. Ditched me.

I still didn't understand why. Was I not enough? Too much?

Whatever the reason, I supposed I should've been thankful he'd done it before we'd gone through with the wedding. Before we had a condo on the East Side and a house in the Hamptons. Before two kids. Before... I sighed.

"What do you want?"

"I made a mistake." He leaned in, his expression softening. "I want...you. I want to go back to the way we were."

I blinked a few times. Stunned. Had he really just said that? When we were together, Erik had rarely showed emotions. Even so, one admission of regret wasn't going to change my mind.

"You're kidding, right?" I glanced around as if someone would pop out with a camera at any time and yell, "Surprise!" But they didn't.

"Can we go somewhere else to talk about this? Somewhere more private?" he asked.

I frowned. "There's nothing to discuss."

He'd left. We were over. I wanted nothing more to do with him.

I turned to walk away, realizing this whole scenario was a ruse he'd concocted to see me. A trap. In the past, I would've been flattered. I'd considered such grandiose gestures romantic. Now I saw it for what it really was—manipulation. A power move.

"Penny." He grabbed my arm. "Wait."

I stilled but didn't turn to look back at him. "We're done, Erik."

"Don't say that. Don't throw away the past three years because of one day."

"*One* day?" I drew back, and he released my arm. "You left me at the altar. On our *wedding* day. Moments before we were supposed to walk down the aisle. And now you want— what? To act like it never happened?"

He lifted his chin but said nothing. Probably because he wasn't used to me speaking up. Speaking out. I'd always kept my feelings, my needs, my emotions, bottled up. No more.

Ever since my dad's death, I'd suppressed my emotions, only ever expressing them in my writing. But my time with Liam had shown me a different way. A better way.

One with communication and trust. Where you didn't have to pretend or wear a mask.

"You're different," Erik said, and I couldn't tell if he thought it was a bad thing. I wasn't sure I cared.

I moved to leave when he blocked my path. I wasn't sure why he was so insistent, other than the fact that he didn't like to lose.

"What's changed?" I asked, wondering what was any different now than it had been six weeks ago.

He stepped closer, his expression softening. "You." He took my hand in his, the other still holding the bouquet. "Please. Give me another chance, Penny." He held the roses out to me, his peace offering, I supposed.

I shook my head and didn't move to take the flowers. "No." The word was said quietly, but there was power behind it.

His expression twisted into a frown. "If I can overlook your indiscretion, surely you can forgive me."

I stilled, my eyebrows nearly rising to my hairline. "Indiscretion?"

"You stayed with another man in *our* honeymoon suite. Did you honestly believe I wouldn't find out?"

I rolled my eyes. I should've known.

This wasn't about me at all. It was about wanting to control me. Claim me. Not that I'd been remotely considering giving him another chance, but still…

"You ended our relationship," I said. "Six weeks ago. Without any sort of explanation. And now you somehow think I owe you something?" I shook my head.

"I fucked up." He tugged on his collar. "I freaked out. I… I'm sorry."

I wasn't sure he'd ever said the word "sorry" to me. But that didn't excuse or explain his behavior. "Why did you do it?"

"Do what?"

"Ask me to marry you? Leave me at the altar? Take your pick."

"Because I love you, Penny. But I was…under a lot of pressure at the time."

I inhaled deeply and let it out slowly. Always with the vague answers. "I'm going to need more than that."

"Can we please not do this *here*?" he asked, glancing around.

I would've told him we didn't have to do it at all, but a small part of me still wanted answers. I couldn't make sense of anything. Why he'd freaked out. Why he wanted another chance. Why I'd agreed to marry him.

At least, apart from wanting that fairy-tale ending. I wanted love. A partner. Maybe even, one day, a family. I wanted to believe in the kind of soul-searching, lifelong love that I wrote about. That I dreamed about.

I just no longer saw myself finding it with Erik. And if I was being honest, I hadn't for a while. I wasn't sure when it had happened, but I'd realized that financial stability didn't necessarily equate to emotional security.

"Look, Erik. I get that you were stressed about…whatever it was. But you should've told me."

"I'm trying to tell you now!" He ignored the curious looks of nearby shoppers and dragged me toward one of the elevators. He jabbed the call button but waited to speak until we were alone in the car.

As soon as the doors closed, he boxed me against the wall, our eyes locking. "Penny," he panted. "I've missed you."

Could I really say the same?

When I searched my heart, I knew the answer was no. If

anything, I felt relief—that we hadn't gotten married. And I couldn't imagine that he'd tell me anything that would change my mind. I was a forgiving person, but the second Erik walked out on me, it was over.

He leaned in as if to kiss me, and I placed my hands against his chest. "Erik. Stop."

He frowned. "Stop? You're my fiancée."

I shook my head. "I'm *not* your fiancée. We're *not* engaged. We're not even in a relationship. And I don't owe you anything."

Wow. Damn. It felt really good to admit that.

The doors opened to another floor, and I took the opportunity to escape. Instead of china and silverware, I was wading through a sea of sexy lingerie. *Awesome.*

"Damn." Erik almost sounded…awed? "All this time, where was *this* Penny?" I rolled my eyes, but he wasn't deterred. "I mean it. What happened to you? To us?"

I paused and turned to face him, softening at the sad tone to his voice. Remembering what it had been like when we'd started dating. Our passionate debates. The sex. The extravagant romantic gestures. I'd thought that was love. And maybe it was, but now I was coming to realize that I'd never felt safe enough to be vulnerable. To be myself.

To gush about a romance novel I'd read or a scene that had blown my mind. To express my deepest desires or hopes for the future. Or even to expect my fiancé to be understanding and proactive about my IBS.

And now that I saw our relationship for what it was, now that I'd seen how different things could be—with Liam—I knew what I'd had with Erik wasn't what I wanted.

"About a month before the wedding," he said, setting the roses on a nearby display. "My dad was diagnosed with early onset Alzheimer's."

I gasped. "Oh no. Erik—" I reached out and placed my hand on his arm. "I'm so sorry."

"Thanks." He stared at the marble floor. "As you can imagine, it means he's no longer fit to lead the company, but the board needed to find a way for him to step down without shareholders losing confidence. Not to mention, we were about to get married."

I swallowed back my hurt and asked, "Why didn't you tell me?"

He dragged a hand through his hair, pacing back and forth between the rows of lace and satin. "I—" He sighed. "I should've. But I was completely overwhelmed. All of a sudden, I was going to be running this huge corporation. We were getting married. Everything was happening so fast, and it felt as if the walls were closing in."

I could understand that it was a lot of pressure, but he'd been groomed for this role his entire life. Maybe it was a different timeline than he'd expected, but he'd always known it was coming.

"I wish you would've talked to me," I said. My heart ached —for his parents and what this would mean for them. But also for Erik. He was an only child, and it was clear that the diagnosis had shaken him.

"So do I. But I panicked."

"But you told me you couldn't see a future for us together," I said. Our last conversation was seared into my brain.

"No." He stepped closer again. "I asked if you could see yourself spending the rest of your life with me. I never said *I* couldn't see a future for us."

I gnashed my teeth. "It was implied. I mean, really, Erik. What the hell was I supposed to think?"

"I just..." He swallowed and took my hands in his, his expression so earnest. So open. "I'm sorry, Penny. I'm so, so sorry. If I could build a time machine and travel back to that moment, I would. It's my biggest regret."

"I wouldn't," I blurted.

"What?" He jerked his head back.

"You're a good man, Erik. But you're not the man for me."

It had taken far too much time, money, and energy to come to that realization, but at least I finally had.

"Is *he?* The guy from the Alondra Valley?"

"Erik." I pinched the bridge of my nose. "This is about us. Not him or anyone else. I'm sorry about your dad's diagnosis, but I'm glad he's getting the treatment he needs."

"Thank you." He smoothed a hand over his hair. "God, I wish I hadn't fucked up. I wish I hadn't freaked out. Then we would still be together."

I wasn't so sure about that. But since Erik seemed more emotional than I'd ever seen him, I decided to stay quiet.

"I think part of the reason I freaked out," he continued, "was because it has a genetic component. I worried—what if I developed it? Or worse still, passed it on to our children."

My heart was burdened by this new knowledge, but it didn't change anything. "I can understand that. It was a lot. But you wouldn't have broken off our engagement if you hadn't had doubts."

"I was wrong, Penny. Please," he begged. He never begged. "Give me another chance. I'm not giving up on us."

I shook my head, striving for a tone that was both compassionate yet firm. "Erik. It's over."

I wasn't trying to punish him. If anything, I pitied him. But I absolutely did not want a second chance. I'd gotten the closure I needed.

"I'M SO PROUD OF YOU," BRINKLEY SAID, LIFTING HER GLASS for a toast a few weeks later. "You released another kick-ass story that readers are loving."

"Thank you." I sipped my martini. Brinkley was right—readers were going crazy for this story about big love in a small town.

I'd had so much fun writing it. The words had flowed faster than they had for any other book I'd written. And readers were raving about the story. They admired the main character. They loved that she was strong yet vulnerable. They swooned over the hero. They loved their chemistry.

I leaned back in my chair and crossed my legs. We were celebrating at my favorite bar, though it always felt like more of a secret garden, with its hidden alcoves and lush greenery.

Brinkley held up her phone, displaying my book's current ranking. *Sixty-nine? Sixty-nine?*

"Top one hundred, baby! Headed toward top fifty. You are on fire, Pen!"

I laughed and drank some more. This was my second book to hit the top one hundred e-books in the entire store, and it was surreal. I was so grateful for each and every reader.

I shook my head, still in shock. "I can't believe it."

"You better believe it." Brinkley grinned. "You're a talented writer."

"Thanks." I bit the inside of my cheek.

She narrowed her eyes at me. "I mean it, Pen."

"I know." I laughed. "And I appreciate all your support."

"Always." She blew me a kiss. "I wish I could go with you to New Orleans for the signing. We could tear it up."

"I know. Did I tell you there's a masquerade?"

She groaned. "Yes. I really want to go just to live out all my dirty book fantasies."

I laughed. "I hate to break it to you, but most of the attendees are women, so it's more about dressing up and dancing."

She frowned. "Don't ruin this for me. I was totally imagining men dressed as aliens from the *Ice Planet Barbarians*. Oh. *Oh.* Maybe a Shibari demonstration like from *Give Me More.*"

"As amazing as that sounds, this is much more sedate." And while I loved reading about sex clubs in novels, I wasn't sure I was brave enough to attend one in real life.

"Penny." She growled.

"Okay. Okay." I held up my hands, trying not to laugh. "I'll leave you to your imagination."

"Good." She crossed her legs in a prim manner that completely contradicted the topic of our conversation. "Now, speaking of dirty fantasies, what's up with your love triangle?"

I rolled my eyes. "I do *not* have a love triangle."

"Did Erik finally see reason and give up?"

I let out a heavy sigh and sipped my martini. Alcohol could irritate my stomach, so I tried to limit it to special occasions and only consume a little. "He keeps sending me flowers and gifts. It's like he thinks he can buy me back."

"Ugh." She leaned forward. "What about Liam?"

"What about him?" I asked, toying with the stem of my glass.

He was never far from my mind. And we texted every so often, usually about surface-level stuff. I'd send him a picture of a bookstore, and he'd send back a picture of Willa the alpaca. But I'd been so focused on writing the book, then releasing it, that I hadn't had time for much else. I'd never felt so consumed by my writing.

"Have you talked to him lately?"

I glanced around at the nearby patrons. A few guys were checking us out, but I wasn't interested. I already had enough drama in my life. And I was perfectly content with my book boyfriends.

Plus, there was the fact that I'd sworn off men. And even if I hadn't, Liam lived across the country. He didn't want a relationship, and neither did I. I needed to learn to be alone for a while. To get comfortable with it.

"Yeah."

"That's all you're going to say?" She gaped at me. "Yeah?"

"What do you want me to say?"

"Are you going to see him again?"

I lifted a shoulder. "I don't know.

"But you want to." It wasn't a question.

I did, but I was afraid to admit it.

My phone vibrated with an incoming text.

> Raven: YOU did it!! You did it!!!

An image came through of my new release and its ranking. My eyes went wide. "Holy shit. I'm number nineteen." I hadn't just cracked the top fifty; I'd blown it wide open.

"Yassss!" Brinkley called for the bartender. "Do you want another, or are you switching to water?" she asked me.

"I'll take a club soda with lime, please."

The bartender disappeared once more as Brinkley turned her attention back to me. "I knew you could do it."

I wasn't sure I'd believed it was possible until now. And I was still in disbelief. I was screenshotting the hell out of my phone.

"Nineteen," she sighed, a huge smile on her lips. "Nineteen, Pen!"

"I know, right? I might have to go back to the AV if this is what happens. I can see why Meghan Hart loves it there."

"Was it the AV or the P in V?" Brinkley made a crude hand motion.

I sprayed my drink everywhere. "Oh my god, Ink. No."

We both started laughing, and a bartender came over to help clean up the mess. She refilled our glasses then disappeared again.

"I'm just going to clean up a bit, then I'll be back." I stood and headed for the restroom.

The bathroom was gorgeous—all moody grays and floral wallpaper. Brass lights.

The setup was clearly intended to encourage selfies. There were several large full-length mirrors, chandeliers, and even a vertical wall of plants with a neon sign in the middle that said, "Hello, beautiful."

I stood before the plant wall and took a selfie before posting it online. I always wanted my readers to feel like they were part of the celebration. Because they were definitely integral to my success.

I did a little happy dance, still in disbelief. Nineteen. In the entire store.

And then my phone chimed with a new email.

PENNY,

Congrats on your new release! You're killing it.

XX,

MH

I FELT LIKE THIS WAS ALL LIAM'S DOING. MY RELATIONSHIP with Meghan Hart. The inspiration for this story. The success of my latest release.

I hovered over Liam's name in my contacts. He'd been my muse for this book. I'd imagined him when writing the hero.

And a number of the scenes had been inspired by our time together in the Alondra Valley.

As excited as I was to celebrate with Brinkley, I wanted to talk to Liam. I wanted to hear his voice.

But did he want to hear from me?

The more I thought about it, the more I realized how often I was the one initiating. As I considered our interactions, it was with a sinking feeling in the pit of my stomach. *I'd* been the one to text him after returning to New York. In fact, I realized I was *always* the one to reach out first. He'd texted, but usually only in response to my messages.

The door to the bathroom opened, and it jolted me from my thoughts. I pushed Liam from my mind. I was doing just fine on my own. I had a new book out. A fabulous best friend. A career I loved. I was friends with my idol. I mean—I couldn't ask for much more. It was everything I'd ever wanted.

Everything except love.

CHAPTER TWELVE

Liam

I stood at the threshold to the ballroom and adjusted my shirt as I scanned the crowd. By and large, most of the attendees were women. They chatted and smiled in groups as they wound around the rows of tables where authors were seated.

All the big names in romance were here, though I wouldn't have expected anything less. It was one of the most popular and well-attended romance book signings in the country. Behind each table—with a few rare exceptions—sat a woman, her name emblazoned on a large banner. The books she'd written were stacked neatly on the table, a line of adoring readers waiting for a chance to meet her and score some swag.

And it wasn't just authors. Cover models. Narrators. So many names and faces I recognized from online, all in one place.

I took my time wandering through the ballroom, studying the attendees and my fellow authors. It was strange—to have so much knowledge about the industry yet be perceived as an outsider. It was like stepping into another world, one where I wasn't sure who I was and what role I wanted to play in it.

For today, though, I was only interested in Penelope Glass. And I couldn't wait to see her.

I was headed toward Penny's section when a woman stopped me. "Can I get a picture with you?"

I tilted my head to the side, taking her in from the lanyard around her neck to the pink graphic tee stretched across her chest. "Um. What?"

"Can I take a picture with you?" she asked again. "You're a cover model, right?"

I shook my head and tried not to laugh. "No, I'm, uh—"

"A narrator?" she asked, her expression earnest.

Was it really so difficult to believe that men loved reading romance too?

"No. I'm just here to see a friend."

"Wow. Okay." Her skin turned the same shade as her shirt. "Sorry."

"No worries. Hey, do you know where Penelope Glass's table is?"

"Just over there." She pointed down the row. Penny had one of the longest lines of readers waiting to meet her. I wasn't at all surprised. "She's the sweetest."

"Thanks," I said and headed that direction.

I should've known hers would be one of the closest tables to the bathroom. I'd read up on IBS since Penny had left, and I worried that the stress from the signing might aggravate her symptoms. I hoped she was drinking her peppermint tea and taking care of herself.

I joined the queue and shifted from one foot to the other as the line shuffled forward slowly. Penny was talking to a reader, posing for pictures with her, smiling. All the while, I wondered if I was about to make a huge mistake.

I'd come to New Orleans on a whim. I knew Penny was a

signing author, and I'd wanted to surprise her. Now it seemed like a stupid idea.

We'd spent a week together months ago. Texted on and off since then. But we'd never discussed meeting up again. What if she didn't want to see me?

Worse still…what if she'd gotten back with her ex? In her emails with Meghan, Penny had mentioned him. But I'd been too scared to pry, and not just because it felt like an even bigger violation of her trust.

But if they were back together, I'd be devastated.

I let out a deep sigh and buried my head in the book I'd brought for Penny to sign. I'd come all this way. I wasn't going to chicken out now.

I lifted the book to cover my face so she wouldn't see me. It was her latest release, and it had hit the top twenty of the entire store. I hadn't had a chance to read it yet—I'd been too busy writing and releasing my own book. But I knew Penny's story would be amazing. I was so fucking proud of her.

I inched closer to the table, closer to Penny. What would she think when she saw me? Would she be happy? Surprised? Mad?

I studied her as she interacted with her readers. She was authentic and warm, and I could see why she was so popular. Why they loved her.

When she stood to take a picture with one of her fans, I drank in the sight of her. Penny was just as beautiful as I'd remembered, if not more so. Her smile was dazzling and genuine. Her fuchsia dress draped over her curves, teasing her cleavage and hugging her waist.

In that moment, I was struck by how much I'd missed her. Despite texting and emailing, nothing compared to seeing Penny in person.

She still hadn't noticed me. She was so absorbed in her task, so giving of her time and herself when it came to her readers. It was something I admired about her. Something I wished I could emulate, even though I knew it was impossible.

Even so, I couldn't help but fantasize about it. And when I did, I nearly laughed aloud at the image that popped into my mind. Of readers lining up to meet Meghan Hart and then discovering a man—me—waiting for them.

I'd been eavesdropping on conversations all day, listening for clues as to what readers thought of Meghan Hart's latest book. So far, though, the online response had been phenomenal. Nearly five thousand reviews already, and most of them were five stars. It was a relief, to say the least.

But there was one reader whose opinion mattered more to me than all the five-star reviews in the world. Which was why—despite the success of my latest release—I was still on edge. Waiting for Penny to read it and recognize some of the scenes from our time together. Wondering if she'd put the pieces together and realize who Meghan truly was.

Right. I was up next. I wiped my palms on my pants and tried to calm my racing heart. I'd never done something like this.

I slid the book across the table.

"And who should I sign this to?" she asked, opening the cover and preparing to sign it.

And then she looked up and met my eyes. Her entire body froze as if someone had hit the "pause" button. The longer we stood there, staring at each other, the louder the murmurs from the people in line grew. But I ignored them.

Penny shook her head as if unable to believe her eyes. "Liam?"

"That works," I said, leaning in so only she could hear me. "Or God." I smirked.

She rolled her eyes, but she was biting back a smile the entire time. "I'll make it special. Just like the recipient." She winked and then stood so we could take a picture together. "Are you here with your mom?"

I shook my head, immediately reaching for her waist. "I'm here for you."

"You…*what?*" She turned to me as her assistant snapped the photo, and it took everything in me not to kiss her.

"I know you're busy with work events, but can I see you later?"

"I'm supposed to go to dinner with some of the other authors and their partners. Well, the few who came. Would you want to…"

"I'd love to," I said. "If it's okay with you, that is."

"Yes," she said, gesturing with her hands more than usual. "Good."

"Penny?" The woman I assumed was her assistant tapped her on the shoulder. "Penny?"

"Sorry. What?" Her attention darted to the woman. "What is it, Raven?"

"Your readers are getting antsy." She smiled.

"Oh right. Of course." Penny waved her hands around then nearly tripped on a stack of books before I caught her. I heard a few gasps from the women in line, and then a sigh of relief rippled through the crowd.

"Thanks," Penny said on a rush of air. She peered up at me, and in that moment, she was the only person who existed.

"I've got you," I said, righting her once more.

She laughed nervously, smiling at the readers waiting in line. "Not every day you get swept off your feet," she joked.

There was a chorus of "mm-hmms" and "hell yeses." I loved how engaged the readers were.

"I have to, um—" She tucked her hair behind her ear. "I need to get back to work. But Raven can give you the details for later."

I nodded, clenching my fist so I wouldn't cup her cheek. "It's good to see you."

She smiled. "It's good to see you too."

"Penny?" Raven said.

"Right. Sorry. Yes." She returned to the table but not without glancing at me once more over her shoulder.

"So…" Raven crossed her arms over her chest. Her red hair was piled high on her head in a messy bun. Freckles dusted the pale skin of her cheeks and the bridge of her nose. And her T-shirt matched Penny's banner in both design and color. "You must be Liam."

I rocked on my heels. "I am. Nice to meet you, Raven." I stuck out my hand to shake.

"Same." She shook my hand then crouched next to a stack of books. She flipped through the covers, looking at the sheets of paper inside. It was all so well organized.

"Penny will be here until five," she said. "Then she'll have an hour and a half to decompress and get ready for dinner."

"Great." I unbuttoned my sleeves and rolled up my shirt. "What can I do to help?"

Her head whipped around so she was looking at me. "Help?" She frowned. "What are you talking about?"

"Looks like you've got your hands full. My mom owns a bookstore. I've helped with a few signings, though not on this scale."

She arched an eyebrow. "You're serious?"

I nodded.

If seeing Penny meant hanging out at the signing, then I was here for it. If it meant packing up her books or taking pictures, I'd do it. I'd flown across the country to see her; this was nothing.

Besides, it was either go back to my room and attempt to write, or I could help Penny. I wasn't sure I'd have the focus to work on a new story, even if I'd wanted to. The idea of being this close to Penny was far too distracting. And I didn't want to waste even a second of my time with her.

Raven explained their system, and then I jumped into action. When I handed Penny her next book, she startled. But then she smiled and mouthed, "Thank you."

I chatted with Raven. Listened to Penny's conversations with her readers. Took photos. Prepped books. And just soaked in the atmosphere.

The energy here was…insane. The readers' enthusiasm. The caliber of the authors. All of it. I'd never felt as much a part of the romance community as I did now. And it made me realize how much I'd been missing out on all these years.

Eventually, the stack of books had dwindled to almost nothing. Penny's energy was flagging—understandably. But she put on a good show. And the ballroom had started emptying out as the afternoon wore on.

"Good job today," Raven said to me as we sorted through the remaining books.

Some were preorders that had yet to be claimed. Others were back stock they'd brought for readers to purchase. I couldn't even imagine the logistics of making this all work. But they'd made it look seamless.

"I'll see you tomorrow." Penny gave her reader a hug. "Thanks for coming."

She turned to Raven. "I have to pee so bad." And then she realized I was still standing there and cringed.

"Go," I said. "I'll finish up here with Raven."

"You really don't have to—" She shifted on her feet.

"Penny, just go." I laughed. "We've got it covered."

"Okay. Okay. Mr. Bossy Pants."

"I'm impressed," Raven said after Penny was gone.

"Yeah?" I closed one of the boxes and then moved to the next.

"Most guys wouldn't attend a romance signing, let alone

help behind the scenes." She stacked the remaining books on the table. "You must really like Penny."

"I do."

Suddenly she was in my face, grasping my shirt. She was surprisingly strong for someone so small. "Then you better not dick her around. Do you understand me?"

"I, uh—" I swallowed. "Yes, ma'am."

She held my gaze, then said, "Good," and released me.

I smoothed down the front of my shirt just as Penny returned and asked, "You ready?"

"Yep," I said, still trying to recover from Raven's unexpected attack.

"Thanks, Raven." Penny hugged her assistant.

"Of course." Raven smiled. But when Penny's back was turned, she pointed at her eyes then me and mouthed, "I'm watching you."

I gulped and placed my hand on the small of Penny's back. "Let's go."

Several readers greeted Penny as we made our way to the elevator. I had so many things I wanted to say to her, but the elevator was packed with attendees. Finally, when we reached her room, she swiped her key card, and I followed her inside.

She kicked off her shoes and dropped her purse on the counter before turning to face me. "I can't believe you're really here."

"I am." I stepped forward so I could grab her hips. I'd been dying to kiss her all day.

She placed her hands on my chest as if to confirm I was real. And that brief contact opened the floodgates. Our lips were colliding, tongues crashing. I swallowed her moan and grabbed her ass, pulling her closer to me. But not close enough.

"God, I missed this." *Missed you.*

"Need you," she said, struggling to remove my clothes.

She eventually gave up and shoved her hand down my pants. She caressed me beneath the material, teasing me like I wanted to do to her. I clawed at her dress, kissing any bare skin I could find until the fabric separating us was gone.

Her eyes fluttered closed as I palmed her breast, bringing her nipple to my mouth. I was desperate for this woman. Crazed.

But she still didn't know the truth. She didn't know who I really was. And she deserved to know.

"I need to tell you something," I said between kisses. I could barely think straight, but this was important.

She yanked my pants over my hips. "First, I want to thank you for all your help today."

"But it's—"

She sank to her knees, her rich brown eyes beguiling as she stared up at me. And then she took me in her mouth, and all other thoughts fled my mind.

CHAPTER THIRTEEN

Penny

I flopped back against the bed, sated and sweating. "I'm going to need a shower before dinner."

Liam pulled me to him and kissed my temple. "Shit. I forgot all about dinner. I wish we could have more alone time."

I rolled over so I was facing him, my chin resting on his chest. I still couldn't believe he was here. That he'd flown in to surprise me. And then he'd spent the day helping with the signing. Seriously? Who did that?

I'd told myself not to immediately jump in bed with him, but after all that he'd done, resisting was impossible. "Me too. Thank you for all your help. That was incredible."

He smiled and tucked a strand of hair behind my ear, his expression filled with pride. "It was fun."

I crossed my eyes and stuck out my tongue. "Maybe you need a new definition of fun."

"I don't know." He pulled my thigh over him and started kneading my muscles, working out any remaining tension the orgasms hadn't. "Anytime I'm with you, I seem to have fun."

"Oh god," I moaned when he hit a particularly sore spot. I leaned back, my body relaxing. "That feels good."

I could hear the smile in his voice. "Good. Maybe you won't kill me for crashing your book signing." Then more softly, he added, "Or for what I have to tell you."

I laughed, opening one eye to peer at him. His body was draped over the bed, his large hands encasing my skin. He was sinful, but he also seemed stressed.

I wanted to ask him what was wrong, but instead, I waited for him to speak. When he said nothing more, I began to wonder if I'd imagined his last comment. So for the moment, I let it go.

"Are you kidding?" I asked. "That was amazing. Do I need to show my appreciation again?" I teased.

"Mm." He hummed, his lips curling into a smile. "Maybe."

"Should I expect to see you at all my signings going forward?"

He continued massaging my muscles, easing the tension from my calves. "Would you pay me in blow jobs?"

I laughed. "Of course."

"Would you want me to come to your signings?"

Of course I would, but… I glanced at the ceiling, trying to steady my heart. I'd sworn off men. And yet, at the first opportunity, I'd jumped into bed with Liam.

As much as I was attracted to him, I'd promised myself I wouldn't rush into anything. Especially not so soon after ending a three-year relationship with a man I'd thought I was going to marry. If I wanted a chance to have a meaningful relationship in the future—with Liam or anyone—I needed to give more consideration to how I'd handled my relationships—both past and future. Not distract myself or try to numb my emotions.

Logically, it made a lot of sense. But my heart didn't want to listen to reason.

Liam took a deep breath. "I know we said this was only for a week, but I also didn't expect to feel the way I do about you."

I... *Wow.* I hadn't expected him to say that. Though, clearly, Liam was full of surprises. It was one of the things I loved about him—how spontaneous he could be.

"Liam," I sighed. "I care about you. A lot."

He groaned. "Uh-oh."

"No uh-oh," I said, removing his hand from his face. "I do care about you, but…well…what exactly are you proposing?"

"More of this."

"More of stolen moments in hotels?"

"Yes." He nodded. "More Netflix and cuddle. More phone calls. More *all* of it."

Was this what he'd been trying to tell me? That he wanted to be together?

"I thought you didn't do relationships."

"No." He dragged his finger down my neck, over my cleavage. "I said I didn't do marriage."

I wasn't looking for marriage. At least not right now. Maybe not ever.

And while I loved the idea of what he was suggesting, the reality was much more complicated. "We live on opposite sides of the country."

"It's a good thing there's texting and FaceTime and airplanes," he teased.

I rolled my eyes. I wanted to say yes. I mean, our week together in the AV had been amazing. But a vacation fling was different from a relationship, and a long-distance one at that.

"Look," Liam said. "I know this is a lot to take in. And I know you just ended a serious relationship."

I nodded, grateful that he understood without my saying anything.

"But I'm a patient man." Liam trailed his fingertips along my skin, leaving goose bumps in their wake. "And I just want to get to know you better. Would that be okay?"

I shivered at his touch.

When he put it that way, it didn't sound so intimidating. We were just…getting to know each other. And considering I liked everything I already knew about Liam, I said, "I like the sound of that."

"There's something else I need to tell you. One of the reasons I came here, actually."

"Okay," I said, trying to push away the sense of unease his words filled me with.

"Penny, I—"

There was a knock at the door, and I groaned. Seriously?

"It's Raven," she called from the hallway.

Raven?

I glanced at the clock and frowned. What was she doing here? We still had plenty of time before dinner.

"Penny." She knocked again, this time more insistent. "It's important."

I huffed and stood, yanking a robe from the hanger and pulling it around me. "I'm sorry," I said to Liam as I headed for the door. "Just give me a sec."

He climbed out of bed, and I couldn't tell if he was upset or relieved by the interruption. Maybe both.

"It's okay." He smiled. "Take your time. I'll run through the shower."

"Good idea." I pulled the bedroom door closed and went to the front of the suite, wondering what on earth could be so urgent.

"Sorry to bother you," Raven said, pushing past me as I heard the shower switch on. "But we have a huge problem."

"We're gonna have a huge problem if you keep barging

into my hotel room like this," I muttered, thinking I'd much rather be in the shower with Liam.

She either hadn't heard me or chose to ignore me. Considering the tightness in her jaw, I assumed it was the former.

"A growing number of readers online are claiming that you copied Meghan Hart's latest book."

"What?" I screeched.

She nodded. "It's bad."

I grabbed my phone from the table and started searching online. Goodreads. Social media. The retailers. It was a shitshow.

"I would never—" I pinched the bridge of my nose. "This is absurd. I haven't even read her latest release. I've been so busy with my own stuff."

"I know," she sighed. "I *know*. But—" Raven shook her head, the phone lighting up her face. "I've been skimming the reader comments." She winced. "They're out for blood."

"How is this *happening*? I thought her release was about a jilted bride?"

"It was. Is."

"And mine is a grumpy sunshine, small-town romance with a wedding hookup." I wasn't sure what the two had anything to do with each other, apart from the fact that they were both romance novels that loosely involved a wedding. And had been released around the same time, though Meghan's had been out for a few weeks before I'd published mine. "They aren't even the same tropes."

"It's not the tropes or even the weddings. The readers pointed to a number of scenes that are too similar to be a coincidence." She grabbed her phone and tapped on the screen. "See?"

I was looking at Goodreads, but it was like a scene from my worst nightmare. It was like a dark hole of dread. A shame spiral. My deepest fears laid bare for the internet to see.

"And everyone knows you're a fan of Meghan," she continued.

I wasn't just a fan. She was my idol. And thanks to Liam, I now considered her a friend.

"Yeah, but to copy her work?" I shook my head. "Our writing styles are different."

In our emails, Meghan and I talked about writing generally and our new releases but nothing of the specifics. And now people were giving my book one-star reviews. They hadn't even read it. They hadn't given me a chance to investigate—let alone explain—the situation. And they were trashing my book. A story that I'd worked my ass off on. This was all a huge mistake.

I checked my email. There were *so* many new reader emails. Some showing support. Others hatred and even some threats. Absolutely nothing from Meghan.

Did she know?

"Should I email Meghan?" I asked Raven.

She shook her head. "I think you need to see if there are similarities first. And maybe consider asking Brinkley for her opinion."

Shit.

Raven was right. I might need legal advice.

"What's wrong?" Liam asked. He was dressed again, his hair still wet from the shower.

Raven deferred to me.

"I-I—" I stuttered. Faltered. What could I even say? He was friends with Meghan too. What if he didn't believe me? What if she didn't?

I shook my head, certain I was imagining this whole thing. There was no way... I didn't understand... I would never... The room spun, and I could feel their eyes on me.

I went to the couch. Lay down. Closed my eyes and placed my hand on my stomach. Counted to twenty. Opened them again.

"What are you doing?" Liam asked me. Then to Raven, he said, "What's wrong?" He came to sit beside me on the couch.

This wasn't a dream. Or a joke. This was my worst nightmare. Worse even than being left on my wedding day. In fact, looking back now, that paled in comparison.

I stood and started pacing. "Readers are accusing me of copying Meghan Hart's latest novel."

He jerked his head back. "What?"

I nodded, wondering why it felt like I couldn't breathe. Wondering if we went outside, if oxygen would fill my lungs again. All the while, I thought about my readers. Of my fellow authors. Authors whose respect I'd worked to earn. Women I admired.

My reputation. My income. My passion…

I doubled over. Before I could collapse on the floor, Liam guided me to a chair and positioned me so my head was between my thighs. His hand was on my back. He said something to Raven, and then the door closed softly behind her.

"Deep breaths, Penny." His tone was calm, but my nerves were so beyond frayed.

Copying? Plagiarism?

I hadn't done it. I would never do something like that. But the accusations alone—the mere whisper of plagiarism— could ruin my career. Ruin everything.

"Hey." Liam pulled me to him. "Hey, come on. Breathe, Penny. Breathe."

"I can't. I won't go back there. I won't."

"Where?" he asked. "What are you talking about?"

I shuddered, just thinking about it. Thinking about the filth and the cockroaches and the worry. I shook my head. "I *cannot* lose everything I've worked so hard for."

"You won't."

"You can't know that. No one can guarantee that."

I remembered the day my dad had died of suicide. My whole life had been torn apart. We'd gone from living a comfortable middle-class life in suburbia to losing our home. Losing *everything*. Though none of that compared to the shock and pain of losing my dad.

"No, but I know you wouldn't copy Meghan—or anyone else, for that matter."

His words were reassuring, but he was biased. "I'm glad *you* do. I wish all the readers did."

"They will. I'll make sure of it."

"And how are you going to do that?" I scoffed. The man was deluded.

"Meghan will tell them."

"Right. I know you're friends with her or *whatever*," I sighed. God, I really hoped they weren't former lovers. I couldn't handle the thought of that. "But she's reclusive and rarely engages online, let alone when there's drama."

I was spinning out of control, and I couldn't stop myself. My footsteps pounded the carpet. *Think, Penny. Think!*

"She will this time." He sounded angry and adamant. Part of me wanted to believe him, and the other part knew that it was my career on the line. This was *my* problem to solve.

I scoffed. "You must not know her as well as you think you do."

"Actually, I know her better than anyone." He grasped my arms, forcing me to stop. "Because *I'm* Meghan."

"You're Meghan," I repeated. Because clearly, I hadn't heard him correctly.

"Yes." He took a deep breath. Let it out slowly. "I'm Meghan Hart. That's what I've been trying to tell you. What I came here to tell you."

I studied him. His eyes held mine, but I shook my head, unwilling to believe what he was saying.

He grabbed his phone from his pocket, then showed me his inbox. "Here. Look."

I stared at the address at the top, "romance-queen@meghanhart.com." I skimmed the screen, knowing it was the same email address I'd been using to communicate with Meghan, but still… My brain wouldn't compute.

So I came up with reasonable alternatives. "Are you her PA? Her lawyer?"

Why had I never pushed for more answers?

"No." He took a deep breath then said, "I write contemporary romance under the pen name Meghan Hart." And then he had the audacity to smile.

"What was the first novel you published?" I asked, prepared to quiz him.

I was the ultimate Meghan Hart fan. If he was lying about being Meghan, there was no way he'd know the answers to all my questions. And while I couldn't think of a plausible reason for him to lie about this, I also couldn't seem to stop myself.

"Technically, the thriller my mom showed you at her store."

"No." I shook my head, my movements agitated. "The first one as Meghan."

"*Hooked.*"

"What is your tagline?"

"A love story for everyone."

"How many books have you published as Meghan?"

"Twenty. Well, twenty-one as of last month."

"Where does the hottest sex scene in *Insatiable* take place?"

"By the pool," he answered immediately. "One of my favorite scenes I've ever written."

I gaped at him, my mind short-circuiting. *Holy shit. He's telling the truth.*

"I had a lot of fun researching parkour for *Flow* and *Leap*. I even learned some moves. It's wicked hard, and you fall a lot."

I remembered him mentioning how obsessed he and River were with Nick Pro, the YouTube parkour athlete. Had Liam been trying to tell me then?

"And the idea for *Honor Bound* came from my grandpa, who was a veteran and later the mayor of Alondra Valley." A look of sadness crossed over his face, quickly replaced by determination. "My favorite trope to write is adventure romance. I will never write a bully romance."

Oh. My. God.

In that moment, everything stopped. The clocks. My heart. The entire freaking world.

Instead of geeking out over the Meghan Hart behind-the-scenes info, I was freaking out at the source of said info. Liam was Meghan was Liam was…

"But you're…"

"A guy?" he asked, rubbing the back of his neck. "Yeah. I know. I'm probably not what you expected, huh?"

I shook my head. Not at all. Not that it mattered.

"So, all this time…"

I tried to replay everything from the beginning. From the night we'd met to the morning after to all our interactions since. Both mine with Liam and Meghan.

He'd recognized me. He'd known that I was the romance author Penelope Glass.

He'd claimed to know Meghan Hart.

He'd given me her email address.

"So this whole time, when I thought I was emailing Meghan, I was actually talking to you?"

I tried to think back on everything I'd told her. *Him.* We'd grown close, and I'd confided in Meghan. I'd shared things about my ex with her. I now realized that meant I'd been talking to Liam about Erik—not that often, but still enough to make me cringe.

He nodded, shoving his hands into his pockets. "Yeah. I didn't mean for that to happen. But I have a hard time saying no when it comes to you."

I softened. At least until I remembered all the times Erik had done something similar. He'd screw up and then try to act like it was somehow my fault. And while I didn't think that was what Liam was doing, I wasn't sure I trusted my instincts either.

"I'm sorry, Penny. This isn't how I wanted to tell you." He held my hands in his. "But I promise we'll find a solution."

I yanked my hands out of his grasp. I couldn't— This was all too confusing. And touching didn't help. It certainly wasn't going to help the fact that my career might be over.

I pulled my lower lip into my mouth and stared at the ceiling, willing the tears not to fall. I needed to figure out how to handle the fact that readers were lambasting me for plagiarizing Meghan's—*his*—book. I'd sort out my feelings about Liam later.

"*We'll* find a solution?" I asked. "*I'm* the one who's being accused of plagiarism."

"I know, but this concerns both our books. I haven't had a chance to read your new release yet, but I never expected that you'd write scenes inspired by our week together," he said, as if it was somehow my fault.

I reared back as if struck. "You're kidding me, right? I could argue the same thing, especially considering I had no idea I was actually sleeping with Meghan Hart. But you...you *knew*."

His expression was contrite, but then a darker thought occurred to me. "Were you using me?"

"Using you?"

"Yeah. All those questions about my books." I shook my head, disappointment and betrayal splitting me apart. "I thought you were such a good listener. So insightful and interested in my passions. But now it seems like you were doing market research on your competitor."

"Hold up now." He lifted his hands as if in surrender. "I wasn't—"

I couldn't handle any more. My career was in shambles, and I needed to work on a plan. Not continue going around and around with Liam.

I swallowed hard and pointed at the door, anger and hurt clogging my throat. "I want you to leave."

He stepped forward, his eyes pleading. I shook my head and dropped my gaze so I wouldn't have to look at him.

"Please, Liam. Please just leave me alone."

CHAPTER FOURTEEN

Penny

I jabbed Brinkley's name in my contacts. "Pick up," I hissed into the phone when it rang, compounding my growing sense of déjà vu. "Please pick up, Ink."

"Hey, Pen. What's up? How's the signing going?"

"Disaster. Complete and utter disaster."

"What are you talking about? Did they ship the wrong quantity of books again or something?" Brinkley knew all about the logistics of attending a book signing. The excitement. The stress.

"I know you're not my attorney, but for a minute, can we just pretend I have attorney-client privilege?" I asked. "So that if I kill someone, you can help me."

"You have something better. Best friend privilege. You know I'd never say anything, Pen. Now, who's on your hit list, girl?"

I gnashed my teeth. "Liam-freaking-Beaudin mother-fucking-Meghan-Hart."

"Huh? Do we have a bad connection or something?"

"No. But I'm about to disconnect his life source." I started pacing, drying some of my tears.

"Uh-oh. What did he do?"

"God, this is such a mess. I don't even know where to start."

"How about at the beginning?"

"Okay." I huffed. "Liam surprised me at my signing."

"Seriously?"

"Seriously. He waited in line, walked up to my table, and asked me to sign his book."

"Cute."

I ignored her comment. I didn't want to think about how cute Liam was or the incredible things he'd done for me. Or how amazing the sex was. Because if I did, I'd open myself up to the possibility of being hurt again.

I'd done it over and over again with Erik, allowing him to manipulate me and my feelings. And I refused to fall into that pattern again.

"He helped Raven all afternoon, and then he told me he wants more."

"Damn. Why are we mad at him again?" I could just imagine her leaning back in her chair, feet propped up on her desk as she stared out over the glittering skyline of Manhattan.

"Liam and I were getting ready to go to dinner when Raven knocked on the door."

"I like how you just glossed over all the juicy bits."

I laughed, though it lacked humor. She was right, but I didn't have time for idle chitchat. So I got straight to the point. "Readers are accusing me of copying Meghan's latest book."

"What?" she shrieked. I could hear her typing on her keyboard in the background and then a quiet, "Oh shit."

"Yeah. Oh shit is right. It gets better." I told her what happened next. How Liam had confessed his identity. How he'd promised to fix everything.

"Holy…wow."

"Right?" I sighed and stared out the window overlooking the French Quarter. "What am I going to do, Ink?"

"What do we always say?" she asked.

"I'm creative. I'm resourceful. And I will figure this shit out," we said in unison.

"That's right," she cheered. "That's my girl."

"But how?" I croaked. "My career could be ruined."

"The good news is, you know that Meghan won't be suing you for plagiarism."

I laughed. "Yeah. I guess that is one bright spot in all of this." Far from it, Liam had promised to help.

"Why aren't readers accusing *Meghan* of copying you?"

"I don't know," I huffed. "I guess because she's the bigger author. More established. Her book came out a few weeks before mine." I was still trying to wrap my head around the fact that *she* was a *he*. Was a she. I buried my face in my hands.

"What does Liam suggest?"

"Nothing specific. He just tried to reassure me that we'd figure something out. He offered to have Meghan post something, but I think that will only add fuel to the fire."

"Mm."

"What are you thinking?" I asked.

"You've seen other authors weather storms like this. What did they do?"

"I've only seen *one* author make it through. And she had to pull the book and rewrite it. She lost all the reviews. She lost readers."

"But she's still writing and publishing books," Brinkley said.

"Yeah, but…" I didn't even know what to say. What to do. I was at a loss, but I was also running out of time. And I had to figure out something.

"Do you want me to fly out there?"

"No." I sniffled. "But thanks for offering."

"I will. And I will beat his ass for making you cry."

I snorted, knowing she would. She was at least a foot shorter than Liam, but she would take him down. The idea was tempting, but I needed to fight my own battles.

There was a knock at the door. "Hey. I gotta go. Thanks for listening."

"Always. I'm sure it's been an emotional evening, but try to get some sleep. Don't make any rash decisions. Call me anytime."

"You're the best."

"So's your face," she teased.

"Love you, Ink."

"Love you too, Pen," she said before we disconnected the call.

"Penny," Raven said, knocking again. "It's me."

"Coming," I called, dabbing at my face and hoping she wouldn't notice my red-rimmed eyes.

"Hey," she said, stepping inside. "So I went through the books and found the scenes readers said are the most similar." She handed me a copy of each, and I was impressed she'd had the time to go to a bookstore and flag a number of scenes.

"Have you read them?" I asked.

"Just skimmed."

I nodded, grabbing Meghan Hart's latest release and thumbing to one of the flags. It was a scene at an alpaca hacienda that sounded a lot like Alpaca Acres. The characters were going for a walk and then taking a picnic. I shook my head and scoffed.

I flipped to the next one. A hot-air balloon ride over the vineyards. And another that was like a playbook for our time together. All beautifully written, of course. But now that I knew who was responsible, I couldn't even enjoy it. I dropped the book on the coffee table.

Wow. Maybe if I weren't freaking out about my career, I would've been flattered. But I wasn't. I felt hurt. Betrayed.

Liam knew how much I'd idolized Meghan Hart. How much I respected her. Had he been laughing at me the entire time?

I mean, he'd spent the day helping me. He'd stood next to me as I signed books—Meghan Hart had stood next to me. Talk about a mindfuck. Perfect for a story, but definitely not what I wanted in real life.

"What do you want to do, boss?" Raven asked.

I sighed. "I don't know." I stood and started pacing. "I don't see how we can come out of this unscathed."

"What if we could get in touch with Meghan and convince her to issue a statement that there was no plagiarism?" she asked, echoing Liam's suggestion.

I shook my head. I still didn't see how that would solve anything. Now that I'd read the scenes, I could understand why the readers were accusing me of plagiarism.

"I'm not sure that's the answer."

"New pen name. Fresh start," she said.

I groaned. "Believe me. The thought has crossed my mind." But I couldn't do that. I'd put in too much work, and I'd done nothing wrong.

"This isn't the first time something like this has happened to a romance author. Maybe you just keep a low profile and weather the storm."

"That's what Brinkley said."

"But you don't like that idea," Raven said, knowing me well enough to anticipate my reaction.

"I just— Ugh." I shook my fists. "I didn't do anything wrong."

"But the similarities are pretty crazy, right? I mean..." She leaned forward, resting her elbows on her knees. "Do you think there's a chance that Meghan copied *your* book? I know hers came out first, but you're friends. Did you share any of your manuscript with her?"

"I—" I opened and closed my mouth a few times, debating my response. As tempted as I was to tell Raven the truth, this was Liam's secret. "No. I didn't."

Maybe if I had, we wouldn't be in this situation!

I lay down on the couch and draped my arm over my eyes. It was nearly midnight, and I was exhausted. But there was no way I could sleep. Forget about dinner. I'd completely blown that off, and I was sure my absence had only sparked more rumors among my colleagues. *Ugh.*

"What am I going to do?" I asked.

"Get some sleep and then reevaluate with fresh eyes in the morning."

I shook my head. "I need a solution before the doors open for the signing. I can't show up in the midst of this shitstorm without a plan. And I can't just *not* show up."

She leaned forward and rubbed her eyes. "I know, but I'm out of ideas at the moment."

I knew she was tired; we both were. God, my stomach was going to be a mess tomorrow. Just what I didn't need.

"Why don't you go to bed?" I said.

"Not unless you are."

"I can't, but you should. You've been working hard all weekend."

"I'm just going to go to my room and rest for like two hours, then I'll be back. But only if you're sure."

"I'm sure. Take all the time you need. You might be out of a job soon, so I wouldn't blame you if you wanted to send out a few résumés while you're at it." I was joking—mostly.

"Oh, come on, Penny. Are you really going to give up so easily?" When I didn't answer, she narrowed her eyes at me.

"Would Jaycee from *Abandon* give up? Would Natalia from The O'Bannon Brothers Series give up?"

"Ugh." I rolled my eyes, hating the way she'd thrown my own characters back at me. She was right, annoyingly so. But I wasn't in the best headspace for a pep talk. "I'm not giving up. I just need to wallow a little bit."

"You can wallow for two hours," she said in a stern tone. "When I come back, we're going to figure out a plan."

I appreciated her confidence, but it felt like my career was over. Everything I'd worked so hard for…

"Just promise me you won't go online until I get back," she said, standing. "In fact—" She snagged my phone from the counter. "I'm taking this with me."

"What?" My jaw dropped. "You can't do that."

"I can, and I am. You'll thank me later."

"I'm not so sure about that," I muttered, though I was grateful not to have the temptation to check. I knew nothing good would come from it.

She shut the door behind her, leaving me alone. I wrote a list of ideas. Threw it away. Lay on the couch and cried. Brainstormed alternate career ideas.

Most of all, I tried to make sense of everything. But I couldn't.

I had whiplash from this afternoon—a high from the signing and the surprise of seeing Liam. To the hot sex that followed and his confession of wanting more. And then everything falling apart and my career being in the toilet.

I lost track of time. The night felt both endless in duration and yet limited. So when there was a knock at the door a while later, I dragged myself off the couch, assuming it was Raven.

I quickly glanced through the peephole and spied a shock of red hair. I sighed and opened the door and took a few steps back. "Liam?"

Raven bounced on her toes, looking surprisingly... excited? "He told me everything, and he has a solid plan."

I held the door open, but Raven shook her head. "I'm going to let you two discuss it, and then you can text me when you decide what to do."

She handed me my phone then turned and headed back down the hall for her room.

That was it? She was going to leave me alone with him?

Liam lingered at the threshold, his eyes filled with sadness and longing. "I know you wanted space..."

"I do. But if you have an idea," I said, "I want to hear it."

At this point, I was getting desperate. The clock was counting down to the signing. My readers would expect a response. And I hadn't come up with any viable ideas apart from abandoning my pen name and everything I'd known and moving to Belize. I'd researched it for one of my novels, and it was gorgeous. Plus, the cost of living was cheaper than New York.

He stepped closer as if to touch me, and I held up a hand to stop him. "Please. Don't."

His expression crumpled.

"I'm already so overwhelmed. Right now, I need to focus on saving my career."

"Then we can talk about us?"

I chewed on the inside of my cheek so I wouldn't cry. "I'm not sure there is an us anymore." *I'm not sure I can trust you.*

"Because I emailed you as Meghan?"

Because you made me feel like a fool.

Looking back now, it seemed so obvious that he was Meghan Hart. And it only made me feel like even more of an idiot. It was almost as if he'd wanted me to figure it out.

But my rose-colored glasses had blinded me to the truth. And now that they'd been removed, it made me question what else I'd missed or misread.

The way he'd acted during our time together. The way he'd treated me. Had I read more into those situations too?

"Penny?" He caressed my cheek.

I shook my head, closing my eyes as I fought the urge to lean into his touch. "Please don't make this any harder than it already is."

He swallowed hard and took a step back. "After you."

Once we were inside, I curled up on the couch beneath a blanket. My travel diffuser was pumping out peppermint oil in the other room, but it did nothing to calm my nerves. "What's your idea?"

"We write a book together. Meghan Hart and Penelope Glass coauthor a book. How epic would that be?"

I shook my head, even though it was something I'd always wanted. Something I'd always dreamed of—the chance to write with my idol. "I don't think that's a good idea."

He frowned. "Why not?"

Because it might break me.

"I just don't think a collaboration is a good idea right now."

"Any collaboration, or a collaboration with me?"

"Either. Both," I said.

"Okay," he huffed. "Do you have a better idea?"

"Besides moving to Belize?" I teased.

He rubbed a hand over his jaw. "A more *realistic* idea."

"Seems pretty realistic to me." Maybe I was being ridiculous, but I just needed a moment.

"I'd rather out myself as Meghan and explain the real reason for the similarity in our scenes."

"I wouldn't," I said immediately. "Do you really want the world to know the most intimate details of our sex lives?"

"That's not—" He pinched the bridge of his nose and sighed. "Honestly, I think more of the focus would be on the fact that Meghan Hart had revealed her identity, and she was a man. Because the only thing that ensures this scandal is forgotten is an even bigger one."

"Okay, Whistledown," I teased, which only made my heart ache more.

Because it reminded me of all the fun we'd had in the past, and everything that would never be.

"I, um—" He cleared his throat. "I prepared a statement in case we go this direction. But I'd like you to review it first."

I sank down on the couch and held out my hand for his phone. We were running out of time, and I still wasn't convinced this was a good idea. But I was curious what he had to say, and I needed time to process.

He rubbed the back of his neck. "I was thinking I'd release it as a video. Will you film it for me?"

I grabbed my phone from the coffee table. "Okay, but that doesn't mean I'm agreeing to this."

He nodded. "Fine. But let's do it so we at least have it prepared."

"Ready?" I asked.

"Yep." He straightened his shirt.

I held up three fingers and counted down quickly.

"Hi." Liam looked up at me—the camera, I reminded myself—and smiled. *Damn.* Why did he have to be so hot? "My name is Liam Beaudin, and for the last six years, I've been writing contemporary romance novels under the pen name Meghan Hart."

Wow. That was a long time to keep such a big secret. I wondered if that had been difficult for him.

"Before writing romance, I published one book under my name. A thriller. It was..." He shook his head and chuckled. "It was pretty awful. My mom disagrees, but you know." He shrugged.

Photogenic. Adorable. Sexy. *Stop!*

"Fortunately or unfortunately, that book did not do well.

I was working full time as a contractor, and I wanted to write. But I couldn't handle more rejection."

It felt as if Liam were speaking directly to me. Pouring his heart out to me as he shared his story, and I wasn't sure I could handle the intensity of it.

"I wrote romance on a dare. I honestly didn't think I'd be any good at it, and I never in my wildest dreams expected it to turn into a career. You guys—my readers—made me a success. Thanks to your support, I've made the best-seller lists multiple times. I was able to quit my job and write full time about a year ago. And I've been privileged to connect with so many of you through my stories. Thank you." He placed a hand over his heart, and I knew exactly how he felt. The longer he spoke, the more it became clear that he was just as passionate—just as invested—in his career as I was mine.

He'd kept this secret for six years. *Six. Years.*

All this time, I—along with all his other readers—had speculated about Meghan's identity. We'd envisioned certain things. Made up stories about who she was.

But that was part of the fun. Imagining what she'd be like. What it would be like to talk with her. To express how much her books had touched me.

But then I looked at Liam and saw how uncomfortable he was, despite the charming facade. And it felt all wrong. There had to be another way.

CHAPTER FIFTEEN

Liam

"This isn't working," Penny said, setting down her phone.

I frowned. "Is it the lighting? Do I need to speak more slowly?"

She glanced at the clock and sighed. "You shouldn't have to reveal your identity if you don't want to."

"Because you think it's a bad move for me or my brand?"

"Because it's your prerogative who you tell. And if you've kept the secret this long, are you sure you want to divulge it now?"

I wasn't sure what I wanted apart from Penny. All I knew was that when she'd started filming, it had all seemed so real. And I'd freaked out. I hadn't even told my family, but I was going to blast this out on the internet?

I cleared my throat, scared to ask. "You think knowing the truth would ruin it for my readers?" When I really wanted to know if it had ruined Meghan for her.

"The mystery is part of the fun. Part of the allure. And if you tell the world, you can't take it back."

I knew she was hurt about the emails. Upset about the

plagiarism accusations. And yet, in the midst of all that, she'd taken the time to consider my needs. To help me determine what *I* wanted for my brand and myself.

"I know, but I'm also tired of keeping this secret. And honestly, sometimes I'd like the recognition. My own family doesn't even know, apart from my grandpa. But he died last year."

She blinked quickly as if her brain was trying to process what I'd said. "What?"

"And Tessa. But she's…" I shook my head. I couldn't make myself say the words aloud. It only made it more real.

"Is—" She cleared her throat. "Is Tessa the reason why you never want to get married?"

"What?" I frowned. What did she think Tessa and I…? "No. Tessa was one of my best friends. She was married to my buddy Tristan. I only recently told him about Meghan. Though I figured he already knew since Tessa was my beta reader."

"Oh." The word tumbled from her lips. "But surely your mom knows, right?"

I shook my head. "Nope."

"That's right. I remember her mentioning something about that when we were at Bibliolater. Your sister?"

"You're *it*, Penny. You're the only one. I mean, apart from Raven now, obviously."

I could tell she had more questions, and I let out a deep sigh. I'd glossed over some of my author history on the video, but only because it was too painful and too private. And while I didn't want to talk about this, Penny deserved an explanation.

"Like I said in the video, I started writing romance as a joke. I was practically begging people to buy my thriller, and I'd go in these online forums and see writers killing it in romance. And at the time, I was—" I shook my head. "Young and stupid. So when this author friend of mine said I didn't have it in me to write a romance, I just *had* to prove her wrong."

"Mm. And then what happened?"

"Well, I wrote *Hooked* and published it. In the first week, I had more sales on it than my thriller had in a year."

"So you decided to write some more?"

I nodded. "Yeah. I was surprised by how much I enjoyed it. I discovered a few craft books I loved, made a beat sheet, and then I never looked back."

She scrunched up her face as if she'd smelled River's wet socks. "Beat sheet?"

"Yeah. You know, the emotional beats of the story."

"Oh, I know what it is, but I could never use one." She cringed. "I like to see where the story takes me."

"Ahh." I tilted my chin back. "You're a pantser."

"Said with such disdain." She rolled her eyes. "Only because you're too scared to deviate from a plan."

"Ironic, coming from you," I teased.

"I'm a discovery writer."

"And I prefer not to *discover* that my plot falls apart in the second act."

She scowled at me. "My plot does *not* fall apart."

"Maybe not after rewrites. But what about during drafting?"

"It's part of the process. You can't tell me you never edit or rewrite."

"All the fucking time."

She sank back against the cushions, arms crossed and a smug grin on her face. "Thus proving my point."

"There are many ways to skin a cat."

Her expression soured. "I always hated the phrase. It's—" She shivered. "Gross."

"You know what's gross? The word 'moist.'"

"Right? Oh. *Oh.* I know..." She tucked her feet beneath her, and I was relieved that she was even talking to me. "Velvet-wrapped steel."

I shuddered. "*The* worst. I feel like I need to make a thesaurus of overused and cheesy romance phrases to avoid."

She laughed, and something in my chest eased.

She'd said there was no *us*, but I didn't believe it. Not when we could talk like this. Laugh like this, especially in the midst of a crisis. And that gave me hope.

She sighed, some of her earlier joy fading. "How did you keep this secret from your family for all these years? And more importantly, why?"

"I just...at first, I didn't want to jinx it. Meghan's novels were doing so well, and I was having fun. And I didn't want them to judge me for it. I'm not proud to admit that my ego was fragile."

"*Was?*" Penny snorted.

I ignored her comment, though she wasn't wrong. "Tons of authors write under pen names and don't tell their families."

"Yeah, but that's usually because they're afraid their family will disapprove. But from everything you've told me about your family, I can't imagine them being anything but supportive."

I shook my head, my skin crawling with shame and regret. "You're wrong," I said more softly.

"Are you referring to your grandpa?"

I nodded. "Tessa had been trying to convince me to tell my family for years. I finally decided to tell them when I quit my job and was transitioning to writing full time. And I started with my grandpa. We'd always been close. He was... everything I'd always wanted to be. Everyone in the AV admired and respected him."

"What happened?" Penny asked.

"He said he was ashamed of me. Said I wasn't a real man because I wrote porn for a living." I rubbed the back of my neck. His words still stung even now, and his reaction had deterred me from telling anyone else. I'd nearly stopped writing because of it.

"He died soon after," I continued, just wanting to get it over with. "And I can't stop wondering if the shock, the bitter disappointment of seeing what I'd become, sent him to his grave."

"Oh, Liam." She placed her hand on my arm. "I'm so sorry. Losing a loved one is never easy. Especially when you feel like there was an unresolved issue. Or that you disappointed them or might have somehow caused it."

"You sound as if you speak from experience."

"My, um—" She tucked her hair behind her ear. "My dad died of suicide when I was in high school. And I've always wondered, what if I could've done something different? What if I could've been a better daughter? You know?"

"Exactly," I said, both saddened and relieved that she understood. "I'm sorry about your dad."

"Thanks." She straightened. "I'm sorry about your grandpa. Both how he reacted to your news and his death."

I blew out a breath, feeling simultaneously relieved and burdened by what we'd shared. I couldn't stop thinking about Penny and her dad. And how that still impacted her, just as my grandpa's reaction and subsequent passing still impacted me.

"The more time that goes by, the harder it becomes to tell anyone else. My parents and Wren were already dealing with my grandpa's death." And then Tessa's. "At that point, I'd kept the secret for so long, and I worried they'd feel betrayed." I'd almost ruined my relationship with my sister and my best friend because of my own stupidity. "And I don't want to lose anyone else."

We were both quiet before Penny said, "There has to be another solution. We're creative people. We should be able to find a way to spin this so you can protect your secret *and* I can protect my reputation." She rubbed her index finger over her lips. I didn't think she had any clue how distracting that was.

I kept staring at her lips. At her eyes. At *her.*

"Why won't you even consider a cowrite?" I sank back down on the couch, this time closer to her.

I knew she was hurt, but the chance to cowrite with her idol? She must really be mad to pass up an offer like that.

I was determined to make this up to her—both the potential damage to her career and the destruction to our relationship. If I were in her shoes, I'd be panicked. I knew how much Penny loved this job. I knew how devastated I'd be if I couldn't be Meghan anymore.

Selfishly, I wanted her to agree. A cowrite would give me the chance to get close to Penny. To spend time with her. If we were writing a book together, she couldn't avoid me.

We'd spend a few months working on it, and by the time we were done, she'd have forgiven me. And she'd remember just how good we were together.

"We have a lot of crossover with our fans," I said. "It would allow both of us to reach new readers. Provides social proof. We can split the cost of marketing." *I could keep going.*

"What about the fact that readers think I'm plagiarizing your material?"

I lifted a shoulder. "We could act like it was intentional." Now that the ball was rolling, it was really gaining speed. "We could say they were Easter eggs for our fans. We wrote the scenes together and put them in our books to see who'd notice."

"Oh, *they* noticed." Judging from her tone, she still wasn't taking this idea—or me—very seriously.

I needed a new tactic. Something that would appeal to her.

"Come on. If you heard that two of your favorite authors were collaborating, don't you think you'd be excited?"

"Yes, but—"

"And everything you do is for your readers, right?"

She rolled her eyes. "Yes, but this is also a business."

"And *this* is a smart business move. It leverages both our brands. Meghan has never collaborated with someone." I was offering her something I'd never offered anyone else. Never even considered, mostly because I couldn't risk revealing my identity. But for Penny—I'd do anything.

"Ugh." She stood and started pacing. "I hate making big decisions under pressure."

I wasn't trying to pressure her, but I knew we were running out of time. And I knew this was a good opportunity —for both of us.

I gave her a moment, then stood and grasped her shoulders. "This could be amazing for both our careers. Don't make a bad business decision because you're hurt by what *I* did. The mistakes *I* made."

"I'm not," she said through gritted teeth. "I'm not trying to punish you."

"Then what's your hesitation? I thought you'd jump all over this."

Unless it was because *I* was Meghan.

I frowned. I hoped that wasn't the reason.

"You want to show the community a united front of empowered, savvy women, right?"

She blew out a breath, her shoulders relaxing. "Been trolling my social media, I see."

She had no idea.

"What better way to do that?"

"You're a plotter," she said it with such disdain.

"And you're a pantser."

"Discovery writer," she corrected. "Our processes are totally different."

"We're both talented writers who are passionate about storytelling."

She nodded slowly, considering. "True."

I tried not to let my excitement show, though it was tinged with wariness. "But…"

"But I don't want you to get the wrong idea. We would have a business relationship, nothing more."

I frowned, her words striking me to my very core. "*Penny.*"

"No." She shook her head. "I need you to hear me on this. I need to know that we can be professionals."

"Anything else?" I asked, without committing to her condition.

"We split the royalties fifty-fifty. We have to agree on all major decisions, like the cover."

"Of course," I said. "Though I'd love to use my sister's studio for the photographs, if you're okay with it. She and Harper photographed my last three releases."

"And she doesn't know?" She shook her head with a laugh. "You're much better at keeping secrets than I am."

"I'm not sure if that's a good thing." I rubbed the back of my neck.

She grabbed her phone from the coffee table. "I want to figure out what we're going to post and how we're going to announce this. We need a plan before the signing kicks off. Raven might have some ideas on how to promote it last minute."

Clearly, she was done talking about us. We were short on time, and right now, we needed to work together. The important thing was that she'd agreed.

"Sounds good."

She texted Raven, and a few minutes later, there was a knock at the door.

"Glad to see you guys kissed and made up," Raven said, taking a seat on the couch.

"Ha!" Penny barked. "I wouldn't say that. But we came to an agreement."

"Okay." Raven glanced between us. "Tell me what you need."

I outlined the plan, and by the time I was done, Raven was practically jumping up and down. "Fuck yes. This is going to be epic."

I gave Penny a look as if to say, *See? I told you so.* And she pretended to ignore me, but she was totally fighting a smile.

"Oh my god," Raven said. "Your readers are going to flip the eff out. We should have something printed for the table."

"Do we have time for that?" Penny asked.

"I'll figure it out. It'll be great promo and shut down any haters."

"What else?" I asked Raven.

"Can you go to the nearest bookstore when it opens and buy a ton of Meghan's books to display on Penny's table? Oh, and sign them."

"Yes." I snapped my fingers. "Good."

"Shoot me your PayPal address, and I'll send you the money from any sales."

"Even better," I said, grabbing my phone to do just that.

"And we should get postcards," Raven said. "No, bookmarks. With a QR code. You could both offer a free book for readers who sign up for your newsletters. Though, this last minute, the printing will be expensive."

Damn. Why hadn't I thought of that?

"I can use *Free to Love*," Penny said. "And I don't care how much it costs."

"Perfect. Liam, does Meghan have a book we can use as a freebie?"

I held Penny's gaze and said, "*Belonging.*" Because I knew it was her favorite. "And I'll pay any fees for the rush job."

"We'll split them," Penny said.

Before I could open my mouth to argue, Raven said, "We'll need some images for social media. Hmm—" She pursed her lips. "How are we going to do this with Meghan being anonymous?"

"Show our books side by side in a flat lay?" Penny offered.

"Yeah. That works. I'll get some fresh flowers."

"I can do something," Penny protested.

"Work on what you want the posts to say. And then focus on being your badass self today with readers."

"God, I'm so tired." She slumped.

"Last day, baby." Raven held up her hand for a high five. "Then we can go home."

"Last day," Penny said with much less enthusiasm.

"It would be nice if you guys at least had a title or an idea what the book was about. Just a little tease," Raven said, lowering her hand. "So it seems like this really was the plan all along."

"Adventure romance?" Penny asked. "Like *Insatiable.* But with a tropical flair."

"I was thinking something with broader appeal. Something that would play to both our strengths."

Adventure romances could be fun, but they could also be a lot of work. A lot of research. Considering the fact that Penny was a discovery writer, I had a feeling we'd both end up frustrated.

"Did you have anything specific in mind?" Penny asked me.

"What's your favorite trope to read?" I asked.

"Brother's best friend."

I groaned, Bennett and Wren immediately coming to mind. "No. I just lived through one of those. I'm not writing about it."

"Love after loss," she said.

I didn't think I could do it. Not after so recently losing Tessa. So I shook my head. "What about on the rocks?"

"I haven't read many of those, but I do enjoy them when done right."

"What about a couple on the verge of divorce? The circumstances force them together, and they realize they love each other." Just like us. Minus the divorce part.

Penny frowned. "Could be depressing."

"I don't know," Raven interrupted. "I think it could be really amazing. And it's got that second-chance vibe that several of your books do."

"See?"

Penny sighed. "It feels rushed. This whole thing feels rushed and sloppy, and I'm the one who's going to have to go down there and sell the hell out of it." She placed her hand to her stomach, a frown creasing her brow.

Despite being a discovery writer, Penny always seemed very methodical about her marketing. Not in an impersonal or automated sort of way. More that she was organized and had it together. I could tell that doing things so last minute was painful for her. And I wanted to support her in any way I could.

"What do you propose?" I asked. I wanted—no, needed—Penny to be confident and comfortable about this. I'd be at her side the whole time, but she was the one on trial with the readers.

"Enemies to lovers."

"Ooh. Yes. So much angst and tension," Raven said.

"I don't know," I hedged. "I don't have much experience with that."

"Enemies to lovers adventure romance. Shove them together. Make it awkward."

The longer she talked, the more excited I was. It sounded hot. Fun. Sexy.

We'd take this risk together. She had experience with enemies to lovers, and I was no stranger to writing adventure romance. We'd marry both our strengths.

"Okay," I said. "Let's do it. Let's be brave together."

CHAPTER SIXTEEN

Penny

"Deep breaths, Penny. Deep breaths." I inhaled slowly then smiled at my reflection, trying to psych myself up for the signing.

I was operating on zero sleep. I'd been accused of plagiarism. And I'd agreed to cowrite a book with Meghan Hart. *Holy freaking shit!*

I should've been happy. I mean, this had always been one of those career goals of mine that had seemed absurd. A collaboration with my idol? With Meghan Hart?

If someone had told me it would happen when I'd begun my author career, I would've never believed it. Even now, I was still in shock. Though perhaps that was due more to the fact that Meghan Hart was Liam Beaudin. Which only compounded my anxiety about writing together.

Oh god. I really hope I can pull this off.

"Penny?" Raven knocked on the bathroom door, and I tried to quell my nausea. "Almost ready?"

How ironic. Every time I was on the verge of finally accomplishing some big goal or dream, my life imploded. My dad died just before I graduated high school. Erik left me at the altar on our wedding day. I was going to get to collaborate with my idol, but only because it might save my career from accusations of plagiarism.

"Yep. Yeah." I sighed and smoothed down my skirt, lowering my voice as I looked at myself in the mirror and imagined Brinkley there with me. Cheering me on. "I am creative. I am resourceful. And I will make this day my bitch."

Okay. I took a deep breath. *You can do this.*

I opened the door, expecting Raven, but instead, I found Liam waiting for me. He scanned me head to toe, his eyes hungry. Wanting.

It didn't matter how much I told myself to act professionally toward Liam, my body still craved him. I blamed it on exhaustion. Stress. Adrenaline. At least that's what I kept telling myself.

But I knew it was more than that. Liam had been there for me after Erik left me at the altar. He'd been compassionate and caring. And he'd helped me move forward during a time that could've been devastating. Plus, his story about his grandpa rejecting him was so heartbreaking that I couldn't help but feel for him.

"You ready?" he asked.

"I thought you were taking care of the books," I said, annoyed by my body's response to him. The things I'd told him when I'd thought I was communicating with Meghan…

"Already done. And I'm staying close—" He placed his hand on my lower back as we headed for the door. "In case anything comes up with the announcement."

"I can handle it." I gnashed my teeth and straightened, taking a step away from his touch.

"Of course you can," he said in a gentle tone. "But we're partners."

That might be true, but *this* partner had a much more public role. For once, I envied him and his secret identity. He could stand back and watch, while I had to deal with upset readers and an even more upset stomach. I'd already gone to the bathroom twice and still felt as if I needed to go again.

"Okay," Raven said, clearly trying to keep us on task. "So, we have the banner set up. Meghan's signed books are displayed on the table and ready to sell. And we have bookmarks with the QR code for the newsletter sign-up."

"Perfect," I said. "Let's go."

We took the elevator down to the ballroom. A number of other authors were already setting up, and I forced myself to smile and act normal, even as my stomach grumbled. Several people turned so their backs were to me as we passed, and I made note of each and every author who slighted me.

"Jesus," Liam whispered. "It really does feel like when the ton snubbed the Bridgertons, doesn't it?"

I laughed, appreciating his attempt to put me at ease by comparing my situation to the fictional one of Julia Quinn's high-class society during the Regency era.

When we arrived at the table, Raven had me pose for a few photos. I smiled through the nausea and posted them to my stories in an effort to distract myself. Then I checked on my most recent post about the collaboration with Meghan. I'd been too busy getting ready to monitor the response, and I'd secretly feared what I'd find when I did.

Last night, I'd had to turn off comments on my posts because they were becoming so vicious. The readers were arguing among one another. Debating the authenticity of my work. I tried not to let it affect me, but it was incredibly difficult.

When I checked this time, though… *"Holy shit."*

"What?" Liam rushed over to me. "What's wrong?"

"Have you seen this?" I flashed him the screen. My post had over one hundred thousand likes, and new followers were pouring in. I'd nearly doubled my number of followers overnight.

"See?" He smirked. "I told you this would work."

"We still have to write the book," I whispered.

He leaned in, close enough that I could smell his scent—clean laundry, fresh air, happiness. "We will."

We didn't have a choice. Both our careers were now depending on it.

"Showtime," Raven said as the doors opened.

"Who's that?" Liam asked as a woman in leather pants and a crop top sauntered down the next row.

"Melanie Hayes. Rock star romance."

"Oh yeah. I've read some of her stuff. Not bad. I'm just not that into rock stars."

I forced myself to smile as she approached my table. Neither was I. No, if someone asked if I had a type, I'd tell them it was the man standing next to me.

"Lucky bitch," Melanie teased, giving me a hug. "A collab with Meghan Hart. Girl, how did you score that?"

I lifted a shoulder. "Luck, I guess."

"Not luck. Talent," Liam said.

Melanie turned to him, her eyes sweeping his body in a way that made me both jealous and uncomfortable. "And you are?"

"Here with Penny," he said, and I tried not to laugh.

"Just a friend," I added, though it was a bit more complicated than that.

But the only future we had together was the one where we coauthored a book. There was a growing pain in my stomach at that thought, and I was pretty sure my IBS wasn't to blame this time.

"Well, congrats," she said again to me. "Let's catch up later."

I waved goodbye and shifted from one foot to the other. I

was anxious about seeing the readers, afraid how they'd react. I wondered if anyone would question the collaboration or if the accusations would just fade away.

Kimmy James approached. Her low-cut top practically revealed her nipples, but if I'd paid as much for my boobs as she had, I'd probably show them off more too. She put on a good act for the readers—pretending she was all for female friendships and empowerment—but she couldn't fool me.

"You really upped your game for this signing," she said. "Male model. A bombshell of an announcement." She studied her fingernails—long, pointy, lethal. "I'm just so glad those rumors about the *plagiarism*," she whispered it like the dirty word it was, "were false."

"Mm." I forced a smile. It was women like Kimmy who gave this industry—and women generally—a bad name. She was catty, competitive, and just...cringe.

"Well, I better get to my table. I already have readers lining up to see me." She turned and left.

"Kimmy James?" Liam asked.

I watched him out of the corner of my eye. "You know her?"

"I know *of* her. Even in the few online interactions I've had with her, I never liked her. She's so fake." He shuddered.

I laughed. He was right about that.

"I bet it's interesting to finally meet everyone in person."

He nodded. "Definitely. This whole thing is wild. I can't even imagine how tired you are at the end of each day."

I tried not to think about how tired I was. And how much my feet already hurt when I had hours ahead of me. "It's both exhausting and exhilarating."

"I'll bet. You make it look easy."

"Thanks." I smiled at him, and my breath caught in my throat. Why did he have to be so handsome? So nice?

"You ready?" Raven asked.

I nodded and took my seat at the table as readers lined up, bracing myself. But there was no need. My readers were thrilled about the collaboration. They asked a lot of questions about it, and I gave only vague answers, but they were used to that. I typically didn't make many announcements about my books until close to release.

During lunch, I crashed on my bed, waking up just in time to refresh my makeup and head back downstairs for more.

"Here," Liam said, handing me a cup of peppermint tea as soon as I arrived at the table. He was always so thoughtful. Always trying to take care of me.

"Thank you." I grabbed it and took a long sip. The nap had helped. The tea was definitely helping. It was almost as if I'd gotten a second wind.

"Have dinner with me tonight," Liam said, bringing me another stack of books to sign. Quickly adding more quietly, "To celebrate our partnership."

I hedged. "I don't know if that's a good idea."

"Please?" He pressed his palms together and batted his eyes.

"Girl, if you don't say yes to him, I will," the next reader in line said. And there was an echoing chorus of Yes, ma'am and mm-hmm. I laughed, mostly to hide my discomfort. The idea of Liam with another woman made my stomach churn.

The group started chanting. "Say yes. Say yes."

It felt as if everyone in the ballroom had turned their attention to us. I couldn't say no. Not now.

"Okay," I said, just wanting to put an end to it. "Fine."

It wasn't like I had to follow through on it, did I?

Everyone cheered, and Liam pressed a kiss to my temple.

"Don't push it," I muttered, pasting on a smile.

"Wouldn't dream of it," he said and returned to his post

but not before drawing his fingers across the back of my shoulders.

The rest of the day flew by. My hand felt as if it might fall off from signing so many books. My feet ached from my heels. And my cheeks were tight from smiling for hours. But I was happy. More than anything, I was relieved.

While I finished signing a few more books, Liam and Raven packed everything up. Liam had been incredibly helpful. He was always friendly and professional with the readers. Always jumping in to assist, whether it was with coffee runs, taking pictures, or lifting stock. It reminded me of all the reasons I'd fallen for him in the first place.

Ugh.

"Okay," Raven said, glancing around one last time. "I think we're good."

"Great. Thanks, guys. I really appreciate all your help. You went above and beyond, Raven."

"My pleasure," Raven said.

"Same," Liam chimed in.

"Take yourself to dinner on me," I said, handing Raven my business credit card as we entered the elevator. "Somewhere nice."

I planned to take a bath, crawl into bed, and order the mildest thing on the room service menu. Probably oatmeal. Maybe a plain baked potato.

She laughed. "I'll take you up on that when we get home. Tonight, I just want to go to bed."

I groaned. Bed. That sounded so nice. "Me too."

"I won't keep you out too late," Liam said with a wink. "Promise."

"We're not going to dinner," I said as the elevator came to a stop at Raven's floor. She handed my credit card back to me, and I tucked it in my wallet.

She smirked at me as the doors closed. "Have fun," she called.

Liam frowned. "You said yes."

"Yeah. Only so they'd let it go."

"Come on," he said, boxing me in. "It's just one meal."

"It's never *just* anything with you."

"Please, Penny." He leaned his forehead against mine, our noses grazing. It was as if my body was hardwired to crave his touch, but I was trying to ignore it. "Give me a chance."

"Liam, I can appreciate that, but I'm physically and emotionally exhausted." I was so tired and overdone, I felt like I was on the verge of tears again. "I just want to crawl into bed and go to sleep. And honestly, after everything that happened, I need some time." To process this information. To work on myself and my deeply defective intuition.

He stepped back as the doors to the elevator opened. "I can give you time. As I told you, I'm a patient man."

I shook my head as we stood in the hallway, his words an echo of promises from yesterday. "Things are different now."

He scoffed. "So, that's it? One hiccup, and we're over? The end."

"Did we ever really begin?" I asked, but even I knew that was a lie.

"Penny—" He opened his mouth to say something.

"Please—" I held up a hand when he took a step forward. "Don't push me on this."

He sighed, resignation in that exhale. "As you wish."

I laughed at his reference to *The Princess Bride*. "Oh no. Don't you dare *Westley* me."

"Classic movie."

"Yes, but I am not your Buttercup."

"That's fine. I always saw myself more as Inigo Montoya."

The vengeful but talented swordsman. An intriguing character but a side one, nevertheless.

"Interesting."

"What's your favorite movie?" he asked.

"I'm not sure I have one."

"What?" He nearly choked on the word. "You're kidding?"

"I typically don't rewatch the same movies. Besides, I'd rather read."

"But you reread books."

"That's different."

"How?" He leaned his shoulder against the wall and crossed his arms.

"It's like revisiting my happy place. It's like coming home. And I prefer to imagine the story the way I want."

"I can understand that. So many movie adaptations of books are…" He shuddered.

I nodded, covering a yawn as I inched closer to the door to my room. I could've stayed up all night talking books with him again, but that was *before*. This was…now.

"It's getting late. I need to pack and get some sleep before my flight."

He pressed off the wall and stepped closer, placing his hand on my hip. "Have a safe trip, Penny." He lingered, our faces nearly touching.

"Thanks." I fumbled with my room key, knowing I'd kiss him if I stayed there any longer. "You too."

I closed the door to my room and sank against it. What I'd told Liam was true—I needed space. Time. But it was mostly because I was scared. We barely knew each other, and it already felt as if he was taking a piece of my heart with him.

CHAPTER SEVENTEEN

Penny

The door to my apartment opened. "Hey!" Brinkley said as she backed in, her arms full of grocery bags.

"Hey." I frowned at her over the top of my computer. "What's all this?"

"You wouldn't come out, so I'm bringing dinner to you." She set the bags on the counter.

"Are you feeding an army?" I teased, standing to give her a hug.

She laughed. "Maybe. I'm hungry. And I know you must be too. I mean—" She gave me a once-over. "When was the last time you left your apartment?"

"Ha-ha. I leave my apartment." I picked through the bags, my mouth watering over the array of goodies in addition to the meal. "Mm. Quinoa puffs and sweet potatoes and…and Hu salty chocolate. All my favorites. Thanks, Ink!"

"You're welcome." She leaned in and sniffed me a few times. "Pen, when was the last time you washed your hair?"

I rolled my eyes. So I hadn't been as thorough with my grooming routine since returning from New Orleans. "Hey! At least I took a shower. So what if I didn't wash my hair every time? I had my period *and* an epic IBS flare. And you know what it's like when I'm immersed in a story."

"Does that mean it's going well with Liam?"

"It's…going." I opened some of the containers and grabbed a couple plates from the cabinet.

We served ourselves then headed to the living room to watch *Friends* reruns while eating. It had been our tradition since high school, when we'd dreamed of moving to New York. To finding friends and love in the city just like Rachel, Monica, and Phoebe. Well, to varying degrees of success. But to small-town girls like us, their lives had seemed so fabulous. Now, we were living them.

"These are pretty," she said, fingering one of the roses on my coffee table. "Did Liam send them?"

"No, um—" I pushed the food around on the plate. "Erik did."

She leaned back against the cushions and crossed her arms over her chest. "I was wrong. He's not persistent, he's delusional."

"I know. I already told him it wasn't happening. I only kept the flowers because they're too pretty to toss."

"Mm," she said around a bite. "I hope you didn't tell him that. Because it doesn't seem like he's getting the memo."

"I don't know what more to do," I said. "He's used to getting his way, and he's not easily deterred."

That was the difference between him and Liam. I'd told both of them I needed space, but unlike Erik, Liam had actually listened. Well, apart from his attempts to sneak personal questions into his emails to me between ones about our story.

His latest—*what's your favorite snack food?*

Why did he even care?

"What is it with you and these guys?"

I slumped in my seat. "I don't know, but I am *over* it. I just want a man like I write about in my books. Honest. Hard-working. Good with kids."

"Right?" She took a bite of grilled chicken.

"If only I could write the perfect man into existence," I sighed.

"Why don't you?"

"Why don't I what?"

She pointed her fork at me. "Write a list of the qualities you'd want in your future partner. Aren't you the one always talking about 'manifest that shit'?"

"Um." I set my plate on the coffee table and hugged a pillow to my chest. "Pretty sure I don't say it like that."

"Whatever." She sliced her hand through the air. "My point is, you manifested your dream collab with your idol. Maybe you can manifest your dream man too."

I barked out a laugh. More like dream turned nightmare. "If my 'dream man,'" I said with air quotes, "turned out as messed up as this collab, I'd be screwed."

She pursed her lips. "Is it really *that* awful?"

"Meghan's a plotter," I said. I'd found that it was easier to think of Liam as Meghan when we were working on the book. Otherwise, I'd get sidetracked, or worse, too emotional.

Brinkley cringed, intimately familiar with my writing process. There was no plotting. The idea of it gave me hives. And any time I'd tried, it had ended badly.

I could outline an entire story, but then I could never write it. I hated knowing the ending. I wanted to be surprised. Once I knew what would happen, the fun was over for me.

Every time Meghan tried to force me into narrowing down a story line, I could feel my skin crawling. So I either avoided answering, or I'd just agree. I had no idea what I was going to do when I had to write and submit my chapters.

She was a brilliant writer, and I was…well, I felt unworthy of her.

"Penny," Brinkley said. "Talk to me. What's going on?"

"I'm stressed." And I was stressed about being stressed, neither of which was good for my IBS.

"I can tell." She gestured to me, waving her hand in a circle. "You've holed up in your apartment since the signing. Been ignoring my texts. Won't go out."

"Ignoring?" I scoffed. "I was a *little* slow to respond."

Brinkley narrowed her eyes at me, and I knew she wanted an answer.

"It all just feels like too much. What if we disappoint the readers? What if they hate our book? What if we can't even write the book because we can never agree on anything?"

"I know this is important to you. But you can't sabotage yourself with worries about the future."

"Are you kidding?" I joked. "I'm the queen of it."

She nodded slowly, taking my hand in hers. "Have you talked to your therapist lately?"

I squeezed my eyes shut. "I haven't had an appointment with her since before the wedding."

"Ooh." Brinkley sucked air between her teeth. "Wow. That's interesting."

"I've been—"

"Don't say busy," she said. "You always make time for therapy. What's going on?"

"I just—" I sighed. "I don't really want to talk about it."

"Is it the stuff with Erik? Liam?"

"All of it. Why I keep repeating the same patterns. Blah. Blah. Blah."

"I'm guessing you know the answer to that. Or at least you have some idea."

"Yeah. I mean, Dr. Hamm and I have talked about it some. A lot of it stems from my dad."

"Not surprisingly. I know you want answers," she said. "Answers you'll likely never have. And that's hard."

I nodded, fighting back tears. Even though he'd been gone nearly a decade, some days, the pain was still very fresh.

"I never told you this, but I was secretly relieved when Erik called off the wedding because I was dreading the fact that my dad wasn't there to walk me down the aisle."

"Oh, Pen." She set down her dish and came over to give me a hug. "I wish you'd told me."

"I just… I wanted to be happy. My mom was so happy, and I didn't want to dwell on it. Nothing was going to change. Dad wouldn't magically appear to give me away—antiquated as the tradition is. Or share a father-daughter dance."

And it had been such a relief not to pretend I was fine. Everything was fine.

It wasn't.

"I know you miss him. And I'm sure that wasn't easy."

I nodded, wiping away a tear. "Thanks for listening, Ink."

"I'm always happy to listen, but I hope you'll consider giving your therapist a call too. I know how much she's helped you in the past."

"I will," I said, and I meant it. Brinkley was right. "Soon."

"Good."

My computer chimed with an alert for an incoming email. Brinkley glanced at the screen on the way back to the kitchen. "It's from Meghan."

I groaned, knowing Meghan either wanted to brainstorm or had sent me her chapters. I had yet to send her mine. "I don't know if I can do this."

"Do what?"

"Coauthor a book with anyone, let alone Meghan freaking Hart."

"What are you most afraid of?"

"Everything."

"Be serious," Brinkley chided. "And dig deep."

"I'm afraid Meghan will realize that I'm an impostor," I blurted.

"An impostor?" She frowned. "Penny, what are you talking about?"

"The only reason I even have this opportunity is because I slept with Liam. And then we both—stupidly—decided to write about our time together. If not, do you really think Meghan Hart would *choose* to collaborate with me?"

"Yes! And she'd be damn lucky to work with you. What's this nonsense about being an impostor?"

"Nothing. Never mind." I wished I'd never said anything.

"Why do you do that?" she asked. "Why do you always shut me down when I'm trying to have a real conversation with you?"

Because I'm afraid to feel too much. I'm afraid you'll think I'm too sensitive. That my friendship requires too much work. That I'm a burden.

Whoa. Where the hell had that come from?

"Look, Pen." Brinkley draped her arm around my shoulder. "You know I only say this because I love you, right?"

I nodded. I wasn't upset with Brinkley. She was my best friend. She was looking out for me.

"And you've been through a lot lately. I'm worried you don't know how to process your feelings about all of it."

"That's why I go to therapy. And why I write."

"Neither of which you're currently doing. Honestly, I'm concerned that you're emotionally constipated."

"Emotionally constipated? Jeez." I shook my head. As if I didn't already deal with enough shit. "Thanks for that lovely mental image."

"Maybe you should talk to Li—" She stopped herself. "I

mean Meghan about it. I bet she's dealt with similar feelings around creativity and her work."

I opened my mouth, ready to dismiss that idea. But part of me knew Brinkley was right. I thought back on my early conversations with Liam. When he'd asked me what I thought about Meghan's latest release. Why I thought it had been unsuccessful.

I'd always assumed that once you reached a certain level of success, it became easy. But that still wasn't the case for me, and I'd passed so many milestones I'd set for myself that the goalposts kept moving. It could be a good motivator, but sometimes I wondered when it would ever be enough.

"Thanks, Ink. You're so smart."

She tilted her head to mine. "Love you too, Pen."

I BLINKED OPEN MY EYES, QUICKLY SQUINTING AGAINST THE harsh white fluorescent lights. It was too much. Too bright.

"Hey, sweetie," Mom said. "How are you?"

How was I? Terrible. It felt as if I'd been run over by a truck.

I squeezed my eyes shut again, trying to remember what had happened. *No. Not a truck...* It all came rushing back to me.

I'd left the coffee shop after writing. It was cold out, and the sidewalks were slick. My stomach had been grumbling. Cramping. I'd been hit with a sudden urgency when I decided to turn back and run for it. And then I'd slipped on ice. And that was the last thing I remembered.

"Thank god you're okay."

"Okay?" I groaned as my vision swam, and a wave of nausea threatened me. "I don't feel very okay."

A nurse peeked her head behind the curtain. "Oh good." She smiled, way too chipper for my head. "You're awake. Feeling nauseated?"

I nodded but immediately regretted it. "Yes," I whispered from behind closed eyes. My throat was tight, my mouth dry, and my hand… I glanced down at my dominant hand, trying not to freak out about the fact that it was covered in bandages. Or was that a cast?

"Wha—"

The room spun, and I closed my eyes again and tried to focus on not vomiting.

"Shh." Mom smoothed back my hair. "You're okay. I'm here. It's going to be okay."

I glanced down at my feet and wiggled my toes. That was a good sign. I felt an immense sense of relief. But my hand…

"What's wrong with my hand?" I asked Mom.

"The doctor will be in soon to explain," the nurse said.

Her smile did nothing to set me at ease. I glanced around the room for my stuff.

"What's wrong?" Mom asked in a soothing tone.

"Where's my laptop? I was holding my laptop when—"

The door opened, and Erik strode in, carrying an obscenely large bouquet. "Sweetheart." He smiled. "You're awake."

"What's he doing here?" I asked Mom through gritted teeth as Erik set the flowers on a nearby table.

She glanced between us, frowning as Erik leaned down to press a kiss to my temple. "What do you mean? He's your fiancé."

I squeezed my eyes shut. Pretty sure I'd remember something like that. But I hadn't remembered the accident. At least, not at first. And even now, not fully.

"No. I don't think—"

"Shh." Erik glanced down at my hands. One was bandaged, and the other had an IV. What a mess. "I'm sure this is a lot to take in. But I'm here now."

I frowned. This felt all wrong. Everything about it was wrong.

I shook my head then groaned. Everything hurt. "Erik and I aren't engaged."

Mom turned to Erik, concern marring her brow. "Do you think she suffered memory loss from the concussion? I don't remember what the doctors said."

I gnashed my teeth. "My memory is perfectly fine. I don't know what Erik told you, Mom. But we're not back together."

The heart rate monitor started beeping louder, declaring my agitation. It seemed mild compared to the storm brewing inside me. Like a Category 5 hurricane building as it headed toward the coast. Intent on complete and utter destruction.

"You just need to stay calm," Erik said, rubbing his thumb back and forth over my shoulder. Stay calm? I was going to explode, especially if he kept doing that.

In the past, I would've stayed quiet to keep the peace, but I was done. I was done shoving my feelings in a box. I was done trying to make everyone happy because I was scared what might happen otherwise.

"No," I said, just as a nurse stepped into the room. "You need to leave, Erik."

He jerked his head back. "Leave?"

"Yes. You're not my fiancé, and I don't want you here."

The nurse raised an eyebrow but soon escorted Erik from the room. *Thank god.*

I rested my head against the pillow, feeling completely overwhelmed. Did everything in my life have to be such an epic disaster?

"You shouldn't be so hard on Erik," Mom said. "He's trying."

"*Mom*, he left me at the altar. Did you really think I'd want to give him a second chance?"

She took a seat next to me on the bed. "We're all fools when we're in love. I certainly was when it came to your father," she sighed wistfully.

And look how well that turned out, I wanted to say but didn't. His death wasn't any more her fault than mine.

"Well, I'm not in love. And I won't be made a fool of again." Not by Erik or Liam or anyone else, for that matter.

"He didn't—" She sighed. "Erik was under a lot of pressure. It's understandable that you're hurt, but he loves you."

I scoffed. "Why are you taking his side? I'm *your* daughter."

Suddenly, I felt so small and alone. And scared. I was completely overwhelmed, trying to process everything that had happened. I couldn't help it; I started crying.

"Hey," she shushed, smoothing a hand over my hair. "Hey, Penny. You're safe. You're okay."

She kept saying that, but I *wasn't* okay. Not at all.

"I'm not okay!" I yelled, surprising myself. "I'm not," I said again, more softly this time. "And I'm tired of always pretending that I am."

"What?" Her hand stilled.

I wasn't sure whether it was the pain meds or the sudden brush with death that had compelled me to be so honest, but now that I'd started, the words came hurtling out of me. All the pent-up emotions that I'd suppressed for years. Decades. Things I'd only ever talked to my therapist about.

"I'm sick of pretending that I'm fine when I'm not. I want it to be okay that I'm not okay."

I never had to pretend with Liam. I never had to be anything but myself. And for a brief moment, I allowed myself to wish that he were here with me. Comforting me and making me laugh. Distracting me from my fear and pain like he did so well.

She furrowed her brow. "You just had a big shock, and it's understandable that you're upset."

"No, Mom." I shook my head, some of my strength returning. "It's not just this accident. For years, I've been holding it all in. Acting like I'm fine, when I'm not. I've just learned how to bury my emotions so deep I'm not even sure I can find them again."

Maybe I was more like Liam than I wanted to admit. Putting on an act. Hiding the truth from everyone.

Why?

Because I was afraid I'd push someone away and lose them like my dad. Or worse still, that I'd end up like him. Because my mom was already overprotective and paranoid enough after his death, I'd never wanted to worry her. But in trying to protect her, I realized I was only hurting myself.

The door opened again, jolting me from my thoughts. A woman in scrubs entered, and her warm smile immediately put me at ease. "Hi, Penny. I'm Dr. Newman. How are you doing?"

I lifted a shoulder, still feeling jarred from the accident and my revelations. "I feel a bit banged up, and I'm really concerned about my hand."

That felt good. Being so honest. In the past, I would've tried to make a joke or downplay my symptoms. No more.

It was like the accident had broken something open in me. Allowed that part that I'd kept hidden, suppressed, for so long to come back to the surface.

Or maybe it was just the drugs.

Somehow, I didn't think so.

"Your wrist took the brunt of the impact, and we had to

realign the bones by inserting a plate as well as several screws."

I cringed. "Wow. That's…intense."

"Yes. The surgery went well, but recovery will take time. Fortunately, with physical therapy, you should recover most, if not all, of your mobility."

"How long?" I asked. All I wanted to know was when I'd be able to write again. To type again.

"Probably a few months for a full recovery."

"A few…*months*?" I choked. "I don't have a few months. I have a book to write, and—"

"Perhaps you can look into dictation," she offered, her expression sympathetic.

I squeezed my eyes shut. *Great. Just freaking great.*

I'd looked into dictation before, and I'd never been motivated enough to try it. It took practice. Time. Two things I didn't necessarily have.

Dr. Newman outlined the rest of my injuries. Fortunately, they were mostly minor and would heal with time. If everything continued to go well, I'd be released tomorrow.

"Do you have any other questions for me?" she asked.

I shook my head. "Thank you. I appreciate everything you've done."

"We're always happy to assist the Cartwright family." She practically bowed before leaving the room.

What the hell?

I turned to my mom for answers.

"Now, before you get upset—" Mom held up her hands. "Erik was the one who called me after your accident. He flew me in on the family's private plane. And he's been working with your medical team to get you the best possible care."

"What?"

"Oh, don't act so surprised," Mom said. "He loves you."

I inhaled deeply and let it out slowly. I couldn't believe I'd forgotten to remove him as my emergency contact. I was changing that to Brinkley immediately.

"I'm not saying what he did was okay," Mom continued. "But he's apologized and admitted his mistake. He's tried to woo you. What more do you want?"

I shook my head. "He should never have left me."

"Oh, Penny," Mom sighed and stood. "Talk to Erik. Give him a chance."

I glared at her. Oh, I'd be talking to Erik, all right. But this time, I was going to make it clear that we were done.

"Can you get me my phone?" I asked. "I need to make a few calls."

Her eyes flashed with hurt or anger, which, I wasn't sure. She said nothing, handing me the phone before leaving the room. Her silence was almost worse than her anger, and I could feel her disappointment binding my rib cage like the brace encircling my wrist.

I took a few deep breaths to center myself as I examined the phone, feeling a bit like the device. A little cracked but mostly intact.

I briefly considered calling Liam but decided against it. Seeking comfort from him would muddle an already complicated situation.

I'd have to confront my mixed feelings about him at some point, but now was not the time. I had enough drama in my life without adding anything else to the mix.

CHAPTER EIGHTEEN

Liam

"Hey, Liam!" Bennett called. I turned off the saw and glanced up to where he was standing by the back door. "Phone call." He waved my phone in the air.

"Who is it?" I asked, thinking it could likely wait. There was a reason I'd left my cell in the kitchen.

He grinned. "Penny."

"What?" Surely I hadn't heard him correctly. Penny had spent the past month communicating with me exclusively through email.

Since the book signing, we'd made little progress on our coauthor project. We were still brainstorming the story and had drafted a few chapters, but I was starting to get antsy. I wanted to know more of a timeline. I needed details. A plan.

As much as I was trying to respect Penny's wishes and give her space, this wasn't working. At least, not for me. So, to hear that she was finally calling me, well, I was elated.

In my haste to get to Bennett and my phone, I nearly tripped over a stack of lumber. Bennett chuckled. "Slow down, man. I don't want to have to stitch you up again."

I rolled my eyes. He was never going to let me live that down, though I was grateful he'd been able to help me during our annual camping trip. We'd been miles from nowhere, but Bennett had known exactly what to do.

I grabbed my phone from Bennett and wiped my face with my sleeve before answering. "Hey, Penny."

I was panting. *God, I sound desperate.* At least this wasn't a video call.

"Hey, Liam."

She'd barely gotten the words out of her mouth when I asked, "What's wrong?"

She didn't sound like herself. A million scenarios ran through my mind, and I didn't like any of them.

I headed around to the side yard for some privacy. Bennett, Tristan, and Asher were helping me build a new pergola for my back deck. Apart from Tristan, I still hadn't told anyone about my writing career or my pen name. I kept telling myself to just do it. To talk to my mom or Wren, but I always came up with some excuse. The timing wasn't right. They didn't need to know. Whatever.

"I, um, I'm not going to be able to send you my chapter on time."

"Are you okay?"

She sighed. "I was in an accident, and I can't type."

I stilled. "What?" I was already putting the phone on speaker so I could look up flights to New York.

"I tried dictation." She started snickering. Why was she laughing? Nothing about this situation was remotely funny. "Get it? *Dictation* sounds like dick, and I'm writing about dicks."

I smirked, and then it hit me that she might be on painkillers. But before I could ask, she continued talking.

"And I tried having Raven type it for me, but it's just not working."

I didn't give a shit about any of that. I just wanted to make sure Penny was okay. "First of all, are you okay?"

"The doctors assure me my wrist will heal with time. But I can barely do anything for myself, and it's frustrating."

"Is there anything I can do to help?"

"I'll be fine. I just wanted to tell you why my chapters were going to be late, and I didn't want to do it in an email because then I'd have to ask someone to type it for me."

She sounded tired. Defeated.

"You should come here," I blurted, wondering if she could even travel. "I'll take care of you. We can write together."

"Oh no. No. No. No. That's way too—"

"It's not too much," I said. "It might help the story gel better."

She sighed. "I'm not coming out there. I can barely go to the bathroom on my own, let alone get on a plane. No."

"I could come to you."

The line was quiet, then she said, "I don't think that's a good idea." But she'd hesitated long enough that it gave me hope she'd been considering it.

"Okay. Well, we could do it over the phone."

"Do it?" She snorted. "Sorry. Sorry."

I chuckled. "Penny, are you on painkillers?"

"What?" She paused. "*Noooo*. That would be *totally* unprofessional."

"Totally, right. Because our relationship has never been anything but professional."

"Meghan is professional," she said. "Liam, though," she whispered, "is a dirty bastard."

"Mm," I hummed. "I thought you liked it dirty."

"I did." She sighed. "God. Why did you have to be so perfect except for the email thing?"

I leaned against the house, the midday sun pouring down

on me. A lawn mower hummed in the distance. "You think I'm perfect?"

I probably shouldn't have asked, considering her impaired state. But I couldn't help myself. It was the first time since the book signing that she'd actually talked to me.

And while I'd told myself to leave it—leave her—alone, to let her be, I couldn't. Not when the universe was practically handing me this opportunity to get her unfiltered thoughts on a platter.

"Sexy. Caring. Good with puppies and kids. I mean, jeez. You meet every criteria on my freaking list."

"You have a list, huh?"

If I'd had a list, I knew she'd hit everything on it. Clever. Kind. Passionate. Resilient. Strong.

"I do. And do you know what's the most annoying part about it?"

"Mm."

"After I made the list, I realized that I'd described you. I was *thinking* of you when I made it."

I rubbed the back of my neck. Suddenly, it didn't feel so right to be privy to these intimate thoughts. It reminded me of when I was emailing Penny and pretending to be Meghan. And I worried she'd be upset with me when the painkillers wore off and she realized what she'd done.

"Penny," I said in a gentle tone.

There was a long silence, then a, "Yeah?"

Had she fallen asleep?

"Get some rest. We'll figure it out. Focus on healing."

"Mm. 'Kay," she said sleepily.

I listened to her breathing for a minute then ended the call with a smile on my face. *She thinks I'm perfect.*

Almost.

When I returned to the back of the house, Tristan was alone. "Hey. Where'd Asher and Bennett go?"

"Pick up lunch. Everything okay? I thought Penny wasn't talking to you," he said, marking off a piece of wood.

After I'd returned from New Orleans, I'd told him everything. The allegations against Penny. The cowrite. Everything.

"She's not, but apparently when she's on pain pills, she's more forthcoming."

He grunted and cut the wood. When the saw was finished buzzing, he handed it to me to lay on the grid we'd set out.

I told him about Penny's accident then blurted, "I think I should go to New York."

"What? Did she ask you to come?"

"No, but—"

He shook his head. "Bad idea."

I sighed. "Yeah. I know, but I'm sick of waiting around for her to forgive me."

"You have to give her time. You can't force her forgiveness, or she'll only come to resent you for it."

"Sounds like you're speaking from experience."

Before he could answer, the back door opened, and Bennett and Asher came out along with Wren. For now, our conversation would have to wait.

"Hey, little bird! What are you doing here?" I gave her a hug.

"Just coming to see your progress. Oh, and I was wondering if I could use your Cortina property for a photo shoot."

"You can, at least until they break ground."

"I still can't believe you donated a portion of your land for a new library. So freaking cool."

"What kind of photo shoot are you planning?" Bennett asked.

"Meghan Hart's new cover."

Tristan coughed, choking on a bite of his sandwich from Larkspur. "What?"

"Harper and I shoot all her covers."

Tristan turned to me, eyebrow raised. "Is that so?"

"You a Meghan Hart fan now?" Asher nudged Tristan with his elbow.

"Tessa was," Tristan said. "And I've read some of her books. They're good."

"Right?" Wren said, lifting her hand for a high five. "Ugh. The best."

Bennett pulled her into his side and whispered something in her ear that made her blush. I glanced away. Oh god…did my books get them aroused? I shuddered at the idea.

"What about you, Liam? Have you read them?" Asher asked.

"Yeah, Liam." Tristan leaned his elbows on his knees. "Have you?"

He knew I'd never outright lie, but I'd never been put in this position before. This was it. My chance to come clean.

And I had a feeling if I wanted a future with Penny, it started with being my fully authentic self with the people I cared about most. At least if the romance novels I wrote were to be believed.

"I, uh—" I cleared my throat. "I have read them. Too many times to count."

"Of course." Wren rolled her eyes. "Leave it to my brother to turn it into a joke."

"I'm not—" I shook my head, but by then, everyone had started talking again, this time about Bennett and Wren's wedding.

The moment was lost. And Wren wouldn't have believed me anyway.

So much for telling the truth.

"OKAY, SO AFTER THE SNOWSTORM HITS, THEN WHAT?" I ASKED Penny.

We'd spent the past few weeks brainstorming and writing over the phone. She hadn't mentioned her painkiller confessions, and neither had I. I was beginning to wonder if she even remembered the conversation.

Meanwhile, I couldn't forget what she'd said. Not that I was perfect, but that she thought I was perfect *for her.* I wanted to make her believe that again. I wanted to be the man she thought I could be.

She sighed. "We've been at this for hours. I could use a break."

"That's fine," I said. "I could use something to eat. Want to hop back on in an hour?"

"Sounds good."

We'd developed a sort of routine, working around our different time zones, her physical therapy appointments, and whatever else came up. But for the majority of the day, I was on the phone with Penny.

We'd write in the morning and afternoon. And then in the evening, I'd clean it all up and send it to her to review. Then we'd start again the next day. It was surprisingly fun. Collaborating with someone else. Brainstorming and daydreaming. Even arguing with Penny was fun.

We'd debate the character motivations. Flaws. Fears. Wounds. I loved learning how her mind worked. It was fascinating, partly because her process was so different from mine.

I'd never seriously considered cowriting with someone in the past, mostly because keeping my identity secret was more important than anything else. But that didn't mean I hadn't dreamed up a list of possible authors I'd love to work with.

Penny had always been near the top. Even before I'd gotten to know her better, I'd always admired her work ethic and her writing style.

"Hey. You doing okay?" I asked.

"Yeah. I'm f—" She stopped herself. I'd noticed her doing that more lately. Where, in the past, she might have defaulted to something like "I'm fine," she no longer was. I wondered what was responsible for the change, but I liked that she trusted me enough to be honest. "My wrist is bothering me."

I frowned. "How's physical therapy going?"

"I've been squeezing this stupid stress ball the entire time we've been talking. And I can sort of almost make a fist."

"That's good, right?"

"It's something, I guess. This experience has been eye-opening. I really took my mobility for granted."

I nodded. "We're fortunate to have that privilege. The ability to take it for granted."

I remembered how much Wren struggled with health issues the first few years after having River. Watching her go through something so difficult and physically limiting was hard. Especially since I'd been away at college at the time. Regardless of distance, I'd helped as much as I could. Just as I always tried to support Penny with her IBS and now this injury.

"I know," she sighed. "I do. I just… Going through this, it makes me want to give my characters more complex issues."

"Like what?" I asked.

"Chronic illnesses. Suicide. You name it."

"So, why don't you?"

"Because I worry readers won't like that. They come to me for an escape, and I would never want to violate their trust by exposing them to a subject that inadvertently hurts them or triggers them somehow."

"First of all, you'll never please everyone."

"I know that," she huffed. "That's not what I'm saying."

"Then what are you saying?"

"Have you—" She paused. "Do you ever avoid reading or writing certain types of stories or tropes because you find them triggering?"

I scoffed. "Hell yeah. I will *not* read a story with cheating. I know some people enjoy them, but that is not for me."

"Were you... Has that happened to you?" she asked.

I pushed back from my desk and started pacing the room. "I...yeah." It was the first time I'd so much as hinted about my past with someone I was interested in romantically. And while I'd blamed my secret pen name for my inability to be in a relationship, I knew there was more to it than that.

"I'm sorry, Liam."

I wasn't sure I was ready to talk about it, and I was glad she didn't push.

"Me too. I know what it's like to be lied to. To feel betrayed. And I'm so sorry for ever doing that to you."

A long silence stretched between us, then Penny said, "I understand why you didn't tell me, truly."

"I was going to. I just..."

"I know." Her voice was soft, almost a faint whisper.

I lay down on the couch in my office. "I've been talking to Tristan about Meghan lately."

"That's great, Liam. I'm sure it's nice to have another person to confide in."

"Thanks. It is."

"I hope you're not going to be upset, but I told my best friend Brinkley about your pen name. I swear she won't tell anyone."

"If you trust her, I trust her. I wish you could tell my friends and family for me," I joked.

"Why? Did something happen?"

"I tried to tell my sister and Bennett recently, and well... yeah." I explained the conversation and what happened.

"You could have Tessa help you. She was your beta reader, right?"

I stared at the ceiling, setting the phone on my chest. "She died earlier this year."

"I'm so sorry, Liam."

"Thanks. It really rocked me, you know? She was my age, and she had surgery for a brain tumor and—" I squeezed my eyes shut and tried to steady my voice. I'd never really talked with anyone about this. Even with Tristan, I'd tried to be strong for him. "It just doesn't make sense. I can't make any sense of it. She was one of the kindest people I've ever known. An amazing mom. And, poof. Gone."

"That's terrible. It sounds like it came as a big shock."

I nodded. "Since then, I've struggled to write. My last release was a flop, and writing it was a slog. But writing with you is fun."

"It is, isn't it?" she mused. "You know, I was worried it would be a disaster."

"Why?"

"I've looked up to Meghan for so long. I mean, this was a dream collaboration for me. And—"

I frowned. "And...?" I asked after a long pause.

"And I questioned whether I was good enough."

I was both angry and surprised that Penny would even think that.

"Of course you are. I've always admired your stories and branding."

"You have?"

"Yeah. You're professional yet personable. And your novels are entertaining and empowering."

"Wow. Um, thanks."

"Never doubt your worth, Penny. You bring something unique to the world, and the romance community wouldn't be the same without you."

"Thanks for saying that. It's something I'm working on with my therapist."

"Is it helping?" I asked. With each conversation we had, and each chapter we wrote, we grew closer.

"Yeah. Things are…" She blew out a breath. "Better. I think it all comes down to the accident. It really opened my eyes to, well, a lot of things."

I was silent, waiting for her to elaborate. Hoping she would.

"For so long, I've been trying to act like everything is fine, and it's exhausting. I think—" She swallowed. "When I'm with you, I feel like I'm free to be myself. Free to express my emotions more fully."

Wow. I…I didn't know what to say to that. But it made me happy that she felt safe with me. And safe to confide in me.

"I'm glad. I'm always here for you. You know that, right?"

"I do," she sighed. "And I'm sorry for overreacting when you told me about Meghan. I was stressed about my career and shocked. And, well, yeah. It's not an excuse, but I wanted you to know that it had nothing to do with you and everything to do with me."

My body went so still, I wasn't even sure I was breathing. "You have nothing to apologize for. I'm the one who screwed up."

"I could've handled it better. And I hope you know that I understand why you didn't tell me. But I'm honored that you wanted to."

"I *did* want to. I was going to," I said. "And despite what happened to get us here, I'm grateful for this chance to work together."

"So am I. It's really nice to have someone to brainstorm with. And it's fun hearing a man's perspective."

I grinned. "Just wait till we get to the sex scenes."

"Oh, trust me. That's one of the things I'm most excited about."

"Really?"

"Yeah. I mean, I know what it feels like to have sex as a woman. But I always worry that I'm not doing the male's point of view justice."

"I've read your books. They definitely gave me book boners."

She laughed. "Book boners?"

"Your sex scenes were so hot, they made me hard."

"Have you ever…" She stopped herself.

"Jerked off to one of your books? I asked, assuming that was her question.

"Yeah." Her voice was breathy and sexy.

"Have *you*?"

"That's not fair. I asked you first!"

I laughed. "Yeah, I have. I loved that scene of yours in *Unbroken*. When they have sex at the rooftop garden. That was hot."

"Interesting," she said.

"Oh, come on. You can't honestly tell me you haven't gotten yourself off after reading a super-hot scene. There's a reason some books are called one-handed reads."

"I have. Wow…I've never heard that term."

"But I bet you've read some."

"Yes, but it's kind of embarrassing to admit."

"What? No way." I shook my head. "Why?"

"I think I was surprised by how hot a few books made me, despite feeling a bit *wrong* about liking it."

"Why?"

"Because it's not something I'd be okay with in real life."

"Back-door action?" I teased.

I'd never seen anal in her books. I'd never put it in mine. Not that our books were necessarily indicative of our sex lives or our preferences. Despite many people's beliefs to the contrary.

"No. I've read a few books with it. It doesn't do much for me."

"Me either," I said. "Threesome?"

"No, but some of the MMF ones I've read are hot. I think they'd be fun to write."

I racked my brain for something else. She'd said it was something she wouldn't be okay with in real life. "Mafia?"

She laughed. "I will confess to enjoying a good mafia romance from time to time, but not without strong character growth."

"That's a given," I said.

"I read one a few months ago that had so much potential, and then...gah. I got to the end, and I was so pissed. The author completely failed to deliver on the promise of the premise."

"Ugh. That's the worst." I was silent a beat, then I said, "You're still not going to tell me, are you?"

"Nope."

"You know you're only making me more curious."

"Well, you just wasted half your lunch break pursuing your curiosity. Gotta run. Talk to you in thirty," she said, laughing as she hung up.

But all I could think was that it wasn't a waste.

CHAPTER NINETEEN

Penny

"Liam asked me to come stay with him," I blurted as soon as I opened the door to Brinkley.

"Well, hello to you too," she teased, standing in the hallway just outside my apartment.

"Hey. Sorry. Hi." I gave her a hug.

Her eyes flicked to my brace. "How's your wrist?"

"Pretty good. I'm still in this thing for a few more weeks, but my doctor and my physical therapist are happy with my progress."

"Good. I'm glad. I still think we should sue the city."

"Brinkley," I sighed. "What would be the point?" This was New York City. It was winter. There was ice.

"The city could've taken better precautions."

I laughed. "Oh, come on. It was an accident. I also could've been paying better attention. Not been in such a rush."

"You could get damages. Loss of income."

I knew she was just trying to look out for me, but it was unnecessary. I was glad it wasn't worse.

"What loss of income?" I asked. "I found a way to make

my job work. And while I appreciate your concern, I just want to move forward."

"Fine," she huffed.

She was more argumentative tonight than normal, which told me something had gone down at the office.

"Rough day at work?" I asked in a gentle tone.

"You could say that." She scowled but said nothing more.

"Are you still looking for another job?"

She laughed, though it lacked humor. "Always."

"Do you want me to see if Erik knows of anything?" I wouldn't have offered, but I could tell Brinkley was desperate for a change. Erik had the connections to find Brinkley a job that would better suit her talents. And I knew he'd be willing to help, even if I was afraid it would give him the wrong idea.

"Are you crazy? Fuck no."

"Just offering." I held up my hands as if in surrender. "I hope the right opportunity comes your way soon."

"Like yours did with Liam?" she asked. "How's the story going?"

"Great. Last night, we were working on this scene, and…" I rambled on, my enthusiasm carrying me away with it.

"I can't wait to read it." Her bemused smile told me that I'd been talking even longer than I'd realized. "And I'm happy it's going well."

"So, you heard what I said when you walked in, right? About Liam inviting me—"

"I did."

"And? What do you think?"

"What do *you* think?" she asked, turning the question back around on me.

"I want to go, but I don't know if it's a good idea."

"Because of the sex?"

I shook my head. "We're just friends."

"Right. *Just* friends who have super-hot sex and are now writing a steamy romance novel together." When I opened my mouth to respond, she added, "Has there been a time that you've seen Liam in person when you haven't jumped his bones?"

I narrowed my eyes at her. "That's not fair."

"Because he's hot?" She'd seen pictures of Liam from my time in the AV and New Orleans.

"Yes, but we're just friends now," I said, more as a reminder to myself than Brinkley. "Colleagues. There's too much riding on this partnership to complicate it by adding something like sex in the mix."

"I hate to break it to you." She hip-bumped me. "When it comes to you and Liam, sex is already in the mix."

I sighed and dropped my head in my hands. Well, my good hand. "Why does he have to be so good at it?"

"Tell me more." She leaned in.

"Liam is a generous lover. He makes my pleasure the goal. No, not just the goal. The center of everything."

"Wow." She was quiet a moment then asked, "What do you think your therapist will say?"

And *that* was the reason for my hesitation. Because I was working on myself, and it finally felt as if I was making some progress. Every day, I felt a little lighter. A little more... connected to my wants and my voice.

"She won't tell me no, but she may advise against it. Mostly by reminding me of my goals."

"Which are?"

"To get comfortable with expressing my feelings. To love myself before considering entering another relationship."

"Good. What else have you been talking about with her?"

"Expectations."

"Yeah?"

"Well, we were talking about my book boyfriends and

how I take all the best qualities and mix them together. But the men in real life…" I shook my head. "Tend to be disappointing. So then she asked if my expectations were too high, and I had an epiphany."

"What's that?"

"It's not that my expectations are too high, but rather, my standards are too low. And for far too long, I've been more concerned with not being alone than with who I was with."

Brinkley started clapping slow and loud. "Amen to that. So you're still intent to swear off men?"

"I'm not swearing them off. I'm focusing on myself and my needs. When it happens, it happens. But the only person whose happiness I'm bending over backward for now is me."

"Yas, queen!" She lifted her hands, pumping them in the air. "But it sounds like *it* could happen if you go to California." She gave me a meaningful look, and we both knew she was referring to sex.

I shook my head and grabbed the remote, mostly so I'd stop thinking about sex with Liam. I told myself we were just friends, but deep down, I wanted more. And I knew he did too.

What message would I be sending if I went to the AV? If I stayed in his house?

Would it be possible to focus on our story and friendship, or would I be too tempted to cross that line?

Brinkley and I watched several episodes of *Friends*, though my mind was stuck on our conversation. On whether or not I should take Liam up on his offer. My gut told me to just do it. Just go for it. But I didn't know if I trusted my instincts, considering my track record.

By the time Brinkley left, I was feeling both drowsy and restless. Normally, I would've done yoga or some writing, but I couldn't do either. At least not the way I wanted when it came to writing. I needed to flop down on the floor on my belly with a pen and notebook. I couldn't wait to use my hand again.

My phone vibrated with an incoming text message. I smiled when Liam's name lit up on the screen. It was as if he knew I'd been thinking of him.

Liam: Hope you had fun with Brinkley.

Liam always knew what I was doing and was thoughtful enough to ask how it had gone. Even though we lived on opposite sides of the country, I spent more time with him than anyone else in my life. I felt like I knew him better too. It was nice. Really nice.

We had fun. How was your afternoon with River?

Though I still sucked at dictating, I'd gotten much better at using the talk-to-text feature on my phone. I didn't know how I would've survived the past month without it. I used it to order food. To look things up on my phone. To play music. To text. It wasn't perfect, but it definitely got the job done.

Liam: Good. Can I call you?

I grinned, loving the idea of Liam being as eager to talk to me as I was to him. Instead of texting back, I selected his name to call. He picked up on the first ring.

"Hey." His rich voice cloaked me in security and warmth.

I'd gotten used to hearing it every day. I tried not to think about what would happen when we were done writing and publishing *Brave Together* and would no longer have an excuse to talk.

"Hey." I lay on my bed, feeling the weight of the silence

between us. It wasn't heavy or tense. It was like my favorite weighted blanket—comforting and safe.

"You sound relaxed."

"It's funny you say that because I feel pretty restless."

"Too much time cooped up indoors?"

"It's so freaking cold here." The high today had been nineteen degrees. Nineteen!

In the past, winter in New York had felt special. Festive. But this year, it just seemed cold. And honestly, kind of lonely.

My mom was coming to visit soon for Hanukkah but only for a week. I wanted something more permanent. A bigger community besides all my amazing online friends.

"I know somewhere warmer," Liam said. "Somewhere you'd barely need a down jacket."

"How'd you know I was considering a trip to Belize?" I teased.

"Oh no. Not that again." He groaned. We both knew Belize was my escape hatch. The place I joked about moving to when writing got tough.

"No. Not that again. Though the beach does sound nice."

"I'm serious, Penny. I want you to come visit."

"So you keep saying." I yawned, my body relaxing at the sound of his voice. My essential oil diffuser was pumping out my favorite peppermint scent, and I grabbed the blanket from the foot of the bed. The one from our first night together at Fall River Estates. I'd curled up under it a lot this winter, always while thinking of Liam.

"Come for New Year's. Stay as long as you like. I'll even show you my cabin."

"Is that a euphemism?" I teased, mostly because I wasn't ready to give him an answer. I couldn't say no.

And while I wanted to say yes, I wasn't sure it was a good

idea. I didn't know if I'd be strong enough to resist sleeping with him.

"No. Though I'd show you that too if you wanted."

"I don't know," I finally hedged. "We're in such a good groove. I don't want to mess that up."

"We're not going to mess up anything. Just think of how much more we could accomplish *together*. In person."

"Oh, I see. You want to speed this up so you can be done with me," I joked, voicing my secret fear.

"If anything, I want to slow it down. Savor every moment with you. Hell, I'd write another book together if I thought you'd agree to it."

"Mm," I hummed, my eyes closing. I liked the sound of that. The longer we wrote together, the more it flowed. The more fun and creative we were. I hoped the readers would have as much fun reading this story as we'd had writing it. "We still have to figure out the ending and finish this one."

"We will," he said.

It was something we'd been debating lately—how the story would end. We weren't close to writing that piece yet, but we'd been brainstorming options.

I wanted them to get married or at least engaged. He was vehemently opposed. Sometimes it felt more like an argument about our life choices than our characters'.

We were silent before I finally said, "I don't get it."

"Get what?" he asked.

"Why you don't believe in marriage when you write some of the most gut-wrenching, heart-breaking romances our generation has ever seen. And they always have a happily ever after."

It was something that had been bothering me. Like a puzzle piece that didn't fit.

"It's not that I don't believe in marriage. Several of my

books featured a wedding, but not every happily ever after needs marriage."

"I know that." I listed off my own books that had different endings. The couple who bought a pied-à-terre in Paris but never married. The couple who drove off into the sunset on their skoolie—an old school bus that had been converted into an off-the-grid tiny home on wheels. The one that had a kid but hadn't married nor did they plan to.

I considered keeping my mouth shut, but then I thought better of it. Since the accident, I'd told myself I wouldn't hold back. I wouldn't push my feelings aside for the sake of harmony.

"But I'm not talking about books. I'm talking about you. And I can't help but feel that when you say you're not interested in marriage, you mean love too."

He scoffed. "Don't be ridiculous. I want love just like anyone else."

He was afraid to trust anyone with his true self, just like I was. Because he'd been hurt. Because he'd dealt with loss. But he trusted me.

And I realized that I trusted him.

"You still there?" he finally asked.

"I, uh, yeah. I am, and—" I cleared my throat, my mind finally made up. "I want to come visit."

"You do?"

"Yeah." I smiled, hearing my happiness echoed in his voice. "I do."

"Okay. Awesome." I could hear him moving around, something rustling in the background.

We talked about my visit, and then he told me about his family's plans for Christmas. He was an amazing uncle, and River was going to love the parkour course Liam had built.

One day, Liam would make an amazing dad.

An image of Liam skipping down the sidewalk outside

Bibliolater with a little girl hand in hand popped into my brain and took hold. She smiled back at me, and so did Liam.

"Are you falling asleep on me?" he asked.

"Maybe," I muttered, not wanting to leave my dreamy state or the images it had conjured. It didn't matter how unrealistic they were, it was a beautiful dream, and I wasn't ready to say goodbye.

"Do you want me to let you go?"

I shook my head and rolled over onto my side with my phone on speaker on the bed. "No." I just wanted to listen to his voice. Wanted to feel like he was there with me. "Tell me a story."

"What kind of story?" he asked, amusement in his tone.

"Not *that* kind," I said, assuming he was envisioning a naughty story. A steamy one. I wanted to hear something real. Something true. "Tell me a story about your family. About you."

And so he did. Telling me stories of his friends, Asher, Bennett, and Tristan, their childhood, and even more recently.

The sound of his voice lulled me to sleep, and when I woke the next morning, I glanced down at my phone. It was still on. Our call was still connected. We'd spent the night together.

I smiled and whispered, "I can't wait to see you," before disconnecting the call.

A LITTLE OVER A WEEK LATER, I WAS PACKING UP MY STUFF FOR my trip to the AV. I was both excited and nervous—and a bit of a mess. Liam and I were in a good place. We'd become close friends. We were having fun writing our book. And I didn't want to jeopardize any of that.

Maybe in the future, we could have something more. But for now, I needed to focus on myself and my goals.

Even so, when I went to my underwear drawer, I hesitated over the options. Sexy or plain? Maybe a few of each? Just for me because it wasn't as if Liam was going to see them.

"Erik told me about your fling," Mom said from the edge of my bed. "Is that why you're going back to the Alondra Valley?"

She'd come to visit for Hanukkah, and she'd insisted that we get together with Erik's family, despite my resistance. The only reason she'd been able to convince me was because Erik's dad wasn't doing well and he was hoping to see me. Mr. Cartwright had always been kind to me, and I felt bad that I hadn't visited since learning of his diagnosis.

It had been a mistake to go for so many reasons. Erik's dad kept asking about our plans for the wedding, the Alzheimer's affecting his memory so that he asked over and over again throughout the course of the evening. Erik, his mom, and my mom clearly held out hope that my presence indicated my interest in getting back together. And all the while, I kept feeling as if I were somehow betraying Liam. Which was ridiculous.

I tossed another shirt into my bag—having long since given up any attempt at folding with my brace—and frowned. I couldn't completely avoid Erik since our moms were old friends, but for someone who claimed he loved me, Erik sure had a funny way of showing it. He was using my mother—manipulating her—against me.

"I'm cowriting a book with Meghan Hart, remember?" I really didn't want to argue about this.

"I know—" She removed the shirt and folded it before

replacing it in the suitcase. "But you're not going to see *him*, are you?"

I wanted to laugh. Of course I was going to see he-who-she-would-not-name. Not that my mom knew Liam's name. Or that he was Meghan Hart. I would never tell anyone that. Well, apart from Brinkley.

I didn't answer. I couldn't. Not without lying.

But she took my silence for a yes.

"I can't believe you're going to throw away what you have with Erik for this—this—"

I had *nothing* with Erik. Not now. Not before. It had just taken me too long to see it.

"This *what*, Mom?"

"Well, I don't know. I know nothing about this new guy. And that's the point. But I do know that Erik loves you. He loves you, and think about the life he can provide for you. The stability."

"I can take care of myself."

"Even so, I worry about you. Your income fluctuates. Readers can turn on you at any time, like they almost did earlier this year."

I gnashed my teeth. "I'm careful. I save my money and invest wisely, and I don't want to live my life in fear." Or only doing what I was "supposed" to do. I'd lived that way for far too long. "And this is an amazing opportunity for me."

"I know. I do, but—" She sighed. "I mean, you've been taking care of yourself for years. You grew up long before you should've had to."

"Then what's this really about?" I asked, knowing that with Mom, it was often about something else, even if it took the long way 'round to get there.

"I'm your mom. It's my job to worry about you. But there was something you said after your accident…"

I frowned, trying to figure out what she was referring to.

I could've said any number of things after my accident, but I'd also been on a lot of painkillers. "What did I say?"

"Something about being tired of holding it all in. It just…" She swiped away a tear. "I worry that I'll miss something like I did with your father."

I sank down on the bed next to her. She rarely mentioned Dad, and I knew it was a difficult subject for her. For both of us. Despite all the hours of therapy, I still struggled with his death. I knew, to some extent, I always would.

It had been so unexpected. And then, when we found out that all our money was gone…

If only he'd talked to us. Told us that he'd lost his job and was struggling to make ends meet. Told us that he'd been draining his retirement funds for months just to keep our family afloat while he looked for other work.

I could see why he might have felt overwhelmed. Like he was somehow a failure. But that couldn't have been further from the truth.

And now Mom was worried I wouldn't confide in her.

"It's difficult to talk to you about my love life when you keep pushing for me to get back with Erik." I knew Mom valued financial security, especially after what had happened with Dad. But I didn't think that was all there was to it.

"It's not about Erik. It's about you, Penelope Pepper." She smiled and so did I, both of us lightening from her use of my childhood nickname. "I just want you to be happy. And for years, you seemed happy with Erik. I'm just trying to understand what changed."

"I think…" I sighed. "I think I *wanted* to be happy, but I wasn't being myself. Not really."

"And with this new guy…"

"Liam," I said. "His name is Liam." Just saying his name brought a smile to my face.

"With Liam, are you able to be yourself?"

"Yeah." I nodded. "I am."

She placed her hand on mine. "I'm glad. Thank you for being honest with me. I'm sure that wasn't easy. But all I ever want is your happiness."

"Thanks, Mom. I know." But it was still nice to hear it. "I think I was afraid to tell you how I really felt because I didn't want to disappoint you."

"Oh, honey." She pulled me to her. "You could never disappoint me. And I appreciate that you were trying to protect me, but that's not your job."

I nodded, knowing she was right. I wasn't responsible for anyone's feelings but my own.

"I wish we'd had this conversation sooner." She kissed the top of my head.

"Me too," I said, feeling like this was one of the first *real* conversations we'd had in years. And it was so nice.

"I'm proud of you, sweetheart. It takes guts to admit when you need something different. And I hope you'll come to me in the future if you need to talk."

I nodded, more at peace than I'd been in a long time. And I felt as if I was finally on the right path. Finally being true to myself.

CHAPTER TWENTY

Liam

I stood at baggage claim, pacing back and forth in front of the window. Penny's flight had just arrived, and I was waiting for them to start unloading. They'd rolled out the ramp and opened the door to the plane, and...*there she is!*

I wanted to run out and hug her, but I also didn't want to start her visit with a trip to jail. This might be AV's small regional airport, but the TSA was still a stickler for the rules. The door to baggage claim opened, letting in a blast of cool air. The sun was setting, and a cold front had come through yesterday, bringing lower temperatures with it.

I rocked on my heels, feeling "nerve-cited" as River liked to say. The thought of River made me smile, and I took a deep breath as I waited for Penny to spot me. When she did, I waved.

"Hey." I smiled as she approached.

She looked even better than I'd remembered. She was wearing a pair of black ankle booties. Black leggings that clung to her legs, flaring out over that ass. A black puffer jacket was open to reveal a cream sweater and the luscious curves of her full tits.

"Hey." Her pale pink lips were glossy and inviting.

I couldn't believe she was here. With me. *For* me. Us.

We hadn't discussed what this meant for our relationship, but I knew it was a huge step in the right direction. Even if she'd only agreed to come for professional reasons, I was so fucking happy to see her I didn't care what had prompted her to finally agree.

"Can I give you a hug?"

"Of course. Just mind my brace." She held up her arm and waved it back and forth.

"Snazzy."

"Right? Really adds to my outfit."

I laughed and pulled her into my side. I couldn't wait any longer to touch her. "Get over here."

I held her close to me, soaking her in. The way she fit beside me so perfectly. Her peppermint scent.

I wanted to kiss the top of her head, her temple, her lips. But I held back. After everything that had happened, and everything she'd told me about her past, I knew I needed to let Penny take the lead. Plus, I wasn't entirely sure where she stood with her ex.

She'd mentioned in passing that she'd seen him and his family for Hanukkah, and I'd nearly crushed my phone. They weren't together anymore, right? So then why celebrate the holiday with his family?

I told myself I was probably just being paranoid. And I really had no right to be jealous. We weren't together. But I hated the idea of Penny with anyone else.

"Good flight?" I asked, removing her tote bag from her arm and slinging it over my shoulder.

An alarm buzzed, and then the conveyor belt kicked into

gear. Bags started appearing on the carousel one after another.

"Thanks. A little bumpy on the flight from LA to here but not terrible."

"If you need a bathroom," I said, hooking my thumb over my shoulder, "it's just over there."

She shook her head. "I'm okay, but thanks."

I couldn't seem to stop grinning. God, it was so good to have her here. In my arms. Not talking on the phone but here with me. By my side.

The luggage conveyor stopped. After a minute, Penny turned to me with a frown. "Where are the rest of the bags?"

A few other people were standing around, but almost everyone else had already taken their stuff and left. "It's not one of the ones over there?" I indicated to a stack of unclaimed bags.

She shook her head. "No."

"Why don't we check with one of the employees?"

She let out a deep sigh, and I pulled her to my side once more. "Don't worry. We'll get it sorted."

We headed over to the desk, and I recognized the clerk. "Hey, Annika. My friend here is missing her bag. Can you help?"

"Sure." Annika smiled at me over the counter then asked Penny for her information.

Annika tapped on the keys then frowned at the screen. "Hmm. I'm not seeing your bag in the system."

"But my—" Penny grabbed her ticket and showed Annika the claim sticker on the back. "Here. Can't you track it?"

"Yes, but it's not showing me where it is. This happens sometimes."

"And then what? Does the bag usually arrive?"

Annika clicked her tongue a few times. "Sometimes yes. Sometimes no. I can call you if it does."

"And if it doesn't?" Penny asked, a wary tone to her voice.

"Then the airline will give you a voucher to replace your things."

"Awesome. A voucher," she sighed and turned away. But at the last minute, she came back. "Sorry, Annika. Nothing personal. I shouldn't have taken my frustration out on you. I appreciate your help."

Annika perked up, her lips curling into a smile. "Any time." Then she turned to me and winked. "You've got a keeper there, Liam."

"Don't I know it?" I said, holding Penny close. "Come on. Let's get some dinner."

"What about shopping?" Penny asked as I led her out to the truck. I took it as a win that she didn't try to pull away.

"That'll have to wait till tomorrow. Everything is already closed."

She cringed. "Seriously?"

"Yeah, but I'll take you first thing. You can borrow some of my clothes until then." I opened the passenger door for her.

"Thank you." She dipped her head.

As I drove through town, I pointed out various places so I wouldn't try to hold her hand or touch her thigh. Since she'd last visited, a new microbrewery had opened. I'd considered taking her there for dinner but hadn't tested the food yet myself. And while that could be a fun adventure, I assumed she'd want something milder to eat after a long day of travel.

"Oh, downtown looks so cute all decorated for the holidays," she said, her nose practically pressed to the window, her breath fogging the glass.

"Yeah?" I chuckled, marveling at her delight and trying not to think about other ways we could steam up the cab of my truck. "I figured it wouldn't compare to the Big Apple."

"New York at Christmas is stunning, but there's definitely

something to be said for the quaint coziness of a small town. It's so magical." Her eyes were wide as she took it all in. "It might seem silly, but I've always loved Christmas decorations, even though I don't celebrate the holiday."

"It's not silly." I smiled and pulled into a parking spot along the street outside Larkspur.

I shouldn't have worried that things with Penny would be awkward; everything was just like before. Fun. Easy. But somehow better. Our relationship now deeper after everything we'd shared.

We'd just finished eating and were heading down the sidewalk when someone called my name. I stilled, recognizing my mom's voice. I knew I couldn't avoid her, but I also didn't want to have to share Penny. Especially not when I'd just gotten her back.

"Mom. Hey."

"You didn't tell me Penny was coming to visit." She hugged me, her bright-red scarf and hat both festive and necessary thanks to yesterday's cold front.

"I was going to bring her by the shop. But no signing this time—" I turned my attention to Penny's wrist, and Mom's eyes followed.

"Oh, that's right. I was so sorry to hear about your accident. But I'm glad you're okay." She hugged Penny gently. "It's lovely to see you again, dear."

"Same." Penny's smile was warm. "I can't wait to stop by your shop again. I would've gone there tonight if we hadn't been held up by my lost bag."

"Oh no. I hope they found it."

Penny shook her head. "I'm not very optimistic. But at least I packed the most important things in my carry-on."

"Oh, you'll have to let me take you shopping. I know all the cutest places. And I've seen your style on Instagram, so I have a good idea of what you'd like."

"I'm not sure—" I started, but Penny cut in.

"I'd love that, Debbie! Thank you."

"Here," Mom said, linking arms with Penny. "Come to Bibliolater. We'll get you some bookish tees and joggers and socks to hold you over until tomorrow. Heck, I might even have some underwear to tide you over until we can go to The Unmentionables in St. Cecilia."

Penny laughed. "Thanks, but you don't have to do that."

"Are you kidding? I want to. And I think you'll love it. It's a boutique lingerie store owned by an eccentric British woman. Come on." She pulled Penny along with her, though it didn't seem to require much convincing.

When we arrived at the store, Mom loaded Penny up with bookish apparel in her size. When Penny offered to pay, Mom said, "Don't be ridiculous. Besides, the cash register is closed."

"I'll have Liam take some pictures of me in all of it and tag Bibliolater on social media."

"What a great idea! That would be awesome."

I smiled and leaned against the counter, watching the two of them interact while I flipped through a book. My mom was always friendly with everyone, but even more so with Penny. It honestly reminded me of the way she'd treated Bennett even before he was with Wren. As if Mom had somehow known that he was family before anyone else did.

"So, Penny. Congratulations on your new cowrite," Mom said, and I paused mid-flip.

"Thank you." Penny ran a hand through her hair. "I'm really excited about it."

"Is that why you're here?" Mom asked with thinly veiled excitement. "To work with Meghan Hart?"

She nodded. "And to see Liam."

Mom lowered her voice, but it was practically a stage whisper. "What's she like—Meghan?"

Fortunately, my mom had given up on getting any information about Meghan from me. But I hadn't considered her plumbing Penny for details. I rubbed the back of my neck while I waited for Penny to respond.

I couldn't see Penny's expression, but I could hear the smile in her voice. "Meghan is funny and creative and so caring."

"It sounds like you've developed a really close relationship with her."

"I have," Penny said more softly. I would've given anything to know what she was thinking.

"I know she's crazy reclusive, but I'd *so* love to meet her someday," Mom said with a wistful sigh.

"You never know." Penny shrugged, then smiled over her shoulder at me.

I couldn't have asked for a more perfect setup. I wanted to do this. I wanted to tell Mom. And I wanted to do it with Penny by my side.

So, I took a deep breath and said, "Mom."

"Yeah, sweetie?" She was still fussing with the clothes for Penny, straightening and folding them just like she would for me.

I swallowed hard. "I have something to tell you."

"You're making me nervous." Mom sank down into a nearby chair, quickly standing again. "Or should I be excited? Oh my goodness. Are you and Penny going to make me a grandmother again?"

She glanced between us and smiled hopefully, and for a moment, I could imagine telling her that. Telling my family that Penny and I were having a child. That I was going to be a father.

I'd always wanted a partner. Children. But after what had happened with Diane, I'd never let myself go there again. But I didn't feel the fear that I'd felt in the past. In fact, the more I thought about it, the more exciting it was to imagine a future with Penny.

"Liam?" Mom prompted.

"Oh, uh, right." I swallowed hard, my throat tight as I tried to force the words past my lips. Penny came to my side and held my hand, likely sensing what I was about to do. "No. We're not pregnant. This is about me and Meghan Hart."

I wasn't sure what Penny and I were, but I knew what I wanted us to be. I hoped to use this time together to show her just how important she was to me. And just how amazing we could be together.

Mom frowned and sat back down. "I'm not sure I understand. What about you and Meghan Hart? I thought you were with Penny."

"I—" I started, and Penny gave my hand an encouraging squeeze when I faltered. "I *am* Meghan Hart. Meghan Hart is the pen name I write under."

Mom stared at me, unblinking. Seconds turned to minutes, and I began to worry that she was having a stroke. Did I need to call Doc Allen?

"Mom?" I waited a beat. "Mom, say something. I'm sorry I didn't tell you, but—"

"Are you kidding?" Mom jumped up and pulled me into a hug, startling me. "This is amazing. *You're* amazing." She drew back and smiled at me. "Oh, I'm so happy."

I searched her eyes for any disappointment or anger. "Really?"

I'd hoped she'd be accepting. Forgiving. But I'd never expected such…enthusiasm. Though, really, it shouldn't have been all that surprising. She'd always been a huge supporter of indie authors and a big fan of Meghan Hart.

"Yeah, really. I know how much you've always loved writing. And the talent you have." She covered her smile with her hand, wearing a dreamy expression.

"Thanks, Mom."

Mom placed her hand on my shoulder. "You are an incredible writer, Liam. And your stories have touched millions of people." Her smile was watery. "I mean…wow. Just wow."

When I spoke, my throat was clogged with emotion. "I wish I'd told you sooner."

"You told me when you felt the timing was right. I'm just happy you told me now."

I nodded, overwhelmed by her love and acceptance. By my own immense sense of relief.

To finally have this secret off my chest felt incredibly liberating. More so than I'd even imagined, especially after what had happened with my grandpa.

"Have you told anyone else? Does Dad know? What about Wren?"

I shook my head, not wanting to ruin the moment by bringing up Grandpa. "Just Tristan, Penny, and now you." I would tell the others at some point when I was ready.

She held my hands in hers. "Well, I'm honored. And I will keep your secret. Of course."

"Thank you."

"Now, Dad's waiting for me. So I'll leave you two to enjoy your evening. You can lock up when you're done."

"What?" Penny shrieked. "We get the bookstore all to ourselves?"

Mom's eyes sparkled. "For two of my favorite authors— anything. Just write down what you take, so my inventory doesn't get screwed up."

"Of course. Thanks, Mom."

She pressed a kiss to my cheek, shaking her head as if in

disbelief. "My son is Meghan Hart. Who would've guessed?" She laughed. "I love you, Liam."

I chuckled. "Love you too."

She smiled and let herself out, locking the door behind her. Penny and I were alone, surrounded by books. It seemed almost too good to be true.

"Are you glad you told your mom?" she asked, perusing the front display table.

I nodded. "More than anything, I'm relieved. Thanks for being so supportive and encouraging."

"Anytime."

"Is this for real?" she asked, moving on, spinning around, taking it all in.

I chuckled. "Yep. Choose anything you like. We'll add it to my tab."

"Wow. I don't even know where to start. Oh my god. I've always wanted to be locked in a bookstore overnight."

I shook my head. "Who said anything about overnight?"

"You're right. I want to sleep in a bed tonight."

"My bed?" I joked.

I expected her to chastise me, but instead, she said, "I, um, that's something I wanted to talk to you about."

"Uh-oh," I teased, though it was mostly to hide the fact that I was freaking out inside. Had she forgiven her ex? Were they back together after all? Was that what this was about?

"I like you a lot," she said, and I pushed away thoughts of exes and fears of cheating.

"I like you a lot too." *God. What am I, in middle school?*

She smiled, but then her expression grew more serious. "Which is why I think we should set some boundaries. Your friendship is important to me," she said. "As is finishing our book."

Damn. She was totally putting me in the friend zone.

She fidgeted with her brace, picking lint from the Velcro

closure. "My therapist thinks we should work on our emotional intimacy more before even considering physical intimacy."

Oh yeah? Maybe I was wrong about being stuck in the friend zone. I felt like a champagne bottle that had been shaken up.

"She thinks this trip could be a good opportunity for us to get to know each other more in person. Which was why she suggested we abstain from sex," Penny said. "At least for this next month. What do you think?" she finally asked.

It sounded reasonable but also absolutely intolerable. Penny was going to be staying in my home—in a bed just down the hall—and I couldn't touch her? Talk about torture.

But I kept circling back to the idea that she *wanted* to be physically intimate. That she *wanted* to deepen our emotional connection. That I had a chance.

"I want whatever will make you happy."

"But what will make you happy?" she asked.

"You," I said simply. Honestly.

Being with her was what made me happy. Talking about books, Netflix and cuddle, all of it.

She dipped her head, tucking her hair behind her ear. And her soft smile told me I'd said the right thing. "You make me happy too."

I smiled and slipped my hand around her waist, leading her deeper into the bookstore. We talked about the books we'd read or the ones we'd wanted to. She'd been on an alien romance kick lately, and I showed her the special edition covers of Ruby Dixon's Ice Planet Barbarians Series. She added a few to our rapidly growing stack of books.

I didn't see the next book she grabbed until she held it out to me with a smile. "Will you sign this for me?"

I looked down at the book. A copy of my thriller. "Ha-ha. Very cute. And you already have a copy."

"But I don't have a signed copy. Please make it out to Penny. I'm a huge fan." She batted her eyes.

I laughed, but I was touched. No one had ever asked me to sign the book I'd written besides my mom. And it meant a lot to me. So I did as she asked and added it to the stack.

"Thank you." She hooked her arm through my elbow and leaned into me as we strolled down the next aisle together. "What do you love about writing romance?" she asked. "I know you started writing it on a dare, but you had to have enjoyed it to some extent to have kept going for so long."

"Well, money—"

She slapped my bicep then winced as she shook out her hand. "Jeez, Liam."

I chuckled and pulled her to me. This was what a friend would do, right? I figured it was okay then.

"It was a fun challenge. And it was cathartic."

"Because of your ex?"

I nodded. "I haven't dated anyone seriously in years."

After Diane, I'd focused on short-term pleasure. Avoiding pain. Then I'd used my travel schedule as an excuse to keep women at arm's length. Then my secret career as Meghan. It was only recently that I'd realized they were just that —excuses.

"Wow. That's a long time."

"I've tried a few times." I wanted to meet someone and fall in love. Have a family. "But…it's hard after what happened."

"Do you want to talk about it?" she asked, then added, "You don't have to."

This was about emotional vulnerability, right?

"In college, I was dating this girl. And I thought she was *it*. The *one*. I could so clearly picture our lives together. Anyway…"

I sighed, trying to ignore the tightness in my shoulders.

The memories that came flooding back. Those feelings of betrayal and hurt. Penny waited patiently.

"We'd been together for two years when I started to suspect she was cheating on me. Graduation was coming up, and I'd asked her to move back to the AV with me. Start a life together. I had a ring and everything."

Penny nodded. "Wow. You *were* serious."

"She was being evasive. I ignored the red flags. Until finally, I caught her cheating on me with one of my friends."

She stilled. "That's awful."

"It *was* awful."

It had made me feel inadequate. Made me wonder what I'd missed or what I'd done wrong. Much like how Penny had described feeling after her dad's death. Not that the two could be compared.

But I understood that feeling of shock and betrayal. I'd thought we were in love. Eventually, Diane had told me I'd pushed too hard and asked for too much. She wasn't ready to settle down. She just hadn't known how to tell me. Even all these years later, I still didn't understand how cheating was the answer.

"I'm sorry, Liam."

"It's affected every relationship I've had since then, even non-romantic ones. Take Bennett and my sister, for example. I cannot tell you how upset I was when I discovered they'd been dating in secret."

All those feelings from when Diane had cheated on me had come flooding back. It wasn't the same thing, obviously. But it definitely compounded the sense of betrayal I felt upon learning that my best friend was sleeping with my sister.

"I think most brothers would feel that way, but it's obviously heightened because of your own past."

I sighed and took her hand in mine, grateful that she

understood without my even needing to explain. "I'm tired of letting my past affect my present. I don't want it to ruin my future. *Our* future." I smoothed my thumb over her skin.

This was big and scary, but Penny made it easier. Seeing how close I'd come to losing her after New Orleans had made me realize how hard I was willing to fight for a future together.

And despite being terrified, I was more determined than ever. Because that's what you did when you loved someone. And I loved Penny.

CHAPTER TWENTY-ONE

Penny

"Come on," Liam said when I yawned for the millionth time. "Let's get you home."

Home. I hadn't ever been to his house, but I liked the sound of it. Of *home.* A home with Liam. Ever since I'd agreed to visit, I'd been imagining what it would be like.

"But I might never get this opportunity again," I pleaded, glancing around the store with longing.

I didn't want to leave Bibliolater. I'd never had so much time in a bookstore. With no one else. It was my idea of heaven. The only thing missing was a charcuterie board and a fireplace.

"My mom will let you come again. Besides, I have a key." He grabbed my stack of books from the table, grunting as he did so. "You want all of these?"

I cringed. "Did I go overboard?"

"Nah." He lifted a shoulder then added the clothes to the top. "You can never have too many books."

I could've sighed at how perfect he was in that moment. His forearms flexing as he carried all my romance novels to the door. His smile soft and full of adoration and directed only at me.

"You can when there's a weight limit on luggage, and I don't even have a suitcase." I moaned. "Ugh. I forgot all about that. Can we run by a drugstore on the way home? Are they even open?"

"I have an extra toothbrush you can use. And some soap. Hopefully your suitcase will still show up."

"I'm not holding my breath." I followed him to the door. He turned off the lights and set the alarm. "But, hey, it's fun to have an excuse to go shopping."

"I didn't think you needed one," he teased.

"I'm not as high-maintenance as you seem to believe."

He leaned the books against the storefront and coughed into his free hand. "A custom Vera Olmstead wedding gown?" Cough. Cough.

"The idea of how much money was spent on that dress makes me want to barf." I paused, watching as Liam extracted his keys from his pocket. "Wait. How did you know that was a custom Vera Olmstead gown?"

"I saw the tag when I helped you take it off."

I laughed at the way he'd phrased that. Taking it off sounded so tame and proper compared to the reality. "You mean when you ripped it from my body."

Our eyes met and held. And suddenly everything I'd been trying to suppress since I'd seen Liam standing there at the airport, waiting for me with a smile, came rushing to the surface.

I wanted him. I wanted him, but I wanted more than a night or a week or even a month. And judging from what Liam had said earlier, he did too.

He cleared his throat. "If we're going to stick to your rules, we should probably avoid talking about that night."

"Yeah." I glanced away. "You're right. Sorry. I'll do my best not to tempt you," I teased.

"Impossible," he said. Or at least that's what it sounded like.

We were both quiet on the drive. I was sleepy but also filled with a growing sense of anticipation. Liam was taking me to his home. I had no idea what to expect.

From the things he'd told me, it was a fixer-upper. I'd pictured something rustic. Definitely not a turquoise Victorian surrounded by acres of fields. The house had a white picket fence, for crying out loud. From the front, it was a relatively modest size. But as he proceeded down the driveway, I began to realize just how large it was.

"You live here alone?" I asked.

What did a bachelor who never intended to marry need all this space for? If I'd read about a male character with a house like this, I would've put them in the "want to get married and have a family" category. Not that people could be put into simple categories, but his house definitely gave me that vibe.

"Yeah." He chuckled as he put the truck in park. "Come on, I'll give you a tour."

He led me in through the laundry room into a huge kitchen which had been updated, though it stayed true to the original feel of the home.

"How old is this place?" I asked in awe. The wood details were incredible. The entire house was so unique and charming. Like the man who owned it.

He set my stack of books on the counter. "It was built in 1893 by the Fernway family. At that time, dairy was big business. And they owned and operated one of the largest dairy farms in the region."

"I didn't realize dairy farming was such a big deal here," I said, leaning against the counter.

"Not so much anymore. Wine has taken over. All the land behind the house used to belong to the dairy, but then it was sold. Luckily, no one's developed it yet."

I nodded. "Have you done all the renovations yourself?"

"Mostly. I hire professionals for electric and plumbing, but I do most of the other stuff myself. Well, with occasional help from the guys."

I knew he was referring to Tristan, Asher, and Bennett. I'd met Bennett, and I'd heard so much about the others, I felt as if I knew them.

"I've been slowly updating the house the past few years. My goal is to maintain the integrity of the original style as much as possible while adding modern conveniences."

I smoothed my hand over the counter. "I can tell. It's obvious a lot of love has been put into this space."

"That's not the case for all of the house," he said, chuckling as he rubbed a hand over his jaw. "At least not yet. Before I give you a tour, do you want anything to eat or drink? Peppermint tea? Gluten-free muffin?"

"No." I shook my head. "But you have those?"

"Of course." He went over to the pantry and opened the door. "This shelf is for you."

I stared at him, mouth agape. "Seriously?"

It held all my favorite snacks. And suddenly, all his seemingly random questions made sense. But even beyond that, there were things we'd never discussed. Like how I ate sweet potatoes and rice when I had a flare-up.

"Of course. I wanted you to feel at home."

Liam wrote stories about love and happily ever after. He treated me better than any book boyfriend. Did we really need to work on our emotional intimacy?

Or did I really just need to work on my ability to trust?

"Yeah, but...how did you know?"

"I've done a lot of reading on IBS and talked to the local GP, Doc Allen."

"Wow." I shook my head, perusing everything on the shelf. I'd never felt so loved or cared for. Just the fact that he'd paid attention… That he'd gone to the effort to research IBS.

"Thank you," I said, genuinely touched by the gesture.

"My pleasure," he said.

I wanted to hug him so badly, but he turned to continue the tour. I followed him to the next room. "I'm surprised you could get all those. Some can be pretty difficult to find in a small town."

"Not when you know who to ask." He winked.

I laughed. "You've always got the hookup, don't you?"

He lifted a shoulder. "I just used Meghan's email, and everyone was *more* than willing to help out."

"I'm glad you're taking advantage of your celebrity status," I teased, knowing it was unusual for him to do something like that. "Are you going to use her name to score us a table at an exclusive restaurant next?"

"Nah. Most restaurants around here don't take reservations."

"And there's free parking," I said.

Both perks of living in a small town. Life in the AV was much simpler. Slower. And I liked the pace of it.

Especially at the holidays. It wasn't nearly as cold as New York, and the decorations were charming. Lights had outlined the historic downtown area, and a big tree was in the center of it all. It was quaint and idyllic and magical.

"Gotta love the AV."

"Would you ever consider leaving?" I asked, genuinely curious. I couldn't imagine him saying yes, but for some strange reason, I wanted to know.

"For the right reason, perhaps." The intense way he was looking at me made me wonder if *I* could be the right reason.

"Would you ever consider leaving New York?" Liam asked.

I got the impression my answer was important to him. And I didn't know what to say. Did I love the AV? Yes. Absolutely. But was I ready to give up my life in New York and move? That was a more difficult question to answer.

"I've always considered moving to Belize," I said, only half joking. "And I definitely wouldn't miss the snow."

He frowned but quickly masked his disappointment. "Belize might be nice for a vacation. But I prefer small-town living in a relatively moderate climate."

I laughed. "What about the cabin? Isn't it cooler up there?"

"A little, but not crazy cold. Here's the formal dining room." He gestured to an empty room. The brown carpet was dated, as was the wallpaper.

"Wow." I glanced around, and from my vantage point, I could see at least four different wallpaper designs. "The previous owners really loved patterns."

"The last one, yeah. This room hasn't been a huge priority for me, as you can see."

"Mm." I hummed, stepping closer to the wall, Squinting to see the design. "Are those..."

"Yep. Everyone totally thinks they look like vaginas."

I laughed. "Seems appropriate for a romance author."

I followed Liam as he explained the history of the house and the steps he'd taken to modernize it. He'd clearly invested a lot of time and money into the place. And I kept wondering to what end. Was it for resale value? Himself?

"Restoring a home seems like a full-time job."

"It can be. I do a little at a time. It helps when I'm stuck on a plot problem. And I like working with my hands."

I nodded. I could see that. The house was just another type of world building. Another creative outlet.

A few of the rooms downstairs were furnished, but most had yet to be updated, including the hall bathroom. It had gotten a facelift in the 1970s, but it was almost as if it had been frozen in time, the tiles and toilet untouched by the years.

I followed him upstairs and into another world. The walls were freshly painted. The wood floor shone. And none of the woodwork was damaged as some had been downstairs.

"Wow," I said, now able to imagine what the house must have looked like in its former glory. And what it might look like once he'd finished. "This is beautiful."

I ran my hand along the banister, admiring a framed set of photographs on the wall. They were scenes of small-town life. Local images. And snapshots of Liam's family. "These are beautiful."

"Wren took them."

"Ah. Right." I should've guessed.

Wren had a photography studio in town with Harper. And Harper was the wife and co-owner of Fall River Estates, where Erik and I were supposed to get married. The more I pieced together the connections, the more I understood how Liam knew everyone in town. It was all so interwoven.

"She's talented," I said. "Though I already knew that from your covers."

"Wait till you see what she came up with for this one." He waggled his eyebrows.

I shook my head. "You can't taunt me with something like that and not show me."

"I will. At the end of the tour."

There were a few bedrooms upstairs, including a generic-looking office that I couldn't imagine him working in. It was so cold. So lacking in the warmth and personality Liam exuded. I stepped closer to the desk and picked up one of the books.

I read the spine. "Mechanical Engineering Reference Manual." I set it back on the desk. "Prop?"

"Pretty much. At least now. I used it all the time when I inspected nuclear power plants."

I laughed, still impressed by his background. "And yet none of your friends or family have questioned it?"

He shook his head. "You're the only one who's seen through my facade. The only one I've let see me."

"And why is that?" I asked. It was something that had been bugging me. *Why me?*

He let out a deep sigh. "I'm not entirely sure. I think part of it was this immediate familiarity I had when we met."

"Because you stalked me online."

"I do not—" He huffed. "I followed you. Casually. It's not like I recognized you right away."

"Mm-hmm." I grinned.

"I had no idea that you were Penelope Glass until the morning after."

I smirked, crossing my arms over my chest.

"And then it was just easy to talk to you," he said. "To trust you. I think because of what you'd been through. I never told you this, but I really admired—admire—your resilience."

I dipped my head and tucked my hair behind my ear. "Thank you. That means a lot to me, especially considering the obstacles you've faced yourself. Actually, meeting you made me realize that I'd been playing it safe for far too long."

"How so?"

"In every part of my life, I was holding back. Keeping myself small. Quiet."

"Really?" He furrowed his brow. "I wouldn't have guessed that from your stories."

"Maybe not, but writing with you, I'm realizing I'm

capable of so much more. I *am* so much more than just the clothes I wear or the body I inhabit..."

He narrowed his eyes. "Your body? Don't tell me that—"

"Having IBS is frustrating and isolating. Especially when there's so much pressure for women to be small. To have curves but only in the right places. To look perfect."

He stepped closer and placed his hands on my waist. "You are perfect to me."

I was far from perfect, but the way he was looking at me made me want to believe him.

He wouldn't let it go. He placed his finger beneath my chin and lifted so I was forced to look at him. "I mean it, Penny. You're fucking stunning, and it's not just your body. It's everything about you."

"Liam," I chided, shaking my head. He was too close. Too tempting. "Don't."

"Don't what? Share my feelings? I thought you wanted emotional vulnerability."

"I do, but..."

"But nothing. The way your mind works is incredible. I've learned so much from writing with you. And from everything you've told me about your past..." He shook his head. "I'm in awe."

My cheeks were hot. I wasn't sure I'd ever been complimented so many times in such a short time span. But he didn't stop.

"In case you didn't realize it—" He cupped my cheeks. "I think you're pretty fucking incredible. As a writer. As a friend. As a person."

"Are you done?" I teased, mostly to distract from the way he was looking at my lips. With such longing and hunger that it filled me with a need so great, I wasn't sure how I'd possibly resist.

"For now." He smirked.

"Good. Because I think you're pretty fucking incredible yourself. You have so many interests, and you're so passionate about them. You have such a generous and tender heart, and I'm grateful you decided to share it with me."

He rubbed his thumb over my bottom lip. I was so tempted to beg him to kiss me, but then he pressed his lips to my forehead instead. My body deflated, but I tried not to let my disappointment show.

He sighed. "Let's finish the tour before I get myself into more trouble."

"Are you ever out of trouble?" I joked.

"My mom would say no." He laughed. "Though she may be singing a different tune now that she knows about my pen name."

I laughed, his hand grazing the back of mine as we continued down the hall. Sparks danced along my skin, stoking the flames of the attraction I'd tried to ignore.

We were being friendly, that was all. Flirting was okay. Hands touching was innocent enough. But my thoughts were far from innocent as we entered his bedroom.

I remembered what Dr. Hamm had said about emotional intimacy and a strong foundation. And I loved that Liam was trying so hard to give me what I needed. Which only made me want him more.

Right. Bookshelf. I refocused my attention there instead of on Liam. My eye was drawn to a framed photo of Liam holding a baby I assumed was River. He was gazing down at the child with such intense love and pride.

"What did your grandpa think of River?" I asked.

It was something that had been bugging me. If Liam's grandfather had considered romance porn, how did he feel about a child like River?

"He may have secretly disapproved, but he always kept his opinion to himself."

"Wren never said anything?"

He shook his head, and I moved on to the next photo. Five little kids covered in mud. I recognized Liam immediately, standing just in front of the group with his hands on his hips and chest slightly puffed out, his blond hair peeking through the mud.

"Let me guess, this is you." Liam nodded, and I smiled.

He indicated to Bennett, Tristan, Tessa, and Asher. I wondered when I'd get to meet the rest of his friends.

"Holy—" I stopped at the threshold to his bathroom and stared. A beautiful, massive claw-foot tub was the centerpiece. And all the tile work was incredible. "Wow."

"Right? This bathroom was a pain in the ass, like *Flow*, which I was writing at the time. But it was all worth it in the end."

"No joke. It's stunning. And you know how much I adored *Flow*." I spun around so my back was to the counter. If this were my bathroom, I'd live in here. But seeing as we'd reached the end of the tour, I was more curious about his workspace and the cover image. "So…where's your office?"

He dug in the cabinet and then handed me a new toothbrush, toothpaste, and a bar of soap. "I showed you my office." He said it with a straight face, but it felt like he was testing me.

"Right." I laughed. "Your *real* office?"

He smirked. "Come on." He went to his room and pulled on the bookshelf, opening it to reveal a hidden staircase.

"No freaking way." I peered through. "No *way*!"

He laughed and tucked me into his side. "Ready to go down the rabbit hole?"

"This is insane!" A hidden door. A secret staircase. What next?

"Yes, I have a sick office. But you're the only person who's ever seen it."

Wait. What?

Before I could even attempt to process that revelation, he flicked on a light switch. The scent of peppermint hung in the air, and it felt like coming home.

At the top of the stairs was a narrow passageway lined with built-in bookshelves housing every Meghan Hart book ever published, many in multiple languages. Nestled among the books were framed images of the *New York Times* best-seller list, the *Wall Street Journal, USA Today*. Some handmade items that I assumed were gifts from readers.

And then the hallway opened up into a larger room with a vaulted ceiling that ran the length of the house. It was split into sections that followed the contours of the roofline, and to the left was a desk and a more formal workspace with a window. To the right were more built-in bookshelves and a daybed that sat beneath another window, a mirror image of the space opposite. I could only imagine having such an incredible place to work. To retreat.

Forget the rest of the house, forget that amazing bathroom; I wanted to live up here.

"Wow. This is…magical." Like my every childhood dream come true. Fairy lights and everything.

"Yeah. It's pretty amazing."

Definitely topped writing at my bistro table crowded in the corner of my tiny kitchen. I continued exploring the space, and I could feel Liam's eyes on me the entire time. I was tired after a long day of travel, but entering a book lover's paradise for fans of Meghan Hart was exhilarating. Like my own magical land of Narnia.

"You're into essential oils?" I asked, noticing a diffuser near the daybed.

He shoved his hands into his pockets. "The smell reminded me of you."

This man... I smiled and went over to wrap my arms around him.

"Hey." His voice rumbled in his chest.

"Hi." I smiled as he rubbed my back. Technically, we were following Dr. Hamm's rules, but we were touching each other every chance we got. "This is nice."

"Yes," he said. "It is. But is hugging against the rules?"

"I don't think so. I'd hug a friend. Wouldn't you?"

"Yes, but I don't consider you a friend."

I stepped back and crossed my arms. "Well, obviously. I'm more than just a friend. I'm your coauthor."

"Speaking of...the preorder went up a few days ago. Aren't you at all curious?" he asked as I sank down on a beanbag and wiggled around like I was making a snow angel.

I'd been talking about it on social media and in my newsletter, but I'd been too afraid to check rankings or ask Liam about actual sales numbers.

"Yeah, but I'm also scared."

"Why?" he asked, joining me when I finally stopped moving.

"Because it only makes me more determined to ensure the story is perfect."

"No story is ever perfect," he said, massaging the back of my neck. It was so incredibly relaxing. It was official: this was my new happy place. "Penny?"

"Hm?"

"I'm really glad you're here."

I let my head drop forward, breathing through my nose as I surreptitiously tried to inhale his scent. Clean laundry. Fresh air. Sunshine. Happiness and a hint of peppermint. I finally gave in and dropped my head against his chest, snuggling into his side and listening to his heartbeat.

"So am I."

CHAPTER TWENTY-TWO

Liam

I shifted, the rustling of material and the sinking feeling of the beanbag making me realize I'd fallen asleep in my office. Something kneed me in the thigh, and I grunted. I felt a hand on my chest. Warm breath whispering across my cheek. Peppermint. I smiled with my eyes still closed. *Penny*.

I reached out and pulled her closer to me. Her body in my arms. It was…indescribable.

And I'd tried. Now that I'd met her, I'd tried to capture what it was like to love someone with words, but it was impossible. And despite all the romance novels I'd written, the love I felt for her was like no other.

I didn't know why I'd been nervous to show her my office. I shouldn't have been. Instead of feeling naked, I felt whole. *Seen*. Accepted.

She had a knack for that. For making me feel good about who I was just by virtue of being myself.

"Ack. Help," Penny said. "This beanbag is like freaking quicksand, and with my wrist…"

That jolted me into action. "Just a second," I said, trying to disentangle myself without hurting her. "Stop wiggling," I said through clenched teeth.

But we'd been lying there so long, the beanbag was practically forcing us together. And the longer we took to disentangle, the more I touched her, the harder I was.

"Liam," she whispered. "You're, um—"

"Hard? Yeah. I know. That kind of happens when you're around."

"No." Her cheeks darkened. "You're sitting on my sweater."

"Oh." I rolled off the beanbag so I was lying on the floor. "Sorry." *Way to go.*

I stood and tried to help her, but it had the effect of pulling her into my chest. Bringing her back close to me. To feel every inch of my desire that was becoming impossible to hide. Especially now that I'd so blatantly announced it.

Penny peered up at me with such trust and need, but I couldn't be the one to make the first move. I wanted to respect her wishes, even if they were killing me. Less than twenty-four hours in, and I was dying.

"Is kissing against the rules?" She stared at my lips as if they were the answer to everything she'd ever wanted.

"Penny," I growled, struggling to restrain myself. I'd always had a very active imagination, and I'd been using it the last few weeks to envision our reunion. It had definitely involved a lot fewer clothes and a hell of a lot more touching. "Don't tempt me."

"I'm just saying. Dr. Hamm probably meant sex when she said physical intimacy. And sex is typically defined as P in V."

I furrowed my brow, still groggy from falling asleep in my office. "P in V?" And then it dawned on me. Penis in vagina. "Right. You forgot to mention oral."

Why was I continuing to torture myself? Regardless of

how you defined sex, we still wouldn't be having any. At least not in the foreseeable future.

"Pretty sure that's still sex."

"Yeah," I sighed. "You're probably right."

"But kissing isn't. Is it? We could just…kiss. Couldn't we? That wouldn't be breaking the rules."

What she was proposing was so tempting, but I was playing the long game. If she thought abstinence was what we needed to build a strong relationship, I'd do it. I'd do anything to be with Penny.

So instead of agreeing like I wanted to, I said, "It's a slippery slope."

"You're right." She shook her head. "You're right. What was I thinking? It's a bad idea."

And with those two words, I was taken back to the night we'd met. The night everything had changed.

"What?" She tilted her head to the side. "What's that smile for?"

"Do you remember what you said the night we met? Just before we kissed the first time?"

A smile slowly crept up her face. "Bad idea."

I nodded. Both then and now, we'd had our reasons for holding back. Would this be like the last time? Would we give in?

Judging from the look on her face, the answer was yes. But I didn't want her to regret it in the morning.

"Time for bed," I said, trying really hard for once in my life to follow the rules. I steered her toward the stairs, ignoring the way she jutted out her lower lip.

"Since when am I the troublemaker?"

"I always knew there was one hiding in there. Just had to let her out."

"Oh, you let her out, all right," she teased, and I smiled.

That was the thing about Penny; she made me want to be a better person. A better writer. A better everything.

I guided her toward the guest room I'd set up for her but stopped just outside the door. "Okay. Well—" I rubbed the back of my neck. "Do you need anything else?"

She glanced back at the room then paused. "A weighted blanket?" She went to the foot of the bed and ran her fingers along the quilted material.

"Yep. There's also a white noise machine," I said, indicating to the dresser. "A sleep mask in the nightstand. And an essential oil diffuser."

She shook her head, slowly turning back to face me before wrapping her arms around me. "You are *so* thoughtful. Thank you."

We stood there for a long time, our chests pressed together, her head resting on my shoulder. I soaked it all in. The feel of her in my arms. We just fit. And when we were together, everything was right.

So while I wanted to strip her naked and toss her on the bed, I wanted Penny's happiness even more. I wanted to respect her boundaries. And I wanted to build something —together.

So, with that in mind, I pressed a kiss to her hair then slid my hands over her shoulders and down her arms. "Good night, Penny."

She smiled, her hands still clasping mine. "Sleep well, Liam."

I doubted that. Not with her just down the hall. It was both a relief and torture to have her so close.

"You know where I am if you need anything," I said, wanting her to feel at home.

She laughed. "Anything?"

"Penny," I growled. I'd give her anything she wanted if she

kept looking at me like that… This woman was going to be my undoing.

"Okay. Okay." She held up her hands and backed into her room. "I'll be good. Promise."

"Mm-hmm." I turned so that my back was to her, calling, "Sure you will," as I headed to my room.

"I JUST DON'T THINK IT'S PHYSICALLY POSSIBLE," PENNY SAID, squeezing and releasing her stress ball. She did it almost constantly, determined to strengthen her muscles so she could regain full use of her wrist and hand.

We'd made it five days and two chapters without touching. Well, not touching more than friends would. There were chaste kisses to her forehead. Hand-holding. Hugs. I felt like I was back in middle school. And it was honestly kind of fun. At least when I wasn't on the verge of exploding.

And I was on the verge of exploding every fucking second I was in her presence. The scent of peppermint was supposed to be soothing, but it made me salivate with want for her. She was currently tantalizing me with her clothes—a pair of bookish joggers from Bibliolater and a soft V-neck shirt that stretched tight over her chest. Then there was the way she toyed with the pen, teasing it with her mouth. *Unh.*

"Liam?"

"What?" I shook my head as if to clear it.

"I said I don't think what you wrote here is physically possible."

"What? Why not?"

"Look." She stood and came over to me. "Can I touch you?"

"Is that a trick question?" I joked.

She straddled me like our character, Bailey, had done to her love interest. Then she said, "Okay. Now put your hands where you think his go."

Even though it felt like a trap, I placed my hands on her hips. "So far, so good."

I mean, apart from my raging hard-on that was becoming more and more difficult to ignore. No amount of cold showers seemed to make any difference. And the fact that we were writing a romance novel together was *not* helping. Especially when we were digging into a sex scene like we were today.

We'd been talking through it as we wrote, working from the outline Penny had drafted. I hadn't completely converted her to a plotter yet, but I appreciated her efforts to be more methodical with our planning. She'd even surprised me with a beat sheet, and it had made my organizing heart happy.

Despite our different methods, I was learning a lot from Penny. Especially when it came to the love scenes. And for not the first time, I wished Tessa were here to see it. To meet Penny and read our story. I had a feeling she'd be proud.

Penny reached behind her to cup my balls like the character had done, though Penny touched my thigh, nothing more. Even that little tease was enough to set me ablaze. Her tits thrust in my face. Her body so close to where I needed it.

"Okay." I swallowed hard. "So, I'm thinking he needs to be playing with her nipples."

Her nipples hardened in response, almost as if they'd heard me talking about them. I inhaled deeply through my nose but immediately regretted it. And when I quickly exhaled, her body responded by breaking into goose bumps.

"Yes," she sighed. "Nipples. Good. What else?" It almost sounded like she was reading a checklist, and I wanted to laugh at the robotic quality to her voice.

Even so, this was the most erotic form of foreplay I'd ever experienced. And this was my job. *God, I am one lucky bastard.*

"He could brush her hair over her shoulder," I said as I did just that. So maybe we were bending the rules a little. "Maybe cup the back of her neck?" I grasped Penny's.

"God." She moaned, her body melting into mine. "I love when you do that."

I pulled her face to mine. "And then maybe he brings her close and looks into her eyes. They both want each other, but they're still denying it. Still fighting it."

"But when they finally give in—" She started rocking against me. We were both fully clothed, but I could feel her heat all the same.

"So. Fucking. Hot," I said, holding her in place. Forcing her to look at me.

"Right?" She swallowed hard, her eyes hooded. "This scene is going to be super hot." She bit her lower lip, and I wanted to sink my teeth into it.

I let out a shaky breath. It was taking everything in me not to rip off her clothes and sink into her until she was screaming my name over and over and over again.

"Then what?" she asked, and I had a feeling we were no longer talking about the characters. But I played along.

At this point, I wasn't sure I could stop. Not with the way she was sliding along my cock, the friction from our clothes only making it worse.

"Then," I said. "Then, he'd tell her how much she means to him."

In the past, I might have skipped that step in the scene. Just like I would've skipped it in real life. Because I'd been afraid. I'd been trying to protect myself. I finally understood what had been missing in my last novel, and it was intimacy. Not physical intimacy, but emotional vulnerability.

My grandpa's disapproval, followed by his death, then

Tessa's, had left me feeling raw. Lost. Penny had made me realize what had been lacking—both in my stories and my life. And I didn't want to hold back anymore.

"Perfect," she hissed, and I wasn't sure whether she meant what I'd said or the feel of our bodies moving together.

"He'd tell her how incredible she is. And how much he loves her." I held her gaze, our bodies slowing as my words connected. I swallowed back my fears and said, "I love you, Penny."

She stilled. "You…you do?"

I nodded, smoothing her hair away from her face. "I have for a while now."

Finally, she smiled and said, "Oh, thank goodness. Because I love you too."

I wasn't sure I'd ever been more relieved or happy. She loved me. She loved me, and that was all that mattered. We would figure out everything else.

"I really want to kiss you," I said, nuzzling against her. Our lips were so unbearably close, but I couldn't take that next step. She had to be the one to do it.

"I think we've earned it." She pressed her lips to mine, and I could feel her smile through the kiss.

I threaded my fingers through her hair, capturing her mouth until we were both breathless.

She tore at my shirt. I yanked it over my head without a second thought. Then I tugged at the hem of her shirt, carefully maneuvering the material around her splint. Her black lace bralette pushed up her tits so they were in my face. Making my mouth water.

"Oh fuck. I want you." I gave them a squeeze, and she moaned.

"I'm yours." She started rocking on my lap again.

I stood and carried her over to the daybed, laying her down on it. I stripped off her pants. Then kneeled before her while she watched from her elbows. She was so beautiful.

My mouth was inches from her pussy when I stopped and squeezed my eyes shut. I'd told myself to think long-term. We hadn't crossed the line yet, but we were dangerously close to going over it. "No. Wait. We can't."

"What?"

I shook my head and rested my hand on her stomach. "You wanted to wait, and I want to respect that."

I also didn't want her to think that I'd told her I loved her just so we could move to this next step. That wasn't why I'd said it. Not at all.

"I take it all back." She looked at me through hooded eyes. "That was a terrible idea."

"It wasn't," I said. "And I can wait. I love you, and I'm not going anywhere."

Penny inhaled then let it out slowly. "What if…"

I shook my head with a laugh. "You're looking for a loophole, aren't you?"

"Dr. Hamm said no physical intimacy without the emotional intimacy. What is exchanging I love yous, if not an act of emotional intimacy? We can have sex."

She seemed almost rigidly tied to the rules her therapist had made. But if that was what made her comfortable… If that was what Penny needed. Who was I to disagree?

"I can't believe I'm going to say this, but I think we should wait."

"Surely we can do something, though, right? Surely we've earned…*something*."

"*Something*?" I laughed. For a steamy romance author, she was being awfully vague. "Like what?"

"You could touch yourself while I watch," she said, all without meeting my eyes.

"Would you like that?" I asked, desire unfurling within

me. I'd certainly enjoy watching her pleasure herself. And…it didn't *technically* seem like it would be breaking the rules.

When she nodded, I shoved my pants down, my cock bouncing toward my stomach. I was hard, aching to be inside her. But I would do it this way if that's what she asked of me.

I certainly craved that physical connection to Penny. Emotional vulnerability was important, but in my opinion, it was definitely enhanced by physical intimacy.

"Oh, I like that," she hissed, using her good hand to rub her breasts. My eyes were on her every move. Every flick of her tongue and shuddering breath.

"Bra. Off," I said through gritted teeth. I wanted to see her.

She took her time, unhooking the bra and removing it around her brace. It only served to make me harder.

I was going to have to go back to The Unmentionables and buy her one in every color. Penny's luggage had finally arrived, though I much preferred her naked or wearing my clothes.

"Touch yourself," I commanded.

She slid her hand between her thighs, our eyes locked as we touched ourselves. It was surprisingly intimate. And I wasn't sure I'd ever felt such vulnerability with another person. Such connection.

"That's it, Penny," I said. "Touch yourself like I would. Pretend it's my hand."

She rubbed herself, but the longer she did, the more agitated she seemed. And not in a good way. Her movements were uncoordinated. Her face contorted with frustration. "Freaking left hand. I need—"

"You want a toy?" I asked.

"You don't…"

"I don't what?"

"Mind?" she asked on an exhale.

"Why would I mind?" I stood and went over to a box of promotional material I'd received over the past few months. Condoms. Toys. Lube. All sorts of fun stuff.

She lifted a shoulder. "Some guys get weird about it."

I wondered if she was referring to her ex, but I didn't want to think about him. He didn't matter. They weren't together anymore.

Because he left.

And then she rebounded to you.

And yet, *he* was the one who'd been at the hospital after her accident. *He* was the one she'd spent Hannukah with. *He...*

"Liam?" she asked.

"What?" I shook my head, forcing away those thoughts. She was here with me. And maybe I'd been a rebound at first, but now she'd chosen me. She loved me.

"I asked what you were doing?"

"Getting you a toy," I said, finally digging two out of the box. "Which do you prefer? Dildo?" I held up a big purple dildo with a spur-looking thing on the front. "Or vibrator?"

She laughed, her eyes darting between the toys and me. "Why do you have those?"

"Companies send Meghan stuff all the time, hoping she'll promote them."

"Yeah, but dildos?" she nearly choked on the word.

"Yep. I have so many, I should set up a trophy wall."

She laughed, her skin flushing with beautiful pink. "Oh my god. That would be hilarious."

"Which do you want?" I asked.

"Vibrator."

"I was hoping you'd say that." I grinned.

"Oh yeah?" She tilted her head. "Why's that?"

I tore open the box and dumped the contents on the table.

"Because this model can be controlled from an app on my phone."

"You're kidding."

"Nope." I handed her the vibrator as I synced everything to my phone. She moved it into place quickly, and I didn't give her any warning, just switched it on.

"Oh fuck." She moaned and threw her head back. Before too long, her eyes were on mine again. "God, you're sexy."

"Speak for yourself," I said, so fucking tempted to kiss her. "I want to pull your lips between my teeth. I want to kiss your entire body."

"Oh god. I want that too," she panted, writhing as I continued to play with the different settings until I came to the ones that seemed to set her off the most. The ones that made her moan. Made her hips buck. Made her hiss and clamp her legs together.

I held the phone with one hand and took myself in the other. I thrust into my fist over and over, watching her slowly unravel from the way I was controlling the vibrator to maximize her pleasure.

"Oh my god. I think I'm—" Her body tensed, back arched as she came on a low moan.

Watching her had been one of the hottest things I'd ever seen. And seeing her let go... it sent me over the edge. My balls tightened, and I grabbed my boxer briefs from the floor. With a few more tugs, I was coming as well. Hissing and clenching my legs as I unloaded into my boxers.

"Fuck." I fell onto the bed beside her.

I was still catching my breath when she said, "That should go in the book."

I laughed, but then I realized she was serious. "Yeah. That was pretty hot," I admitted.

"Right?"

"I mean, sex with you is always my favorite." I grinned over at her.

"And another thing. With the scene we were working on —and generally—why don't we just remove some of the references to specific body parts? Let the readers use their imagination," she said.

"Are you seriously talking about work right now?" I slumped back, my body still recovering. "Clearly, I didn't make you come hard enough," I joked.

"I often get my best ideas after an orgasm."

"Mm." I captured her lips for a kiss. "I see a lot more orgasms in our future."

She smiled at me. "So do I."

CHAPTER TWENTY-THREE

Penny

I turned off the stove and set two plates on the counter. "Here you go," I said to Liam. "Breakfast is served."

"Mm. Looks delicious. Thank you, babe." He gave me a kiss and poured a coffee for himself and a mug of peppermint tea for me.

I took a seat in the chair next to him, enjoying this quiet pause in what had otherwise been a busy month.

I'd gone back to New York for a few weeks to check in with my doctor and see my physical therapist in person. They were both pleased with my progress, enough to let me try going for longer stretches without the brace. During that time, I'd missed Liam like crazy.

I'd had a few more sessions with my therapist. Dr. Hamm had been pleased with Liam's and my progress, though perhaps that was because I hadn't confessed to having sex. Liam and I had made it nearly a month before taking that step. And when we finally had, whew, had it been hot.

Since I'd left the AV, Liam and I continued to talk every day, and we were making good progress on *Brave Together*.

We'd hoped that he'd be able to come to New York, but he'd been too busy in the lead-up to Bennett and Wren's wedding. As the best man, he'd planned the bachelor party and was involved in other preparations for the celebration.

He'd invited me to attend, but I'd had a book signing in Rome. Not that I'd actually *signed* any books. My wrist wasn't healed enough to handle that kind of abuse, but none of the readers seemed to mind that Raven used a stamp for my signature. They were even more excited than usual, and my line was one of the longest at the event. I'd gotten so many questions about my cowrite with Meghan from both readers and authors.

I was glad I'd insisted on taking signed copies of Meghan's books. Raven had handled all the logistics like the pro she was. And we'd sold a ton of books for Liam and given away even more swag.

I'd been filling Liam in on the signing as I cooked our breakfast. I knew he'd only attended the one signing with me in New Orleans. And it was clear that he sometimes wished he could take a more active role with readers, despite his desire to keep his identity a secret.

So I'd taken it upon myself to help make that happen. And once I'd explained my plan, he'd enthusiastically agreed. I just hoped he'd like the other surprise I'd prepared.

It was part of the reason life had been so hectic the past few weeks, and I was both anxious and excited to see how he'd react. It was finally almost time for the big reveal, and I was finding it difficult to sit still.

"What do you want to do today?" he asked.

Yes. Perfect setup. Now I just had to act casual. Pretend this wasn't all preplanned.

"I was hoping to stop by Bibliolater. Your mom mentioned that she could use our help for the special event today."

"Oh yeah. The big surprise celebration, right?"

I nodded. "Yep. That's the one."

"Do you know what the surprise is? She wouldn't tell me."

I lifted a shoulder. "I guess we'll see when we get there," I said, knowing full well what it was about but not wanting to give anything away.

I was shocked we'd been able to keep it out of *The Vine*, but Debbie had done her best to hype up the event without giving away the most important details. Like the fact that it was going to be Meghan Hart Day.

With the anniversary of Meghan's first book coming up, and a new cover to match, I'd wanted to do something special for Liam. Something that would let him see just how much readers loved his books. And, hopefully, even allow him to interact with them, all while keeping his identity secret.

When I'd pitched the idea to Debbie, she'd been one hundred percent on board. Raven had helped us organize it, and we'd spent weeks working on this secret. I only hoped Liam would like it. I was honestly really nervous about his reaction.

I finished my breakfast and carried my plate to the sink to rinse it off.

"I'll take care of it," Liam said, joining me. "Why don't you finish getting ready?"

"You sure?" I asked.

He nodded. "The sooner we help my mom, the sooner I have you all to myself again."

"Good point." I smiled, giving him a quick peck.

But he grabbed me around the waist and pulled me to him for a long, sensual kiss that made me crave more.

I was only here for a few days, and already I was dreading the goodbye. This constant travel and jet lag were getting old. My stomach didn't know whether I was coming or going. And my lack of sleep and altered eating habits were not helping. Despite everything, I was excited to be back in the AV. Back with Liam.

Our bodies were pressed together, his hips anchoring me to the counter. I lost myself in him and the moment.

And then my phone vibrated.

Oh, right. The celebration.

Debbie's name flashed on the screen, and I grabbed it before Liam could read the message. We'd kept Meghan Hart Day a secret this long; I wasn't going to blow it now.

"Everything okay?" Liam asked.

"Hm?" I read through her text, then realized I hadn't responded to Liam's question. "Oh. Yep. I'll be ready in a few."

I bounded up the stairs, responding to Raven's and Debbie's texts. They wanted to know when we were going to arrive and if I'd told Liam yet and so many other questions. Ack!

When I finally made it back downstairs, Liam was sitting on the back porch, book in hand.

"Whatcha reading?" I asked, leaning against the door-frame. Could he be any sexier?

He held up the cover for me to see. It was a book we'd been buddy reading while we were apart.

"How far in are you?" I asked.

"About halfway. You?"

"A little further. I read a lot of it on the plane last night. You ready?"

He sighed and closed the book, placing it on his lap. "Are you sure you want to go to Bibliolater? It's going to be a madhouse. And you know people are going to recognize you and stop you for autographs."

I waved a hand through the air, trying to at least appear

nonchalant when I was freaking out inside. Not go? We had to go!

"It'll be fine. Everyone's cool."

He chuckled. "You spend a month here and think you know everyone? You probably think you've seen everything too."

I lifted a shoulder. "Well, it is a small town," I teased, mostly to goad him.

He narrowed his eyes at me, and before I knew it, he'd pulled me into his lap. "The AV is full of surprises. You could spend a lifetime here and never discover them all."

"Is that so?" I asked, our teasing making way for something more serious.

"Yes." His eyes were such a dark blue that they were almost black. Like an inky night sky. Beautiful, dark, magical.

"Well then, even more reason for me to go today. I wouldn't want to miss out on any of those surprises you mentioned." I grinned.

"Mm." He held me close, looking out over the fields behind his house with a contented smile.

I rested my cheek against his chest, listening to his heartbeat as the wind swayed through the trees. And the birds sang a beautiful song. It was so peaceful here.

I didn't want to leave. And not just for the day.

I'd honestly begun to feel like part of the community. Part of Liam's family.

I peered up at Liam and smiled. "I love you."

He caressed my cheek, tilting his head down to meet my lips. "I love you too."

I smiled, reveling in this quiet moment. In this man. At some point, Liam had become my everything.

But we'd only been together a short time. My mom hadn't said it, but I knew she thought I was moving too fast. And part of me worried she was right. Part of me worried that my reluctance to tell Dr. Hamm about Liam and me taking that next step was because I knew she'd disapprove as well.

Deep down, I loved Liam, and what we'd done together felt right. But I also didn't want to fall into the same mistakes I'd made in the past.

"We should get going," I said, pushing myself off his lap before I could get too comfortable.

He stood and followed me to his truck, opening the door for me before going around to the driver's side. As we drove through town, I mentally practiced my speech one last time, hoping Liam would like this surprise as much as I thought he would.

We pulled into the parking lot down the street from Bibliolater, and he put the truck in park. He unbuckled his seat belt, and I placed my hand on his thigh before he could open the door.

"Is everything okay?" he asked.

I nodded, swallowing back my fear. "So, I planned a surprise for you, and I really hope you're going to like it because I'm scared I may have crossed the line."

He arched an eyebrow, his blue eyes swimming with curiosity. "Okay."

"I wanted to do something special to celebrate the anniversary of publishing *Hooked.* And every time we talk about signings and author events, I can tell there's a part of you that wants to participate. That wants to interact with readers and receive the recognition you deserve."

He furrowed his brow. "Yes, but we both know that keeping my identity a secret is more important."

"Yes." I nodded. "Which is why I'm telling you about this event now. And you don't have to attend if you don't want to. No one there will ever know that you're Meghan." Oh god, I was rambling, but I couldn't seem to stop. "You have two perfectly legitimate reasons to be at Bibliolater that have nothing to do with the event. Your mom owns the store and requested your help. And you're my boyfriend, and I dragged you along."

"Dragged me along to what?" He smoothed his hands down his thighs. "Will you please just tell me what this secret event is?"

I opened my purse and extracted some heart-shaped confetti, tossing it in the air as I said, "Happy Meghan Hart Day!" with a huge, cheesy smile.

Liam watched the confetti as it rained down all over the cab of his truck. "Was that really necessary?"

I cringed. "Sorry. I'm super nervous. Didn't really think it through." And I still had no idea how he felt about this big thing I'd planned. "I'll vacuum it later. Promise."

He chuckled and shook his head. "I was just messing with you. Don't worry about the confetti. I'm sure River would love to help me wash my truck."

I laughed. "True. So, um—" I fiddled with the seat belt. "What do you think? Do you want to check it out? No pressure either way."

"What are people expecting? Like, do they think Meghan Hart will be there in person?"

"No." I shook my head. "We always said it was a surprise event. Until this morning when the store opened, only a handful of people knew it was for Meghan Hart. And we made it very clear that it's a celebration in her honor, but that she would not be attending."

Liam nodded. "Wow. You really thought this through."

"Of course," I said. "I would never reveal Meghan's true identity. You know that."

"I do, but—" He rubbed his jaw. "Damn. I'm just… I never thought I'd get to have an opportunity like this." He placed his hand on my thigh. "Thank you, Penny. I'm touched."

I smiled, relief washing over me, followed by excitement. If he was already getting choked up, I couldn't wait till he saw everything we'd done to celebrate him and his achievements.

"You've always been so supportive of me and my author career. I just wanted to do something special for you."

He leaned across the console and captured my lips for a sweet kiss. "Thank you."

"My pleasure." I kissed him again.

"Oh. There will definitely be a lot of pleasure coming your way later." He kissed me back, unwilling to let me go. And I didn't want him to.

"That was cheesy," I said, breathless. "But I don't mind because—"

"You love cheese."

"That." I laughed, thinking back to the night we'd met. "And I love you."

"I love you." He slid his hand over my thigh, nearing the apex. I groaned as he began to rub me through my pants.

"Liam," I chided. "What if someone sees us?"

"Then everyone will know you're mine."

"Um. Pretty sure they already do," I joked. Though his possessive tone both gave me pause and made me hotter. *What the hell is wrong with me?*

He sped up the pace, and I arched my back to add more pressure. I'd never realized I might like the idea of someone catching us in the act. But then my phone buzzed again, and we both groaned.

"Come on," I said. "We'll finish our celebration later."

He smiled back at me then opened the door to the cab and hopped out. "Fuck yes. Let's go!"

"Okay. Okay." I laughed, scrambling to get out of the car.

We took a few steps before Liam paused and stopped to stare at the sidewalk. I smiled as he read a line from one of his books. I'd selected all the quotes, and Raven had commissioned a local artist to write them on the sidewalk with chalk. This was one of my personal favorites.

"Love is trust. And where lies live, love can't flourish. But where trust lives and breathes, that's where you will find love. Sometimes it is as small as a seed. It's tender and needs frequent nourishing. But other times, it's as large as an oak tree. Strong and steady."

The artist had added tree branches, and it was so stunning I took a picture.

"Wow," Liam said. "That's really cool."

"That's just the beginning," I said, linking my arm through his.

As we neared the bookstore, a line stretched out the door and around the corner.

"How the heck are we going to get past that?" he asked.

"Through the back door, of course," I teased.

He threw his head back and laughed at my innuendo. And then we went around to the back of the store and let ourselves in. Raven glanced up from the stock section.

"Oh, good. You're here," she said, breathless.

I widened my eyes and cleared my throat. She stood and swept her hair away from her face. "Right. Sorry. Happy Meghan Hart Day!" She wiggled her hands.

Liam and I both laughed, then I said, "Don't worry. She's getting paid extra for this."

"Thank god." Raven slumped. "This might be more intense than any signing I've ever attended. The minute people heard who the celebration was for, they went crazy. We're going to need more cookies."

"Cookies?" Liam tilted his head.

"Come on." I grabbed his arm and pulled him toward the store. He should be out there—enjoying the celebration. Not stressing over the details. This was his big day. Even if no one else would ever know it.

As soon as we stepped through the door to the shop, I could see why Raven had been overwhelmed. People were *everywhere*. Mostly women, but there were a few men too. Liam's dad smiled from across the room, and I waved.

"Tristan!" Liam called.

A tall man with dark hair glanced up and then smiled when he caught sight of Liam. He waded through the crowd to join us.

"Tristan, hey." Liam pulled him in for a hug. "What are you doing here?"

"Celebrating Meghan Hart, of course. I mean, she did dedicate a book to my wife, so it only seems right." He winked.

I laughed, and his attention turned to me. Liam made the introductions and then asked Tristan where the kids were.

"Probably with Ellie. They haven't left her side since she arrived from Australia."

"Oh. I didn't realize she'd already moved back," Liam said. "Where is she? I'll have to say hi."

Tristan sipped his coffee. It was from Pore Over, but we'd had custom sleeves made in honor of Meghan Hart Day. "Last I saw, she was over by the register with Lizzie."

I followed Liam's line of sight, curious who they were talking about.

"Where?" Liam asked, frowning.

"Next to Lizzie. In the lavender shirt and ripped jeans."

Liam's jaw dropped. "*That's* Ellie?" His attention whipped to Tristan, who nodded. "Tessa's younger sister, Ellie?"

Tristan shifted. "Yep. Can you believe it?"

"Oh my god," Wren said, joining us along with Harper. "Isn't this amazing?"

"Look at all the covers with the photos we've taken." Harper glanced around in awe.

"And these cookies from Wildflour Bakery are insane!" Wren held one up for us to see. "I took that picture!" She pointed at the image printed on the icing, and we all laughed at her enthusiasm.

Every time I looked at Liam, he was beaming, and my heart was filled with happiness. Everything about the event was perfect, from the company to the wild flowers dotting the tables, to the love and support for Meghan and her books.

"I can't believe Mom kept all this a secret," Wren said then lowered her voice to a whisper. "Do you think Meghan's here?"

I wanted to laugh. To think that Meghan was standing right next to her. When I glanced at Liam, he was definitely fighting a smile. I knew he'd tell her when the time was right, but in the middle of a crowded bookstore packed with Meghan Hart fans was not it.

Debbie climbed the stairs to the small stage. She tapped the microphone, and the room quieted down.

"Hello." She smiled out at the crowd. "Thank you all for coming today. I'm so excited to celebrate Meghan Hart and her accomplishments. She's a local author with an incredible talent for writing about love, and I've long been a fan. With the anniversary of her first novel, *Hooked,* I wanted to do something to celebrate her and all that she's accomplished. Thank you all for joining me."

The audience applauded, and while no one was watching, I saw Liam swipe a tear from his cheek. I placed my hand on his back and rubbed gently.

Debbie then said, "I'd like to invite Penelope Glass up here to say a few words. As many of you know, she's been cowriting a book with Meghan and perhaps knows her best. So please, welcome Penny."

Liam leaned in to kiss my cheek and whispered, "Can you mention that a portion of the proceeds from today's sales will be donated to the new library?"

I smiled, completely in awe of this man and everything he did. Not just for his family, but for this community. And they had no idea he was behind it. He was so unbelievably selfless. And I couldn't love him more. I nodded and headed for the stage.

"Thank you all for coming today. And thank you to Debbie and the team at Bibliolater for hosting such an incredible event." There was a round of applause. "A special thanks to my assistant, Raven, for helping organize everything as well." More applause.

"I started writing romance because of Meghan Hart. Her books have always been my escape, especially in difficult times. And rereading them still feels like coming home."

I took a deep breath then continued, my eyes on Liam. I might be addressing the crowd, but this speech was really meant for him. His gaze was intense, and it was as if we were the only two people in the universe.

"The past few months, I've had the honor of cowriting a book with Meghan. And it has been the biggest privilege of my career and a highlight of my life. Meghan may not like the spotlight, but she deserves all the praise.

"She is a talented writer who makes readers feel seen. And an incredible person, always supporting both the online book community and the Alondra Valley. So—" I forced myself to smile so I wouldn't cry. "I hope you'll show her just how much she means to us by leaving a note in the guestbook or picking up a signed copy of one of her books. I talked to her earlier, and she's dedicating a portion of the proceeds from today's event to the new library."

Everyone started cheering, and suddenly Liam was being yanked into a hug by Tristan. I didn't know what was being said, but both men were clearly emotional.

When Tristan released Liam, Liam smiled up at me and mouthed, "Thank you." And I knew I'd done the right thing. I was thrilled that I could finally show him just how much he —and Meghan—meant to me.

CHAPTER TWENTY-FOUR

Liam

"Um, that was fucking amazing," I said, practically floating down the sidewalk.

Penny laughed. "I'm so glad you enjoyed it. I was really nervous."

"About the event or about telling me?" I asked.

"Both, but mostly about telling you. I didn't want you to feel pressured to attend or like I was trying to push you to reveal your identity."

I wrapped my arm around her, kissing her hair. "I would never think that. Honestly, it was one of the coolest things I've ever experienced. Better than making the best-seller lists."

She stopped and gaped at me. "You did not just say that."

I knew how much she wanted that accolade, and I was doing everything I could to make that happen for *Brave Together*. I'd secretly thrown extra money into the advertising and was pushing the book in all the places.

"That was an amazing accomplishment, but I didn't have anyone to share it with. Plus, aren't we always saying we do this for the readers?"

She nodded. "Yeah, but—"

I placed a finger to her lips. "No but. Today was incredible. Thank you for giving me that experience."

"You're welcome. And I'm so glad Tristan and your family were there for it."

"So am I. He doesn't go out much since Tessa's death." Apart from Friday night drinks with Asher, Bennett, and me. Though even that had been a rare occurrence the past few months. "So it was nice to see him doing something that wasn't an obligation for the kids."

"Wren and Harper were so funny," she said. "I didn't even think about the cookies having their photos on them."

I chuckled. "Those cookies were so good. And today made me realize how badly I want to tell Wren. I'm ready to tell the rest of my family and Asher."

"Wow, Liam. That's big."

"I know." I took her hand in mine and led her down the path by the pond. "But I've been thinking about it for a while."

She gave my hand a squeeze, and we passed by Lick ice cream and several families strolling down the sidewalk with ice cream cones. I led her to a bench overlooking the gazebo and pond.

"I was wondering if you'd go with me when I tell them."

"Of course," she said. "When are you thinking about doing it?"

"At family dinner this Sunday."

She leaned over and placed her head on my shoulder. "I'd be honored."

"So…" Penny asked from the passenger seat as the fields rolled by. "How are you feeling?"

It was the night of family dinner. The night I'd decided to tell them about Meghan Hart. And I was… "Nervous."

"That's understandable," she said, her smile reassuring. "Maybe we can be brave together?"

I smiled at the reference to our book title. It was something we'd started saying anytime we got to a scene one of us had reservations about. We'd remind ourselves that, together, we could do anything.

"Brave together," I said, feeling stronger and more confident with Penny by my side.

Penny placed her hand on my thigh. "I have to admit—I'm excited. Just think of how thrilled and proud your mom was when you told her."

"Yeah, well, we'll see…" I blew out a breath and twisted the steering wheel in my hands.

I reached for the dashboard, turning up the radio. It was still too chilly to roll down the windows, but I couldn't wait to experience Penny's first summer in the AV with her. We'd go berry picking. Spend lazy days in the hammock. Have as much leisurely sex as we wanted.

I hadn't asked her to stay—not yet. But I was going to. I couldn't wait much longer. She was flying back to New York again tomorrow. The only reason I'd put it off was so she wouldn't feel pressured to decide while we'd been focused on finishing the book. That, and I was scared she'd say no.

I pulled up the drive to my parents' house, my nerves mounting with every second that passed. I wanted to believe Penny was right. And I hoped my family would be supportive, but I was afraid.

Penny slid her hand into mine as we walked up the path to the house. "Brave together, right?"

I nodded, but I couldn't force myself to say the words. She

made me feel braver, that was for sure. I still couldn't believe she'd organized Meghan Hart Day for me. Seeing everyone in town so excited and supportive had been everything. And it had made me realize just how much I wanted to share my success with my family and friends.

I knocked on the front door once before letting myself in. "Mom? Dad?"

"In here," Mom called, and I followed the sound of her voice back to the kitchen.

"Hey, sweetheart." She gave me a hug and then Penny. Over the past few months, they'd become friends. Any time Penny was in town, Mom would take her shopping and to lunch. I knew Mom was secretly hoping Penny would stay.

She just fit. In my life. In my family. In my heart.

"Mm. I'm so glad you're here," Mom said to Penny, releasing her. "We've missed seeing your face at family dinners."

"I've missed you too." Penny smiled. "Dinner smells delicious. Can I do anything to help?"

"I've got it covered." Mom winked. "Besides, we don't want to overtax your wrist when it's doing so well. And—" Mom turned to us, resting against the counter. "While we're alone, there's something I want to talk to both of you about."

"What's up?" I asked.

"Well, I don't know what your plans are for *Brave Together*, but I would love to host a signing at Bibliolater in a few weeks. Liam, you could pre-sign a bunch of copies. And then Penny could sign them for readers live." She turned to Penny. "If you're willing. And able," she added, giving Penny's wrist a pointed look.

Penny placed her good hand on my mom's shoulder. "I'd love to, Debbie. That would be amazing. And I think I should be up to it, but we'll see what my doctor says. I have my final appointment later this week, and then I can let you know."

"Oh." Mom frowned. "I didn't realize you were leaving again so soon."

"Yeah. Quick trip," Penny said.

Then Mom turned to me. "So…what do you think about the signing?"

"Great idea. Thanks, Mom. And thank you for Meghan Hart Day."

She smiled. "Of course. That was fun. Why do you think I'm proposing a signing?"

"Because you're my biggest fan?" I teased.

"What?" Penny jerked her head back. "We all know that title belongs to me."

I laughed. "Of course it does, babe."

Mom watched us with a secret smile. "I would only relinquish my title as number one fan to someone who's worthy. And you, Penny, are definitely worthy."

Penny stilled, and I had a feeling we were talking about more than just rights to the Meghan Hart fan club. "Thank you, Debbie. And thanks for offering to host the signing."

"Absolutely," Mom said. "Meghan Hart Day is going to be an annual event. It broke all of Bibliolater's sales records."

I gaped at my mom. "Seriously?"

"Yes, seriously. The library is going to be getting a big fat check from us."

"I didn't—" I pinched the bridge of my nose. "I was going to donate from a share of my proceeds, not yours."

"Don't be ridiculous. We can both donate. And next year, we can choose another charity if you want."

"That's a great idea."

"We're making a huge impact on the community, and all because of Penny," Mom said.

"Oh, I don't know about—"

"Yes," I said, cutting Penny off before she could downplay

her role. "This was your idea. And it was brilliant. Did you want to give Mom her present?"

Penny and I had wanted to do something special for Mom to thank her for hosting Meghan Hart Day. We'd just gotten a few advance paperback copies of *Brave Together*, and we immediately knew who we wanted to give one to.

Penny pulled the package out of her purse and handed it to Mom. Mom wiped her hands off on her apron then removed the tissue paper to reveal one of the first copies of *Brave Together*.

"Oh. My. God. Is this for real?" She glanced up at us then back down at the book. We'd both signed her copy, and her hands were shaking as she flipped through the pages. "This is amazing. And I'm trying really hard not to fangirl." Though, she practically squealed as she said it.

"Who's fangirling?" Dad asked, joining us.

I tensed. But if he'd overheard anything about my pen name, he didn't act like it. He hugged Penny then me before leaning against the counter.

"That would be me." Mom raised her hand.

"What's new?" he teased, giving her a kiss. Then he saw the book. "What's this?"

"Meghan and Penny's new book," Mom said, clutching it to her chest.

There was another knock at the door, followed by River's exuberant "Hello!" and the sound of Toodles's nails scratching against the floor. My mom lit up and hid the book in a cabinet as Dad went to greet them.

He soon rejoined us, along with Bennett, Wren, River, and Toodles.

"Hey, River. Love your skirt," Penny said, crouching down to his level.

"Thanks." River beamed, always proud of his bold fashion

choices. "I'm really glad you're here. I wanted to talk to you about a story I've been working on…"

"I'd love to hear all about it!" She ruffled River's hair, and he smiled up at her as if she'd hung the moon. I understood because it was how I felt about her.

Bennett nudged me with his elbow. "Looks like you've got some competition."

"Yeah. Yeah." I smiled and shook my head as Wren pulled me in for a hug. "Hey, Liam."

"Hey, little bird. How are you?"

"Good." She smiled, but her skin seemed paler than usual.

"You sure?" I held her away from me, taking a good look at her. "You look tired." I turned to Bennett. "Are you taking good care of my sister?"

"Of course my husband is," Wren said, smacking my chest with her hand before beaming up at said husband. I still couldn't believe it sometimes—my best friend was married to my little sister.

I narrowed my eyes at Bennett, but we both knew that everything he did was for Wren and River.

Dad nudged me. "Be nice."

Wren rolled her eyes and pulled Bennett closer. He wrapped his arms around her, holding her to his chest and whispering in her ear. I wanted that. I wanted what they had. A loving home. A happy family. It was what I'd always wanted, but for years I'd been too scared to let myself believe it could be real.

Until now. Until Penny.

I glanced over at Penny and smiled. I wanted it with her.

"All right," Mom said, clapping her hands. "We've got hot dogs, grilled veggies, and hamburgers. River, sweetheart, what would you like?"

"Hot dog, please," River said, eyes focused on the paper he was showing Penny. "No bun."

Penny and I glanced at each other, our eyes meeting as we shared a secret smile. I assumed that she—like me—was thinking about the time we'd hot-dogged it, as she'd called it.

I fell in line behind Penny as everyone served themselves. We sat down at the table, and not for the first time, I was struck by how well Penny fit in with my family. She belonged here. With me. Just like Bennett belonged with Wren.

How could I ever have been opposed to this? To Bennett with my sister? He was my best friend, my brother. And now, he was family.

I sipped my beer slowly. It was a new brew from Faulty Brewing, and it was good. Everyone chatted around me about work, about their latest projects, whatever.

After a while, Wren turned to me. "It feels like it's been months since you went on an inspection."

I nodded and wiped my mouth with my napkin. "Actually, I have some news about my job." Penny gave my thigh an encouraging squeeze.

"Oh yeah?" Dad smiled, helping River cut his hot dog.

I took a deep breath and opened my mouth to tell everyone the truth when Wren stood abruptly. "I'm sorry." She held a hand to her mouth. "I'll be right back." Then she ran off.

Penny and I glanced at each other and frowned, but my parents continued eating as if nothing had happened.

"Sorry about that," Wren said when she returned. Her skin was still pale, but her smile was wide. "What did you want to tell us?"

I waved away her question. It could wait. "Are you okay?" I asked, watching Wren closely.

Bennett merely rubbed her shoulder and asked if she needed anything. She shook her head and sighed. "Should we do it? Should we tell them?"

"Tell us what?" River asked.

Bennett nodded, grabbing her hand. "Go for it, baby."

Wren took a deep breath and smiled. "We're pregnant!"

"What?" River froze, and for a second, I worried he was upset. But then he jumped up and threw one arm around Wren's neck and the other around Bennett's and said, "Best. Day. Ever!"

We all started laughing, and I was so happy. But I was also scared. My sister hadn't had the easiest time after delivering River, and I worried about her health.

"And you're healthy? The baby's healthy?" I asked.

"Very healthy." She placed her hand on her stomach and smiled up at Bennett. "Doc Allen and my OB have been keeping a close eye on things. And Bennett has been taking excellent care of us."

I nodded, some of my concern abating. She wasn't alone. This wouldn't be like last time.

And with that admission, something in me eased, allowing fear to fade and happiness to flow in. I was going to be an uncle. Again!

I stood and pulled her into a hug. If she hadn't told me she was pregnant, I wouldn't have known. She wasn't showing yet. "This is wonderful news."

"Thanks, Liam." Wren was tugging at the corner of her eyes to hold back tears.

I turned to Bennett and hugged him. "Congratulations, man. I'm so happy for you."

He patted my back. "Thank you." His smile was watery when he pulled back. "That means so much to me. I was honestly concerned how you would take the news."

"Nah." I wrapped my arm around his shoulder. "You're my best friend. I want you to be happy."

"I know. I just—" He sighed. "I hate keeping secrets, and I never want you to feel like I'm choosing Wren over you. You're both important to me."

"She's your wife," I said, guilt swirling in my gut at his admission—both from the secret I was keeping, and the fact that I'd placed additional stress on him during a time that was already emotional enough.

I placed my hand on his shoulder. "You're a couple now. Of course she comes first. That's how it should be. I hate that you were worried about telling me such happy news."

Wren nudged him. "See?" And then she moved on to talk to Mom.

"Bennett," I said, wanting to reassure him, to let him know that he had my full support. "You have to do what you both think is best. I know it's customary to wait to tell anyone until after the first trimester. I'm just glad Wren and the baby are healthy."

His answering smile was brilliant, and I could feel his shoulders relax. Though his next words severely undermined his calm exterior. "Me too. I might give myself an ulcer before this baby is born."

I chuckled and patted his back before returning to my seat beside Penny. Wren could take care of herself, but Bennett was the best partner I could've imagined for her. He was loving, attentive, and protective.

"Have you discussed names?" Mom asked.

Wren nodded. "A little, but we might wait to find out the baby's sex."

"Wait?" Penny's eyes went wide. "People still do that?"

We all chuckled. Conversation soon turned to other matters, and after a while Dad asked, "Liam, what did you want to tell us about your job?"

I considered telling them the truth, but I couldn't. I told myself this was Wren's moment, and I didn't want to ruin it. But secretly, I was relieved.

"Nothing nearly as exciting as Wren's big news." I forced myself to smile.

"I'm sure that isn't true," Mom said.

But I subtly shook my head, silently begging her to drop it. I didn't want to overshadow Bennett and Wren's happy news. Tonight should be about them.

I'd already waited six years. What was a little longer?

CHAPTER TWENTY-FIVE

Liam

Penny was quiet on the drive home from family dinner, and so was I. I couldn't believe I was going to be an uncle again! I also couldn't believe that the night I'd finally decided to tell my family about Meghan Hart was when Wren and Bennett had announced they were expecting.

"You feeling okay?" I asked Penny.

She continued to stare out the window and nodded. "Yeah. It was nice of your mom to prepare sweet potatoes and rice for me."

"It's not a big deal," I said, knowing Mom was more than happy to do it. Penny had been dealing with a flare-up lately, and I'd wanted her to be able to eat something that wouldn't aggravate her stomach.

"It feels like a big deal. No one's ever gone to that kind of effort for me."

"What about your ex?" I asked, unable to stop myself. Thanks to *The Vine*, I knew Erik's family was loaded. So loaded that I assumed they had a private chef.

She shook her head. "I usually eat something before I go over since I can't have most of the stuff they serve."

I stared at her a beat then refocused my attention on the road. "Seriously?"

She nodded. "Yeah. Though some of that's my fault. I should speak up and advocate for myself."

I scoffed and pulled into my driveway. "You were together for three years. He should've known better."

"Perhaps," Penny said. "But enough about him. It's in the past."

She said that, but was it? She'd seen him only just recently for Passover. I gnashed my teeth, incensed by the fact that he hadn't looked out for her. And the idea that they'd spent time together—*again.*

"I really like your family," Penny said as I put the truck in park and shut off the engine.

"They really like you too," I said. Dad had told me as much.

I climbed out and went around to her side, spinning her so her back was pinned to the truck, my hands on her hips. Penny blinked up at me.

"Um, hi." She laughed.

"Hi." I tilted my forehead to hers. It was now or never. I had to just— "I don't want you to go back to New York. And I know this isn't something we've talked about." I squeezed her hips. "But I want you to stay. I want you to move in with me."

"What?"

I was sick of being so far apart. I'd given this a lot of thought, and I wanted her to see that it could be possible. "Your lease is up soon, isn't it? You could just—"

"Liam—" She dipped her head. "I-I... I don't know."

Well, that wasn't the reaction I'd been hoping for.

"I know I'm asking a lot, but I know how much you love it

here. How much I love having you here. And you've said it yourself—we can do this job anywhere."

She nodded, and I hoped that meant I was persuading her. "That's true, but moving in together is a huge step. And we've only been together for a few months."

"It feels like longer." When she frowned, I added, "In a good way. What I'm trying to say is that we've spent a lot of quality time together. Living and working together?" I shook my head. "That isn't easy. Let alone writing a romance novel together. And we did it."

"True, but…"

"But what?" I asked. "I want to be together. I mean, haven't these past few months been amazing?"

"Yes, but—"

"And don't you want more of that? And less travel?" I kept talking, afraid that if I stopped, she'd say no. Until then, I'd do my best to make her see what a great idea this was.

"Of course. And maybe it's something we can discuss in the future."

I sensed there was something else holding her back. Something besides the quick timing. And I wasn't ready to give up just yet.

"Is there anything I can do to help convince you? To make you feel more comfortable with the idea?" I didn't think I was being unreasonable. In fact, I'd asked her because I'd thought it would make her happy. I thought *I* made her happy.

"I just…need more time." She dropped her head. "Less than a year ago, I was about to walk down the aisle and marry another man."

I didn't want to think about Erik or her past. I wanted to focus on us and our future. It rankled that she was still in touch with him. That she still saw him for holidays and family events. She might act like it wasn't a big deal, but it bothered me.

I couldn't take it anymore. "Is this about him?"

"What?" She frowned. "No, Liam. Why would you think that?"

"Because you've been so distant the past month. Secretive. And even when you've been here, you're sending all these texts and stuff."

"What?" She jerked her head back. And then she started laughing.

"This isn't funny." I hated the petulant tone to my voice. It made me sound needy, desperate. I'd promised myself I'd never put myself in that position again.

"I'm sorry. You're right. But I was texting with your mom and Raven. If I've seemed distant, it's only because I've been busy planning Meghan Hart Day, and I didn't want to blow the surprise."

"Oh." Well, shit. I felt like an asshole.

"And yes, I saw Erik at Hanukkah and Passover. But I told you about that. And you knew I didn't want to go."

"Then why did you?"

"Because our moms are old friends. And even though Erik and I may not be together anymore, they're still family."

Family? It didn't sound like family to me. What kind of family didn't look out for each other, especially when it came to the most basic needs like food?

She placed her hand on my arm. "I've made it very clear to Erik that we are over. You believe me, right?"

"I—" I hesitated. I certainly wanted to believe her. "I don't like it."

"As long as I live in New York, he will probably continue to be part of my life."

"Even more reason for you to move here," I blurted.

She scoffed then realized I was serious. "Liam." Her tone

was gentle, but her expression was firm. "I'm with *you*." She placed her hand over my heart. "I love *you*."

"Then why won't you move in with me?" I pleaded, feeling as if I might break. Why couldn't she just say yes?

"I love you, but it's too soon. Too fast. I'm not ready to take that next step. I know that's not what you want to hear, but that's how I feel."

"Is it because I didn't tell my family tonight?"

"What?" She jerked her head back. "No, Liam. I know you want to tell them. And maybe someday you will, but that's your decision."

"Then what?" I asked.

"I have to do what feels right for me. I can't keep jumping into relationships and making the same mistakes."

A hole formed in the pit of my stomach. "So, I'm a mistake."

"No. Absolutely not." She huffed. "Clearly I'm not explaining this well."

We were both quiet, and I felt as if I might explode. With every second that ticked by, I tried to make sense of her decision. But I couldn't.

Penny was the first person I'd let in. The first person I'd trusted since my ex. I'd thought we were on the same page. But now, it felt just like it had with Diane. I wanted to take the next step, and she wasn't ready.

"I want to do this right," Penny said.

I dragged a hand through my hair. "How is what we're doing 'wrong'?"

"It's not *wrong* per se. It's just...fast."

"Is that you or your therapist talking?" I snapped, immediately regretting it. I fully supported talking to someone. And I fully supported Penny taking care of her mental health. "I'm sorry," I said. "That was uncalled for."

"No. You're right. I know I use her to justify my decisions sometimes. But that's only because I trust her."

"Sometimes it feels like you trust her more than yourself. More than you trust me."

"I-I—" She shook her head and then stopped herself as if clawing back from the ledge of something we couldn't move past. The trouble was, we were already rapidly approaching that point.

"Is that it?" I asked, latching on to her hesitation. "You don't trust me?"

"I just don't understand why you're in such a rush? What's the big hurry?"

"The rush?" I stepped closer. "There's no rush apart from the fact that I love you, and I don't want to spend another fucking second without you."

How could she not understand that?

And if she couldn't, then maybe she was right. Maybe we weren't ready for such a big step after all.

She was quiet, and when I turned back to face her, her head was bowed. A tear leaked out, cascading down her face. And then she finally admitted, "I love you too, but I just… I can't."

"I know it's a big step, but it's not like I'm asking you to marry me."

"Right?" she scoffed. "Like that would ever happen."

I frowned. "So that's what it would take? A proposal?"

"No," she sighed. "I think we're getting off track."

I wasn't so sure about that. "But you want to get married."

"Maybe someday. I don't know what the future holds."

I was beginning to realize that this went deeper than just moving in together. We fundamentally disagreed on the future of our relationship. And I wasn't sure how to reconcile that.

"I don't know what the future holds either," I said. "But I can't keep living like this."

We'd done the long-distance thing for months now, and it sucked. Penny loved the AV, and I loved her. This seemed like a no-brainer.

"So what?" She crossed her arms over her chest. "That's it? I move or we're done?"

"What?" I jerked my head back. "No. That's not what I said."

"Are you sure? Because that's how you're acting."

I pinched the bridge of my nose and sighed. "It's been a big evening. I think we're both tired, and we should discuss this again when we're in a calmer space."

"Fine," she said through gritted teeth.

"Great." I clenched my jaw.

She said nothing more, then turned and headed for the house.

"Fuck." I kicked at the tire.

That hadn't gone at all the way I'd hoped or planned.

AFTER A SLEEPLESS NIGHT SPENT ALONE, I VENTURED DOWN the hall to find Penny so we could talk. But when I reached the guest room, the door was open and the bed was made. There was a note on the comforter, and I picked it up to read it.

LIAM,
   I'm sorry. I can't.
   Penny

. . .

I SANK DOWN ON THE MATTRESS, THE SCENT OF PEPPERMINT lingering in the air. For all her talk of emotional vulnerability, Penny had bolted. She hadn't even given us a chance to talk. To try to move past this.

I shook my head, crushing the note in my hand. "So much for being braver together."

CHAPTER TWENTY-SIX

Liam

I lifted the hem of my shirt to my forehead. I was covered in dust and dirt and sweat. I bobbed my head to the music, using a hammer to smash the tile flooring of the downstairs bathroom. It was an eyesore from the seventies, and it absolutely did not belong in this house. Smash. Smash. Smash.

I was on a roll. Tearing up the tile. Gutting it.

The past few days, I'd taken my anger and frustration and hurt out on that bathroom until my limbs were too exhausted to continue. And then I fell into bed, only to wake up and do it all again.

The music cut off. "Hello?" Mom called. "Liam?"

I frowned. "In here."

"Wow. Looks like you've been busy," she said, surveying the damage from the doorway.

I lifted my safety goggles and glanced around, realizing just how big of a mess I'd made. It felt a bit like my life at present.

Which was why I'd spent every waking moment in this hideous bathroom, needing space from the memories of

Penny that floated around my house like ghosts. Everywhere I went, she haunted me.

My bedroom.

My office.

Bibliolater.

I couldn't go anywhere and not be reminded of her.

How did Tristan do it? Live in the town he and Tessa had spent their entire lives in. Surrounded by the memories of his late wife.

If I was hurting this much after a few months with Penny, I could only imagine the devastation Tristan felt from losing the woman he'd loved for fifteen years.

I thought back to that day with Tristan at Tessa's grave. When I'd told him my secret, and he'd given me advice about relationships. About it being worth the effort. At the moment, I wasn't sure I agreed.

"What's wrong?" Mom asked.

"Nice to see you too," I said in a sarcastic tone that only deepened her scowl.

She crossed her arms over her chest. "Did something happen with Penny?" When I said nothing, she said, "Oh no. I'm right?"

I squeezed the hammer. "I don't want to talk about it."

She stepped closer, mindful of the broken pieces of tile littering the floor. "Are you okay?"

I didn't answer her question, instead asking one of my own. "What are you doing here anyway?"

"Family dinner. Your week to host. Remember?"

Had it really been a week since Penny had left? It felt more like a year.

"Aw. Shit." I rubbed a hand down my face just as Dad appeared in the doorway and Mom said, "Language, William."

I sighed. It didn't matter how old I got or how famous my

books became, my mom would always scold me. "Let's reschedule."

"What's wrong?" Dad asked.

Mom rolled her eyes but didn't answer Dad's question, though I assumed it was only a matter of time. "We're not rescheduling. Wren and Bennett just pulled up."

"Mom? Liam?" Wren called as if to prove my mom's point.

"In here," Mom said. "No, wait—" She stuck her head out into the hall. "You should stay there. I don't want you and the baby around any chemicals."

"Can I come see?" River yelled down the hall.

"I think we should all give Uncle Liam a minute to clean up, and then he can join us out back." Mom glared at me, her look a silent command to get my shit together.

"What about dinner?" River asked as Dad steered him toward the kitchen.

"We'll order pizza."

"Good idea. Dad will want a Giada. And I'll have…"

Their voices faded just as Bennett appeared on the threshold of the bathroom.

"Shit, man. You really did a number on this bathroom. You break up with Penny or something?" he teased.

I sighed and rubbed a hand over my forehead. "Yeah. Something like that."

"Oh." He cringed. "Sorry. You okay?"

I shook my head. "No."

He rapped his knuckles on the wood casing. "I'm here if you want to talk."

I nodded. "Thanks. Maybe some other time. Just give me a minute to clean up, then I'll be out."

I shook the dirt off my clothes then removed my work boots and stomped upstairs to shower. After showering and changing, I headed back downstairs, filled with dread. The second I slid open the door to the backyard, all eyes turned toward me. *Fucking awesome.*

"You broke up with Penny?" River asked in a strangled voice.

I glared at my mom. "Seriously?"

Mom lifted her hands palms up and shrugged. "I'm sorry. River asked where Penny was. Then Wren guessed what had happened and started to cry."

"I'm sorry." Wren held up her hands, her eyes still rimmed with red. "Pregnancy hormones."

Bennett nodded, his eyes wide as if to say, "Yes. Lord help me."

I scrubbed my face with my hands. "Penny went back to New York. And yes, we broke up. Okay? Now, let's drop it, everyone." I narrowed my eyes at each and every one of them.

Dad nodded. Bennett sipped his beer, his arm around Wren. I glanced away. I couldn't watch them. It was too painful after knowing what it was like to be with Penny.

River was sitting with my mom, glitter shoes catching the sunlight and tossing sparkles around the patio. And, as usual, I was all alone.

And then it dawned on me that part of the reason I felt that way was my own fault. My family was *always* there for me. Always loving. Just like Penny had been before I pushed her away.

I smoothed my hands up and down my thighs as if that would ease the anxiety coursing through me. I wanted to hide and run and stay in place all at once. "I'm glad you're all here. I need to tell you guys something."

Everyone was somber. Silent.

I was quiet for so long, formulating what I wanted to say, that Wren finally asked, "Liam, is everything okay?"

When I met her eyes, they were filled with worry. "I, um

—" I cleared my throat. "You know how I mentioned some news about my job the other week?"

"Yeah," Bennett said, his voice marked with confusion.

"Well, I—" I glanced at Mom, and she gave me a reassuring smile. Encouraging me to continue. I inhaled slowly and let it out shakily. "I—" I stood abruptly, nearly toppling my chair. "Maybe it would be easier if I showed you."

"Showed us what?" Bennett asked.

"Just, um—" I headed for the house and waved them on. "Follow me."

I led them through the house, up the stairs to the second floor. Then my bedroom. With every step closer to my office, I questioned whether I was doing the right thing. Because once I told them, it was out there. I couldn't take it back. I couldn't undo the hurt I'd caused or the betrayal they might feel. But I also knew I didn't want to keep this from them anymore.

"This is strange," River said, not too quietly.

Wren hushed him. "Let's pay attention to Uncle Liam."

There was a collective gasp as I pulled open the bookshelf leading to my secret office. I braced myself for their reaction. Because if this was a surprise, I could only imagine their shock upon discovering what was waiting upstairs.

Since I was in the lead, I couldn't see any of their faces. But I could hear their silent questions. Their confusion was so loud, it was as if they were shouting.

I tried to imagine it from their perspective. And I knew they were all taking it in. The awards. The books. The... everything. Fortunately, the dildos and other toys were all well hidden.

Everyone seemed similarly affected. Wide eyes. Gaping mouths. Confusion.

Well, everyone except for Mom, who was practically giddy. I chuckled at her reaction, some of my earlier tension dissipating. My mom was such a book nerd, I should've known she'd enjoy this. But I hadn't worried about her reaction—not like the others.

"Welcome to my office. For my company—Meghan Hart."

"Why…" Wren's mouth kept opening and closing. "How?"

Bennett placed his hand on her lower back. "Are you okay, baby?"

"Meghan's first book was published years ago," Wren said, seeming to collect herself. "Are you trying to tell us that you've secretly been writing as her for all this time?"

I braced myself for their reactions. "Yes."

"I—" Wren went over to the shelf and picked up a book. *Belonging. Penny's favorite.* I pushed away thoughts of Penny. She'd left. "*You* wrote this?"

"Yep." I shrugged.

She flipped to a page and started reading aloud. Though I wanted to cringe, I was grateful it wasn't a sex scene. She slammed the book shut. "*You* wrote that."

I wasn't sure whether she was asking or merely restating it.

"Yes. I wrote that. I wrote all of these."

"Wait…so you and Penny were writing together? Did she know?"

"Not at first."

Bennett shook his head. "Damn, Liam. Next, you're going to tell us you're a spy."

"No. Because then I'd have to kill you," I deadpanned.

"I'm glad your books are more original than that line," Bennett teased, and I gave his shoulder a playful shove. If anything, I was relieved he didn't seem mad at me.

Wren just kept shaking her head in disbelief. Flipping through the pages. Reading the back covers. Inspecting my office.

"I think this is super cool, Uncle Liam," River said, giving me a hug.

"Thanks, kiddo." I gave him a squeeze, hoping the rest of my family would be as supportive.

"Well, I certainly didn't expect this," Dad said, finally breaking his silence and hugging me. "But I'm proud of you."

"Thanks, Dad. That means a lot."

Wren was quiet, drinking in all the details that made the space. Then she turned and walked over to me and slugged me. "I can't believe you kept this from me all these years."

This was what I'd been afraid of. The disappointment. The anger. The sense of betrayal.

"I'm…sorry?" I couldn't quite gauge her reaction.

"I'm Meghan's photographer. *Your* photographer." She shook my shoulder. "All this time…"

"I know. I know." I cringed.

"Are you even still doing inspections?"

I dropped my head to my chest and shook it. "No. Not for the past year."

She furrowed her brow. "Where the heck do you go when you're on 'inspection'? Do you just hide up here?"

I laughed. "No. I usually go up to the cabin."

"Why do I get the feeling Mom already knew?" she asked, eyes narrowed as she glanced between us.

"I told her earlier this year."

"Please don't tell me I'm the last one to find out that my brother is secretly my favorite romance author."

I chewed on my lip. "Not the *last* person, but Tristan knows because Tessa was my beta reader."

She gasped. "What? No freaking way!"

"Does anyone else know?" Bennett asked. "I mean, are we allowed to talk about this openly, or is it a secret?"

"I want to tell Asher at some point, but I'd like to keep my circle small. So I'd appreciate your discretion."

"What?" Wren asked. "No! Are you kidding? My brother is *the* Meghan Hart. I want to shout it from the rooftops."

"Yeah, but his readers love the secrecy. The mystery. It's part of Meghan's brand," Mom said, echoing Penny's comments from the past.

"Now we understand why." Bennett chuckled, gesturing to me.

"Right?" Wren laughed, and my shoulders eased. She wasn't mad. She was proud. Excited. They all were.

"What do you think I should do?" I asked my family.

Everyone blurted something different, except Mom. I turned to her. "I think you should do whatever you think is best for you as a person and as a business."

"Whatever you decide," Dad said, clapping a hand on my shoulder, "we'll support you."

When I glanced at everyone, they were nodding. My heart was full. I only wished I'd told them sooner.

"I'm going to expect advance copies of every release going forward," Wren said, wagging her finger at me as the doorbell rang.

"That's probably the pizza," Dad said, heading for the stairs.

"I mean it," Wren said to me.

I laughed. "Done."

"And signed copies," she called as River tugged her toward the stairs.

"I already send you and Harper each a copy at the studio."

"Oh. Right." She laughed. "Okay. Fine."

Everyone headed down for dinner, but Mom hung back with me.

She cupped my cheeks. "I could not be more proud of you."

I dipped my chin, but she forced me to hold her gaze.

"I mean it, Liam. I've always believed you were a talented

writer. And I'm so glad you're sharing your gifts with the world."

"You don't think it's strange that your son writes romance?" I knew how much she loved books, especially romance, but still…

She jerked her head back. "Why on earth would you think that?"

I explained what had happened with Grandpa. I didn't think it was right to tell the whole family, but I needed to tell someone. I needed to understand.

"Oh, sweetheart." Her expression was pained.

I dipped my head. "It really made me question myself and my choices."

"I can imagine. And I'm not sure if this will make you feel better or worse, but toward the end, Grandpa was suffering from rapidly progressing dementia."

"He was?"

"We didn't find out until later, but yes. Doc Allen told me it can cause sudden changes in mood and behavior. Which would explain his uncharacteristic response to your news."

"You're right. That does make me feel both better and worse. I'm sad for him, but…"

"Relieved?" she offered.

"Yeah." It felt as if a weight had been lifted from my shoulders.

"Good. Because I know that Grandpa would never have been ashamed of you. He loved you."

She pulled me in for a hug, holding me close and tight. Just like she would've when I was a child. She smelled of books and roses, and I felt more at peace than I had in a long time.

"So, what happened with Penny?" she asked in a gentle tone after I'd had a minute to process this revelation.

I shook my head. "I asked her to move in with me," I said then explained what happened. The fight. Everything.

Mom nodded. "So you had a fight. But I have faith you two will work it out. Because what you and Penny have is…" She placed her hand over her heart. "It's all I ever wanted for you. Wren found it with Bennett, and now you have it with Penny."

"It's not…" I shook my head. This wasn't just a fight. "Besides, Wren and Bennett are different."

"Why? You think they're somehow more deserving of love?"

I shrugged, not entirely sure how to answer.

"You—" she tipped my chin up so that I was looking at her "—my darling, are worthy of a big love. A great love. A love that eclipses moons and sails among the stars. A love that is written in the very fabric of the universe. Undeniable. Immovable. Like gravity."

I laughed. "Did you just quote my own book to me?"

The corner of her mouth tipped up. "I couldn't have said it better myself."

"You must really like Penny," I joked.

"I do, but I love you even more. At the end of the day, your happiness is my sole concern. And I've never seen you as happy as you were with Penny."

I let out a heavy sigh. "Sorry to disappoint you, Mom. But I don't think it's going to happen."

"Bullshit."

I stared at her, mouth agape. I wasn't sure I'd ever heard my mom cuss.

"You're scared," she said.

"I-I—" I stammered. "What?"

She rolled her eyes. "Look, I get it. After what Diane did, no one is blaming you. But Penny is not Diane."

"I know *that*."

"Do you?" Mom asked. "Because as much as I know you want Penny to move here, I'm guessing some of your haste may have been motivated by fear."

"Fear?" I jerked my head back.

"Fear that she would get back with her ex? Fear that your relationship couldn't continue to withstand the distance? You tell me. What are you afraid of, Liam?"

Wow. Was Mom right? Was that why I'd pushed Penny so hard? Because, deep down, I was afraid of losing her?

And if so, how ironic was that? In my desire to cement our relationship, I'd pushed her away. I'd pushed too hard.

My mind went back to Diane. I'd pushed her away too, all because I was scared. I'd wanted to cling to her when life was changing too much for my comfort. And instead, I'd had the opposite effect.

And here I was, making the same mistake again, albeit for different reasons.

Did I really want to miss out on the chance to be with Penny because I was scared of losing her? How ridiculous was that? To sabotage any joy I might have because I was too afraid.

Mom tapped the side of her nose. "Ah. I see. The wheels are turning."

I nodded. "I think you might be right."

"Of course I am." She smirked. "Now what are you going to do about it?"

CHAPTER TWENTY-SEVEN

Penny

Ten long days passed in silence.

During that time, I'd buried myself in promo for the book, telling myself it was because we had a real chance of making one, if not more, best-seller lists. Liam and I emailed about business, but otherwise, we didn't talk. And the silence was glaringly obvious.

I knew he was pissed that I wouldn't move to the AV, but he wouldn't listen. Why couldn't he understand? Why couldn't he be patient, like he'd promised? Instead, he'd just kept pushing and pushing until I couldn't take it anymore.

I couldn't stay if it meant losing myself—my voice—again.

Unfortunately, while I could leave the AV, I couldn't avoid Liam entirely. We had a book to promote, and the readers were counting on us. Not only that, our businesses were on the line.

But all of that felt so…unimportant. Who cared about a love story when my own heart was breaking?

The more time that passed, the more I missed hearing his voice. The more I wondered if I'd made a mistake. I wondered if I was being a coward.

And now that *Brave Together* had been published, we'd have fewer reasons to talk. The thought should've filled me with relief, but all I felt was an overwhelming sense of dread.

It wasn't that I didn't love him. I did.

But why couldn't he understand that I needed more time? Why was he demanding a future together, but only on his terms?

I was responding to a comment on social media when there was a knock at the door. I padded over to the peephole.

"Let me in!" Brinkley called from the hallway.

"Hey." I opened the door and stepped aside for her to come in. My joggers were frumpy in comparison to her sparkly cocktail dress and heels. "Well, don't you look fabulous?"

"Thanks. Soon, you will too." She winked. "Get ready, Pen. We're going out!"

"Oh yeah?" I raised my brow, surprised by her attitude. She seemed more lighthearted and excited than she'd been in a long time. "What's the occasion?"

"Double celebration. Your book release, and..." She leaned in and grinned. "My new job."

"What? You got a new job?" When she nodded, I said, "Ink, that's great."

"I can't wait to tell you all about it." She steered me toward my bedroom. "Over drinks. You can get a nojito if you want. But let's get moving. You shower. I'll pick something for you to wear."

My shoulders slumped. I didn't want to disappoint her, but... "Ink—"

"Nope. No excuses." She shook her head, her lips set in a firm line. "I've let you wallow long enough."

I barked out a laugh. Even if she'd let me wallow for a lifetime, I wasn't sure it would be enough. I was miserable without Liam.

"Come on, Pen. We *always* celebrate your book releases," she said. "It's tradition."

"Okay. You're right," I huffed, heading toward the bathroom. A book release deserved a celebration, and so did her new job. "And I really want to hear about this new job."

When I returned from the shower, she held up two dresses—a red one that was tight and sexy and a floral patterned one with a plunging neckline. "This one or this one?"

I lifted a shoulder, trusting her sartorial judgment more than my own. "You pick."

She sighed and laid them both out on the bed before taking a seat at the edge of the mattress. "Have you talked to him lately?"

I shook my head. "Only about business stuff."

"You've certainly buried yourself in work lately. What are you going to do about the book signing at Bibliolater?"

I wanted to laugh at that question or maybe cry. Because it was the same one I'd been asking myself in my rare quiet moments.

Brinkley was right—I'd buried myself in work, trying to forget about Liam. But my heart wouldn't let me. And the idea of returning to the AV was… Well, I didn't know how I'd survive.

I let out a sigh and started applying my makeup before even considering responding. Previously, I would've been looking forward to the signing. Eager for another excuse to return to the AV and Liam. But so much had changed since then.

As much as I didn't want to go, I also knew I didn't have much of a choice. Debbie was counting on me, and the readers were too. I'd heard from a number of fans who planned to attend, some of them driving hours just to see me.

"I have to go," I finally admitted as much to myself as to Brinkley. "I promised."

I didn't know how I was going to do it. How I was going to face his mom. The AV. All the reminders of Liam. Let alone the man himself if it came down to it.

"I'm sure Debbie would understand if you canceled."

I shook my head. "I don't want to let her down. And a ton of readers preordered the book for the signing. This could impact her business and my relationship with my readers."

She grabbed one of the throw pillows from my bed, punching it down before leaning on it. "Will Liam be there?"

I stared at myself in the mirror, running my hands down my dress. It was easier to smooth the wrinkles in the fabric than soothe the ache in my heart.

"I have no idea."

"But part of you is hoping to run into him, right?"

I lifted a shoulder, but Brinkley wouldn't let me get away with my nonanswer. As hurt as I was, I still missed talking to him about the plot and characters as if they were real. I missed hearing the sexy rasp of his morning voice. I missed going to sleep with his words in my ear. I missed *him.*

"Have you considered calling him?" she asked.

"Only about a million times," I sighed.

"What's stopping you?"

"He wants to be together but only on his terms. Sound like anyone else you know?"

She furrowed her brow. "Erik?"

"Yes. He kept pressuring me to move in with him, even after I said I wasn't ready. And then he made me feel guilty for attending functions with Erik's family."

"Can't say I blame him for that. How would you feel if Liam was still spending holidays with his ex and her family?"

The idea made me want to vomit.

"That's what I thought," Brinkley said.

"Fine. You're right, but I have no interest in getting back together with Erik."

"Obviously. But you can see how it might look to Liam, right?"

My shoulders slumped. "Yeah." And that realization only made me feel even worse. I knew he'd been cheated on in the past, and while I'd done what I could to assure him, perhaps I should've been more sensitive. And firmer with my mom and Erik.

"Be honest. Do you have any interest in moving to the AV?"

"In the future? Absolutely."

"The future, as in when? A month? A year?"

"I don't know." I threw up my hands. "Does there need to be a timeline?"

"No. And please don't think I'm advocating for you to move. That's the last thing I want. But I know how hard city life can be, especially with your IBS. You love the AV, and you seemed happy with Liam."

"I was. And if he hadn't pushed me so hard to move, we would still be together."

"At some point, one or both of you was going to want to take that next step. The man loves you. Why is this a bad thing?"

"Because we haven't even been together for a year. He never wants to get married. And I'm afraid to give up my apartment and uproot my entire life in the hopes that he won't wake up someday and realize he doesn't want to be with me." My eyes went wide. Had I really just said all that?

"Oh boy," she sighed. "This is just like with Erik."

I frowned. "What are you talking about?"

"You were engaged to Erik. You were going to marry him. And yet, you were afraid to take that final step. You refused to get rid of your apartment."

"Do I need to remind you how hard it is to find good apartments in New York that don't cost an arm and a leg?"

"No." She shook her head. "But I don't think it was about that. I think it was about needing an escape plan. Needing an out for when—not *if*—things went south."

I stared at her slack-jawed. "Are you forgetting the fact that Erik left me?"

The smile she gave me was soft and yet filled with pity. But she was quiet, waiting for me to continue. Giving me the space to sort it out myself.

"I was with Erik for three years, and I'd known him for many years before that. And I still never saw it coming. Just like with my dad, I was completely blindsided."

She nodded. "And that has to be so hard. But, Penny." She wrapped her arm around me. "There was nothing you—or anyone—could've done."

I leaned into her touch. It didn't matter how many times I'd told myself. How many times I'd heard it from my therapist or anyone else. I still wondered...

A horn honked, then more joined in. There were sirens blaring. It made me miss the quiet serenity of the AV. I'd always felt so at home there. A sense of community and belonging.

"And there are some things you can't prepare for, no matter what you do," she finally said. "You have to take a risk and hope it works out."

"But what if it doesn't?" I asked.

"What if it does?"

I hadn't thought about that.

When had I stopped believing that happily ever afters could happen in real life? Who said they were attainable only in fiction? Or that men like the ones I wrote about couldn't exist?

"I'm scared," I finally admitted.

"What would a character in one of your novels do in this situation?" Brinkley asked. "Would she give up and live with a broken heart?"

I laughed. "No. Of course not." My readers knew that my stories came with a happily ever after guaranteed. "But I can control the outcome in my stories. I can make the characters behave how I want them to."

"But Liam isn't a character, and you can't control him."

"I know that," I sighed. "But I'm scared he'll change his mind about us without warning. That I'll lose myself in him, only for him to hurt me."

She couldn't deny it wasn't a risk.

"Have you read Brené Brown?" Brinkley finally asked.

"No," I sighed. "I'm sorry. I know you love her, and *Daring Greatly* is on my TBR list. But I haven't had time."

"Read it at some point, but for now, I'll give you the Brinkley's Notes version. Which is that trust is like a marble jar. We often think of trust as something that's broken in one big moment—"

"Like Erik leaving me at the altar."

"Yes. And that can definitely be the case. But a lot of times, it hinges on the little moments. The times that someone does something caring. That they turn toward us instead of away. When they show up again and again."

Hm. I could think of a million instances where Liam had turned toward me. He was always supportive about my IBS, going above and beyond to make sure I was comfortable. I mean, the things he'd done to make me feel welcome as a guest. He'd really paid attention. But it was more than that.

He'd always followed through on business commitments and personal ones. He'd always been supportive of me, as a writer and a person. He'd helped me grow in all areas of my life.

Liam had only ever encouraged me to be more of myself. To try new things. To use my voice.

And yet, when he'd asked me to move in with him, when he'd tried to give me something he thought I would want, I'd freaked out.

The longer I sat there, the more I realized how badly I'd screwed up. And all for what? An arbitrary timeline that seemed "reasonable"? When, really, I'd been clinging to some external metric to make myself feel more secure.

Nothing in life was guaranteed. Except for the fact that if I closed myself off to vulnerability, I'd *never* experience the depth of love or the true meaning of joy.

"I think I made a huge mistake," I finally admitted.

CHAPTER TWENTY-EIGHT

Penny

"Hey, Willa," I said, smiling at the alpaca as she trotted over to the fence to greet me. "It's good to see you again."

At least someone seemed happy to see me.

I'd landed in the AV an hour ago. I was disappointed but not surprised when Liam hadn't been at the airport to pick me up. He knew I was coming. Thanks to *The Vine*, everyone in the AV knew all about my visit.

I'd taken the local ride service, stopping by his house on the way to Alpaca Acres. He either wasn't home or hadn't answered, and I was afraid he didn't want to see me. Worse still, what if he'd gone to his cabin purely to avoid me?

I didn't have a plan. All I knew was that I wanted to see him. I wanted to talk to him.

And while I could've called him, this was the type of conversation you had in person. I'd realized that the timing didn't matter. There was no "right" way. And the only way to find out if this could work was to take the leap and trust that Liam would be by my side just as he'd always been. Because we were braver together.

"You're such a cutie, aren't you?" I watched as Willa ate some hay and nuzzled with Larry.

Finally, I forced myself to head to my yurt to get ready. Debbie was picking me up in an hour to attend the VIP wine tasting she'd arranged for some of Meghan's and my superfans. She'd also insisted on putting me up at Alpaca Acres, in addition to hosting a book signing at Bibliolater. I'd never felt like such a rock star.

Usually, I had to pay my own way for signings. Organize everything with Raven's help. This time, Debbie had taken care of everything. I wondered if she was doing it because she secretly wished Liam and I would get back together. Was it wrong that I hoped that was the case?

I sighed and started to unpack while sipping some peppermint tea. When that was finished, I showered and took my time getting ready, mostly in an effort to distract myself. All the while, I wondered when, or even *if*, I'd see Liam.

I'd been a coward before, but he made me want to be brave. I just hoped I wasn't too late.

Don't think like that. One way or another I was going to see him, and we were going to talk about this.

A while later, there was a knock at the door. "Penny. It's Debbie," she called in a chipper voice.

"Hey!" I was breathless, rushing to get my shoes on. "Be right there."

"Penny!" Debbie smiled brightly when I opened the door. "It's so good to see you."

I smiled and accepted her hug while one of the alpacas hummed loudly. "Thanks. It's good to see you too."

Debbie updated me on life in the AV as she drove, asking about my writing and how I'd been. The closer we got to town, the more my nerves increased until my anxiety was as big as the balls of yarn in the window of the knitting store—Get Knotty.

Everywhere we went, I looked for Liam. A few times, I even swore I'd seen him walking down the street, only to realize my mind was playing tricks on me.

"How's…everyone?" I asked Debbie as she turned toward the wineries. When, really, I wanted to know how Liam was.

"Good." She smiled, her eyes on the road. "Harper and I are planning Wren and Bennett's baby shower. It's going to have a *Great British Bake Off* theme."

I grinned. "That sounds fun." And like something the two of them would totally love.

"Bennett finally found a home for the last puppy," she said, turning on her indicator.

I smiled, remembering the day Liam and I had spent at Bennett's clinic, helping with the adorable pups. I glanced out the window and tugged at the corner of my eyes. Being back in the AV was even more emotional than I'd expected.

"I'm glad." I didn't mention that I'd seen that in *The Vine.*

I'd been reading the gossip blog religiously ever since I'd left. No mentions of Liam. One brief post about our book coming out and the signing. The VIP wine tasting had sold out almost immediately, which was gratifying.

Debbie hadn't disclosed the location to me, though I figured it was more of an oversight. And I hadn't asked, too afraid to know the answer.

I told myself it didn't matter. What mattered was that the money from the ticket sales was being donated to an organization that supported children's literacy, which pleased me.

I was grateful Debbie carried the conversation. I was far too nervous to contribute much beyond the basics. But I appreciated the distraction, especially as we neared Fall River Estates.

When she pulled off the road and into the parking lot of

the winery, I glanced over at her. Did she know this was where Liam and I had…

"Here we are," she said, putting the car in park.

I forced myself to smile and follow her inside. I had no idea how I was going to do this. How I was going to smile and pretend with the readers, when all I could think of was Liam and the last time we'd been here together.

The hostess smiled and greeted Debbie by name. "Right this way."

As we headed down the hall toward the dining room, the hostess paused in front of the tasting room. My heart was pounding so loud, it was the only thing I could hear. I held my breath as she pushed open the door.

I finally stepped inside, only to discover the room was empty. I didn't know why I'd expected Liam to be here. I hadn't called. Hadn't texted outside of discussing professional matters. And yet, I'd hoped he'd magically know I wanted to see him and be here. It just seemed like something he'd do.

Not that he could read my mind, but he was always very perceptive and attentive. Not to mention romantic. Arranging for us to see each other again at the winery where we'd had our meet-cute? That was totally something he'd do.

But he hadn't…

"Is something wrong?" Debbie asked.

"Oh, um—" I fidgeted with the strap on my purse, finally taking in the room. "No. Everything looks lovely."

"Great. I need to go check on a few things," Debbie said, giving my shoulder a gentle squeeze.

As soon as she was gone, my shoulders deflated. I trudged over to the table where several of my books were on display. As I got closer, I noticed a book I'd never seen before.

Love Like No Other," I said, frowning at the cover.

It was an object cover, almost designed like a scavenger

hunt. There were alpacas and peppermint leaves, books and other little details that reminded me of my time with Liam. I'd never heard of this book, but it had both our names on the cover as the authors. Our real names.

What the...

I opened the cover, and my hands were shaking so badly I nearly dropped it. A piece of paper fell to the floor. I reached for it and immediately recognized Liam's scrawl.

PENNY,

As you know, the best stories are the culmination of months of work. Draft after draft, honing the words until they're just right.

No book is perfect—fictional or not. But our story is as unique and beautiful as the romance novels we both love to create. And it's my favorite story yet.

I love you, and I want to keep writing our story—together. I promise to listen to your ideas and go at your pace. We'll find a method that works for us. I just want a chance at happily ever after with you.

Love,

Liam

I GASPED, GLANCING AROUND THE ROOM FOR ANY SIGN OF HIM. I couldn't believe he'd done this. *How* had he done this?

We'd been apart for a few weeks, and all this time, he'd been pouring his heart out into this story. *Our* story. It was incredible.

I shook my head and smiled at the first words on the page as I took a seat at the table. And then I lost myself in his words, in his storytelling that was both breathtaking and magical. It was our story. Our story from his point of view.

It was all there, from his first impressions of me to our

alpaca walk and even the last time I'd had dinner with his family. It was raw and honest and beautiful.

I cried as I pored over the pages, wanting both to savor his words and speed to the end. About halfway through, I got to this section.

THIS ISN'T THE END. IT'S JUST THE BEGINNING OF OUR HAPPILY ever after. I intentionally left these pages blank so we could write the rest together.

I want to be where you are. You are my heart, and I love you.
Let's build the life we want together. On our own terms.
Let's be brave together.

LOVE,
Liam

I FLIPPED THROUGH THE REST OF THE BOOK, AND THE PAGES were indeed blank. It was the best story I'd ever read. Certainly my new favorite by him, and it was the story of us.

I pulled out my phone to text him when the door opened. Liam appeared in the doorway, and I stilled. I took him in. From those soulful blue eyes I'd missed. To the hands that held me close. And the arms that kept me safe.

The door shut behind him with an audible click, emphasizing the fact that we were alone. After weeks apart. Weeks of silence. Liam and I were alone.

"Oh my god," I gasped, holding a hand to my mouth. "You're here."

He chuckled and took a tentative step forward. "Where else would I be?" His attention was focused solely on me. Drinking me in the same way I was eyeing him.

"I don't know." I stared at the floor, my confidence suddenly vanishing. "I stopped by your house earlier to talk…"

"You did?"

"Yes. I-I'm so sorry, Liam. I screwed up. I freaked out."

He shook his head and blew out a breath. "I'm sorry too. I'm sorry I didn't listen to you. I shouldn't have pressured you into moving here. I wanted—*want*—to be with you. And I only pushed so hard because I was afraid of losing you."

I nodded. "I should've been more sensitive to how you might feel about my relationship with Erik and his family. And you were right—I was scared. I was scared of losing myself and my voice, but I know you'd never let that happen."

He'd always given me the courage to speak up. To be honest about my wants and needs. And he'd always supported me as a writer, reminding me that the world needed my stories.

His expression was solemn. "I wouldn't."

"I'm sorry I ran. I don't want to make decisions based on fear anymore. I want to be brave together."

"Brave together." He smiled, taking my hands in his.

"I'm ready to start our next chapter. I love you, and my home is here. With you. In the AV."

"Fuck yes, it is." He cupped the back of my neck, his dark blue eyes intent on mine. "It hasn't been the same without you."

He flashed me a watery smile, cupping my cheek before crashing his lips to mine. His kiss was searing, and I'd forgotten how all-consuming Liam's touch could be. He was everywhere. It was everything.

"I love you," he said between kisses.

"I love you so much," I said, unable to stop touching him.

"God, it's good to be home." It hadn't truly felt like home until now. Until I was with Liam.

"How long are you here until you fly back to New York?"

I grinned. "I'm here to stay. I bought a one-way ticket and terminated the lease on my apartment." That was how confident I was in my decision. I didn't need an escape hatch, and I didn't want there to be any doubt in Liam's mind. Because there was certainly none in mine.

"Best thing I've ever heard." He tore at my clothes, but then I heard laughter echoing in the hallway.

"Um, Liam?" I asked, placing a hand to his chest. I was trying to catch my breath and hold on to my train of thought, but he was making both impossible.

"Yeah?" He didn't stop, his hands roaming my body, cupping my ass and pulling me into him.

I moaned at the feel of his erection nudging my center. "What about the VIP tasting?"

"Haven't you realized by now that I'm your number one fan?"

I giggled as he kissed his way down my neck. But then I pushed on his chest. "I'm serious. I don't want readers to bust in on us." Or Debbie. Talk about mortifying.

"They won't." He continued kissing me. Touching me. As if he were afraid I'd vanish if he stopped.

"How can you be so sure?" I asked.

"Because I *am* the VIP."

I frowned. "No one else came?"

"No one else was allowed to buy tickets."

I gaped at him. "What?" I glanced around. "Seriously? There's no VIP tasting?"

"That's right." He smirked. "Though I will certainly be tasting you."

I shook my head, but I couldn't hide my smile. "Liam Beaudin, you are something else."

"And you, Penelope Glasner, are mine."

Yes, I was. In every sense of the word.

And I didn't need a piece of paper or a wedding ring to tell me that. I just needed him. He was my happily ever after. But even that seemed trite in comparison to the depth of our love. We were made for each other, and our story was timeless.

He picked me up in his arms, and I laughed and squealed as he carried me over to one of the tall chairs that matched the height of the pub table. "I may be yours, but we are *not* reenacting our first night together."

"Maybe not all of it," he teased, pushing my dress up over my hips. "I'm not going to rip your dress," he said, pulling the straps down gently. "But I might rip your panties."

"Liam," I gasped as he palmed my breasts. His words and his touch were making it difficult to think straight. "Oh God."

He smirked. "Yes, dear?"

I rolled my eyes. "Were you always this full of yourself?" I teased.

"It's all thanks to you, my love. I mean—Meghan Hart Day? What did you think that was going to do to my ego?"

I laughed. "That's it. Meghan Hart Day is officially canceled from now on."

"Shut your mouth." And then he kissed me hard, claiming my mouth with passion and need. "Fuck, Penny. I need to be inside you."

"I need that too." I hissed when he started playing with my clit through my panties. He knew exactly how to touch me.

"It's been too long," he groaned when I reached into his jeans and started stroking his length.

He grabbed my panties, and the next thing I knew, he was

shredding them. I stared at him, mouth agape. "I would've taken them off."

"Not nearly as fun."

I pouted. "But I really liked those. Your mom bought them for me in St. Cecilia."

He closed his eyes and pinched the bridge of his nose. "Can we *please* not talk about my mom during sex?"

I smirked. "Only if you promise never to rip my underwear again."

"I'll buy you another pair. I'll buy you a pair in every color of the rainbow."

"Deal. Oh, and I want to add custom built-ins to the closet."

"Sure. Fine." He gnashed his teeth, rubbing a hand over his bulge. "Anything else?"

I laughed, knowing I was torturing him and loving every minute of it. "Mm." I tapped a finger to my lips. "I think we should adopt a dog."

"Anything you want."

"Anything?" I teased.

"Yes, Penny. *Anything.* If you want to adopt a dog, we'll adopt a dog. If you want to get married someday, we'll get married. Have kids. The whole nine yards."

I placed my hand over his heart, appreciating his willingness to compromise as well. "I don't care if we ever get married. I just want to be with you."

He placed his hand over mine. "I'm sure we'll figure out what's best for us. Together."

"Together."

He kissed me long and hard. A kiss that spoke of forever.

And then he kissed his way down my body until he was crouching in front of me. After that, I was silent apart from the cries of pleasure he evoked. He kept licking my clit, maintaining a steady rhythm until the pleasure built and built. Until I was immersed in a beautiful, incandescent light. And through it all, the scent of sunshine and happiness grounded me and made me smile.

I was still recovering when he stepped closer, cock in hand. He reached for his wallet when I stopped him. "I was tested recently, and I have an IUD."

"I haven't been with anyone but you, and I've been tested too." He lined himself up with my entrance. And then he slammed into me, stealing the breath from my lungs.

He gripped the back of my neck, his gaze intense as he thrust into me. Over and over again. Adding his thumb to my clit until my hips were bucking and we were both chasing our release.

"That's it," he said. "Come for me, Penny."

I shook my head. "Together," I panted. "I want to do it together."

"Always," he panted.

And then we fell over the edge. Because everything was better when we were together.

CHAPTER TWENTY-NINE

Liam

Six Months Later

I STARED AT THE SCREEN, WONDERING WHAT WAS MISSING FROM this chapter. I could've just asked Penny for advice, but I preferred to figure it out myself first. Besides, she was downstairs making breakfast and probably dictating the next chapter in her novel. Though her wrist was fully functional, it tired easily. And she'd discovered that she actually enjoyed dictating once she'd gotten the hang of it.

I stood and stretched, gave Bailey a pat on the head. Made a lap around the office then returned to my seat.

A few weeks after Penny had moved in, Bailey had joined us. She was a lively and energetic Cavalier King Charles Spaniel, but she seemed happiest hanging out on the daybed in the attic. Penny and I had named her after the main character in *Brave Together*. And as much as I loved Bailey, I hoped getting another dog for every new coauthored release wasn't going to become a tradition. Even as adorable as she was.

I checked my emails, responding to a few as Meghan. The new branch of the library would be completed soon, and the mayor—who also happened to be Tessa's mom—was trying to schedule the grand opening party. I was looking forward to the completion of the new library, but it was also bitter-sweet. I knew it was a space Tessa would absolutely love, but she'd never get to see it.

I continued to visit her at the cemetery and talk to her, and so much had changed in the year and a half since her death. The grass had grown over on her grave. Her children were getting bigger every day. And Tristan had seemed happier lately. I had a feeling it had something to do with Ellie, and I secretly wondered if there was more to it than her helping with the kids for the summer.

Though, the summer had ended months ago, and she'd moved to Japan. And she seemed to have taken his good mood with her.

I seriously doubted they'd hooked up, but it was fun to imagine for a story. If Tristan and Ellie were characters in a romance novel, what would their tropes be?

He was thirteen years older than her. Age gap. *Yes.*

Late wife's sister. *Oof.* That sounded taboo and angsty as fuck.

That could definitely be a hot story. Not that Tristan would ever act on it. But still…I grabbed a pad and pen. I had to write this down. I started scribbling on the page.

She was living with his family for the summer. Helping with his kids. *Boom!* Forced proximity.

"What are you doing?" Penny asked, startling me from my thoughts.

"Working on a story."

She narrowed her eyes at me. "Let me guess. It's not the one you're supposed to be working on."

"No, but—"

"Oh boy." She shook her head.

I grabbed her waist and pulled her into my lap. She squealed, writhing when I started kissing her neck.

"Listen to this," I said. "Widower and single dad. His late wife's much younger sister. Forced proximity."

"Holy shit. That sounds hot."

"Right?"

I hung my head. The more I thought about it, the more wrong it felt. Capitalizing on Tristan's pain. And while I wanted him to find another happily ever after, I wasn't sure I could be the one to give it to him. "You should write it."

"What?" She jerked her head back. "Why? It's your idea."

"I based it on Tristan and Ellie."

"Ohh." She gasped, her eyes going wide. "Do you think they…?"

I shook my head. "No. No way." Though… "No. I just was using them as inspiration."

"We could write it together," she offered, trailing a finger over my cheekbones, down my jaw. Then my neck.

"Hmm. Tempting," I said, referring more to the way she was touching me. Though I was always game to write another book together.

I smoothed my hands up her ribs, over her breasts, squeezing them through her shirt. This was the best part of working at home together. She rarely wore a bra, and we could have sex whenever and wherever we wanted.

"Mm." She moaned. "I signed us up for sweet potatoes and cranberry fluff for Friendsgiving."

"Excellent. When does Brinkley fly in?"

"The nineteenth."

"And your mom?" I asked, hoping to make a good impression on both of them.

"The twenty-first, but she's going to stay with your parents."

"Great." I captured her lips with mine, kissing her slowly. Savoring the taste of her as I nipped at her lips. Tangled my tongue with hers.

I continued to palm her through her shirt, and Penny moaned. The sound went straight to my cock, and I ached to be inside her.

Bailey barked, and I squeezed my eyes shut. "Get naked. I'll put Bailey in her crate."

Penny laughed, nearly falling over herself in excitement as she climbed off my lap. "Deal."

I set Bailey up with some toys and food then returned to the office. Penny was naked as promised, kneeling on the floor with her hands behind her back.

"Oh fuck." I groaned into my fist, recognizing the scene she'd set. It was just like the one in the romance novel we'd been listening to together at night before bed. "We're doing that one now?"

She nodded, though the movement was barely perceptible. She was really committed to staying in character. And that suited me just fine. Because, damn, this was hot.

I walked to my desk, my eyes on Penny the entire time. On the delicate slope of her back. The flare of her hips and curve of her ass. *Mm. Mm. Mm.*

I rummaged around in our toy box—we'd decided against a trophy wall of toys and dildos since River came up here from time to time. But we'd gone through the rest of them and kept the ones we liked or wanted to try.

Since I was trying to stay true to the scene, I grabbed a silk blindfold, and a flogger. I let the lid of the chest fall, watching Penny when she jumped.

"You okay?"

She nodded again.

"Need to hear you say it, princess," I said, paraphrasing from the book.

She was breathless when I took her chin in my hand, her big brown eyes peering up at me with lust and trust. Love and a twinge of excitement.

"Yes," she whispered.

I lifted her chin. "Say it again, Princess. Tell me what you want."

"I—" She swallowed hard as I moved my hand down her neck, keeping my grip loose. "I want you."

Her breasts were magnificent, and I was tempted to touch them. But then I knew she'd scold me for breaking the scene. And I *really* didn't want to break this scene. I had a feeling we were both going to enjoy it.

"What's your safe word?" I said, knowing she wouldn't need it. I would never push her *that* far, but it was fun to pretend.

"Pickles."

I tried not to laugh as I slipped the blindfold over her head. "Good."

Her breasts were begging for my touch. But not yet. I wanted to please her, and that meant sticking to the script. I was supposed to be the Dom, but it felt more like she was the one in control.

I unzipped my pants and pulled out my cock, teasing her mouth with it. She parted her lips, her breath warm on my skin. Driving me fucking wild. There was no way I was going to make it through the whole scene. No fucking way.

I staggered backward and admired her. Dragged the flogger gently over her shoulder and down her back. She shivered, goose bumps rising on her skin.

"Crawl to the bed," I said. Even blindfolded, she obeyed. "Climb onto it and get on your knees."

She did as I'd asked, presenting her perfect ass for me. *Goddamn.*

I smoothed the leather tail of the flogger with my hands. Enjoying the weight and feel of it as I padded closer to Penny. And then I used it to give her a tap on the ass. Gentle but startling all the same. At least, I assumed it was startling since Penny jolted, gasping at the same time.

"Do you remember your safe word?" I asked.

She nodded.

"Princess?" I growled.

"Yes."

"Good. Do you need to use it?"

"No, Sir."

Satisfied, I reared back and let the flogger hit her ass with a pleasing thwack. She whimpered, but I knew it was a sound of pleasure and delight. So I kept going. All the while, she moaned and wiggled her ass, gripping the sheets but never saying her safe word.

Finally, I made my way over to her and smoothed my hand over her ass. Her skin was pink, but I could smell her arousal. And when I slid my thumb over her pussy, it was dripping.

I pried her cheeks apart and pressed my lips to her folds. She let out a deep, throaty moan. So I kept at it, devouring her like a starved man. Until finally, I flipped her over onto her back and spread her legs.

The blindfold had already shifted, and I tore it off. *Fuck it.* I needed to see her. Connect with her. So what if I was going a little off script? It didn't seem like she was going to complain.

I kissed my way up her body. When she reached for my

hair, I stood once more. "Keep your hands to yourself until I say otherwise."

The corner of her mouth lifted. But apart from her dreamy smile, she stayed in character. "Yes, Sir."

But then a moment later, it was as if she'd forgotten. And she was reaching for my pants again. Trying to touch me through them.

"Princess." I narrowed my eyes at her, power and desire flowing through me to her.

She pulled her lip into her mouth, and it was my undoing. Suddenly, I didn't care that I was breaking the scene. I didn't care about anything but making her feel good.

I smashed my lips to hers, settling over her so that my arms were bracketing her head.

"You'd make a terrible Dom," she teased, laughing between kisses.

"You're one to talk. Miss Disobedience."

She stuck her tongue out at me. "That's part of the fun. Now, aren't you going to punish me for it?" she asked with a cheeky grin.

"Mm. Later. You liked the flogging, huh?" We hadn't tried it before, and while I could tell she enjoyed it, I wanted to hear it from her lips.

"God, yes. It felt amazing."

"Maybe I need to start spanking you more too."

"Mm," she moaned when I turned my attention to her nipples, taking my time to address each one thoroughly. Her hands were in my hair, on my shoulders. "Yes, please."

"I love you," I panted as she arched her hips against me. "You are my heart, and—" I squeezed my eyes shut. If she kept doing that, I was going to come.

When I opened my eyes, she was peering up at me with such love and trust that I was in awe. Honored. "I love you."

We could act out any scene. We could pretend to be any

characters. But I liked who we were best of all. Who I was when I was with her. And who she was with me. Because it was only with each other that we'd found the safety and courage to be our true selves.

PENNY'S FEET POUNDED ON THE STAIRS UP TO OUR OFFICE. MY heart started beating the same cadence. Bailey lifted her head and barked.

We'd been on baby watch for weeks. Wren had already gone to the hospital once with false labor pains, and while she had a planned C-section, I was worried the baby would come before then. We all were.

"Wren's in labor," Penny called. "They're headed to the hospital."

"What?" I leaped out of my seat and headed for the stairs, nearly tumbling down them in my haste. It didn't help that Bailey was constantly underfoot. "Ugh. Bailey, stop." I picked her up and carried her down to the laundry room. "Sorry, girl. Gotta go help your aunt Wren."

I gave her a little hug, nuzzling her fur. I put her in her crate and shut the laundry room door behind me. But when I went to grab my keys from the bowl on the counter, they were missing.

Penny jingled the keys and shook her head. "I'll drive."

"But you'll go too slow," I whined, following her out to her new car, a VW SUV.

"And you'll end up getting a speeding ticket," she said, heading for the driver's side.

She was probably right, but still… I was impatient to get

to the hospital. Bennett had to be freaking out, and River would need someone to hang out with, and…

I was so worried about Wren, and if Bennett was with River, then she was all alone. After what had happened with her ex Kade, I wanted to make sure she felt nothing but love and support. Especially from Bennett.

"Hey," Penny said, placing her hand on my thigh. "It's going to be okay."

I blew out a breath as she pulled out of the driveway. "I hope so."

When we arrived at the hospital, Penny dropped me off and went to park. I headed inside and asked for directions at the front desk. I sped down the halls, following the signs for Labor and Delivery. When I reached the waiting area, Bennett glanced up and smiled with relief. River ran over to me, clinging to my legs.

"Hey. I've got River. Go be with Wren, yeah?"

He nodded. "I can't believe we're going to meet our baby."

My smile was so big, it nearly split my face. "Not if you stay out here all afternoon." I shooed him toward the door. "Now, go."

He chuckled and jogged toward the doors, already in his scrubs.

"Hey, kiddo." I ruffled River's hair. "This is exciting, huh?"

River nodded, though his expression was somber. I led him over to some chairs, and we sat down. He was abnormally quiet, and I waited for him to say something, but he didn't.

"You okay?" I asked.

He nodded quickly.

"Hey!" Penny said, breathless. She pushed her hair aside, slowing as she likely read the serious mood of the room. "Hey, Riv." She sank down next to him and pulled him into a hug. "How are you?"

"I'm scared," River whispered, and I was glad he'd decided to open up to her.

"That's totally understandable," Penny said. "You love your mom, and you want her and the baby to be okay."

River nodded. "I'm worried she's going to die like Miss Tessa."

Penny frowned. "Savannah's mommy was sick. But your mommy is having a baby. And that's an exciting thing, even if it feels a little scary too."

"Yeah," River said, scrunching up his nose. "I don't like it here. It smells funny. And there are weird noises."

"I'm not sure many people *like* hospitals," Penny said. "But the doctors and nurses are here to help people. Your mom has a great team taking care of her. And she has your dad there with her. And she knows that you're out here, supporting and loving her."

"Yeah, but Miss Tessa had all that too, didn't she? And she still died." River dropped his shoulders.

Penny and I shared a quick glance. River had always been tenderhearted, and while I'd known Tessa's death had impacted him, I hadn't realized the extent of it until now. Though I guess I should've anticipated it would've hit him harder, considering he was best friends with Tessa's daughter, Savannah.

I racked my brain for something to say to reassure him. To help him feel less afraid.

"My dad died when I was young too. I wasn't as young as Savannah, but I wasn't much older either."

"He did?" River asked.

"Yep. And it was really hard. But you know what got me through?"

"What?"

"My best friend, Brinkley. She was always there for me.

Just like I know you and Aiden are always there for Savannah."

River perked up. "We are. We totally are."

"I know you are." She smiled at him. "And Savannah has lots of people who love her and watch out for her, just like you do. You have your dad, your grandparents, Uncle Liam, and now, me."

He wrapped his arms around her waist. "Thanks, Penny."

"Anytime," she said, holding him close. "Anytime, kiddo," she said more softly, smoothing her hand over his hair.

Damn. How did she do that?

More than anyone, she seemed to just *get* River. We all loved River. We were all supportive and accepting. But Penny understood his emotional needs better than anyone else. And it only made me love her more.

Even before Penny, our family had been complete. But she made it whole.

"Thank you," I mouthed over River's head. Penny smiled back at me.

I went to get us some snacks from the cafeteria. And by the time I'd returned, Mom and Dad had arrived. Dad and Penny were talking with River.

"Hey, sweetheart," Mom said. "You doing okay?"

I nodded, though that was mostly because I knew I had to stay calm for River. I was sure Bennett would text or come out to update us when he could. And I tried not to take his silence as an indication of bad news.

"What story are you working on?" Mom asked, and I knew it was mostly to distract me.

I dragged a hand through my hair. "The Olympic skier."

"Ooh. I can't wait to read that one."

"Thanks. I'm excited about it. It's been a nice change of pace." And fun to research. "Penny and I are planning a trip to Vail."

"That will be fun. And Penny's working on her wedding series, right?"

I nodded. "Yep."

"Who do you think will finish first?"

I choked on my laughter at her seemingly innocent question. Penny's eyes met mine, and her smile told me she was thinking the same thing. Which was why I answered, "Penny. Penny always finishes first."

Penny bit her lip as her cheeks turned pink. But she knew it was true. I always made sure she came first and often. It was a rule in our house. Just like we had a rule that we didn't talk about work in the evenings or on the weekends. And we would always put our relationship first.

"When are you going to write another book together?" Mom asked, as she often did.

She wasn't even pushing us to get married or have kids. She just wanted to know when our next book baby would be published. We definitely wanted to write more books together in the future, but we also wanted to continue to write our own stories too.

Brave Together had been a best seller for several weeks. Readers had raved about it and continued to do so. Mom could barely keep the signed paperbacks stocked before they'd sell out again. It had taken both Penny's and my career to new levels.

"Probably after we finish our current projects."

"Good. I'm not the only reader begging for it, you know."

I chuckled and pulled her into my side. "I know, Mom. I know."

Finally, after what felt like forever, Bennett emerged from behind the doors. "It's a girl!"

There were congratulations all around, and then he offered to take River back first to meet the new baby—Hazel.

My parents had gone to grab coffee, and I wrapped my arms around Penny. "Thank you."

"For what?" she asked, turning to face me.

"Being amazing. For not being afraid to be you."

She smirked. "It's only because you made me feel safe to be myself."

"Yeah, but what you did with River..." I shook my head. "You're really good with him."

She tucked her hair behind her ear. "River's a great kid. He's already got a lot more figured out than I did at his age."

"Yeah?" I tilted my head to the side. "Like what?"

"River's not afraid to express himself. To be loud. To have emotions. To take up space."

I smiled and shook my head. "No. He's not. And I love that about him."

"For years, I was afraid of being seen as 'too emotional.'"

I scowled, and she laughed and tried to smooth away the lines in my face.

"Thank you for loving me as I am," she said. "I'm so glad I found you."

I pulled her close, holding her to me. "So am I, Penny. So am I. You are the best thing that's ever happened to me."

"Even better than writing romance?" she teased.

"Yes," I said. "Even better than writing romance. Because when I'm with you, I'm myself. I give you all of me, and I love all of you."

"Always," she said, kissing me.

"Always," I repeated.

I couldn't have written a better ending myself. But that was the beauty of our story; our happily ever after was just beginning.

CHAPTER THIRTY

Penny

Brinkley spun around in a circle, the gravel parking lot crunching beneath her heeled booties. "Can you believe it's sixty-four degrees? On Thanksgiving?"

"Right?" I laughed and peered up at the beautiful blue sky. "God, I love living in the AV."

I met Liam's eyes that were the same color as the sky, the color of home and happiness, and we smiled.

I'd moved to the AV over six months ago, and I'd never second-guessed my decision. I loved small-town life. I loved Liam and his family and the sense of community. I delighted in running into people at the grocery store and having them greet me by name. Plus, the amazing food and the weather.

"And we're having Thanksgiving at a winery," Brinkley said on a sigh. "With free parking. It really is perfect here."

"Does that mean you're going to move here?" I teased, knowing how much she loved her new job for the famous self-made female billionaire Sloan Mackenzie. Even if it meant we didn't get to see each other as often.

"No, but I'll definitely vacation here every chance I get."

I nodded. "Good."

Liam held open the door to Fall River Estates, and we were greeted by a steady hum of conversation. We weren't the first to arrive, and I'd spotted Tristan's SUV in the parking lot, along with Debbie's and a few other cars I recognized.

I'd been looking forward to my first AV Thanksgiving for weeks. Ever since I'd read about it in *The Vine* last year. The whole town came together to celebrate, and everyone was invited. It was a tradition started by Harper and Enzo a few years ago, and I was excited to be part of it.

Harper waved to us, beckoning us in. Enzo stood on one side of her, his wedding ring glinting against his olive skin as he ran a hand through his hair. On her other side was a tall blonde.

When the other woman turned to face us, I realized it was the famous wedding planner Juliana Wright. I'd seen her around town a few times since moving here. She and her husband, Harrison, had a vacation home. But I didn't recognize the other women standing with them, or their partners.

"Hey. Welcome." Harper smiled. "Happy Friendsgiving."

"Happy Friendsgiving," I said. "Thank you for inviting us. Harper, this is my best friend, Brinkley. She's visiting from New York."

"Oh, awesome. Nice to meet you, Brinkley," Harper said. "You've met Juliana." She indicated to the blonde. "And I'll have to introduce you to Lauren and Alexis. They're visiting from LA with their families."

"I'd love that. Maybe after we ditch the food. Where should we put our dishes?"

Harper gestured to a long serving table overflowing with covered plates. "Anywhere you can find an empty space on the table. We tried to label it by group, but it always ends up a bit crazy."

"That's part of the fun." Brinkley grinned.

"Very true. It's much more of an adventure that way."

I laughed. "You got it."

Brinkley and I went over to the table and set down our offerings before glancing around. Fall River Estates was always beautiful, but this was my favorite time of year to visit. It was a big part of the reason I'd planned my ill-fated wedding to Erik during the fall.

It was funny to think of how many big life moments this vineyard had seen me through. I'd been left at the altar here. I'd met Liam here. Then, after we'd broken up, this was where Liam and I had reunited. And now, it was a regular gathering place for my friends and me. Not just for Friends-giving, but all the time.

Today, the tables were topped with vases of local wild flowers from Alpaca Acres. The bouquets were a testament to fall—gorgeous reds and deep oranges, a mix of colors and textures that somehow all looked beautiful together.

"Are you thinking about your wedding day?" Brinkley asked.

I laughed. "Yeah. I was, actually. I'm grateful for how everything turned out."

"So am I," Brinkley said, nudging me with her elbow. "I really like Liam. And I really like the two of you together."

"Thank you. I'm glad." Brinkley's opinion meant a lot to me.

But she didn't have to tell me how much she liked him for me to know. She'd only been here a few days, and already they seemed like old friends.

She smiled. "Crazy how much has changed in a year, isn't it?"

I nodded. "Yeah. But it's good change. I mean, look at my mom." We both glanced over to where she was walking around with Hazel, talking to the newborn. "I haven't seen her this happy in years."

"Do you think she'll move here?"

"I hope so. I asked her to."

"Wow." Brinkley smiled. "That's big."

After everything that had happened with Erik and then my accident, my mom and I had grown a lot closer. We had a better relationship than we'd had in years, and I wanted to spend more time with her. Not just at the holidays.

When Debbie had heard my mom was coming for Thanksgiving, she'd insisted on putting her up at her house. She said it would allow Brinkley and me to have time together. But I knew Debbie secretly wanted to get to know my mom. I appreciated that Liam's parents had welcomed Mom into the family as quickly as they had me.

"Mm. Who's *that*?" Brinkley asked.

Asher had just walked in, carrying a large tray of pastries. "Asher Hansley. Famous pastry chef. One of Liam's best friends."

"He's hot. And, damn. So is that guy." She tilted her head to indicate Tristan. "I mean, those forearms." I smirked, watching as he lifted his son Maddox over his shoulder. "Mm."

I laughed, but I only had eyes for one man, and he was on the opposite side of the room, talking with Doc Allen and his wife, Linda.

"What's his story?" Brinkley asked, still focused on Tristan.

"Tristan?"

"Yeah. If that's the name of the tall, dark-haired man with the cute kid. I didn't see a wedding ring."

"He's a great guy, but…I get the impression his love life is complicated," I added, unwilling to say more. I had a feeling Liam's theory about Tristan and Ellie was more accurate than he imagined.

"What about Asher?"

"Very *uncomplicated*," I said. "But, Ink—" I placed my hand on her arm when she stepped forward in Asher's direction. "Be careful. Gossip spreads quickly, and everyone in the AV is here. Which means V from *The Vine* is likely watching."

"Ooh. So scared," she joked, shaking her hands as if she were frightened. Then she laughed. "It's a local gossip blog, not the *New York Times*."

"Okay, but don't say I didn't warn you."

"Consider me duly warned." And then she headed in Asher's direction.

I stood there, reveling in the scene before River ran up to me. "Hey, Penny!"

"Hey, Riv. Why are you out of breath? Are you okay?"

"Just—" He panted, hands planted on his knees. "Playing a game with Savannah and Aiden. Oh, and some of Aiden's mom's friend's kids."

I laughed. "That was a mouthful."

"I know." He stuck out his tongue. "But I forgot their names already." He cringed.

I laughed. "Just ask again. Or wait until another kid uses their name."

He perked up. "Great idea!"

"Have you seen your mom?"

He turned and pointed across the room. "Over with Dad."

"Thanks. I'm going to go say hi."

"'Kay. Bye!" River ran off, joining his friends once more.

I shook my head with a laugh and headed over to join Bennett, Wren, and Liam, whose back was to me. When I got there, I realized Liam was now holding baby Hazel, and her lips were parted in sleep, her long, dark eyelashes fluttering softly against the skin of her cheeks.

"Oh, she's so beautiful," I cooed, taking a seat next to Liam as I turned to Wren. "How do you not take a million pictures a day?"

"She does," Bennett said with a wry smile, toying with her bare shoulder where her sweater was artfully draped.

"Hey," she chided. "I'm not the one crying every night because 'our baby's growing up too fast,'" she teased, but we all knew it wasn't a joke.

Hazel had everyone wrapped around her little finger, especially Bennett and Liam. It was pretty funny, but also incredibly adorable. She'd only been here a few weeks, and already, she was more loved than she could ever know.

Soon, it was time for dinner, and Liam carefully handed Hazel back to her dad. We joined everyone at the table, taking our seats for a toast.

My mom was sandwiched between Debbie and Doc Allen, and I wasn't sure I'd seen her this at ease in years. She winked at me from across the table, mouthing, "Love you." I smiled and placed my hands over my heart, hoping she knew just how happy I was to have her here.

Brinkley leaned in to whisper something to me, and I laughed. When I settled back in my chair, Liam draped his arm over my shoulder, pulling me to him for a kiss.

A little over a year ago, we'd been gathered here for an entirely different reason. And as I thought back to what would've been my wedding day, it was with gratitude. At the time, I couldn't see the future. I couldn't see how being a jilted bride might be the best thing to ever happen to me. How it would lead to meeting Liam and collaborating with Meghan Hart and finding a place where I belonged.

And as Enzo spoke of gratitude for family, love, and community, I knew I was exactly where I was meant to be. And I finally had everything I'd ever wanted and so much more.

And it was only just the beginning.

Want to see grumpy, single dad Tristan find a second chance at happily ever after with his late wife's younger sister? Keep reading for a sneak peek!

Read *A Love Like That* now
(Free with Kindle Unlimited)

Love playlists, reading recommendations from Penny and Liam, and other bonus goodies? Sign up for Jenna's newsletter and have the exclusive content delivered straight to your inbox!

Click here to sign up!

PENNY & LIAM'S FAVORITE WRITING RESOURCES

Since the publication of our debut collaboration, *Brave Together*, Penelope and I have received numerous requests for our favorite writing resources. We have compiled a list of podcasts, books, and other resources that we've found helpful. We hope it helps you too!

Podcasts

The Screenwriting Life Podcast with Megh LeFauve & Lorien McKenna

Self Publishing Authors (SPA Girls) Podcast

Wish I'd Known Then for Writers Podcast with Jami Albright & Sara Rosett

Books

Deep Work by Cal Newport

Essentialism by Greg McKeown

Write Naked by Jennifer Probst

Creating Great Character ARCs by KM Weiland

The Plot Whisperer by Martha Alderson

Romancing the Beat by Gwen Hayes

Make a Scene by Jordan Rosenfeld

Goal, Motivation, Conflict by Debra Dixon

Happy Writing!
Meghan & Penelope <3

BIBLIOLATER STAFF PICKS

Bibliolater is an indie bookstore located in downtown Alondra on Main Street. We are proud to feature a wide array of books, and are the sole outlet for signed paperbacks of Meghan Hart novels. We hope you'll join us for our annual Meghan Hart Day celebrating our favorite local author to raise funds for the community.

Please stop by anytime. Our friendly and knowledgeable staff are always happy to help find the perfect book for you.

Here are a few of our staff member's favorite reads.

Debbie
Owner

Debbie has been obsessed with books even before she could walk. She's the proud owner of Bibliolater, and loves having the opportunity to share her passion for the written word while serving the community.

1. *The Ghostwriter* by Alessandra Torre
2. *Becoming Cliterate* by Laurie Mintz
3. *Brave Together* by Meghan Hart & Penelope Glass*
4. *Nothing Feels Better* by Brit Benson
5. *Unpredictable* by Jenna Hartley
6. *Atlas Shrugged* by Ayn Rand
7. The Filthy Rich Americans series by Nikki Sloan
8. The Harris Brothers series by Amy Daws
9. The Bergman Family series by Chloe Liese

Lizzie
General Manager

Lizzie loves nothing more than escaping into a world where anything can exist from vampires to dragons. She wants to experience something different and new. And she resents having to narrow down a list of favorite books.

1. *The Once and Future Witches* by Alix Harrow
2. Neon Gods series by Katee Robert
3. The Secondborn series by Amy A. Bartol
4. The Blood and Ash series by Jennifer Armentrout
5. The Six of Crows series by Leigh Bardugo
6. A Court of Thorns and Roses series by Sarah J. Maas
7. Throne of Glass series by Sarah J. Maas
8. The Legend series by Marie Lu
9. The Folk of the Air series by Holly Black
10. The Nevernight Chronicle series by Jay Kristoff
11. The Ice Planet Barbarians series by Ruby Dixon

Kristen
Book Buyer

When she's not reading a book, Kristen can be found strolling through the AV, listening to her latest audiobook. She loves books in all forms, chocolate, and her rescue puppy. In her free time, she volunteers at the animal shelter.

1. *Iona Iverson's Rules for Commuting* by Clare Pooley
2. *Carrie Soto is Back* by Taylor Jenkins Reed
3. *Lessons in Chemistry* by Bonnie Garmus
4. *Project Hail Mary* by Andy Weir
5. *The Song of Achilles* by Madeline Miller
6. *The Last Mrs. Parrish* by Liv Constantine
7. *Outlander* by Diana Gabaldon

Eli
Bookseller

Eli's a recent college grad who loves to read poetry, general fiction, LGBTQ+ fiction, and memoirs. They like board games, smashing the patriarchy, and have a general aversion to cooking.

1. *Us* by Sarina Bowen & Elle Kennedy
2. *Red, White & Royal Blue* by Casey McQuiston
3. *Work for It* by Talia Hibbert
4. *Real Queer America* by Samantha Leigh Allen

Jade
Book Buyer

Jade is passionately curious. She's fluent in three languages, has traveled extensively, and is training to be a pastry chef.

Jade is obsessed with books and dreams of having her own giant home library some day.

1. *Anxious People* by Fredrik Backman
2. *The Reading List* by Sara Nisha Adams
3. *The Good Neighbor* by Maxwell King
4. *The Push* by Ashley Audrain
5. *The Henna Artist* by Alka Joshi
6. *Why We Sleep* by Matthew Walker
7. *Same Kind of Different as Me* by Ron Hall and Denver Moore with Lynn Vincent

Brave Together is a fictional work written by Penny and Liam in *Love Like No Other*. The rest of the books listed are real and can be found at your favorite bookshop.

Book Signing & VIP Tasting

POSTED: MAY 6, 2023

To celebrate the release of *Braver Together* by Meghan Hart and Penelope Glass, Bibliolater is hosting a special book signing. Penelope Glass will be attending, and the event is free of charge.

Bibliolater is also hosting a VIP Wine Tasting with Penelope Glass at Fall River Estates. All proceeds benefit Dolly Parton's Imagination Library. Tickets are selling fast, so be sure to stop by Bibliolater or call to snag one for yourself.

<3 V

A Big Hart

POSTED: APRIL 4, 2023

Thanks to Bibliolater, Meghan Hart, and the generous people of the AV, the library received $20,000 from Meghan Hart Day. This will be an annual event going forward, and Bibliolater would love to hear what charities you think should be considered as future recipients for next year's donation.

<3 V

SEARCH HERE

ALONDRA VALLEY
FARMERS MARKET

Fresh and Locally
Grown Produce
Gifts & Goods

Every Saturday 9am-2pm

Alpaca Acres

Comings & Goings

POSTED: MARCH 16, 2023

After spending nearly two years in Australia, Eleanor "Ellie" Curran is coming home. Please give this AV native a warm welcome if you see her around town.

<3 V

Ring My Bell

POSTED: FEBRUARY 28, 2023

Wedding bells are ringing today. Wren Beaudin is tying the knot with Bennett Nash. We are so happy for this couple and wish them all the best, even if we are sad to see Dr. Sexy off the market for good.

All of the AV will be at the wedding, with no shortage of eligible bachelors. The groomsmen are particularly delicious.

Who's calling dibs on Bennett's sexy best friend (and brother of the bride), Liam Beaudin? Rumor has it he's been getting cozy with a romance author. And no, it's not Meghan Hart.

Asher Hansley is certainly available. Or is he? Sometimes it's so difficult to tell.

Wishing you all love on this beautiful day.

<3 V

Come relax let us take care of you.

5-star Spa & Resort in St. Cecilia

Tea with the Mayor

POSTED: DECEMBER 1, 2022

AVers,

Join Mayor Curran this Friday, December 4 at 4pm for a holiday tea at City Hall. She'll be talking about upcoming city initaitives and answering questions.

There will be a tree-lighting ceremony following the tea. Please join us downtown for this event. It's free to all and includes carols, games, and a scavenger hunt for the kids.

<3 V

Library News

POSTED: NOVEMBER 22, 2022

After a long search, a new site has been selected for the new branch of the library. Liam Beaudin has graciously offered a portion of his property in Cortina to be used for the library. It will be named for late librarian and AV sweetheart, Tessa Lockwood.

The library is raising funds for construction and to help expand the book collection. Please visit their website for details.

<3 V

Live Music Thursday Nights
Wine Flights 1/2 off

11616 FM 428
Fall River, CA 98145

Friendsgiving

POSTED: NOVEMBER 12, 2022

AVers,

You're invited to attend the annual Friendsgiving celebration at Fall River Estates. Everyone is welcome to this potluck dinner on November 22 from 3pm until...whenever. Sign up to bring a dish at www.fallriverestates.com

Everyone welcome!

<3 V

Adopt-a-Dog

POSTED: OCTOBER 28, 2022

AVers,

Looking for a new companion? There's an entire litter of pups at the Alondra Valley Animal Clinic. Dr. Nash is seeking loving homes for these adorable fluffballs.

Please call 707-AV-CLINIC (707-282-5464) for details.

<3 V

Come check out
our new yurts!

133 Sparkle Lane
Alondra Valley, CA 98175

Kick Axe New Place

POSTED: OCTOBER 13, 2022

AVers,

We have it on good authority that a new axe-throwing place is coming to town. It's one of several new developments that were recently approved by the City. And certainly one of the most intriguing.

<3 V

It Pays to Read

POSTED: OCTOBER 4, 2022

Has anyone else seen the contests popping up in the little lending libraries around town? If not, check a box near you.

Gift cards to local shops and restaurants. Cash prizes and more! It really does pay to read.

<3 V

yarn | expertise | classes

Wednesday – Saturrday
10am to 5pm

www.LetsGetKnotty.com

Apples

POSTED: SEPTEMBER 29, 2022

They say the apple doesn't fall far from the tree. And in the case of Asher Hansley and his gran, we have to think it's true. Gran has been seen cavorting around town with no less than three men.

Is she building a harem? We wouldn't be surprised.

Hey, Gran. If you're reading this and would like to submit some tips. We're all ears.

<3 V

A Walk Down the Aisle

POSTED: SEPTEMBER 3, 2022

Big things are happening at Fall River Estates, and I'm not just referring to harvest. Rumor has it there will be a wedding with 500 guests for the heir to a pharmaceutical fortune and his bride.

Prepare for traffic in that area later this month. And be sure to have a smile and a kind word for any non-locals.

<3 V

Back to School Bash

POSTED: AUGUST 10, 2022

AVers,

Let's kick off this school year on the right foot!

Donate unused school supplies to help our students achieve their goals! You can find teacher wish lists here on Amazon using the link at the top of this page.

<3 V

Happy Independence Day

POSTED: JULY 3, 2022

AVers,

Join us in downtown AV for a celebration. There will be bounce houses, farmer's market, free activities for the kids, a parade. And of course, fireworks! Hope to see you there.

<3 V

Free beer!

POSTED: MAY 3, 2022

Calling all beer fans! Faulty Brewing has a new IPA, and they're offering samples of "What the Hayes" at their brewery. Stop by for a taste and stay for a tour.

This brew is named for retired Hollywood Heatwaves player, Harrison Hayes. He frequently visits the AV with his wife, Juliana Wright. And he recently invested in the brewery after it was taken over by the Arcenaux family.

<3 V

Volunteers Needed

POSTED: APRIL 24, 2022

Calling all volunteers!

With tourist season upon us, the Alondra Valley Visitor Center is seeking volunteers. Must have a pleasant disposition and knowledge of the area. Stop by the AVVC if you're interested!

<3 V

wedding | newborn | boudoir

Capturing your most
important memories

www.littlebirdstudios.com

Squak!

POSTED: FEBRUARY 28, 2022

This cheeky bird has been seen flying around town, spouting off to locals. He's a rather friendly fellow, trying to pick up chicks with cheesy pick-up lines. Have you been victimized by Sqauk?

Owner unknown
Please email with any details as to who he belongs to:
VtheVine@gmail.com

<3 V

I Hart Romance

POSTED: FEBRUARY 9, 2022

Rumor has it that local, reclusive romance author, Meghan Hart will be releasing another book soon. It's a steamy contemporary romance and will be available May 30 from all major retailers.

As always, Bibliolater will have exclusive signed paperbacks for purchase. Please visit their website for details on how to get your hands on a copy.

<3 V

Open Daily
8am-4pm

1246 Mockingbird Lane
Alondra Valley, CA 98175

Dr. Bennett Nash

Sending All Our Love

POSTED: APRIL 23, 2021

It is with a heavy heart that we share the following news.

Teresa "Tessa" Lockwood, local sweetheart, librarian, and life-long resident of Alondra, died on April 22, 2021, at the age of 32, from complications following brain surgery.

Tessa is survived by her parents—Tim Curran and Gloria Curran, the current mayor of Alondra; her younger sister, Eleanor "Ellie" Curran; her husband, Tristan Lockwood; and her two children, Savannah and Maddox.

Tessa was known for her generous heart and her love of family. She will be greatly missed.

In lieu of flowers, the family asks that you donate to the Brain Tumor Research fund in Tessa's honor.

To assist the Lockwood family in this time of need, please visit MealTrain.com/Lockwood to assist with meals and childcare.

<3 V

Free Donuts

POSTED: APRIL 20, 2021

Wildflour Bakery is feeling generous after they got an extra shipment of flour. Free donuts--today only, until they run out.

Open Daily
6am-4pm

1245 Harrington Drive
Alondra Valley, CA 98175

Positive Vibes Needed

POSTED: APRIL 14, 2021

We were shocked and saddened to discover Teresa "Tessa" Lockwood has been diagnosed with a brain tumor. We will update this page when we have more news.

For now, please keep the Lockwood Family in your thoughts.

To assist them in this time of need, please visit MealTrain.com/Lockwood to assist with meals and childcare.

<3 V

Tickets Selling Fast

POSTED: APRIL 5, 2021

Don't forget to grab your ticket for the annual Alondra Valley Food & Wine Festival this weekend. Tickets are selling fast, and you're not going to want to miss this amazing event.

This year's proceeds benefit the Ronald McDonald House, and everyone in the AV will be there. Silent auction. Dancing. Wine tasting. And food you won't want to miss!

<3 V

Lucky in Love

POSTED: MARCH 30, 2020

Is sweet Wren Beaudin finally getting lucky in love?

After years, it looks like the single mom and resident town photographer has taken on the role of AV's local bachelorette.

Who will she give her rose to?

The mysterious newcomer or our beloved local vet, Bennett Nash. Neither is a bad choice. Though I for one would be sad to see Dr. Sexy off the market.

<3 V

Charity Calendar Now on Sale

POSTED: DECEMBER 1, 2020

Love animals and want to give back? Alondra Valley Animal Calendars are now on sale! Grab your copy online, at the Alondra Valley Animal Clinic or shops around town. All proceeds benefit the animal shelter.

Photography: Little Bird Studios

Calling All LoveBirds

POSTED: NOVEMBER 30, 2020

Move over Match.com, Alondra Valley's got a new dating app. LoveBirds seeks to match singles who are looking to mingle. Booty-callers beware, this app is for serious love birds only. If you're looking for true love, this is the app for you.

One of the best things about LoveBirds is how user-friendly it is, lowering the barrier for the more...technologically impaired residents of our community. And the selection—mm yes. Considering the small size of the region, there are a wide array of candidates to suit anyone's preferences.

The app is currently in beta testing, and free to use. It's open to all genders and orientations. One of my favorite things about it is the inclusivity and options it offers potential matches. Will I see you on there, AVers?

<3 V

Perfect Pairing

POSTED: NOVEMBER 2, 2020

We're pleased to report that Fall River Estates has found a new pastry chef. Owner, Lorenzo Mancini, announced that Asher Hansley would be taking on the role. Hansley is a local who spent the past few years as a pastry check in a three-star Michelin restaurant in Los Angeles.

locally owned
providing jobs and homes

www.gotiny.com

BOOKS BY JENNA HARTLEY

<u>Love in LA Series</u>

Inevitable

Unexpected

Irresistible

Unpredictable

Irreplaceable

<u>Love in LA Series novellas</u>

Perspective

Unwritten

<u>Alondra Valley Series</u>

<u>Feels Like Love</u>

<u>Love Like No Other</u>

<u>A Love Like That</u>

For the most current list of Jenna's titles, please visit her website
www.authorjennahartley.com.

Or scan the QR code on the following page to be taken to her author
page on Amazon.com

SCAN ME

Acknowledgments

Thank you for reading *Love Like No Other*. I love writing for the pure pleasure of it, but seeing all your reactions is definitely a highlight. To all the bloggers, bookstagrammers, booktokers, and readers who get excited, who post about my books, and who have shown me a sense of genuine community and support—thank you!

To all the authors who have been so kind and generous. Who have welcomed me into this community and been so supportive. Not to mention all the authors who have joined me for Writer Wednesdays. Talking to each and every one of you has been both fun and inspiring!

A big thank you to the Hartley's Hustlers and my Girl Gang (not just for girls!). You rock! I cannot possibly tell you how much your support means to me! I appreciate everything you do to promote my books and to encourage me throughout my writing journey.

To Angela. I appreciate your attention to detail. Your encouragement and support. And your willingness to dive in on this adventure with me. Thank you.

I didn't intend for there to be such a large gap between the first book in this series—*Feels Like Love*—and this one. But sometimes that happens. Life happens.

It was fun to finally revisit characters from the Alondra Valley series. Bennett and Wren and River (and baby Hazel!), to peek in on Tristan and Asher as well.

That said, it wasn't all smooth sailing, but I did it! And

there are a number of people I have to thank for helping me get to "The End" of this story. Because, whoo boy, crossing the finish line was particularly difficult, and I couldn't have done it without some AMAZING people cheering me on.

Thanks to Emily for your early review of the story, and your suggestions on plot. Your insight was so targeted and really went to the heart of the issues.

To my editor, Lisa with Silently Correcting Your Grammar. I so appreciate your attention to detail, and your patience with my questions. You always go above and beyond and this time was no exception. Seriously—you know I tried to add more breathing room to my schedule, and it backfired in a major way. Thank you for being flexible about my dates and for always magically making it work. My books wouldn't be the same without your eye. And I value your insight and your friendship.

And thank you also, Lisa, for hooking me up with Franci this time in my last-minute moment of panic. A HUGE thank you to Franci for coming in as a very last minute beta reader and providing such useful insights. I so so appreciate you.

Thank you, Emily, for providing your input at an early stage of the story. I can usually tell where there are issues, but you really helped me drill down on what they were.

Thank you to Najla Qamber for designing such a gorgeous cover that really captures the feel of the story and characters. You always exceed all my expectations.

Thank you to Ellen, as always. Thank you for being so supportive and positive, for being a friend. And thank you for sharing your incredible eye for detail. Your comments are always priceless, and this book was no exception! You always help add the small details that provide a richer reading experience.

A huge thank you to Kristen for being such an amazing friend. I value your judgment and honesty, and I so appreciate your support. We've been through so much together, and I treasure your friendship and advice. Seriously, I cannot thank you enough for all that you do. You're always willing to read "just one more time," and I so appreciate it. And your pep talks made all the difference! Thank you for helping me at the eleventh hour and providing your honest and thoughtful comments.

Thank you, Jade. If I hadn't already dedicated *Perspective* to you, this book would definitely be yours. Seriously. I am so incredibly grateful that you had the courage to give me your honest opinion and feedback. You cracked this story right open, and it's because you were brave enough to point out where the characters or story were lacking. Thank you for speaking your mind.

Thank you to Brit! I love writing strong, badass female main characters, and you help ensure that they live up to their potential. And that the men who dare to love them do too.

Thank you to JudyAnnLovesBooks for providing some last-minute ideas to improve the story. I always appreciate your insight, and I value your candid responses. And I know this book is stronger because of your suggestions.

A huge thank you to all my beta readers. Thank you for making me a stronger writer, for offering your unique insight and advice. You each bring something different to the table, and I'm always amazed and impressed by your suggestions. I'm so incredibly honored to have you on my team!

Thank you to my husband for always encouraging me. For always supporting my dreams. You are better than any book boyfriend I could ever imagine. And to my daughter, for always putting a smile on my face. You are spirited and independent, and I wouldn't have it any other way. Dream big, my darling.

And a big thank you to my daughter for her "I'm so proud of you" song that she sang when I was close to the end but struggling. You make me smile, and you help me stay focused on my goals.

Thank you to my parents for always being so encouraging. For reading my books. For being my biggest fans!

And to my in-laws for their continuing support!

Dear reader, if this list of people shows you anything, it's that dreams are often the effort of many. I'm grateful to have such an awesome team. And I'm honored that you've taken the time to read my words.

About the Author

Jenna Hartley is USA Today bestselling author who writes feel-good forbidden romance, much like her own real-life love story. She's known for writing strong women and swoon-worthy men, as well as blending panty-melting and heart-warming moments.

When she's not reading or writing romance, Jenna can be found tending to her growing indoor plant collection (pun intended), organizing, and hiking. She lives in Texas with her family and loves nothing more than a good book and good chocolate, except a dance party with her daughter.

www.authorjennahartley.com